The Family Friend

The Family Friend

CLAIRE DOUGLAS

PENGUIN MICHAEL JOSEPH

UK | USA | Canada | Ireland | Australia
India | New Zealand | South Africa

Penguin Michael Joseph is part of the Penguin Random House group of companies whose addresses can be found at global.penguinrandomhouse.com.

Penguin Random House UK,
One Embassy Gardens, 8 Viaduct Gardens, London SW11 7BW

penguin.co.uk

First published 2026

001

Copyright © Claire Douglas, 2026

The moral right of the author has been asserted

Penguin Random House values and supports copyright. Copyright fuels creativity, encourages diverse voices, promotes freedom of expression and supports a vibrant culture. Thank you for purchasing an authorized edition of this book and for respecting intellectual property laws by not reproducing, scanning or distributing any part of it by any means without permission. You are supporting authors and enabling Penguin Random House to continue to publish books for everyone. No part of this book may be used or reproduced in any manner for the purpose of training artificial intelligence technologies or systems. In accordance with Article 4(3) of the DSM Directive 2019/790, Penguin Random House expressly reserves this work from the text and data mining exception

Set in Garamond MT
Typeset by Couper Street Type Co.
Printed and bound in Great Britain by Clays Ltd, Elcograf S.p.A.

The authorized representative in the EEA is Penguin Random House Ireland, Morrison Chambers, 32 Nassau Street, Dublin D02 YH68

A CIP catalogue record for this book is available from the British Library

HARDBACK ISBN: 978–0–241–76427–5

TRADE PAPERBACK ISBN: 978–0–241–76429–9

Penguin Random House is committed to a sustainable future
for our business, our readers and our planet. This book is made from
Forest Stewardship Council® certified paper

www.greenpenguin.co.uk

For Mum

'Art is a lie that makes us realize truth, at least the truth that is given us to understand.'

Pablo Picasso

PROLOGUE

5 January 2025

If Dorothea had known this was the day she was going to die, she would have spent those precious remaining hours differently. Instead of hiking in the hills surrounding her home in the mud and the rain when it made her ageing joints ache, she would have finally said yes to dinner with Dennis and eaten something rich and creamy like steak with a béarnaise sauce. And she would have certainly spent longer in her studio breathing in the familiar, comforting scent of oils and acrylics, her beloved Golden Retriever Solly at her feet, instead of wasting time on boring admin.

All this filtered through her mind as she lay at the foot of the stairs, her body at an odd angle and her cheek pressed against the cold flagstones. She could already smell the smoke and hear the crackle and hiss of fire, and she pictured the destruction of it all: her paintings and sculptures, the flames licking at the edges of her canvases, turning it all to ash. Her life's work.

She should have been more on her guard but she'd misjudged the sounds of the intruder for the creaks and groans of an old house. Yet there had been no mistaking the sensation of someone standing too close behind her on that twisty staircase, or the hands that had shoved her, or the flash of a dark-clothed figure as they darted past her prone body and into her studio.

So, he'd come for her, at last.

Solly stood over her now, by her side as he'd always been, loyal to the end. He emitted a low, desolate bark, his breath hot on her ear, and she tried to reach out a hand to comfort him, but she couldn't move. She wanted to tell him to get out of the house. To run. But the words wouldn't come. There was a metallic taste of blood in the back of her throat and her legs were numb.

This was it. This was how she was going to die.

And as she closed her eyes for the last time, her final thought was of Imogen and the letter, half-finished, that was now going up in smoke.

Tuesday, 7 January 2025

THE SUNDAY TIMES

ARTIST DOROTHEA ROE KILLED IN HOUSE FIRE

A RENOWNED artist specializing in macabre sculptures has been killed in a fire at her Somerset home.

Dorothea Roe, 73, is thought to have fallen down the stairs in her haste to vacate her Regency villa on the outskirts of Bath in the late hours of Sunday night after a fire broke out in her downstairs studio. A concerned neighbour raised the alarm and the fire service and ambulance were called, but unfortunately Ms Roe died at the scene.

At the time of her death, Roe was working on a new collection, more than fifteen years after her last, but reports suggest most of it was damaged in the fire.

Born on 17 June 1951, not much is known about Roe's early life. She was notoriously private and gave only a handful of interviews, although she is quoted as once saying she never went to art school and was 'self-taught'. Roe's paintings and sculptures were hugely popular in the late 1980s and are now in museums around the globe. Inspired by artists like Paula Rego, she was particularly interested in working with papier-mâché to craft life-sized creations, often depicting the darker side of life and relationships. Roe specialized in the macabre, playing with misconceptions of the female form, distorting and warping ideals about beauty and relationships, and many of her sculptures are considered sinister, with one critic describing them as 'having a nightmarish quality'. Her most famous is *Woman in Turmoil,* a surreal sculpture of a woman with four heads, each with a different horrified and twisted expression of inner anguish.

In her later years, Roe concentrated more on her philanthropic work and was one of a small group of women who set up a successful art therapy business.

Roe was fiercely guarded about her personal life, but in an interview given to this paper not long before she died she said she had never been married.

Roe's agent Gabe Mitchell issued a statement today that said: 'I have worked with Dorothea for over forty years and I am devastated to learn of her death. She was a wonderful, caring, strong-minded and creative soul with a sharp wit who worked tirelessly to help others. She wasn't just my client, but also a dear friend and I will miss her terribly.' An investigation into the cause of the fire is ongoing.

I

IMOGEN

End of April 2025

Josh is jiggling along to 'Mr. Brightside' while stirring a Bolognese on the hob when I walk into the kitchen. He finishes work early on a Friday so regularly cooks – nothing fancy, usually the basic dishes we've been having since we first moved in together – but it's cheaper than going out and we are trying to save money.

I stand and watch him for a while unnoticed as he sings at the top of his lungs, endearingly out of tune: his muscular shoulders (despite never going to the gym), his slim hips, his long legs, the thick, conker-brown hair that just skims the neck of his navy hoody which he would have changed into as soon as he got home, all his movements so familiar I'd know them anywhere. I creep over to him and snake my arms around his waist, making him jump. He swivels around to face me, his smile wide, his hazel eyes twinkling. 'Hey, you,' he says, planting a kiss on the side of my mouth, and then turns back to the pan.

I'm still wearing my gym gear, which smells of the Pilates studio: warm wood, stale sweat and Dettol.

I move away from him and lean against the breakfast bar – the kitchen is too small to fit a dining table, so we always sit here, side by side on the high stools. It's one of the many reasons we never have friends over for dinner. Late last year we were seriously discussing putting the flat on the market and buying a house, but then, a few weeks ago, everything came crashing down.

My boss, Chris, said he was being lenient in not firing me from my job as a journalist at a TV station because I did something illegal on a case I was investigating. And I got caught.

I'd previously been behind the conviction of local businessman Jeremy Filcher, whose plumbing company had been installing substandard products and ripping off their customers. He is now serving a prison sentence for fraud.

If only that had been the end of it.

One night, Filcher's thug of a son, Dominic, followed me to my car and threatened me after he was tipped off that I was investigating the phoenix company he'd subsequently set up. It was only thanks to a passing couple who called out asking if I was okay that he was frightened off. Yet his threats made me even more suspicious that he had something to hide. I'm not proud of myself for what I did next, but I broke into Dominic Filcher's office in an attempt to obtain proof of him evading debts and committing fraud. I didn't find anything, although a security guard saw me and contacted the police. Thankfully I wasn't charged, but Chris was furious with me, saying he had no choice but to suspend me indefinitely while the company investigated it further.

'Good day?' Josh asks now.

'Great,' I say, trying to inject as much enthusiasm as I can into my voice. Josh thinks the break will be good for me, but the truth is I do miss the hub of the TV station. I miss getting my teeth into a story, leaving no stone unturned until I've exposed corruption, or illegal activity. It made me feel alive. It made me feel I was doing something worthwhile to make up for . . . well, for my family. Josh, on the other hand, has had the same job since we both graduated from the same university nine years ago, slowly climbing the ladder of the engineering company he works for to become a project manager. My older sister, Alison, calls him Steady Eddie and I suppose he is – most of the time. But that implies that he's boring and one-dimensional when, like all of us, he's complicated, layered, although Alison never delves beneath the surface, only ever sees what she wants to see. She doesn't notice Josh's insecurities from growing up without knowing his father. Or how protective he is of his mum. When I met Josh I saw the chink of darkness he masked with his chirpy exterior because I did the same. We could relate to one another. We were only eighteen when we met, and he was my first serious boyfriend. I'd retreated further into myself after my mum died, but Josh had seen something in me. Something broken that he wanted to mend. He made the world colourful again. He made me want to live.

The kitchen window has fogged up from the heat of the hob and the enclosed space makes me feel drowsy. I reach over and turn the radio down. Josh always plays music way too loud. I prefer peace and solitude. It already feels as though I have hundreds of different instruments crashing inside my skull at the best of times. And despite loving my job, it had started to add drum and bass to the haphazard cacophony already in my head.

'Glass of wine?' Josh goes to the window where a bottle of Pinot Noir sits, unopened, on the shelf.

'Ooh, yes please.' I watch as he pours me a glass, and I try not to guzzle it back in one go. Josh doesn't like it when I drink too much. He turns back to the pan and chatters away about his day as he stirs and I'm only half listening as I slump onto one of the bar stools. He dishes up the spaghetti Bolognese and then joins me. 'Thanks, babe,' I say to him, reaching over and rubbing his back. 'I'm starving.'

He grins in response, like a child who's just been praised, offering me the bowl of grated cheese, which I turn down, before he scatters a generous portion over his food. He shovels a forkful into his mouth like he hasn't eaten for a week. He always misses lunch, surviving on coffee and adrenaline, so by dinner time he's ravenous. We fall into a companionable silence as we eat. It's one of the things I love about Josh: he doesn't feel as though he has to fill in the gaps between conversations and, over the years, I've learnt how to do this too. My friend from work, Rachel, teases me that we're more like a couple in middle age than people who are just thirty, but that's the beauty of being with the same person for twelve years. We know everything about each other. Well, mostly everything. Of course, there are some things I don't tell Josh. Things I know he wouldn't appreciate, and I'm sure the same applies to him. Over the years we've learnt what we can and can't talk about in order to keep our relationship on an even keel. And, inevitably, there are things I don't love about Josh. Things that I wish were different, although I've had to accept them because the pros outweigh the cons. At least, most of the time.

'Oh,' he says casually after we've finished. 'A letter arrived for you earlier. I've put it on top of the microwave.' I can tell by the twitch of the muscle in his jaw that he's feigning nonchalance. I can just imagine him puzzling over it when he got home, tempted to rip it open. Josh is the nosiest person I know. I used to joke that *he* should have been the journalist. Not that he would have opened it without my consent. It would have been a lesson in constraint, a mental task he'd set for himself: wait until after dinner to mention the letter.

'It looked pretty official,' he says now, his back to me as he stacks the dishwasher.

I tense. 'Is it from the prison?'

He spins around to face me with a plate in his hand. 'What makes you think that?'

It's something I've been dreading. Every time I get an official-looking letter, I wonder if it's about my dad. 'It's been nearly sixteen years,' I say quietly.

Concern floods his face. 'Yes, but he got life.'

'You know as well as I do that life isn't actually life . . .' He was sentenced to a minimum of twenty-five years, but our solicitor warned us at the time that he could serve less.

Josh dumps the plate in the sink and moves to the microwave, taking the letter from the top, his expression grave as he examines the envelope. 'Well, I can't see a prison stamp.' He hands it to me. 'The only way you're going to know is to open it.'

The letter says 'Private and Confidential', and I have to swallow down the nausea. I glance up at Josh, who is trying his best to hide his curiosity. 'What if he's going to be released?' I don't want to see him. I never want to see him again.

'Ims . . .' Josh sounds exasperated. 'Just open it.'

My fingers tremble slightly as I rip it open. It's from a firm of solicitors in Bath. I read it quickly, hardly daring to breathe as unexpected words jump out at me. *Estate. Wills. Dorothea.*

'Well, it isn't about my dad,' I say, frowning, after I've read it. 'It's . . . well, it's about a will.'

'A will?' He moves towards me, and I hand him the letter to read, my mind racing. He's silent as he takes in the information and then looks up at me, his mouth hanging open. 'Who the hell is Dorothea Roe?'

'She was this artist friend of my mum's.' I realize, even as I'm saying it, how much I'm downplaying how important Dorothea once was to me. I've never told Josh about that summer. I clear my throat, trying to find the right words. 'Mum was her cleaner. Had been for a few years and they'd become friends . . .'

Josh snorts in response and I half expect him to make a quip about how posh old ladies aren't ever really friends with their cleaners, but he doesn't.

'Dorothea helped us out after . . . after Mum left my dad.'

'Your mum left your dad?' He hands me back the letter.

'Yes. For about four months during the summer of 2008, Dorothea let us stay with her at her beautiful house in Bath while Mum figured out what to do . . .' I swallow. The memory of that last idyllic summer is still too painful to think about, a bittersweet moment in my adolescence that I'd buried away. I'd been fourteen and it was the last time I'd been truly happy before my world was turned upside down. By mid-September Mum had decided to go back to my dad and, apart from twice, I never saw Dorothea again. I'd contemplated visiting her many times, but Alison always persuaded me not to, saying Dorothea obviously didn't want to keep in touch. I'd tried to push away my feelings of abandonment, but it still hurt.

And now it's too late. I'll never see her again.

'I can't believe you never told me about your mum leaving your dad. Or Dorothea,' says Josh.

'I wanted to forget.' The letter trembles in my hands. 'I didn't even realize she'd died. Why would she leave me anything? Could it be a hoax?'

'She might have left you money. Or a family heirloom. Ring the number to check.'

'I can't now. They'll be closed. It's gone five.'

'Just try them! You never know, they might still be open. Where's your phone?'

I go to the hallway to fetch it from my bag, Josh following close behind. He's fizzing with energy and the hallway feels cramped. 'Don't get too excited,' I warn as I tap in the solicitor's number. 'This could be a scam.'

'Actually, google the solicitor's first. Just in case it is.'

I do a quick search. 'Yep. They're a real firm. The contact details on their website are the same as on this letter.'

To my surprise someone picks up straight away. I ask to speak to Lawrence Kemp, the probate solicitor named in the letter, and I'm put through.

I can feel Josh's eyes on my back as I explain to the solicitor why I'm calling.

He explains that he can't reveal the details of what exactly I've been left without seeing some ID, but he makes me an appointment to visit him first thing on Monday.

'Well?' probes Josh when I've ended the call.

'It's true . . . she's left me something. I just don't know what, exactly.'

'It could be some crusty old doll or one of those ancient rocking horses posh people used to have in their homes. Or it could be a fortune.'

'I doubt it's a fortune, Josh. I haven't seen her in sixteen years. Why would a woman I spent one summer with, a million years ago, leave me anything substantial?'

'Maybe it's because of what happened after you'd stayed with her. Wasn't it that autumn that your dad . . . you know . . .?' He lets the rest of the sentence hang in the air, his eyes sliding away from mine, a sudden awkwardness between us.

Because we very rarely talk about why my dad is serving a life sentence.

For killing my mum when I was fourteen.

2

Dorothea didn't leave me an ancient rocking horse or an old family heirloom. She left me her house. Her beautiful Regency villa in Bath.

Josh gasps and reaches over and grabs my hand, squeezing it in excitement. We're sitting side by side in the solicitor's office in Bath. It has high ceilings and views over the Georgian buildings opposite. I keep thinking Lawrence Kemp is about to tell us he's made a mistake, that the house wasn't meant for me after all, because how can this be true? Things like this don't happen to me. They just don't.

'Ms Roe has some stipulations in her will surrounding the house,' Lawrence says, pushing his little round spectacles further onto his face, turning away from the screen to give us his full attention. His beard is so thick and bushy it's hard to see his lips unless he opens his mouth. 'You cannot sell the house for a minimum of one year, which is fairly unusual. And she's left you enough money for the continued upkeep. Congratulations, Imogen.' He reaches into his drawer and pushes a set of keys across his desk. There's a buzzing in my ears as I take them. Lawrence explains that I've inherited the bulk of her estate, with the rest going to charity, and I try and concentrate on what he's saying but all I can think about is Dorothea's house. The house that I'd loved so much as a teenager. The house my mum used to clean. It's mine. It's actually mine. I don't care that I can't sell it for a year. I don't want to sell it anyway.

Lawrence hands me some paperwork to fill out. Josh is peering over my shoulder as I write down my bank account details. We have a joint account for the mortgage and bills, but we also have our own separate accounts too, which is the one I stipulate that I want the money to go into.

'Thank you, Miss Cooke,' says Lawrence when I hand him back the forms.

'And how much money will she get?' Josh asks, much to my irritation. I'm desperate to know too, of course, but I can't help but feel it sounds greedy. Dorothea has already given me her house.

Lawrence glances at me for approval, and I give an embarrassed nod. 'Let me have a look,' he says, turning back to the screen. 'Yes, it looks like there will be an initial sum of £250,000 and whatever her yearly royalties will be, which will, of course, change every year.'

Josh is tipping forwards in his chair and whistles in surprise. And then he's standing up and I follow suit as though in a trance. Lawrence passes me a folder full of paperwork to take away, shakes our hands and then ushers us out, seemingly unconcerned that he's changed my life.

It's not until we are standing on the street outside that Josh begins to laugh. 'Oh. My. God. This is crazy! We need to go there. I need to see this house for myself. Come on, Ims. What are you waiting for? Let's go.'

He pulls my hand and tries to lead me down the hill, but I can't move. 'I just . . . I can't believe it.'

His eyes light up. 'Well, believe it, babe! Didn't you hear what he said in there? You're now a very rich woman. You never have to worry about money again.'

And then my emotions play catch-up and I squeal in delight – startling a couple walking by – and throw my arms around Josh's neck.

I peer through the bars of the wrought-iron gates like an orphan from a Dickens novel, the rain falling softly on my hair. Everything around me feels hazy and slightly unreal, like I'm in a dream that I don't want to wake up from.

'Fucking hell,' exhales Josh, his breath dissipating into the damp air. 'Villa Oiseau.' He reads from the inscription on one of the stone pillars to the side of the gate. 'Isn't that French for bird?'

'Oh yes. I remember she always had birds in her art.'

It's been over sixteen years since I was last here but my memories from that summer are pin-sharp: the lush green lawn out the back, Dorothea's glass studio overlooking the Royal Crescent and the streets of Bath, the three hyper dogs, the fluffy grey and white Persian cat, Casper, flopped on the back of the sofa, my mum, happy and relaxed for the first time in years as she took a batch of cakes from the

Aga, a slant of sunlight picking out the red in her brunette hair, the wood fragrant with sweet scented honeysuckle, and Harry, the boy who used to live next door and who I'd had my first kiss with one night under a starry sky.

The villa is shabbier than I remember and the gravel driveway could do with re-laying. But the creamy Bath stone walls, the majestic portico and the sash windows with original shutters look as imposing as ever. I can't see any evidence of the fire, although Lawrence told me at our appointment this morning that there is damage around the back of the house, mainly to the studio.

I've never had much money. My mum was a cleaner and my dad worked in a warehouse. I grew up in Keynsham, a small town between Bristol and Bath, and we never went on fancy foreign holidays, or even on day trips, and any money my dad had would be spent down the pub. After Dad went to prison I lived with Alison. Seven years older than me, she was twenty-one when Mum died. She'd escaped our aggressive father and moved to Cardiff three years earlier, only returning now and again. After our mum died she reluctantly moved back to Keynsham in order to sell the family home and, with the little money we received from it, she rented a flat near to my school so that I had some continuity.

Josh makes a disbelieving sound that brings me back to the present. 'I can't believe this is our house,' he says.

My house, I think. And then I instantly feel guilty after everything Josh has done for me, how kind he's been about my suspension. 'It's amazing, isn't it?'

'You never said it was anything like this. I mean, it's got a wood out the back. Its own fucking wood.' He laughs. 'It must be worth millions.'

I picture my sister in her tiny new-build semi in Cardiff. What will she think about this? It doesn't seem fair. Why did Dorothea leave this to me and not to both of us? Although I think Alison only met Dorothea twice, and that was after Mum had died. Alison had already moved away to Cardiff when Mum started her cleaning job for Dorothea. She worked for a chain of hair salons so managed to get relocated to the Bristol branch after Mum died and Dad was arrested. We rubbed along together well enough for those four years. I had a part-time job after school as a cashier in Tesco so that I could help Alison with the rent. After I followed Josh to Nottingham University, Alison moved back to Cardiff, met and married Gareth, and now they have a little girl, my six-year-old niece, Lila. Even after everything we've been through I wouldn't say we are close. We've rarely talked about our parents. We've buried it all under hard work and polite small talk. It's been our way of coping, I suppose. Heads down and carry on.

I wonder why there is the clause in the will that won't allow me to sell the house for the first year.

Josh is opening the gates with a code the solicitor gave us. He suggested we change it as soon as we can. Josh is wearing wellies over his work trousers and the fabric has puffed around his knee, making it look as though he's wearing old-fashioned breeches. I want to laugh at the absurdity of it all. It's like we've abruptly been transported to the early 1900s and Josh is standing at the foot of his estate.

'What?' he asks, noticing my expression.

'Nothing. This is all a bit surreal, that's all.'

'Too bloody right.' He hasn't stopped buzzing since we left the solicitor's office. I'm excited too, of course. It's the most amazing thing that's ever happened to me.

Almost too amazing. As though something is about to go wrong.

Josh returns to the car and drives it through the gates, and I follow behind, preferring to walk over the gravel, which is sparse in places. In my peripheral vision I see something yellow fluttering in one of the bushes by the front porch. It looks like a piece of ribbon and then, with a stab of revulsion, I realize what it is. Police tape. I untangle it from the branches and pocket it. Then I walk up to the front door with the arc of stained glass above and wait for Josh to get out of the Vauxhall. His car, a decade old, looks out of place next to this beautiful house. He comes over to me, his expression softening. 'Are you okay, Ims?' He takes my hand. 'I can imagine this must all be weird.'

I squeeze his hand. 'I'm happy – about the house and everything. But also sad, for Dorothea.' I think of the police tape lining my pocket and it hits me again that Dorothea died here. Since Friday I've read everything I could find online about her death. It sounds as though she fell down the stairs in her rush to escape a fire which had broken out in her studio, and it saddens me that she died all alone. I can just imagine the fear and sheer panic she must have felt when her house started to fill with smoke. She had no family, no children, and another pang of regret hits me that I didn't try harder to get back in touch. That I let my hurt pride get in the way of reaching out to her.

'You never talked about her to me,' he says gently, rubbing his thumb against mine.

'It was all tied up with my dad.' I swallow. 'And after Mum's funeral, Dorothea never got in touch and so I . . . I pushed it all to the back of my mind.' I'd felt so close to her when we stayed here that summer. This was the last place where me and my mum were truly happy.

I picture Dorothea as she was back then. A woman in her late fifties with long, sandy-blonde hair held back from her face with a red neckerchief and wearing paint-splattered dungarees. She was tall, willowy, attractive, with the most beautiful silvery grey eyes I'd ever seen, well-spoken, blunt, quick to laugh and, well, like nobody I'd ever met before. Her outfits were always thrown on haphazardly and she favoured suede Birkenstock clogs with socks, yet on her, it all worked. She was stylish, like an elegant, ageing supermodel. I'd liked her instantly. I was a nervous, meek teenager, used to making myself small, so as not to take up too much space in the world, trying to be unseen by my bad-tempered father, but there, in Dorothea's studio, sitting cross-legged in a patch of sunlight as I devoured my mum's old Penny Vincenzi novels, Casper on my lap, while she painted, I felt calm. I felt safe. I thought her paintings were strange and floaty, like a confused dream, but I'd admired her creativity.

I'd confided in Dorothea, once, about my wish to be a writer one day. She hadn't sneered like my father had, her brow hadn't crumpled with worry like my mother's had at the notion of chasing an impossible fantasy, she hadn't scoffed and taken the piss like Alison. Instead, Dorothea had listened seriously and told me I could do anything, be anyone I wanted to be if I worked hard enough. She'd cupped my chin with her long, slender fingers, the nails encrusted with paint, and sighed, almost wistfully. 'It's so much easier for your generation,' she had said. 'You're not bound by convention or forced to marry young. You're not restricted by an outdated class system.' I hadn't understood what she'd meant, not really, not then. As far as I could see, Dorothea was a strong, independent woman, free.

Josh lets go of my hand and I reach into my coat pocket for the keys to let us inside.

Instantly we are rendered speechless. I'd forgotten just how huge the space is. There are doors facing each other across a wide hallway, an intricate archway and the magnificent staircase, carpeted with a duck-egg blue runner. The floors are a creamy stone and the walls are painted a pale blue. Original cornicing runs around the high ceilings and there is an antique dresser to my left. Next to the stairs is a coat stand with a red mackintosh hanging from it and a checked umbrella that I assume belonged to Dorothea. My eyes rove around the hallway, taking in the photographs and framed artwork that I recognize as Dorothea's on the walls going up the stairs. I feel a pang when I realize it's barely changed since I was last here. I almost expect Dorothea or my mother to come out of one of the rooms to greet us and I'm hit by melancholy. But I also can't help but imagine Dorothea's prostrate body lying here, at the foot of the stairs, and I blink the image away.

The air is musty and the withered flowers that droop sadly over the side of a narrow glass vase have cast their crispy dead leaves along the top of the bureau like a foul-scented potpourri. It's so at odds with how the place used to smell: a mixture of Dorothea's Givenchy perfume and the cut roses, sweet peas and irises from her garden which she'd always dot around the house in anything she could get her hands on – empty milk bottles, old champagne flutes, vintage glass medicine bottles she'd found in charity shops.

'I didn't realize it would be furnished,' says Josh, stepping further into the hallway and running his hands over a Louis XVI-style chair that has been pushed against the wall. 'But then I suppose she has no family, so where else would it go? It all belongs to you now. To us. Do you think this is an antique? I bet it's worth a bit.' He runs a finger along the dresser, and I want to tell him to stop. He's like a magpie. These were Dorothea's things, not items to be pawned. I feel a surge of protectiveness towards the house and everything in it. I want him to go.

To leave me to wander the house by myself, to let myself wallow in my memories of that idyllic summer before everything changed. But I can't say all this to him, of course. He wants to share in my joy. He's never going to fully understand my oscillating feelings.

Thankfully his phone rings and he retrieves it from his pocket with a frown. 'Damn it. It's the office. I better take this,' he says, pulling off a glove with his teeth as he heads out of the open front door. I can hear his voice floating towards me, his words clipped and polite, which makes me think he's talking to his boss. When he returns he's wearing an apologetic smile. 'I need to go into work. I'm really sorry, babe, but we can come back at the weekend.'

I can't leave. Not yet. I've not had the chance to look around the rest of the house, let alone the grounds. 'Um . . . why don't you go and I'll get a taxi to the train station.'

His smile wavers. 'Really?'

'Yes. I want to have a proper look around.'

I can tell he's disappointed, but he gives a small nod. Then he kisses the side of my head. 'See you later, then.' I watch as he reverses out of the driveway and backs out onto the narrow country lane, and I'm thankful to be alone at last.

Silence rings in my ears. That summer I was last here the place had been buzzing with people and animals and life. In my mind's eye dust motes floated in the sunlight that slanted through the windows, beaming down on well-worn Persian rugs; dogs lolloped on squishy sofas; chickens strutted across the lush green lawn; birds twittered in the wood and the honey scent of buddleias filled the air.

I'm probably looking back at that time through rose-tinted glasses.

I retrieve my phone from my bag and scroll to Alison's number. And then I hesitate. How am I going to tell her? I stare down at my phone for a couple of seconds, before changing my mind and slipping it into my coat pocket.

I sigh as I make my way through the hall and down the short flight of stairs into the kitchen. The runner is more faded than it was sixteen years ago but the kitchen is exactly the same: cream-painted French-style cabinets, rustic stone floor tiles and the black Aga on the far wall, the wooden table with mismatched chairs in the middle of the room. I picture the functional but ugly kitchen in our tiny flat with its sharp-edged modern units, black work surfaces and odd shape. This kitchen was always the beating heart of the house. It was where we all congregated, where Harry would come and visit me and we'd sit drinking homemade lemonade, giggling over some shared joke while my mum pretended not to listen. I close my eyes, remembering it all.

When I open them again I jump in shock.

A man is standing in the garden, watching me.

3

DOROTHEA

A Month Before

Dorothea had been expecting this visit.

Every morning she got up, made herself a cup of tea and then sat in her favourite wing-backed chair in her studio, which had the best views of her garden and wood. In winter, a wraithlike mist clung to the branches and obscured the tops of the trees, and, as she sat there watching in anticipation, she imagined him emerging through the woods like the apparition, the ghost, that he was. Haunting her. Taunting her. Was she scared? She didn't like to admit to any kind of vulnerability: she was proud she'd carried on living alone in the villa, long after her friends told her she should downsize, even as her body began to decay. She made sure to keep fit and dexterous with her art and her hiking, but there was no slowing down the hands of time that were ticking too quickly for her liking.

The final sculpture was her insurance. Her secrets set in papier-mâché. Other people's secrets too. This last collection had featured some of her best work. It was the sequence of her life – yet without the last sculpture it was a sentence without a full stop, a story without an ending.

But there was an ending, of course. There was always an ending if you waited long enough.

Solly started whining by her side, his ears pricked forwards, his nose pressed to the studio's sliding doors, leaving a mark on the glass. 'Can you sense it?' she whispered, placing a hand on her dog's large head. Solly answered by whining some more, high-pitched and chilling. Her eyes were trained on the area of garden where lawn met bracken, until she was certain that she too could see him materializing from between the trees, as though he'd been living in the woods all these years. 'He's coming for me,' she said to Solly. 'He's finally coming for me.'

4

IMOGEN

My first thought is that it's him. Dominic Filcher. The man I lost my job over. I shrink back in terror, knocking my hip against the wooden table. And then, as the man walks brazenly across the terrace and right up to the French doors, I realize this man is at least thirty years older. Still, I'm shaking as I remember the night I was accosted by Filcher and I stand frozen for a few seconds.

'I can see you,' he calls, peering through the glass pane. 'Who are you? What are you doing in Dorothea's house?' He has the kind of voice that BBC newsreaders had back in the 1960s.

I creep forward, softening when I see he has a Golden Retriever and a black Labrador by his side. 'Who are you?' I call back. The man is stocky, with white sideburns poking from his flat cap, and he has a matching neat beard. He looks to be somewhere in his mid-seventies and is wearing a padded, waterproof jacket. How threatening can a man with a Goldie and Lab be?

'My name is Dennis. Dennis Creasy. I was an . . . um . . . friend of Dotty's.' Dotty? She was only known as

Dorothea during that summer. 'I like to keep an eye on the place since her . . . um . . .' he clears his throat, '. . . since she passed.' Something in the way his expression softens and his pale eyes water when he mentions Dorothea makes my heart go out to him. He obviously cared for her. I search around for a key to open the doors and find it on a little hook on the end of the butcher's block.

'Sorry,' I say, when I finally open it, letting in a gust of wind and rain. 'I don't know anyone around here and . . .' I shrug apologetically. 'I'm Imogen. It's . . . well. Dorothea left me the house,' I add in a rush.

'Oh, right. I see. That would explain why you're here, then. I just wanted to check to make sure the house wasn't being broken into.'

I bend down to stroke the dogs' floppy ears which have gone silky in the rain. 'Gorgeous boys.' I'm obsessed with dogs. Every time I see one I have to stop to coo over it. Josh always says we can't get one because our flat is too small.

'This is Solly. He belonged to Dorothea. Thankfully he managed to escape the fire and I've taken him in . . .'

'Solly was here when she died? That's so sad.'

'Yes. He was the one who alerted Mick next door that something was up. He wouldn't stop barking and practically led Mick here.'

Mick. That was Harry's dad's name. 'Mick and Sue still live next door?'

He nods. 'That's right. You know them?'

'From a long time ago. I was friends with their son, Harry. I hadn't seen Dorothea in years, but she was always so kind to me.'

'She was an amazing woman. The best.' His voice cracks and he turns it into a clearing of the throat.

'Had you known her a long time?'

'We've been friends and neighbours for the last ten years.'

'My solicitor said there wasn't a funeral for her.'

'No. Just a very small cremation. No service. That's all she wanted. No big fuss. We – me and three of her closest friends – scattered her ashes there . . .' He turns and points towards Dorothea's woods and the wind picks up, rustling the branches. From somewhere nearby I can hear windchimes. 'That's what she wanted,' he says again. 'Small, intimate. Despite being a famous artist, Dorothea never did like being the centre of attention.' He smiles sadly.

I stroke the black Lab. 'What did you say his name was?'

'Her. Cady. As you can see, the dogs get on well together. Dorothea adored her animals.'

'I remember.' I stand up. The air smells of petrichor and wet dog. 'I know it sounds an odd question, but did Dorothea ever mention me? She left all this to me, and I don't really know why.'

'What did you say your name was again, dear?'

'Imogen. Imogen Cooke.'

His face falls. 'I'm sorry, she didn't. But then Dotty was very private.'

I feel a stab of disappointment.

'You said she left this whole place to you?' His eyes darken in suspicion.

'Yes.' I shuffle, feeling embarrassed. 'It's so generous of her.'

'Well, yes. She was like that, was Dotty. I assumed she'd give all her money away to charities. That's what she always said she'd do.'

'She left some of it to charity.'

He lifts his chin so he can see me more clearly under his flat cap. 'There's no family resemblance between the two of you,' he says briskly, no doubt taking in my dark hair and eyes, the negative image of Dorothea. 'Dotty said she had no family.'

'I'm not family. She was a friend. Of my mother's mainly but also . . . to me. A long time ago.'

'Right.' A pause. 'Do you have any plans for the house?'

'I . . . no, not really. I'm, well, I'm still trying to get my head around it all. I only found out about the house this morning.'

'Ah yes, a bit of a shock suddenly inheriting all this, I imagine.' We fall silent and I'm not sure what else to say. 'Anyway,' he says eventually. 'If you need anything, I live further down the lane, at Plato House, the other side of Mick and Sue.'

'Okay, thank you. Nice to meet you.'

He nods without smiling and I watch as he leads Solly and Cady further up the garden, his wellies sinking into the wet grass, and then out of the side gate almost hidden in the high stone wall. I remember that the gate leads onto the lane. I really should check to see if it has a lock.

I'm just about to go back into the house when I notice a flicker of movement between the trees at the bottom of the garden where it leads into the wood. Is someone there?

I step onto the patio, straining to see, a cold sensation creeping over me, but there is nothing there apart from the gossamer mist that hovers between the branches.

I go back into the kitchen and through an entrance that I know leads to a kind of scullery before a door opens up to Dorothea's studio. There is another small, spiral staircase that leads to the main hallway upstairs which the servants would have used once upon a time. I wonder if this was where Dorothea's body was found. I glance down at the tiles and notice something rust-coloured in the corner of one. I kneel down to get a better look, running my fingernail over it. It looks a lot like dried blood. I straighten up, surveying the stairs: uncarpeted and hazardous with just a thin metal rail on one side. It would be easy to stumble on a staircase like this and an image of Dorothea falling and cracking her head on these hard, unforgiving tiles shoots through my mind.

The door to her studio is closed but I notice the smudges of soot on the frame, and I hesitate before turning the handle. Dorothea's studio had been like an emporium of wonder: of light and colour and space. I push the door open, immediately engulfed by the smell of burnt wood. Disappointment flares in my chest. The once beautiful glass studio is now a sad, dingy husk. The sliding doors that had opened onto the garden have been boarded up and one wall completely consumed by the fire has been replaced with more boarding. The remaining wall is intact, but the fire has eaten away most of the plaster, revealing sections of exposed brick, like bone through open flesh wounds. The whitewashed floor is warped and damaged and all the furniture and paintings and sculptures that once inhabited this studio are gone. This had been the place Dorothea had loved the most and where I'd been my happiest, and to see it like this makes my eyes smart.

'I'm going to restore it for you, Dorothea,' I whisper into the cold, dank air. 'I promise.'

I make my way upstairs to Dorothea's bedroom. I still feel like I'm trespassing and never more so than here, in this room. Everything is how she must have left it before she died. The double bed with the pink satin eiderdown is neatly made, the brush with her hair tangled in the fine needles sits next to her creams and make-up on the dressing table.

Her clothes are still hanging in the large walnut armoire, and I open the door and look through them, her scent still lingering on the fabric. On one of the shelves is a pile of neatly folded scarves and I can't resist picking up a pink cashmere one and draping it around my shoulders. I survey myself in the full-length mirror. The pink brings out the colour in my cheeks and contrasts nicely with my dark hair. I instantly feel more polished and elegant. I finger the soft material and lift the end to my nose. I inhale deeply, instantly reminded of Dorothea, of that perfect summer and my mum. She loved pink. She wore it often. This all belongs to me now and it's an unsettling, if not unpleasant thought. I've never owned anything expensive, and I can tell by the fabrics that all these clothes are of exceptional quality. I carefully part the hangers, marvelling at the clothes: jumpsuits, trousers and blouses, and I can see straight away that none of it would fit me. I'm a good five inches shorter than Dorothea was. My eye goes to a navy chunky-knit jumper with an orange, pink and cream Fair Isle print around the neckline. I can't resist trying it on and whip off the scarf and pull the jumper over my head. The arms are slightly too long but it's stunning with the jeans I'm wearing. It looks almost new. I decide to keep the jumper on and then I wrap the scarf back around my neck and close the wardrobe door.

Nobody has been here to clear out her things as far as I can see. She had no family left after all and the huge weight of responsibility suddenly threatens to floor me. How do I sort through seventy-odd years of someone's life? I don't even know where to begin.

Feeling disheartened, I go into the room next door, Dorothea's study. She wasn't particularly tidy but she was meticulously organized, and I'm relieved to see the box files lined neatly on the top shelf of her bookcases and clearly labelled. Her antique walnut desk is bare. I pull down a file marked SCULPTURE IDEAS, but there's nothing inside. I pull out another box file labelled IMPORTANT DOCUMENTS but that's also empty. That's weird. I look through the others, but they too are empty. I don't understand why she'd keep the box files if she'd decided to dump their contents.

And then something on another shelf catches my eye and I start in surprise. A lidded box, different to the other files. IMOGEN is written on the front in – presumably Dorothea's – handwriting.

I open it, half expecting it to be empty like the files, but sitting on top of a wad of papers is a short story I remember writing when I was staying here. My heart tugs at the thought of Dorothea keeping it all these years. Underneath are old yellowing newspaper clippings which I recognize from when I worked at the now defunct *Wiltshire Gazette* after leaving university. Everything I'd written for the newspaper is in here. I rummage through them noticing the investigative stories I'd covered as a freelancer before joining Broadcasting House in Bristol. And then, buried right at the bottom of the box, is an old, battered silver Zippo lighter. I take it out and turn it over in my hands. It's heavy and beautifully engraved with swirls. Underneath is a Post-it Note with three words scribbled onto it: *weld sheet faster*. Sellotaped next to the words is a small key. I slip it into the pocket of my jeans.

I drop the lighter back into the box and replace it onto the shelf, my mind ticking over.

The empty box files. Dorothea following my career. The key left where she knew I'd find it. It all means something. My journalistic antenna is twitching and I can't ignore that familiar sensation in the pit of my stomach: a mixture of adrenaline and instinct that tells me I'm on to something.

Dorothea knew I could sniff out a scandal. A story.

And I'm suddenly convinced this is why she left me her house.

5

It's already dark when I get back to the flat in Bristol and Josh opens the front door before I've had time to put my key in the lock.

'I was starting to get worried,' he says, the overhead light in the hall illuminating the flicker of a scowl. 'It's gone seven.'

'You knew where I was,' I reply mildly as I step inside and hang up my coat. I kick off my trainers but keep hold of my bag. 'I got immersed in Dorothea's things. Turns out she still had a dog. Solly. A Goldie. So cute.' I turn to him with a smile, hoping to jolly him out of his mood. My friend Rachel always says I give in too easily for, as she puts it, 'a quiet life'. But that implies I'm a walkover, and I'm not. Rachel, who is naturally bolshie, believes that the louder you are the more confident you are, that somehow that equates to strength, but I don't agree. My mum wasn't a pushover either. She was one of the strongest people I've known. It took strength and determination and bravery to walk away from a destructive drunk like my dad, even if she did go back to him. No, I just hate rows, that's all.

Arguing with Josh makes me feel sick to the pit of my stomach. Not that Josh shouts. He understands that's something he must never do.

'But don't worry,' I continue, in that same jovial tone, 'Solly won't be moving in with us. Can you imagine! Dorothea's neighbour is looking after him.'

'Babe, I was genuinely worried.'

I turn and face him. 'I'm sorry. But I'm fine.'

'And what are you wearing?' His eyes narrow as he takes in Dorothea's pink cashmere scarf and navy jumper.

I explain about finding them in her wardrobe.

He wrinkles up his nose. 'Isn't that a bit weird? Wearing old lady clothes.'

'They're not old lady clothes! They're classics.'

He looks like he wants to say more but doesn't. Instead he gives me a half-smile. 'Okay. Now, tell me all about the house. I'm gutted I was called in to work.'

He clatters around emptying the dishwasher while I sit at the breakfast bar and explain about Dorothea's empty files and my theory about why Dorothea left me the house. I'm about to tell him about finding the Post-it Note with the key attached when he interrupts.

'You're having a break from all that investigative stuff, remember?' He hands me a mug of tea. Josh once told me that he found my obsession with my job and trying to call out corruption 'troubling'. Even more so after the Filcher incident. 'I think this is all a reaction to what happened to your mum,' he had said gently after I was suspended from the station. 'You work long hours and get yourself into some dangerous situations and all for what? To try and right the wrong your dad did? To try and get some kind of justice? It won't work, Ims. I'm worried about you.'

I decide not to mention the key and Post-it Note after all. He looks so disapproving. 'True,' I say instead.

Josh smiles, satisfied, and then moves to the worktop and picks up his mobile. 'Do you fancy a pizza tonight? We can afford it now.'

'Sure, thanks.'

He orders the usual without even needing to ask. Once he's ended the call, his eyes are shining. 'I've been thinking . . .'

'Uh-oh.'

'. . . about us moving into Dorothea's place. I love what I saw of it. It's huge and we can't just leave it standing empty, can we? What if squatters decided it was a great place to . . . well, squat?'

I can tell that the house has already worked its magic on Josh and he hasn't even seen the rest of it yet. The wood. The studio. The high ceilings and large, airy rooms. The cornicing. 'Sure . . . I mean, I'd love to. I love it there, I always have, but what about this place? Would we sell it?'

'No. We should rent it out furnished.' He begins pacing the kitchen, something he always does when he's fired up about something. 'I've been thinking about it all afternoon. Dorothea's furniture is in the villa, yeah, so we won't need any of our own stuff. We can take our personal belongings, sentimental stuff, whatever, and my TV of course.' His huge TV has always been a bone of contention. 'We'll have space now for ten TVs!' He laughs and I can't help but join in. This is the Josh I fell in love with. The Josh high on life and the future. He made it seem so exciting, yet so safe.

'Okay,' I say. 'Let's do it. Let's move to Bath!'

He picks me up and spins me around and I hug him tightly, happily, all of our problems, my worries, Dorothea, my parents, all of it, leaving my mind so that there is nothing but this moment, this feeling of joy and love.

I come back down to earth with a bang the next morning when the doorbell rings. Josh has already left for work. I answer it, expecting to see the postman, but standing there are two strangers, a youngish man with glasses and a tuft of white-blond hair, and a woman in her late fifties, scruffily dressed in a scratchy-looking brown coat over black jeans and biker boots. She has a very stern face offset by a cloud of soft auburn waves.

'Imogen Cooke?' the woman says, holding up an identification card, and my insides turn to ice, thinking of Josh. 'I'm DI Erica Shirley and this is DC Colin Hurst. We wondered if we could come in?'

6

DOROTHEA

Six Weeks Before

Dorothea didn't trust journalists. Yet, against her better judgement, here was one tripping over her driveway in impractical heels and a flimsy coat despite it being late November. It was raining heavily yet the woman didn't have an umbrella and was trying to shield her blonde curls with a leather tote bag while the wind whipped at the hem of her trench coat.

It was Gabe who had convinced her to speak to this young woman, even though he knew she rarely gave interviews – not because she believed she was somehow above it but because she had to be on her guard. She knew any journalist would be very interested to know about who she'd been before becoming the enigmatic Dorothea Roe, a persona she had carefully cultivated over forty-five years.

'No, Gabe,' she'd said when her agent had called her a week earlier to tell her that a journalist from a broadsheet wanted to interview her for their Sunday supplement. 'It's not a good idea.'

'Of course it's a good idea, darling. You've got a new collection you're about to release. It's great publicity. You've been off the scene for years. This is your comeback.'

'I'm seventy-three years old . . . it's hardly a comeback.'

'One last hurrah. That's what we agreed.'

'I don't have anything to say.' Which, again, wasn't strictly the truth.

'Just tell them a little about your life now, what you've been up to these past fifteen years, and hint at what's to come in the new collection.'

So she'd agreed. And only to keep Gabe happy.

Solly suddenly growled next to her, alerting her to the knock at the door, and she reluctantly left her position by the living-room window to go and answer it. The journalist, Maria something or other, seemed nice enough even if she was wearing totally impractical shoes which she offered to take off at the door. 'No, don't worry about that. Your feet will freeze.' Maria's eyes widened in awe as she stepped over the threshold. All Dorothea could see were all the things that needed doing to her house, but most people were blinded by the original features and airy space. They sat in the cosy, warm kitchen and ate the pancakes that Dorothea had made on the Aga's hob the day before and drank tea while the sky outside darkened and thunder rolled overhead. Maria's damp coat was slung over the back of her chair and, too late,

Dorothea realized she should have offered to hang it up. She often forgot her manners, so seldom did people now visit her. Maria was complimentary about Dorothea's house, her work, her dog and even her pancakes. She told Dorothea she didn't look a day over sixty, even though Dorothea wasn't vain enough to believe it, and she said how powerful she'd found Dorothea's most famous sculpture, *Woman in Turmoil*.

And then, with her Dictaphone placed in front of her on the wooden table, Maria leaned forward conspiratorially and asked the one question Dorothea had been dreading.

'One of your collections, called *Dangerous Love*, is about a toxic relationship? Was this because you'd experienced this yourself?'

'Well, not in a romantic relationship,' Dorothea replied, firmly and without a beat. 'But I saw it in my parents. My father was physically abusive towards my mother, and back then there weren't many places a woman could go to for refuge. Not in the South West area, anyway. Domestic violence wasn't taken seriously by the police back then. So my mum put up with it.' Dorothea pulled the cuffs of her oversized cable-knit cardigan over her hands and sat back in her chair, hoping that would be the end of that line of questioning. She hated talking about her father.

'And what about partners? Were you ever married or had any serious relationships?'

Maria's eyes gleamed and Dorothea wondered what

she knew. 'No. There were relationships, of course, but nothing that lasted. I prefer my own company these days.'

'And children?'

Dorothea lowered her guard, just a little, while also reminding herself that she was speaking to a journalist who might twist her words. 'I found out at a young age that I couldn't have children.' She coughed into her sleeve. She didn't want this journalist to feel sorry for her. 'Would you like more tea?'

'No, thanks. I've drunk three cups since I've been here.'

'Sorry, it's my vice, I'm afraid. Caffeine is my only drug.'

Maria smiled and tapped the tips of her too-long taupe gel nails against her mug. Dorothea eyed them curiously, wondering how she could possibly do everyday tasks with such talons. 'What made you decide to set up an art therapy centre in the late 1970s?'

'I'd met Annette by this point, and after I'd started to have some small success with my own art . . .'

Maria consulted her notes. 'You mean Annette Baker-Hume?'

'Yes. That's right. Annette told me her idea about the centre, and I loved the sound of her vision, so I offered to come on board. I wanted to do something to help others. There was a small group of us back then, all connected to art in our own way. Annette and Maisie both trained as art therapists . . .'

'And that's Maisie . . . ?'

'Hill. Annette's friend Rosemary Farrington was also involved – she put up the capital. We were quite the campaigners back then, always on a protest or a march. We fought for women's rights.' She smiled sadly at the memory, remembering the type of young women they'd been. Feisty, dogged, idealistic.

'And is the business still running today?'

'Yes. Although a couple of us have taken a step back, the centre is still running.'

'It's very inspirational,' Maria said, tucking a blonde curl behind her ear. It occurred to Dorothea how easy it was to spin a version of the truth of her life, like creating a drawing but not colouring it in.

'And when did your career really start to take off?'

'When I met Gabe, my agent. He was still up-and-coming back then, but he had great contacts and he helped me get my work seen by the right people. I got lucky,' said Dorothea. 'I'd always been arty, but I came from working-class roots, and my parents thought art was frivolous and that I'd be forever poor. I never went to art school. Shall we move on to my collection?' She didn't want to talk about the past any more. It was all so long ago.

'Yes, of course,' Maria said, sitting up straighter and adjusting the neck of her blouse. 'So, your new collection is mainly sculptures? The papier-mâché ones you're famous for?'

'That's right.'

'And what can your fans expect?'

'It's probably my most controversial yet,' she said.

'How exciting. Can you give the readers a hint?'

'Magpies.'

'Magpies? As in the birds?'

'That's right. You remember the rhyme? One for sorrow, two for joy . . .'

Maria took up the mantle in a sing-song voice. 'Three for a girl, four for a boy. Five for silver, six for gold . . .'

Dorothea was enjoying this. '. . . Seven's a secret, never told.'

Maria leaned back in her chair and assessed Dorothea carefully. 'So, the secret?'

'Oh, now, that would be telling,' Dorothea said with a wink. 'You'll have to wait and see.'

7

IMOGEN

I stare at the two police officers, taking in their plain clothes and their identification cards and their grave expressions. It's all too familiar and I'm suddenly fourteen again, unwittingly opening the door to a future without my lovely mum.

'Has something happened to Josh?' I blurt out.

DI Erica Shirley's jaw softens slightly and she raises her eyebrows, and something about the way she does this tugs at my memory. 'No. Nothing like that. We'd like to talk to you about Dorothea Roe, if we may come in?'

Relief surges through my body. 'Sure. Yes . . . of course . . .' I step back to allow them into the tiny hallway. 'Please. Go through to the kitchen.'

I close the front door and follow them. I offer them a drink, which they both decline, and then the three of us stand awkwardly by the breakfast bar. The male detective whose name I've already forgotten gets out a notebook from inside his jacket and then perches on a stool, with one foot resting on the metal bar. I notice his trouser legs are too short, revealing a slice of very pale skin above his schoolboy grey socks.

DI Shirley does all the talking and I wonder if they tossed a coin to decide before they came in.

'We understand that you are the main beneficiary to the estate of Dorothea Roe,' she says, studying me closely. There's something earnest and trustworthy about her face, but her gaze is intense. She has head-teacher energy.

'Yes, that's right.'

She assesses me for a few seconds. She has a cluster of sunspots on her cheekbones and deep nose-to-mouth lines, and I feel as though I've met her before.

'Did you know that Dorothea had planned to leave you her house in her will?'

'No! Of course not! I hadn't talked to her, or seen her, in years. I . . . it was – is still – a shock to me.'

The detectives stare at me silently, judgement rolling off them, and I wonder if they know about my father and what he did. Is that why they're looking at me like that?

'Her death was an accident, wasn't it?' I say, remembering a newspaper article I read online after discovering Dorothea had left me her house. 'I read somewhere that a candle started it?'

DI Shirley purses her lips together and the two detectives exchange glances.

The male officer says, 'I'm afraid the fire investigations team found evidence of an accelerant used.'

'Accelerant? But . . . she would have had turps, paints and all sorts of combustible stuff in her studio,' I say.

'Petrol was found,' says DI Shirley gravely. 'And we've only just been told that you've inherited her house.'

There is a loaded pause.

'Wait! You don't think... you don't think I had anything to do with her death, do you?' I blurt out.

'You're the only one to benefit from her death,' the male detective pipes up and I want to slap him.

'But... I haven't seen her in years.'

'Strange, then, that she'd leave everything to you,' muses DI Shirley, her eyes not leaving mine.

'Yes. Absolutely. I'm still trying to get my head around it. I don't know why she left it to me.'

'Where were you,' asks the male detective, somewhat smugly, 'on Sunday the fifth of January?'

My mind races. Where was I? I can't remember what I did last night, never mind five months ago. Oh yes, thank God. 'I went to visit my sister, Alison Davies, in Cardiff,' I cry out jubilantly. 'For my niece's sixth birthday. I was there until the Monday morning when I got the train back. You can ring her to check if you like.' I pick up my phone from the worktop and reel off her phone number, which the male detective scribbles down. Then he tucks the book back inside his jacket and hops off the stool.

'There's something else,' says DI Shirley. 'We're not totally sure, but it looks like Dorothea might have been pushed down the stairs.'

'What?' I can feel the blood draining from my face. 'Pushed? Someone pushed her? But why?'

'That's what we're trying to find out,' says DI Shirley.

'But . . . there's been nothing in the press about murder.'

'We haven't revealed it yet,' she explains. 'The fire investigation team took a while to submit their report. I know you're a journalist, but we'd be grateful if it's kept out of the press for now.'

'Of course,' I promise. Tears burn the back of my eyes at the thought of Dorothea being pushed down the stairs. Someone wasn't content in just torching her studio, they actually wanted to make sure she died. The realization sends ripples of shock through me.

'That's all for now. We'll be in touch,' says the male detective.

As I'm showing them out, DI Shirley turns to me and adds, under her breath, 'Will you be moving into Dorothea's villa? A house like that probably shouldn't be standing empty.'

'Um . . . yes, we are,' I say while thinking it's none of her business.

She waits until her colleague is at their car before adding, 'You probably don't remember me. I was one of the detectives working on your mother's case.'

That's why she'd looked familiar. I nod. 'Oh yes, I remember now, meeting you in court . . .'

Something shifts in my memory and an image of her rushing over to me and Alison as we entered the lobby of Bristol Crown Court on the first day of my father's trial pops into my mind. A younger DI Erica Shirley appearing through the throng of people (which I'd later realize were the CPS solicitors and barristers); her kind chestnut eyes and general air of dishevelment had put my nerves at ease. She'd escorted us to the right court room, insisting we find her if we needed anything.

'You and your sister were very brave,' she says with a small smile, bringing me back to the present. Then she turns and joins her colleague at the car.

I contemplate calling Alison but I talk myself out of it, reasoning she'll be busy in the salon as she works Tuesdays. I decide to ring Rachel instead. I haven't spoken to her since being suspended. She'd tried to call me a few times and she left messages asking if I was okay, but I didn't have the energy to call her back. I was too ashamed. I still feel ashamed. But I was a good journalist, before.

'Immy!' she exclaims as soon as she picks up her phone. 'I was worried I'd never hear from you again.'

I hop onto a bar stool, slightly disgusted to see the imprint of the male detective's bottom in the leather. 'I'm so sorry. So much has happened. I'm just so embarrassed about it all. I mean, it's just so . . .'

'Oh Immy,' she sighs. 'Anyway, you've still got your job for now, so that's something.'

'I don't know if I have. I've been suspended while they look into my conduct, apparently.'

'You're a brilliant journalist. He'd be a fool to sack you.'

I press my foot against the panel of the breakfast bar. 'Has he said anything to you?'

'No. Not really, just something about how lucky you are that Dominic Filcher didn't press charges.'

'He didn't press charges because he knows how fucking guilty he is.'

'Hmmm. Well, I can assure you he's on my radar.'

'Thanks, Rach.'

'We'll get him eventually. Don't worry about that. God, you must be bored. I know what you're like! At least you're still getting paid. You *are* getting paid, aren't you?'

'Nope.'

'Oh . . . shit.'

'But it's okay because, well, the strangest thing happened.' I tell her all about the villa but I don't reveal the visit from the police. It's not that I don't trust Rachel, but she is a journalist after all. The temptation to report on it would be too strong.

And if anybody is going to report on it, it will be me. When the time is right.

'Wow,' she says when I've finished. 'Great news about the inheritance, but I'm sorry to hear about your artist friend. Dorothea Roe. Yes, we covered her death at the station back at the start of the year.'

I don't know how I could have missed it. But then I had been in the middle of the Filcher case at the time.

'She was pretty well known,' I say, 'at least she was in the eighties and nineties.' I can hear Chris's booming voice in the background shouting at someone, and I flinch. 'I better go,' she whispers. 'I'll see you soon.' She ends the call before I've had the chance to reply.

When Josh gets home from work I tell him about the police visit and how they think it's arson. I don't mention that Dorothea might have been pushed down the stairs. He doesn't need to know that detail for now, it will only make him worry.

Straight away his body language shifts and I can sense his anxiety. 'Maybe we should stay here now we know someone torched Dorothea's place?'

Disappointment floods through me. 'Why would someone want to hurt us, though?'

He perches on the stool next to me and loosens his tie. He looks tired. 'I hope you're not thinking of investigating this, Ims. Leave it to the police.'

'Of course not,' I lie. 'And if we move into the villa we can get security cameras, make sure everything is locked and secure.' I can't admit that one of the reasons I want to live in the villa is so that I can chase the truth more easily. 'Come on, Josh, we were so excited by this. The villa is amazing. And it's ours. It's all ours!' I want him to revert to the fun Josh of last night when he was spinning me around in excitement and making plans for his ugly TV. I watch his face, willing him to say yes.

And then he flashes me an indulgent smile. 'You're right. We'll be fine. Whatever happened to Dorothea has nothing to do with us, and she was an old lady. Vulnerable. But I'll call the security firm straight away, okay?'

'Okay, great idea.' I jump up and give him a quick kiss and ruffle his hair, which makes him laugh.

I'm willing to do whatever it takes to get my job back.

8

That Friday Josh takes the day off work and we move into Villa Oiseau. As we unload the car, Josh's mum, Jackie, asks me when Alison is coming to visit. Jackie had jumped at the chance to help us move in (probably because she'd like a good nose around).

I squirm inwardly because I still haven't told Alison. I know I can't keep putting it off. It's not that I'm scared of her reaction per se, it's more that I don't want her to be envious.

'I . . . well . . .'

'She still hasn't told her,' announces Josh with an eye-roll as he closes the car door with his foot, weighed down by the TV.

'What?' Jackie cries in surprise. She stops dead in the driveway with a cardboard box containing mugs in her arms, an overly exaggerated move, but then that's Jackie. Nobody loves a drama more.

I pull a face. 'I know. I know. I've been putting it off.'

'Well, she's not going to be happy when she hears you've inherited all this,' she inclines her head towards the house, 'and she gets diddly squat.'

I can feel my cheeks flame. 'I don't know how I'm going to tell her.' It's going to be another thing that divides us. I balance my box of bedding against the wall with my hip while I unlock the front door.

'Maybe face to face. Might be easier.' Jackie's expression softens in sympathy as she passes me. She knows how complicated my relationship is with Alison. Jackie has been there for me since I was eighteen and treats me like the daughter she never had, but she's also searingly, sometimes crushingly, honest. She only ever tries to sugar-coat what she's said after she's already said it, and by then it's too late. She means no harm, and I love her. She just doesn't have much filter, and over the years I've grown a thicker skin.

'Holy shit!' she exclaims when she steps over the threshold. 'This is impressive.' She follows Josh into the living room and deposits the box there, even though it's clearly marked KITCHEN.

'We have so much space, you could move in too,' suggests Josh when he's set down his TV. Dorothea's telly, old and tiny in comparison, has already been discarded.

I prickle. I love Jackie but I definitely don't want her moving in. Her personality is too big to share a house with. Plus, as much as she views me as a daughter, I'm not flesh and blood. Josh will always come first, and even though she tries to play devil's advocate when we disagree, she always ends up taking Josh's side. I'm annoyed with him for mentioning it, even if he was joking. I don't want him to give Jackie any ideas.

The awkward silence stretches before Jackie says, 'I couldn't leave Bristol. My life is there.'

'You mean Tony is there,' he says with a laugh. Tony is Jackie's 'man friend'. Josh never knew his dad. He walked out when Josh was a baby and it has always been just him and his mum, until five or six years ago when Jackie went on Tinder and met Tony, a barrel-bellied man with a ready laugh and a sleeve of tattoos. They refuse to move in together. 'We're both too stuck in our ways,' Jackie says when we probe her on it. 'We're nearly sixty and we've both lived on our own for a long time.'

I pick up the box of mugs, offering to make tea, and Jackie follows me down the stairs into the kitchen. I feel like I'm play-acting as I go to the kettle – Dorothea's orange Le Creuset – fill it and then place it on the hob.

'Wow,' says Jackie, seeing the kitchen for the first time. 'This is totally lush. Look at that Aga. I've always wanted an Aga, not that I could fit one in my kitchen.' She moves to the French doors. 'And that garden. Just amazing.' She throws open the doors and steps outside. 'Is that . . . is that an actual wood?'

'Yep. It was all Dorothea's.'

'Bloody 'ell.'

I laugh. 'I know.'

She steps back into the kitchen. 'What a great place to bring up children,' she says wistfully. Then her gaze lands on a cream-painted display cabinet with bone china plates. 'All this stuff,' she says, her eyes roving over the wooden dining table and the armchair in the corner, by the French doors. 'It's just so . . . much.'

Josh and I have already agreed not to tell Jackie for now about the arson because she would worry about us being in this huge house by ourselves. It's something that's constantly on my mind as it is, and I haven't even told Josh the half of it. It's hard to imagine something so horrible happening here. This house had been my safe space all those years ago, the kind of place where I could never imagine anything bad ever happening. Anxiety twists in my gut at the thought of this house as a crime scene when it's so beautiful, so idyllic. I'm suddenly seized by doubt. Are we doing the right thing? I still have so many questions about the night Dorothea died. But how can we back out now? We're planning to rent our Bristol flat out, and who wouldn't want to trade that for this stunning villa? We've already arranged for a security firm to come out and put measures in place, but it's more than that. If I want to find out more about Dorothea's life, and death, if I want to be in with a chance of getting my job back, then I need to be here, right in the thick of things.

'Are you all right, love? You've gone a bit pale.'

'I'm okay,' I say as I start to unpack the mugs. But they look clunky and ugly against Dorothea's bone china teacups and so I put them back in the cardboard box, using the teacups instead.

Jackie sits down at the table. 'I imagine it must feel strange suddenly inheriting all this,' she says, glancing around. 'I mean, it's beautiful, don't get me wrong. But definitely different to what you're used to.'

I nod and busy myself with the tea. I hand Jackie a cup and she comments on the 'posh china'.

I pour tea for Josh and then tell Jackie I'll take it to him. 'Go ahead, love. I'll help unpack these boxes if you like.' But she doesn't move, her eyes still on the garden.

Josh glances up when I enter the room. The massive TV looks incongruous amidst Dorothea's antiques. 'Thanks, babe,' he says as he takes the cup. 'Where's my Yoda mug?'

'I haven't unpacked it yet,' I lie.

He slurps the tea and then sets it on the coffee table behind him without using a coaster and I fight the urge to pick it up again. 'I'm going to have to drive Mum home soon. She's going out with Tony tonight. And then I'll come back with the last of the stuff from the flat. All the guys at work are so jealous!'

'You told them already?'

'Of course. Why wouldn't I?' He bends down and starts fiddling with another lead. Without saying anything else, I leave him to it.

Josh and his mum leave an hour (and a tour of the house) later. Jackie had been impressed with it, especially the studio. 'I know it needs renovating, but it would be a great place to use as a reading room, or a library. I know how much you love your books,' she had said. Josh had nodded in agreement, while I pretended this was something I hadn't even thought about.

And now, at last, I have the house to myself for a precious ninety minutes or so.

I haven't told Josh about the key I found in that box with my name on it. I keep it tucked away in my purse along with the Post-it Note. I take it out now, examining it. It's a generic Yale key and I go around the house trying it in different door locks. It doesn't fit any of them and I wonder if it was the key to the studio. It doesn't fit the back door either. She must have left it in that box hoping I'd find it, so it has to mean something. I don't remember there being any sheds or outbuildings in the garden, but I vow to have a look later and I slip the key into the front pocket of my jeans.

I take a few of the lighter boxes up to the room we've chosen to sleep in: I don't want to use Dorothea's bedroom, so we've picked one at the back of the house, with windows at the side and rear looking out over the gardens and woods and fields beyond. It was the room I stayed in all those years ago, and the bed is the same – a sleigh-style double in a sleek chestnut wood – although the mattress looks new. The room has since had a refurb – a fresh, French grey paint on the walls and new, cream-painted wooden wardrobes. I wonder who else inhabited this room after I left. The bed is stripped and I find fresh duvet covers and fitted sheets in the wardrobe, but I decide to use our own duvet and throw it on the bed, although the bright pattern looks too modern for this room. For now it will do.

It's turned into a surprisingly sunny afternoon after a grey start, so I grab my jacket and venture outside, keeping an eye out for a shed. I haven't really had the chance to explore the grounds yet, even though my memory of that summer is still clear in my mind. I remember how much I'd loved the fact Dorothea had her very own wood. It felt magical. Harry and I had spent hours lying on a blanket beneath the canopy of leaves, talking about books and music and films, content that we wouldn't be disturbed. I get that queasy pull in the pit of my stomach. I feel guilty that Dorothea had to die for me to get all this. I feel guilty that I am the one to benefit, and not my sister. I feel guilty that I could be happy when my mum never got the chance. And now, learning that Dorothea was murdered makes me feel even more uneasy. Ever since the visit from the police earlier this week, I can't stop thinking about those empty box files, imagining someone rifling through them. I wonder why they didn't empty the one with my name on it. Were they disturbed? Was it the night of the fire?

I cross the lawn – fluffy-edged but otherwise neat – until I reach the path between the trees. It feels like yesterday when I last stepped into the dark undergrowth. The wood is smaller and less dense than I remember. If I recall correctly, the path takes you right to the edge of the woods where a six-foot fence separates it from a farmer's field. The only access to the woods is through Dorothea's garden. I trudge along the path, past huge oaks and pines, light flickering between the leaves. It's colder here, without the full force of the sun, and I pause to do up my bomber jacket. I breathe in deeply, all the worries and fears leaving me just like they did back then every time I came here. I can almost hear Harry's laugh and my mum calling us in for tea. I wonder what Harry is up to now. I once tried to find him on social media but there was no trace of him and I'd been surprised by how disappointed I'd felt.

The path is more overgrown than it was the last time I was here. I take a left off the main path, stepping carefully over large roots and fallen branches. I keep thinking of Jackie's mention of children. Josh and I have talked about marriage and kids over the years, but he still hasn't proposed even though we've been together so long. Both of us have trepidations about marriage, which isn't surprising considering our backgrounds, but we both agree that we'd love children a few years down the line. Lack of money has also held us back, but the thought of children growing up in this idyllic place, of having the kind of childhood I never had, fills me with hope.

The wood is denser the deeper I go, and just when I'm beginning to worry I might get lost I catch a glimpse of the cognac-coloured fence in the distance and the small clearing next to the old, disused well where Harry and I used to hang out. I walk to the well and look down into darkness. I remember how Harry and I would yell into it, enjoying the echo it made. I walk around a bit more, prodding the earth with the toe of my trainer, amazed to see a patch of bluebells at the root of one of the trees, when my phone's ringtone startles me. I reach in my pocket and my heart sinks when I see Alison's name flashing up on the screen. I consider deliberately not answering it but then realize I can't avoid her forever. We haven't spoken since I went to visit her last month.

'Hey, Immy,' she says as soon as I answer. 'Long time no speak. You okay?'

I have the sudden paranoid thought that she's somehow heard about the inheritance and this is a test. Has DI Shirley called her yet to check my alibi for the day of Dorothea's murder? Would she have let slip about the house?

'I'm good. You?' I answer carefully.

'Yeah. All good here.'

'Lila and Gareth?'

'Yep. Lila got the main part in the school play.'

'Maria! She got it! That's brilliant.' I smile when I think of how excited Lila must be. She'd spent hours the weekend I was there practising for her audition, singing 'The Hills Are Alive' over and over again while I curled up on her bed and watched her with awe, amazed at her confidence. 'Where does she get her talent from?'

'Not us! I'm so proud.' Alison sounds so happy, I don't want to burst her bubble by telling her about Dorothea and she hasn't mentioned the police so maybe they haven't contacted her yet.

There's a beat of awkward silence, but then that's not unusual. Neither of us is great at small talk, especially on the phone.

'So, um, Immy. I wanted to have a chat with you about something . . . sensitive.'

I brace myself. So she does know. 'Okaaay.'

'Can we meet? I'd rather do this face to face.'

I feel sick. But she's right. We are always – marginally – better in person. 'Sure. When?'

'Tomorrow? I could get the train to Bristol.'

'Could you come to Bath?'

'What? Why?' She sounds confused; maybe she doesn't know about Dorothea's will after all? I mentally kick myself for mentioning Bath.

'Long story. But we can talk properly tomorrow.'

'Sure. I'll meet you outside the abbey. Say one p.m.? We could grab some lunch?'

Bath will be rammed on the weekend, so I tell her I'll book us a table somewhere.

'Perfect. See you tomorrow. Gotta go. Bye.' She mimics two kisses down the phone and then she's gone.

I stand looking down at my mobile, my head spinning. If Alison doesn't know about Dorothea's will, then what does she want to talk about so urgently?

The woods feel chilly, so I turn around and head back the way I came. But I must have taken a wrong turn, distracted by Alison's call, and I end up walking back a different way. At least I think it's a different way. I'm getting disorientated as it all looks the same. I'm not yet on the main path so I walk through the trees, turning to make sure the fence is behind me, and I stumble into a thicket. I definitely didn't come this way but the wood isn't very big. Even so, I don't fancy the idea of getting stuck here in the dark. I quicken my steps. The day might feel spring-like but I always forget darkness comes down quicker than I expect. I continue walking, relieved when I see glimpses of the house in the distance. I push my way through a group of close-knit trees and then I stop dead in horror, clamping my hand over my mouth.

Hanging on the branches of a tree right at the edge of the wood is a dead bird, strung up by its neck. I baulk, nausea rising, as I take in its black and white feathers, bony feet and crooked neck. A magpie.

A twig snaps behind me and I let out a yelp of fear. And then I run, as fast as I can, back to my new home.

9

ALISON

Imogen is standing at the entrance to the abbey, her arms wrapped around her body as though trying to make herself look smaller. She used to do it as a little kid, and usually only when something was troubling her. Alison wonders if she's got a juicy case at work. Journalism is perfect for Imogen. Even as a child she was always asking why this and why that. It used to drive Alison mad. 'Just because!' she'd often snap back. Thank goodness she's more patient now she's a mum.

Imogen looks fresh and young in her black jumpsuit and denim jacket. She's wearing a beautiful pink scarf, her long, wavy hair cascading over her shoulders, and Alison feels a maternal tug at her heart. Why do they have such a distance between them? Why can't she throw her arms around her sister? She steels herself. She's been dreading this conversation. She doesn't know how Imogen is going to react, and the last thing she wants to do is upset her.

'You just need to rip the plaster off,' Gareth had said that morning. 'You can't keep it from her. It's not fair. She has a right to know.'

Gareth, her lovely, even-tempered and kind husband. Primary-school teacher and voice of reason. With his large, welcoming family and bantering siblings, it's hard for him to understand the fractured dynamics of the Cookes. When Alison first met him she didn't tell him for months about her dad, worried he'd see her differently, think she was weird or damaged or dark. How could this man, from a family of cockapoos, ever relate to her family of wolves?

Alison pulls at her blunt bob, momentarily regretting cutting off her long hair when she sees how lovely Imogen looks. She strides across the square towards the abbey, weaving in and out of people who are standing around listening to a busker – a woman in her twenties – singing 'Hallelujah' sweetly into a microphone.

Imogen looks up when she arrives and adjusts her expression from one of mild anxiety into a welcoming smile. 'Ali, hi,' she says. 'Thanks for coming to meet me.'

'I asked you to meet me,' replies Alison curtly, and then inwardly berates herself for sounding so abrupt.

'Oh, yes. Of course. Sorry.'

'You don't need to say sorry.'

'No. Sorry.' Imogen laughs and it breaks the ice. Are they always this awkward around each other? They fall into step as they head towards the restaurant Imogen has booked. Imogen asks about Lila and the school play, but every now and again, when Imogen thinks she's not being watched, her expression floods with anxiety.

'Okay, what's up?' Alison says eventually once they've been shown to their table by the window and sat down, menus in hand. She moves a small vessel of fake carnations to the side so that she can see her sister clearly.

'I have something to tell you, something totally mad,' Imogen blurts out. 'I've inherited a house.'

Alison is thrown. 'What? Which house?'

'Dorothea's. The villa.'

'I have no idea what you're talking about. Who the hell is Dorothea?' And then it clicks. The boho arty woman their mum had worked for. 'Do you mean the artist?'

'That's right.' Imogen rests her elbows on the table and leans forward. 'That's not why you're here? You haven't heard from the police?'

Alison shakes her head, confused. 'No. But now that I am, you better tell me what's going on.'

The waitress arrives to take their order. Alison hasn't even had a chance to glance at the menu, and it doesn't look like Imogen has either, but her sister orders the avocado on sourdough and Alison follows suit. Once the waitress has gone, Alison leans in to meet her sister's gaze. 'Come on, spill.'

Imogen sighs, something she often does when she is putting off telling the truth, but those sighs speak volumes.

'Remember when Mum and I went to stay with Dorothea after Mum had left Dad that . . . that last time?'

Alison nods, biting her lip. She remembers how relieved she'd been that her mum and little sister had left at last and how excited that she could just concentrate on being a twenty-one-year-old girl, dancing and flirting and drinking, without the weight of her family on her shoulders, and how gut-wrenchingly disappointed she'd been when she found out that her mother had gone back to him.

'Your dad's changed, love. He's given up drinking and he's so sorry for everything,' her mum had said during that last phone call. Her words still so fresh in Alison's mind that even now, all these years later, just thinking about them can bring tears to her eyes. 'He's going to get counselling for his anger. He's promised. No more flare-ups.'

And he *had* appeared to have changed. He did go to counselling. He did stop drinking.

'Well, she left me her house! It's mad, Ali, totally mad! I still don't fully understand why – although actually I might just be beginning to – but . . .'

'Wait.' Alison sits up straighter. 'Let's get this straight. A woman you haven't seen for years left you her house? Her actual house? Her whole house?'

Alison can feel a white-hot flame of envy ignite in her belly as Imogen explains about wills and Regency villas in Bath worth millions and antique furniture and bluebell woods and burnt-out studios, and, as she speaks, an image comes back to Alison, one she thought she'd forgotten, of an attractive older woman in a sombre black dress, her face drawn as she spoke to her at their mother's wake. She remembers she had beautiful grey eyes that had seemed both watchful and full of sadness that day. Dorothea Roe. She'd met the woman twice. The first time had been the day they found out their mother was dead. Dorothea had been waiting at their family home in

Keynsham with Imogen when Alison had arrived from Cardiff. But they'd barely spoken then. Dorothea had tried, but all Alison had wanted to do was be with her sister so had ushered the older woman out, assuring her that the two of them would be fine by themselves.

Alison doesn't want to be jealous. She wants the best for Imogen, of course she does, especially after everything that has happened to their parents. And there is some part of her that is pleased for her sister, but another part of her can't stop thinking about the mounting bills and the extra hours she has to put in at the salon to make ends meet when she'd much rather be spending time with Lila.

Imogen falls silent as the waitress reappears with their food and Diet Cokes.

'And I'm not allowed to sell it – at least for a year,' Imogen continues when the waitress has gone. 'I still don't know why Dorothea put that stipulation in her will.' She looks up at Alison with a guilty expression on her face. 'But I also get royalties too – from Dorothea's artwork – which I can use to keep up the villa and also . . . to help . . . you.'

'I don't need help,' Alison finds herself saying even though this isn't true. But how can she accept anything from her little sister? She picks up her knife and fork. 'So, you're saying that this woman has left you everything? Why?'

Imogen launches into – what sounds like – a well-rehearsed speech about her job as an investigative journalist and how she believes Dorothea knew her life was in danger.

'Christ, murdered!' Alison can feel the knot of worry in her chest. Why do dark things seem to follow them around? Isn't it enough that their father is in prison for killing their mother, for crying out loud? And now this. More drama. More crime and heartache and darkness. All Alison wants to do in this moment is hotfoot it back to Cardiff to be with Gareth, kind, cuddly Gareth who always makes her feel better. She wants to be curled up on Lila's bed, amongst Lila's teddies, in her lovely pink bedroom with the fairy wallpaper, listening to her daughter talking about her friends and the school play. Not this. Not murder and death.

Imogen nods gravely as she chases a cherry tomato around the plate with her fork. 'The police have evidence that the fire was started on purpose, and they think that Dorothea was pushed down the stairs.'

'And now you're living in the house? Is that safe?'

'I think so. I hope so . . .' Imogen's eyes cloud over, which makes Alison wonder what else she's hiding.

'What?'

'It's nothing. It's safe, yes.'

'Well,' Alison says, swallowing a mouthful of sourdough, feeling like it might choke her. 'I'm pleased for you. What does Josh think? He must be over the moon.' Alison has never taken to Josh, truth be told – although she's never said as much to Imogen. She prides herself on getting the measure of people, yet Josh is a hard one to read. It doesn't help that he keeps her and Gareth at arm's length, never making an effort to get to know them even though he's been with Imogen since they were eighteen. Alison had voiced her concerns to her sister when she said she was following Josh to Nottingham University. Imogen hadn't listened, of course, and it had all worked out fine, but she wonders if Josh harbours some resentment towards Alison because he knows she didn't approve. Imogen insists on spending every Christmas with Josh and Jackie ('because she's on her own') and Alison gets it, she does. Jackie is a surrogate mother, just like Gareth's family are to her. Apparently – according to her sister – Josh doesn't like large groups and, she suspects, he doesn't much like kids. Every time Alison asks her sister about marriage and babies she is dismissive, trotting out the same story about how Josh doesn't believe in marriage after his dad abandoned him, but maybe kids one day. Alison can't help but feel it's all an excuse. Which is fine, if Imogen is happy.

'He is over the moon. We moved in yesterday. It's going to take a bit of getting used to. I haven't told him everything, about Dorothea.'

'What do you mean?'

'I've said about the arson. Not about her being pushed. He worries.'

An uneasy feeling washes over Alison. Why is Imogen keeping things from Josh? She tells Gareth everything.

'What about your job? Won't it be a bit of a commute to Bristol every day?'

Imogen shifts. 'It's about an hour at that time of day. Anyway, it won't matter because I'm . . . er . . . taking a break.' Imogen flushes and takes a sip of her drink.

'But you love being a journalist!'

'It's . . . just for a bit.' She puts the glass down but she's avoiding eye contact. 'I might go freelance. I haven't decided yet.'

Another jab of envy hits Alison under the ribs. She'd love to take time out from working.

Imogen finally meets Alison's eyes. 'Hey, why don't you come back with me and you can see the villa?' And then her face falls. 'Only if you want to. I don't want it to look like I'm . . .'

'Rubbing my face in it?' Alison laughs to take the sting out of her words. 'I'm pleased for you. Honestly.' And she really is trying to be. 'It's about time something good happened to our family. Some light in all that darkness.'

'Thanks, Ali. I would really love to help you out, though. I don't need all the money.'

Alison shakes her head. 'No way. Gareth would never hear of it. It would wound his stupid male pride. You know what men are like. Josh must be the same?'

'Nope. Not Josh. He's only too happy to embrace my new-found wealth. Lila, then. Can I do something for her? Give her some money? Put it in savings?'

Alison hesitates. 'Look. Let things settle first. You don't know how much money the upkeep of a Regency villa is going to take. If you still want to do something for Lila in the future, then that would be lovely, thank you.'

Imogen's expression floods with relief and Alison knows this will go some way to appeasing her sister's guilt. Although Alison has got enough guilt of her own to contend with.

'Now there's something I need to tell you,' Alison says.

10

IMOGEN

Alison's expression is grave and my guts twist in apprehension. 'So what is it? What was so urgent to make you come all this way on the train?' I ask in a bid to keep things light.

Alison very rarely visits. I'm always the one trekking over to see her in Cardiff. I assumed it was because of Lila, although I know my niece would love Bristol – and now Bath – but I wonder if it's because Bristol especially holds too many bad memories for Alison.

She looks down at her plate. She's hardly touched her food. She mumbles something.

'What did you say?'

Alison glances up, her eyes softening. 'I went to visit Dad in prison.'

It's as though I've taken a punch to the stomach. I stare at her, unable to breathe for a few seconds. Eventually I manage, 'You went to see Dad?' Neither of us have ever visited him – at least, that's what I always thought. 'What do you mean? When? Why?' I shake my head at her. 'What the actual fuck, Alison?'

She swallows and pushes her plate away. 'Last week. For the first time.'

'But . . . why? Why now?'

'He wrote to me. He's been writing to me for a while, after he didn't get parole, and I've never read his letters or replied. I always threw them straight in the bin as soon as I saw they were from him. And then, last year he stopped, he just . . . Stopped. And I was relieved, but then a few months ago he started up again, and I suppose curiosity got the better of me because I read this one. He wrote that he has liver disease and he didn't know how long he had left and that he wanted to see me.' She pauses and looks at me, breathlessly. 'And, I dunno why, maybe because I'm now a parent, maybe because he's dying, but I suddenly started panicking and thinking that if I didn't go to see him I'd never have any answer. There was a time when he was a good dad.'

I almost choke on my drink. 'Oh, come on!'

'What? He was. To me, at least.' Her voice softens. 'I know it wasn't the same for you . . .'

She was always his favourite. Going by Alison's memories of her early years, she started off with a very different childhood – a very different father – to the one I had. She was nearly seventeen when he started drinking. I was ten with fewer memories of happier times with him: me sitting on his shoulders at the balloon fiesta, him teaching me to ride my bike, to swim. But they get fainter and fainter every time I try and recall them.

In the summer of 2004, my grandparents – my dad's parents – were killed in a helicopter crash while on a once-in-a-lifetime holiday to the US. They'd moved to Cornwall so we didn't see them that often, but it had devastated our father. Alison said he was never the same afterwards: the odd evening down the pub became a regular thing. Alison likes to blame the drink for his violence – but I don't agree. Yes, he was a nasty drunk, but the anger, the resentment, the aggression, must already have been in him. I've always suspected that Alison had more compassion for my father than I had, even after Mum's death. But I still never expected her to forgive him.

'So you went?' I sit back in my chair, disappointment lodged in my chest. 'And did you get the answers you were looking for?'

The waitress pops up again, preventing Alison from replying. We both order a latte and she takes our plates away, our food unfinished.

'In some ways, maybe,' Alison says when the waitress has gone. 'He's aged so much. He seemed so shrunken and old.'

'He's sixty-seven. Hardly old,' I say, somewhat petulantly.

'He looks way older. Like eighty-odd. Honestly, I was shocked. I was expecting him to look . . . well, like he did back then.'

He had been broad-shouldered and strong at fifty. Intimidatingly tall with a thick neck that flushed red when he was angry and deep grooves between his eyebrows that spoke of a life lived in disappointment. Although he hadn't always looked that way, of course. His wedding photos tell a different story – handsome, optimistic, gazing adoringly at his young, pretty wife.

The waitress is back with our coffees. She sets them down in front of us and then moves to clear the next table. Alison stares at me silently. I'm not sure what she expects me to say.

'He seemed so sincere, this time,' she says as she spoons the froth from her coffee. 'He told me he didn't want to die with me – and you, he mentioned you too, of course – still thinking the worst of him. Even after all these years, he's insisting he didn't kill Mum.'

I laugh bitterly. 'You're joking. He actually said that? Even before he killed her, he beat her up, on more than one occasion. I saw it with my own eyes.' I take a deep breath, fury lapping at the back of my throat. 'He made us all sit through a trial because he refused to plead guilty.'

'I know, I know . . .' She looks down at the tablecloth and a surge of anger almost lifts me from my seat.

'You don't believe him . . . do you?'

'I . . . don't know. Why would he lie now, when he's dying? He's served most of his sentence. What would he gain by insisting he was innocent again now? There was always something about that night that didn't make sense to me. He had stopped drinking. He was having therapy. Why would he suddenly flip?'

She'd intimated this to me before, when we were much younger, but I'd always refused to listen, so she'd stopped telling me about her doubts. But they must have been there, all this time, hidden beneath the surface, which was why she'd opened his letter and gone to see him.

I push back my chair and stand up. 'I can't listen to this.'

'Immy, sit down,' she says firmly when the diners from the next table turn to look. I sink back into my seat. 'I'm not denying he hit Mum when he was drunk,' she says in a hushed tone. 'I'm just saying I think he might be telling the truth about not killing her.'

'A jury found him guilty. He was seen on CCTV arguing with Mum before she headed down the towpath. Eyewitnesses saw them arguing before that at that Halloween party. She had his skin under her fingernails, he had a scratch on his face. The mask to his Halloween costume was found chucked in the river . . .'

'Yes, they argued. They always argued. But the evidence was circumstantial . . .'

'Are you telling me that, for all these years, you've believed he was innocent?' I'm aghast. I can't believe what I'm hearing.

'No. Of course not. I'm not going to deny I've had doubts, you know that. But it's only after I went to see him. Would he still continue to lie when he knows he's dying? What would be the point?'

'You can't believe a word he says, Ali.'

'But it was always the drink . . . you know that. He had stopped drinking when Mum died and he wasn't drunk that night. He said he wouldn't have put us through a trial if he *had* been guilty. You know the prosecution conceded he could have pushed her by accident, and she hit her head. He said if that had been the case he would have admitted it. Gone for the lesser manslaughter charge.'

I'm absolutely speechless that she's defending him like this, after everything that man put us all through, and I feel her betrayal like a sharp slap.

'He wants you to visit him,' she continues, her eyes not leaving mine. 'He asked me to put in a good word.'

'Jesus,' I splutter. 'He's deluded. It will never happen. I still can't believe *you* went.'

'I think you should visit him, Immy. You need closure. He's going to die. Don't you want to hear his side of things before he does?'

'One visit and he's completely brainwashed you?'

'That's not true . . . I . . .'

But I can't hear any more. I push my chair back, opening up my purse and throwing down two twenty-pound notes. 'I'm sorry, but I can't do this.'

'Immy . . .'

'I need to go.'

And I storm out of the restaurant leaving her sitting there alone.

11

DOROTHEA

Three Months Before

Dorothea was nearly finished with her seventh, and last, sculpture. Her most important. Her most telling. She had always processed her emotions through her art, her way of making sense of the world, and never more so than with this collection. Her anger and frustration were evident to see, but her sorrow and regret too, she hoped.

The sky was a powder blue with the suggestion of sunshine beneath the swirling vanilla clouds. The kind of sky she liked to paint. No hint of rain, which meant it was safe to go into the woods today. That was one of the worst things about getting older, her deteriorating suppleness, her concern about falling, although she was fit. Fitter than some half her age, she reckoned, judging by some of the forty-year-olds she'd seen huffing and puffing as they tried to climb the hills by her house. And her trusty old hiking boots still had enough grip to stop her slipping. Still, she always took her old Samsung phone with her. And Solly, of course. He was getting on – in dog years not much younger than her – but he still loved the walk through the woods, barking at birds and trying to chase squirrels. His hearing wasn't as good these days, another thing they had in common.

Dorothea shifted her tote bag full of paints and brushes further up her shoulder to stop it digging in as she made her way through the winding tracks to the outer part of the woods. It was one of the reasons she bought this house almost thirty years ago. Not many places came with their own wood but were still close enough to walk into the city, should she choose to do so, though she rarely did nowadays.

She stood for a few moments in a patch of sunshine, breathing in the tangy mid-morning air. Birds tweeted overhead and she closed her eyes. Things were bad, that much was true. And she was so angry. God, she was angry. But she could fix it. Well, no, not *fix*, exactly. But maybe she could right some wrongs. 'There's no fool like an old fool,' she murmured to Solly, who barked at her in response.

She continued marching through the woods, Solly trotting by her side. She was nearly there now. Sunlight dappled the path in front of her and she felt that sense of freedom that was synonymous, to her at least, with being alone in the woods with the great expanse of sky above her.

And then a twig snapped from somewhere behind her.

Dorothea froze and so did Solly, his ears pricking forwards.

These woods were private land. *Her* private land. There was no public access. No right of way. The only way was through her garden and she always kept the side gate locked. Slowly she turned around. She refused to be scared but her palms started to sweat anyway. 'Hello?' she called. 'Is anyone there?' Her voice echoed among the branches. She stood for a few moments, watching, waiting, but there was no other sound except the rustle of leaves in the breeze, the cooing of a rook and the far-off rumble of traffic.

She continued on her way, casting the thought from her mind. It was only later, while she was walking back to the house, that she noticed it. Propped up against the trunk of a tree was a postcard with a woman's face on the front and letters that she couldn't clearly see without her glasses. She paused, frowning, before bending down to pick it up, her stomach clenching when she realized the woman on the front was her when she was younger. Her hands shook as she took out her reading glasses from her jacket and put them on, the words finally coming into focus.

COMING SUMMER 2025

A WOMAN IN TURMOIL?

The unauthorized biography of Dorothea Roe

by Sidney S. Crane

She looked around to see who could possibly have put this here, although she had a good idea. She turned the postcard over and on the back someone had scribbled:

I've been waiting a long time for this. Will we get to the truth at last?

12

IMOGEN

'It's here,' I say to Josh the next morning. It's Sunday, the sky is a bleached white, dew still on the lawn. I wasn't going to mention the dead magpie I'd found the other day to Josh but knew I couldn't hide it, because he'll eventually see it, and I'm too squeamish to take it down myself.

This place, once so magical to me, so safe, now feels threatening. It's as if that halcyon summer I was last here was just a fever dream, or a figment of my imagination, conjured up from the pages of a romance novel to be replaced by a thriller.

It's rained overnight and the bird's black and white coat looks scrawny and decayed. 'I don't know how long it's been there.' I shiver and wrap my coat further around my body.

'What the hell? Why would someone do this?'

We stand and stare at it, unsure of what to do. Neither of us are outdoorsy types or gardeners; we're used to inner cities and concrete, not woods and bird carcasses.

'Someone wanted us to see it. It could be a warning. For us. You know the rhyme. One for sorrow . . .'

Uncertainty crosses Josh's face. I can see him oscillating between wanting to reassure me and admitting I might be right. He lands somewhere in the middle. 'Maybe it's a country thing. Some kind of ritual? Or perhaps someone found out you'd inherited the house and is pissed off. Wanted to leave a little message. I wouldn't worry about it too much. Let's get back in the house. It's cold out here. I'll find some scissors and cut it down.' He wraps an arm around my shoulders and steers me away from the dead bird, pulling me closer to him as we cross the lawn so that I'm snuggled tight against him, wrapping my arm around his waist. Thank goodness he's here. And I think again of Dorothea, all alone in this huge house, perhaps being watched, threatened, with dead birds strung up on trees for her to find. Except the magpie was fresh when I first found it. It hadn't been there long. I know it and Josh knows it too, we're just not admitting it to each other.

Josh is already being extra protective because of my fight with Alison yesterday. He was as appalled as I was about Alison's suggestion that I visit my dad in prison. 'I don't get your sister sometimes,' he'd said, his expression darkening. 'She's being really unfair, but then, that's Alison. She doesn't get that you had two very different experiences with your father – she was much older when the violence started.' And I know he was only sticking up for me, and I love him for it, but still, it niggled that he was putting Alison down.

I'd texted Alison as soon as I got home yesterday to apologize for walking out on her. I'm still mad at her but she is the only family I have left. When she replied with a brusque, *It's fine. Talk soon,* I wished I hadn't bothered.

I leave Josh rummaging through the kitchen drawers for scissors and I go back upstairs to unpack. I try not to let the dead bird unsettle me but it's lingering in the back of my mind. I'll be alone in the house tomorrow when Josh is at work, and, not for the first time, I wish we had a dog. This house seems empty without animals, especially as last time I was here there was a menagerie milling about the place. I vow to myself that I'll bring the subject up with Josh tonight. He's in such a great mood at the moment, so happy with our windfall, that I might be able to persuade him. Maybe Dorothea's neighbour, Dennis, would consider letting me have Solly. This was his home after all.

Half an hour later I'm in the bedroom, sorting out my clothes and hanging them up in the wardrobe, when I hear a clatter and the sound of Josh swearing under his breath. I go into the hallway to see him trying to manoeuvre a huge cardboard box full of electrical stuff through the doorway of Dorothea's study.

What the hell is he doing? I march down the hallway.

He sets the box down on Dorothea's beautiful 18th-century walnut desk. 'I thought this could be my office.'

'What? No!'

He turns to me in surprise. 'Why?'

'Because . . . because this was hers.' I can still picture Dorothea sat at this desk, her eyes softening every time I'd shyly poke my head around the door, wanting her attention. It was here that we discussed art and history and novels. It was where she'd peruse her bookshelves looking for my next read, whether it be a tome on the Russian Revolution, which I was studying at school, or the autobiography of Agatha Christie. 'It's important that you know the difference between a biography and an autobiography,' she'd said to me as she pressed it into my hands. 'These are Agatha Christie's very own words. No one else's.'

I'd asked her then if she would ever write an autobiography. 'Oh no, I don't think so,' she'd replied. 'I'm better at expressing myself through art than I am with words.'

This room is where Dorothea came up with her ideas for her art. Signs of her particular taste are everywhere, from her Louis XVI-style armchair to her antique furniture. It's a room for a woman, and the thought of Josh in here with his gadgets and his maleness changing the energy just feels wrong. 'It's so . . . Dorothea,' I finish lamely.

'So we're just going to leave this room empty as some kind of shrine to Saint Dorothea?' His tone is cutting. Josh likes to get his own way and he certainly doesn't like being told what to do.

'Well, I was thinking I'd like to have this room as my office . . .'

'But you're not working at the moment.'

'That's not going to be forever, Josh. I'm considering perhaps freelancing . . .'

He sighs in irritation. 'Fine. Whatever. You have the room, then. It's your house after all.' He makes a great show of hugging the massive cardboard box and hoisting it up from the table. 'Excuse me.'

I step aside so that he can leave the room. 'Oh, wait,' he says. 'You better tell me which room I'm allowed.'

My heart sinks. 'Don't be like that . . .'

'Like what? You're obviously the boss.'

'What about this one?' I indicate a bigger room next door to the study. It's empty apart from a built-in wardrobe and a single bed. 'It has the same views.'

'It doesn't have a desk.'

'We can buy a desk. And get bookshelves built.' I push down my irritation – it's not like he ever works from home anyway.

Without saying anything else, he carries the huge box into the room and plonks it on the floor. He kneels down to go through it, keeping his back to me. I leave him to it.

When I wake up the next morning, Josh has already left for work without saying goodbye. We'd barely spoken last night so this doesn't surprise me.

I'm alone in the house, and I try not to flinch every time I hear the hiss of an electrical appliance or the hum of the fridge. I feel oddly stranded with Josh gone. We only have one car between us, which is Josh's as I used a company car when I worked at the station. When Dorothea's money comes through I'm going to buy myself one. Nothing too expensive and it will be second-hand, but I've always fancied a Mini.

I try to distract myself by researching Dorothea. I'm curled up with my laptop and a notebook in what has already become my favourite spot: a wing-backed armchair in the corner of the kitchen by the patio doors with views overlooking the garden and the wood beyond. The chair is covered in a cream fabric with blowsy pink roses, which has now faded in places and still smells faintly of dog. I remember Dorothea had a very similar one in her studio and I wonder if it also got destroyed in the fire.

This isn't the first time I've tried to find out more about her, but there is still surprisingly little personal information online. A few news reports about the fire and her death, a Wikipedia page, but it's only a few lines long and vague, reviews about her past exhibitions and the agency that represents her. I manage to find a website about the art therapy centre that she set up in the late 1970s along with three other women – Annette Baker-Hume, Maisie Hill and Rosemary Farrington – and read an extract:

> Annette, whose own husband had gone to prison ten years earlier for fraud, subsequently taking his own life in his cell, trained as an art therapist. She was looking for like-minded individuals to set up an arts therapy institute for women. Dorothea, already a friend of Annette's, agreed and the art

therapy centre was born. A few years later the centre took off when Dorothea became critically acclaimed in the art world.

Annette and Dorothea bonded over their commitment to the institute. At that time there weren't many places in the West Country where women could go to seek therapy, and a lot of their clients were women who were recovering from violent relationships. One of their first clients, Maisie Hill, whose ex-husband was serving a long prison sentence for attempting to kill her, joined Annette and Dorothea to become a founding member of the institute. Maisie, while being unable to draw or paint, was very talented at knitting and crocheting and later studied for her art therapy qualifications. Rosemary Farrington started off as a silent partner but then slowly became more involved as their success grew.

I write the women's names down in my notebook, planning to track them down along with her agent, Gabe Mitchell.

And then I see the headline and click on to a newspaper article:

SEVEN'S A SECRET NEVER TOLD

What secrets lie in artist Dorothea Roe's past?
By Maria Hensley

Dorothea Roe is warm and charming when I meet her in her stunning Regency villa on the outskirts of Bath. Famously private and perpetually single, not much is known about Dorothea's past and she has rarely given interviews over the years. Over copious amounts of tea and pancakes, and with the rain battering the single-paned windows, she eventually admits to me in a moment of vulnerability that she was unable to have children, and I can sense the sadness beneath her gruff . . .

I scroll down, but it won't allow me to read the rest of the article unless I subscribe. This is the only interview with Dorothea I can find, so I use the station's password to access the rest of the article – after all, I reason, I am still an employee. The journalist has written a lovely insight into Dorothea's world and I can just picture her here, in the kitchen, offering pancakes and numerous cups of tea, although I can see she refuses to be drawn on romantic relationships. And then I read something that makes me sit up straight, my heart thumping:

There is a playful twinkle in Roe's eyes as she discusses her new collection. Secrets, she says, will feature heavily in her sculptures. 'And lots of them.' When I press her on what kinds of secrets, she refuses to be drawn. 'You'll have to go and see the exhibition next year.'

I ask her if they are her secrets, or do they belong to other people? She appears introspective when she says, 'I find that secrets are like lattice pastry; there is always a point when yours will criss-cross with someone else's.'

The theme of the collection, says Roe, is magpies. She's done seven to correspond with the rhyme. 'I've always loved birds, and what bird is more magnificent than the magpie? The keeper of secrets, the stealer of trinkets.'

'But seven is a secret never told,' I say recalling the rhyme. 'Does that mean you'll be holding some secrets back?'

'Well, that would be telling,' Roe replies. 'Let's just say that my seventh sculpture is my most explosive.'

I check the date on the article. It was published just a week before Dorothea was murdered. Did someone see this interview and panic that Dorothea was going to spill their secrets? Is that why her studio was torched and the sculptures destroyed? But why push her down the stairs? Why kill her?

I'm just about to read more when something makes me start.

A loud thud overhead.

I freeze.

Another, fainter noise. Footsteps perhaps.

It sounds like it's coming from the room above.

Dorothea's study.

I cast around for something to use as a weapon, my heart in my throat. The studio is still boarded up and the back door is flimsy. Josh was on the phone on Saturday lining up a builder, but they can't start for another month or so. We only moved in three days ago – someone could assume the house is still empty. Or it could be Dorothea's killer.

I grab a bread knife from a block by the Aga and slowly walk through to the pantry, hoping I'm being overly dramatic and that the sounds I can hear are just the moans and groans of an old house. If someone has entered through the studio, they would have taken this spiral staircase up to the first floor. I glance towards the studio and my heart drops. The door is ajar. Was it like that before? I creep up the stairs, brandishing the knife as I tiptoe along the hallway, the floorboards creaking underfoot, until I'm standing outside Dorothea's study. The door is closed and I push it open.

Going through a box, the one with my name on it, is a man.

I gasp in alarm and the man drops the box, spilling the contents, and pushes past me so that I stumble backwards and fall against the banister, the knife clattering out of my hand and onto the bare floorboards as he makes for the winding staircase.

'Oi!' I shout, getting to my feet, grabbing the knife and following him down the stairs. He is wearing a hoody that hides his hair and forehead but I'd been able to see his face: blond stubble, very blue eyes, a long nose. He's in his twenties, and wearing baggy jeans and chunky Nike trainers. I race to the bottom of the stairs but there is no sign of him. The studio door is wide open and I run through it but the room is empty, a gap in the side of one of the boards. I head through it and stand in the garden. Has he gone into the wood? The only other way he could have feasibly escaped is if he managed to vault the six-foot fence. But then I see that the side gate that leads to the lane is wide open. It was definitely locked. I follow through the gate, stepping out onto the lane, my knees shaking.

'Are you all right?' a voice asks. Dennis is walking past with Solly and the black Lab.

I explain what's happened and he gently takes the knife from my trembling hand and helps me back through the garden and into the house, sitting me at the table and making me a cup of tea with heaps of sugar. 'For the shock,' he says quietly as the dogs lie at my feet. He takes off his coat and flat cap and he looks weirdly naked without the hat. Dennis exudes a grandfatherly presence and I'm relieved when he joins me at the table. I could see for myself how much he seemed to care for Dorothea and I can't imagine this elderly man would want to hurt her. 'You shouldn't have chased him,' he admonishes, raking his hands through his white hair. 'He could have been dangerous, and you must get a new lock for that gate. It looks broken.'

It wasn't broken yesterday.

He clears his throat. 'I think I should call the police, dear. It was devastating to hear what happened to Dotty, and it could all be connected. The man might come back.' He gets out his glasses and an ancient iPhone from his coat pocket and begins punching in a number. 'And you should have a dog about the place. A big house like this.'

I glance at Solly, at his massive fluffy head resting on his massive fluffy paws. I'd love a dog. I'm tempted to ask

Dennis if I can have Solly. Josh won't like it, of course, but what's the alternative? I doubt he's going to want to move back to the flat.

Dennis stands up, phone to his ear. 'Did he steal anything?' he asks me.

'I don't know. I should go and check . . .'

'Yes, you go, dear. Oh hello, yes . . .' he says loudly into his phone. 'I need to report a crime.' I leave the kitchen and head back up to Dorothea's study. Something niggles. It's not until I'm in the study that I realize why. The house is full of valuable antiques and yet the man had been rummaging through a box, the only one left in the study that still held papers. In his haste he dropped it and the newspaper cuttings are spread all over the wooden floor. I pick them up and start to put them back in the box. The man had been wearing gloves so there will be no fingerprints left behind. I notice the old Zippo lighter is missing. Surely the man didn't break in here just to steal that?

And then I remember the key with the Post-it Note. Was this what the man had been looking for? I run to my bedroom and fetch the jeans I was wearing yesterday from where I'd slung them over a chair. The key is still in the front pocket. Then I dart back downstairs to get my purse from my bag in the hallway. I retrieve the Post-it Note and unfold it. I look at the three words scribbled on the yellow square: *weld sheet faster.*

'The police are on their way,' Dennis says when I enter the kitchen.

I hand him the Post-it Note. 'Do you have any idea what this means?'

He squints. 'There's just three words here. They make no sense.'

'Why would Dorothea write three random words down . . .' I trail off as it clicks.

Of course. Three words. I was so stupid not to realize earlier.

'What three words!' I cry.

He reads them out and I laugh. 'No, I mean, it's co-ordinates.' I take out my phone and open up the what3words app and type in the words from the Post-it Note. Instantly the blue dot highlights an area in Dorothea's woods. I head out the patio doors, with Dennis and the two dogs following close behind, a familiar fire in my belly. I'm on to something, I just know it.

It doesn't take me long to find the spot with the help of the app.

'Here,' I say to a befuddled-looking Dennis who still doesn't understand what I'm talking about. We both glance around the small clearing surrounded by trees. I bend down and examine the ground. This must mean something. It has to.

And then, partially covered in soil and leaves, I notice a piece of metal protruding from the ground. 'This looks like a handle,' I say, dusting away the debris surrounding it to reveal a hatch door.

Dennis exhales in surprise. 'Well I never. It's one of those old bunkers.'

'What? Like a World War Two air-raid shelter?'

'It looks like it. I never knew that was here.'

Solly starts to sniff the hatch and then barks twice. I try the key in the lock on the original hatch door. It fits perfectly. Every nerve feels charged with excitement as I inch closer to knowing more about Dorothea.

Dennis helps me lift the metal door but it's much lighter than either of us was expecting and it opens easily, crashing back against the ground. I use the torch on my phone to shine a light into the dark void, illuminating a set of stone steps that leads down into a large room.

'You're not going down there, are you?' Dennis asks, his bushy brows furrowed.

'Of course,' I say, wielding my phone. I shiver – in anticipation or fear, I can't decide – and wrap my cardigan further around me, wishing I'd brought my coat.

'Be careful,' he says from behind me as I slowly descend the steps. The air smells of acrylics and something strong like turps.

And then I let out a shriek of horror.

A pale face looms out of the darkness.

13

At first I think it's a person until I step forward and see it's a life-sized papier-mâché sculpture of a woman, about my height with her arms out wide like a scarecrow. Magpies sit on each arm, and one more on the left shoulder. I blanch, remembering the gruesome find at the weekend. I already guess before I've even counted them that there are seven magpies.

'Well I never,' exhales Dennis from behind me. It's only then I realize he's followed me down the steps, leaving the dogs behind.

A frizzle of excitement sears through me and my hands are trembling as I hold my phone up close, the triangle light picking out each detail. And detailed it is. There are so many different things to take in. The woman resembles Dorothea, wearing a silvery-blonde wig and a wool jacket. On her feet are heavy hiking boots, at odds with her thin cotton skirt. She's clutching some dark fabric in one hand, the other is covered in red paint – which I'm assuming is supposed to be blood. A closer look at the magpies reveals miniature items pinned to them: I notice a Christmas card and a cat brooch.

I've seen Dorothea's work in museums before – mostly her paintings, but once I went to see a sculpture exhibition with my mum not long before she died. I remember finding the papier-mâché sculptures frightening even then.

The skin on the back of my neck prickles and I'm relieved that Dennis has followed me down here.

'There's a light switch here,' he calls from behind me. He presses it and the room floods with light, instantly making everything less scary. I turn off the torch on my phone. There is no reception down here. I scan the rest of the piece – so many details, too many for them to sink in. I take some photos with my phone to pore over later.

'Lordy. It's like a secret studio. She never once said she had this here.' Dennis pulls at the collar of his jumper. 'I'm not a fan of enclosed spaces, truth be told.'

'Why don't you go back up?'

He nods but he doesn't take his eyes from the sculpture.

I cast my gaze around the windowless room which is roughly ten foot by twelve foot – smaller than the glass-walled studio attached to her house and with a very low ceiling. Anyone above six foot wouldn't be able to stand up tall in here. A workbench runs along one side of the room with chicken wire, paints, brushes, white spirit and other bottles of unidentified liquids cluttered along it. Chucked in the corner are head-sized balls of papier-mâché, as though Dorothea was going to use them but then decided against it. Clothes and pieces of fabric spill from a big bin liner. A cluster of wigs in different colours hangs on a coat rack, which gives the impression of a group of women all huddled together. Cobwebs sparkle from dusty corners and the air is cold. The whole room looks like what I imagine you'd find backstage at a theatre.

'I don't understand,' mutters Dennis, mirroring my own thoughts. 'What's this one doing down here? Is it unfinished?'

'I think she made it here.' I indicate her materials on the bench.

'But why not use her studio? It's like she didn't want anyone to see this one.'

I feel like I've betrayed Dorothea's trust by bringing Dennis along with me. She left that Post-it Note and key for me to find. In the article I read earlier, Dorothea had told the interviewer that the theme for her new collection was magpies. Was this sculpture here because she hadn't finished it – although it looks completed to me. Or had she always been planning to keep it down here for me to discover?

Seven's a secret never told.

'There's something quite frightening about this,' Dennis says, not taking his eyes from it. 'She told me she was working on a bird theme for her new collection. Did you know her real name was Dorothy Bird?'

I turn to him in surprise. 'No, I didn't. Did she tell you that?'

He nods, looking pleased. 'She was quite private, as you probably know, but slowly, very slowly over the years, little things would come out.' He coughs into his hanky. 'The dust down here isn't good for my chest.'

There is a loud bang and I jump, heart thumping.

The hatch door has closed.

We turn to each other in alarm. 'The wind's blown it shut,' Dennis says, but I can hear the uncertainty in his voice. It's not particularly windy outside. We head for the stairs and I walk up first and push at the hatch. My throat goes dry when it won't budge.

'Here, let me,' insists Dennis and I take a step back so he can get past. He reaches up and pushes against the door with all his strength.

The hatch still doesn't move.

'What's going on?' Dennis cries. 'Who would do this to us?'

We both try it again, shoving our shoulders against it, but it's no use.

We're locked in.

14

DOROTHEA

Ten Months Before

It was finding the Zippo lighter that was the defining moment, she thought afterwards. She'd been out walking the dogs with Dennis, and her blood had run cold as she'd bent down to pick it up, nestled in the long grass on the edges of the wood, glinting in the late summer sunshine, knowing before she even whipped her glasses from the pocket of her dungarees that it would have the initials RF inscribed on it. The silver was tarnished with a slight dent in the corner and her hand trembled as she pocketed it, straightening up and glancing about frantically. Dennis must have noticed because he came straight over, concern on his face.

'Dotty, is everything okay?'

Her fingers closed around the lighter.

'What's that?'

'Oh, it's nothing . . . it's . . . an old lighter . . . I must have dropped it.'

He knew her too well. He wouldn't have missed how shaken up she was.

'Can I see?'

She didn't want him to see it but it would look odd if she refused, so wordlessly she handed it over to him.

He held it in the palm of his hand. 'Looks like silver. Expensive.' He turned it over. 'Who's RF?'

'I don't know,' she lied. She'd assumed the Christmas card she'd found a few years ago was a coincidence, but now this. Could it be true? Could he really be back? No, it was impossible. She needed to talk to Annette.

'Right.' He handed it back to her with a puzzled expression, presumably not understanding why an old Zippo could warrant such a reaction.

She slipped it into her pocket. 'The sun's gone in. Shall we go inside for a glass of wine?' She needed it for her nerves.

He hesitated and she could almost see the questions forming on his lips. Dennis was one of her most trusted friends, but she couldn't tell him this.

It was lonely keeping secrets. She'd realized that long ago. She thought how true Sir Walter Scott's poem was. 'O what a tangled web we weave, when first we practise to deceive!' And her web was so tangled it was threatening to strangle her.

But here was Dennis, with his flat cap that he wore all year round and his open, trusting face, wanting nothing from her but companionship. A true gentleman. She liked who she was when she was with him.

'Come on then, Dotty,' he said, breaking into a smile. 'Let's get in and have a cuppa. I think it might be a bit early for wine.'

As she took his arm she tried to push away the thought of the lighter and what it signified, knowing that she wouldn't be able to sleep that night.

Because she couldn't ignore the truth any longer.

15

IMOGEN

'What are we going to do?' I wail.

We've tried everything. We've tried endlessly to move the hatch door, we've shouted for help, we've drummed our fists against the metal, but to no avail. It won't budge. We could hear the dogs barking at first but now there is just an eerie silence.

Dennis looks grey and keeps pulling at the collar of his jumper. He clutches his chest and I'm worried he's about to have a heart attack.

'Come on, let's sit down and think about what to do,' I say, helping him back down the steps. He perches on the only chair by the bench and I get out my phone, but there is still no reception down here. I'm trying to repress the feelings of terror but they threaten to bubble over. I have to keep my head. There is no point us both freaking out, and I can see that Dennis isn't coping well. He keeps rubbing his chest and sweat has broken out on his forehead. 'It will be okay,' I say, pacing the room, but I can't stop myself from catastrophizing. Nobody knows we're here. Nobody even knows this place exists. Josh will come home and wonder where I am. How long would we survive down here without food or water?

'My chest is hurting,' mutters Dennis and I'm seized with panic. How is this happening?

'Take deep breaths. It's probably an anxiety attack.'

He does as I say. A hot feeling rises from my feet, up through my body and to my face. I used to get anxiety attacks when I was a kid but I haven't had one for years. And I can't afford to have one now.

'What about your phone? I don't have any reception, do you?'

Dennis taps his trouser pockets theatrically. 'I left my phone on your kitchen table after I called the police.' His eyes are dark with alarm. 'What are we going to do?'

'Someone will come for us.' I try to sound more confident than I actually feel. 'At least we're not in darkness. We have electricity.'

'Great,' mumbles Dennis. 'Electricity but no air. Or food or water.'

'This was an air-raid shelter, wasn't it? People would have been down here for hours.'

'But not days . . . not . . .' He pulls at the neck of his jumper again. 'Oh God. Oh Lord. I can't . . . I can't do this . . . I'm sorry . . .'

'Dennis!' I say firmly. 'Stop it. It's going to be okay.' I need to take his mind off it. 'Someone will come for us. The dogs. Someone will notice the dogs.' I stop pacing. 'Tell me. Are you married? Do you have children?'

At first I don't think he's going to answer, then he eventually says, 'Yes. I was married. A long time ago. She left me in the end. Had an affair with one of the neighbours.'

'Oh Dennis, I'm sorry.'

He shakes his head. 'It's okay. It was when we were living in the Chew Valley. I moved here ten years ago.'

'Children?'

'A daughter. She's married and lives in Liverpool.'

'Any grandkids?'

'Two.' He smiles at the memory of them. 'Two boys. Twins. They're amazing. Thirteen now but I go and visit them every few months.' His face falls. 'I might never see them again . . . my daughter. Stella. She'll be devastated. We're really close . . .' He clutches at his heart again.

I need to get us out of here otherwise Dennis could keel over. I dart back up the stairs and start pushing on the door again, ramming it with my shoulder, trying to heave it open. And then I start yelling. 'Help. Help. We're locked in here. Help. Help.'

A sound. Footsteps perhaps. And then a dog's bark.

Dennis looks at me, round-eyed.

And then, much to my utter relief, the door is pulled back, showing me a wonderful, exhilarating slice of grey sky. I gulp lungfuls of fresh air and sprint up the rest of the stairs before it can close again, my legs weak. I turn to help Dennis. I've never seen him move so fast. He almost runs up the stairs too.

'Thank God,' he says and we step out of the bunker and into the woods. 'Thank God.'

And then I turn to our rescuer. 'Hello, Imogen.'

It's DI Erica Shirley. She's standing with Solly and Dennis's black Lab, Cady.

'We were locked in . . .' Dennis manages as he tries to catch his breath.

DI Shirley's expression is troubled and I follow her gaze to a large stone boulder set next to the hatch. 'That was on top of the door,' she says gravely. 'If it hadn't been for the dogs here, leading me to this area of the woods, then I wouldn't have found you. We need to find out who did this.'

16

'I'll need to take a statement,' says DI Shirley when we are back in the kitchen. She hands me and Dennis a cup of coffee that she kindly made for us and I warm my hands on the hot mug. My teeth are chattering. The room smells of dogs and coffee. Dennis is talking too fast as he fills DI Shirley in on what happened, starting with the man in Dorothea's study, as though he's afraid he won't be able to get it all out if he doesn't say it quickly.

'What did he look like?' asks DI Shirley gently, directing her question at me.

'Late twenties, I think. Blue eyes and slim build. Tall.' I describe his bulky trainers and baggy jeans and dark hoody. 'He didn't seem to take anything apart from an old Zippo lighter. But I think he was looking for the key to the bunker.'

After DI Shirley had rescued us she wanted to check the bunker out for herself, but then Dennis took a funny turn, slumping to the ground. While she was seeing to him I took the opportunity to run back down to the bunker on the pretence of leaving my phone behind. I threw an old sheet over the sculpture and moved it to a corner of the bunker, surrounding it with other art paraphernalia. When DI Shirley did go into the bunker, the only things she noticed were a load of old art supplies.

'You don't know that for certain,' DI Shirley says now. 'There's nothing of interest down there that I could see.'

I hesitate. Dorothea left the key for me to find. She didn't want anyone else knowing about the sculpture. It could be a clue, and if that's the case then I already feel bad enough that Dennis knows. 'That's what we noticed too. Just a load of old art supplies.'

I shoot Dennis a look over the detective's head and he gives a very slight nod of understanding.

'Perhaps someone thought she had valuables in the bunker,' muses DI Shirley. 'But then why not take any of the antiques in the house?'

'He might have been about to steal all that but Imogen disturbed him,' suggests Dennis. He still looks a little pale, his fine white hair standing up on end.

'Are you okay?' I ask, concerned for him as he pulls at the neck of his cable-knit jumper.

'I'm grand, thank you,' he replies. 'Just a bit of a shock, that's all.'

Cady barks, making us both jump as Josh walks into the kitchen carrying his briefcase. He stops in surprise when he sees us all.

I introduce him to Dennis and then DI Shirley, and he stiffens when he realizes she's a detective. 'Is everything okay?' He sidesteps both dogs who have trotted up to sniff him.

DI Shirley tells him why she's here.

He looks appalled as he puts his briefcase down and pulls a chair out next to me. He takes my hand and rubs it between his own. I'm relieved that he's forgotten about yesterday's disagreement and I'm grateful for his presence. 'We need to do something about that boarded-up studio,' he says. 'We could change the back door to something more secure. It's only a single wood internal door with a stupid makeshift lock. We need something double glazed. Triple glazed, even. Especially as the builders won't be able to renovate the studio for a few months.' Over the last week we've both rung around to see if any other builders are free sooner, but we haven't been able to find anyone who can start before July.

'That all sounds like a good idea,' says DI Shirley, standing up. 'I'm going to send over a team of forensics for fingerprints, so please don't touch the study.' She shrugs on her scratchy-looking overcoat. I notice white hairs among the fabric and wonder if she has a cat or dog. 'Hopefully they can come first thing.'

'Did Imogen tell you about the dead magpie?' Josh asks.

'Not yet,' I say quickly. 'I was just about to.'

DI Shirley looks at me questioningly but Josh jumps in to explain. I don't mention the seven magpies on the hidden sculpture, but I can tell by Dennis's expression that it's not lost on him either.

'I'll leave you to it for now, but I suggest you sort out that back door as soon as you can,' she says.

'We've got a security firm coming tomorrow to install cameras in the garden,' Josh says, sitting up straighter, like he expects DI Shirley to give him a gold star. He's always like this around authority, desperate to please. 'I'll show you out,' he says to her.

DI Shirley promises to be in touch and tells us we can call her anytime, and then follows Josh out of the kitchen.

'Well,' says Dennis, standing up too and putting his coat on. He picks up his flat cap and places it on his head. 'Do you want Solly to stay here with you?'

Josh appears back in the kitchen and can't hide how horrified he is by Dennis's suggestion.

'It's just, it might help,' Dennis explains. 'Extra security.'

'Having the dog here didn't really help Dorothea though, did it?' Josh replies bluntly. Dennis's face falls and I could kick Josh for being so insensitive.

'I think it's a great idea . . .' I start to say but Josh interrupts me.

'Thanks, mate, but let me and Ims discuss it and we'll get back to you. Is that okay?'

'Of course.' Dennis snaps the leads back on the dogs' collars and then flashes me a kindly smile. 'See you, Imogen. If you ever need anything . . .'

'Thanks, mate,' Josh says again, taking his coat off. I can tell he's itching to get rid of Dennis and I cringe inwardly. 'We'll let you know.'

I show Dennis out, stopping to give Solly and Cady a

quick pat. 'Thanks so much for your help today, Dennis. I'm so sorry about what happened in the bunker.'

'You won't go down there again, will you, dear? Not on your own?'

'No. I promise. I've taken some photos but . . .' I lower my voice. 'Please don't say anything about the sculpture. I want some time to try and work out what it could mean before I share it with anyone she might not have trusted . . .'

He taps the side of his nose. 'I promise to keep schtum.'

'Thank you.'

I watch as he leads the dogs down the path next to our driveway and out of the side gate. He turns and gives me a quick wave and then he's gone.

When I return to the kitchen, Josh has a pan of pasta boiling on the hob.

'Are you okay, babe?' he asks with concern. 'It must have been really scary. Dennis seems a nice fellow. A bit nosey, perhaps. What was he doing here anyway?'

I explain how he helped me after I found the intruder. 'The whole thing was really horrible, Josh.' I slump onto a seat. 'Can I help?'

'No, of course not. You've had a shock.' He's silent for a few moments and I can tell he's chewing something over. Then he says, 'Why were you and Dennis in the bunker in the first place?'

I explain about the key I found and the what3words on the Post-it Note.

'Why didn't you mention this before?' He stirs the pasta more vigorously.

'I forgot about it. It wasn't until the man broke in and I realized he was looking for something that I remembered about the key.'

'Right.' A loaded pause. 'And what was down there?'

'Just . . . some art supplies.'

If I tell him about the sculpture he'll only worry. And he'll know I won't be able to resist trying to figure out what it means.

'Look, about Dennis's offer,' I say to change the subject. 'I know you're not a fan of dogs, but I'd feel more comfortable . . .'

Conflicting emotions pass over his face.

'I don't know. A dog is a big responsibility.'

'If we continue to live here we need a dog. For security.'

'A Golden Retriever is hardly a bloody guard dog.'

'He saved my life today.'

Josh dishes out the pasta without speaking. The sky is darkening outside and I push away the unease that grows in the pit of my stomach. Is someone prowling around our grounds right now? Killing magpies and thinking up new ways to threaten me?

'Right, fine,' announces Josh as we sit down. 'We can take Solly. But he'll be your dog. Your responsibility.'

'Yes, thank you, thank you, thank you,' I cry, jumping up and kissing him. 'You won't regret this.'

'I better not.'

*

The next morning, while Josh is busy showing the security firm where he wants the cameras to go, I head over to Dennis's house to get Solly. A forensic van turned up at 8 a.m. and the officers are currently in Dorothea's study dusting for prints.

It rained in the night and as a result the air is clear and fresh, the lane muddy. I'm wearing an old pair of Dorothea's wellies and one of her quilted jackets that was hanging on the coat stand and it still smells faintly of her perfume, which takes me right back to the summer of 2008. As I head down the lane, splashing through puddles, I pass Mick and Sue's house and think fondly of Harry, wondering how he is. Their house is similar to Dorothea's but much smaller and with less land. I slow down to glance through their wrought-iron gates. The driveway is empty. I might call in on them in a day or two, when Josh is out at work. He doesn't know about Harry and I'm not going to tell him, as it would only make him jealous. He likes to believe he's my first boyfriend.

Plato House, where Dennis lives, is the other side of Mick and Sue's. It's a pretty, semi-detached Georgian cottage with ivy growing up the Bath stone walls and the name of the house pressed into the gatepost. The front door is on the side of the house, surrounded by a stone porch. I push open the wooden gates to the drive where an old Skoda sits. Rubber dog toys are scattered on the gravel.

I knock on the door and instantly there is the sound of dogs barking. I wait, expecting to hear Dennis calling to them or maybe his footsteps. But there's nothing. Maybe he's out, although he said himself he leads a small kind of life these days. Unless he's visiting his daughter. He mentioned yesterday that he often goes and stays with her. But I heard him say to DI Shirley yesterday that he'd be in today if she needed to ask him more questions, and there is no way he'd leave the dogs alone in the house to visit his daughter all the way in Liverpool. And his car is in the driveway. The first stirrings of anxiety ripple through me as my second knock goes unanswered. I remember how he clutched his chest yesterday while we were locked in the bunker, and I hurry around the side and into his back garden.

I press my nose to the glass plane in the back door, which has a view of the kitchen. The dogs rush to the door barking wildly, jumping all over each other in their eagerness, and then Cady starts to whine. I cup my face with my hands and then my heart stops.

Lying on the tiled floor, a halo of blood around his head, is Dennis.

17

DOROTHEA

Two Years Before

'Can you be persuaded to come out of retirement and do one last collection?'

Dorothea's heart sank at Gabe's question. She could almost hear him holding his breath on the other end of the line. She glanced around her studio at the half-finished paintings and sculptures. At one time you couldn't move in here for all the canvases and the art paraphernalia, but these days the studio was mostly used as a garden room, somewhere she sat with a cup of tea and the wireless radio that Rosemary had given her for her birthday, looking out over the garden with Solly at her feet. Her fingers weren't as supple as they used to be, despite all the cod liver oil tablets she washed down her throat.

But more than that, she had nothing left to say.

'I don't know, Gabe . . .' The truth was she didn't need the money and she enjoyed her quiet way of life. She still saw the girls – they were always the girls, despite being in their seventies – their bond could never be broken. And she enjoyed pottering in her garden, going for walks with Dennis and the dogs. It was a life she felt lucky to have. In her heyday she'd made Gabe a lot of money, and he still benefitted from her royalties, but she knew she remained his biggest client. Of course he'd want her to continue working, and he knew a brand-new collection could fetch a great price.

He'd become her agent when she was about thirty and noise had begun to surround her creations. He'd visited the gallery in London where some of Dorothea's work was being exhibited and had given her his card. He'd been up and coming himself back then, five years her junior but hungry for success. They'd risen through the art world together and as a result they'd formed a close working relationship. She thought of Gabe as the younger brother she never had. He had been the one who had suggested the name change all those years ago; it had come at just the right time.

'It would be amazing. A new collection after all these years. Just imagine how surprised and pleased your fans would be.'

She had to put a stop to this. She didn't want to hear Gabe waxing lyrical about what could be. 'Let me think about it,' she said curtly. That was the best way to handle Gabe.

'Do you mean it? You'll really think about it?'

'I said so, didn't I? Now I have to go. I have a paper to read and you're disturbing my morning routine.'

She could almost see him rolling his eyes in mock frustration. 'Have it your way,' he chuckled.

It was peaceful in the morning, her favourite time of day, the grass ice-tipped and crunchy, the sun low in the sky, making the trees in the wood look black. Gabe was disturbing all that with his talk of new collections.

'One more thing . . .'

'Gabe.'

'It's important, Dot.'

'Fine.' She suppressed a sigh and smoothed down the newspaper that she'd laid across her lap.

'A man has called here a few times, asking questions about you.'

She froze, alarmed. 'What? Who?'

'His name is Sidney Crane and he says he's writing a biography.'

'A biography? Whatever for?'

'Money, I suppose. He wants information. Obviously, I haven't given him any.'

'I should hope not.' Her mind raced. Why now? Could this biographer have found out what she had done? Images from that terrible night flashed through her head: the chip in the glass ashtray, that spot of blood on the mushroom-coloured carpet. And then an even more horrifying thought occurred to her. If he knew about that, did that mean he also knew what happened afterwards? 'And it's doubtful he'll find anyone to talk to,' Gabe continued, and Dorothea had to zone back in to what he was saying. 'But maybe you should warn

Annette, Maisie and Rosemary. Just in case he tries to harass them.'

'You don't have to worry about them,' she said confidently. She trusted the three of them with her life. 'Thanks for letting me know. Now, can I get back to my paper?' She tried to sound nonchalant, but she felt sick.

'Absolutely. Remember to think about the collection.'

'Goodbye, Gabe.'

Her heart was still thudding as she ended the call, and she placed a hand on her chest and breathed deeply.

She needed to find this Sidney Crane. She couldn't allow that book to be published. She had to put a stop to it at once.

18

IMOGEN

Josh comes into the kitchen carrying one of Dorothea's throws and drapes it over my shoulders. 'You're shaking,' he says, running his hands up and down the top of my arms. 'Do you want a cuppa?'

I nod, thanking him, while trying to push the image of Dennis's prostrate body from my mind. His face had been so pale and there was so much blood. Josh keeps throwing me looks of concern as he puts the kettle on the hob. The two dogs are lying by my feet under the kitchen table. I had to bring Cady back with me, I couldn't just take Solly.

'I can't stop thinking about Dennis.'

'Well, he's lucky to be alive by the sounds of it.'

'I wonder what happened. Do you think he had a heart attack and then hit his head or something?'

'God, it's like *Midsomer Murders* around here.'

'Don't say that. Dennis hasn't been murdered.'

But I can't ignore the possibility that Dennis was attacked. First someone locks us in the bunker and now this.

The sound of the kettle whistling gets Josh's attention and he turns away from me to make the tea. I watch his body language, his rigid shoulders, his tensed jaw, and I bite back my annoyance. I get the impression he's still cross with me for not letting him have Dorothea's study but trying to hide it on account of everything that has happened since.

As soon as I saw Dennis lying there on the floor I tried the door, but it was locked, so I called for an ambulance straight away. Around five minutes later they arrived and managed to get into his house. I followed them inside the kitchen and tried to calm the dogs down, but it took a while to persuade Cady to leave her owner. There were bloody pawprints all over the floor. I can still spot flecks of blood on one of Solly's paws.

'At least I've got Rachel coming over later. She'll take my mind off it,' I say.

He hands me a mug and then sits down next to me. 'Oh, you didn't mention she was coming today. Is that a good idea with the security firm here?' He once told me he thought Rachel was 'too loud, too brash and too forthright'. He's not entirely wrong – but she's so much more as well. Fiercely loyal, funny, sharp and kind. Josh doesn't seem to think we need friends. He has workmates that he never spends time with outside the office and he's in a football WhatsApp chat with a group of mates from university, but he never makes the effort to see them.

'We'll make sure not to disrupt them. How are they getting on?'

'They're busy right now installing some at the front, but they'll also do the back of the house – overlooking the wood. We should probably put one on the gate so that it alerts us if someone enters the property, and they're putting a new lock on the gate. Oh, and there's a bloke coming later to replace that flimsy door that leads to the studio with a proper back door, double glazed – so even if anyone does get into the boarded-up bit around Dorothea's damaged studio, they won't be able to get into the house.'

'Thanks for organizing it all.' I sip my tea, feeling slightly calmer now after the shock of finding Dennis like that.

Josh is on a roll. He's always at his most animated when he feels like he's being useful. 'And they're going to install an alarm system. I can't believe that Dorothea never had one, living in a house like this.' He rolls his eyes. 'These old people, it's like they don't trust technology. Dennis wouldn't have been attacked if he'd had security.'

'Stop saying he was attacked. We don't know that for definite!'

I think of his back door, locked, with no signs of forced entry. The same with the front door, and none of his windows appeared to have been broken. I'm hoping that Josh is wrong and is just understandably paranoid after what happened to Dorothea.

I gave my name and number to the paramedics in case Dennis's daughter wanted to speak to me. She might want to take Cady, but if not, I'm determined to look after her. It's the least I can do.

Because deep down I'm terrified that Dennis was attacked, and if he was, then it's my fault for dragging him into all this.

'And this is where I found the intruder yesterday,' I finish. Since Rachel's arrival, I've talked non-stop about everything that has happened, knowing that her natural inquisitiveness will mean she's all ears. Josh, predictably, has made himself scarce. 'And I think he was after the key to the bunker.'

'Why? What's so special about the bunker?' asks Rachel, stepping into the room and surveying the shelves.

I explain about the sculpture I found. 'Look, I took photos. They're not very clear, so I need to go back down there.' I lower my voice. 'I haven't told Josh. He'd only worry, and after Filcher and everything . . .'

She gives a brisk nod of understanding as she takes the phone and starts scrolling through the photos. 'Dorothea's sculptures are sinister. What's with all the magpies?'

I explain about the rest of the collection that was destroyed and how I believe she'd left this one behind for me to find.

'Is it true that Dorothea was murdered?' she asks to my surprise as she hands me back the phone.

'What makes you say that?' Have the police decided to release that information to the press after all?

'Something that came in last night about a possible arson. I'm so sorry,' she says when she notices my expression.

I sigh. 'I think it was because of this sculpture, Rach. I found an article published the week before she died where Dorothea was interviewed, talking about her new collection and alluding to knowing all these secrets.'

'But if the person who set Dorothea's studio on fire thought they'd got rid of all her artwork, why would they be looking for the bunker? How would they know about it?'

'Hmmm. I dunno. It's like they knew where to look.'

'Who else knows about the bunker?'

'Well, the neighbour, Dennis, who was with me when we got locked in. Josh knows about the bunker but not what's in it. And a detective called DI Erica Shirley who rescued me and Dennis from the bunker, but I haven't told her about the sculpture. I made out that it was just a load of art supplies down there.'

'You don't trust the police?'

'It's not that . . . it's just . . .' I try to organize my thoughts. 'She left it for me to find for a reason. I think she knew she might have been in danger and potentially even from whom. And she didn't go to the police herself.'

'But you could be in danger, Immy. However, I think you're right to keep the bunker to yourself. Don't tell anyone else about the sculpture.'

'I won't.'

She moves to the study's sash window that overlooks the edge of the woods. When she turns back to me her expression is serious. 'Let's take the dogs into the woods with us and I can take a proper look. No offence, but your photos are pretty shit and I need to see this sculpture for myself.'

As we cross the lawn I spot one of the security team by the patio doors. I wonder how much this is all going to cost and if Josh has gone overboard. And then I remind myself that we can never be too safe. It's great I've been left all this money from Dorothea, but I can imagine maintaining this place will become a financial drain. We can't waste it.

'Everything okay between you and Josh?' asks Rachel, linking her arm through mine.

'What makes you say that?' The wind has picked up, sending a flurry of leaves into the air.

'Just . . . you keeping things from him.'

'You know how he worries.'

'Hmmmm. He seems to think you're made of glass.'

'It's worse since that whole Dominic Filcher thing.'

She rolls her eyes. 'No, it's not. He was like that before. He always insisted he wait for you if you were working late.'

'He was worried about me. I liked it. I've never had anyone worry about me before.'

'And now you find it stifling?'

'Um . . . no, I didn't say that . . .' I blush because, despite my protestations, she's right.

'It's okay if you do. You are nearly thirty years old, you can look after yourself.'

'Rachel,' I inject a warning tone into my voice. 'Everything is good between me and Josh, okay?'

'Fine. Do you think you'll be able to come back to work? It's more of a commute now you live in Bath.' She puts on a plummy voice when she says Bath and I laugh. 'Although you don't need to now, I suppose. Not now you're minted. You probably never need to work again.'

The subject of money makes me feel uncomfortable. And now I'm concerned that all this will change the dynamics of our friendship – that Rachel will stop seeing us as being 'the same'. We were always bemoaning our lack of money, our long working hours, our big mortgages and outstanding student loans.

'I like working, so I hope so. And also Dorothea stipulated that we can't sell the house for a year. Don't you think that's odd?'

'Actually, it makes sense if it's linked to the sculpture. Maybe she wanted to give you enough time to work everything out.'

A chill settles over me. 'Which means she must have known she was in danger.'

'It looks that way, yes.' A disbelieving noise escapes Rachel's lips as we walk further into the woods. 'I can't believe you have a whole wood!' The two dogs lollop in front of us, making me feel a whole lot safer.

It's not long before we reach the spot where the bunker is and I pull out the key from my jacket pocket. Rachel stares down at something on the hatch door. 'What's that?'

I follow her gaze and frown. I kneel down to pick it up, confused.

'A Zippo lighter?' she says, taking it from me. 'Is it the one stolen from the box?'

I push my hair out of my eyes. 'It looks like it, which means he was here, in the woods.' The hairs on the back of my neck bristle. 'What does he want?'

'He must know about the bunker and possibly the sculpture as well.'

I glance about, wondering if we're being watched, but then I reason that surely they'd be put off at the sight of the security men on the driveway.

Satisfied we're alone, I bend down and put the key in the lock.

'I'll stay above ground to make sure we don't get locked in,' I say to Rachel as I open the metal door. It clanks back against the ground.

She nods, staring down at the open space. 'Wow, this is so cool. Bit dark though.'

'There's a light switch, just on your right. The sculpture is in the corner, covered by a sheet.'

She hands me back the lighter and descends the steps with trepidation. I keep watch as she disappears into the bunker. A rook caws overhead and I shiver, thankful that the dogs are with me. I don't like being out here alone and I have to keep telling myself that the security guys aren't far away. I turn the lighter over in my hand, noting the engraved swirls. It's definitely the one I first found in the box. Why would that man steal it just to then dump it here again? Is it a warning?

Eventually Rachel emerges from the bunker, dusting

the shoulders of her coat. 'It's so strange,' she says. 'All those magpies with the little trinkets attached. They're obviously clues. And is the sculpture supposed to be of Dorothea?'

'I assume so, yes.'

Rachel keeps watch this time while I go back down. I try to imagine Dorothea coming here, working on this sculpture in secret. 'What are you trying to tell me?' I whisper into the damp air as I study the sculpture again, hoping that, this time, something makes sense to me, but nothing does. I always feel this way when studying a piece of art, totally baffled as to its meaning. The only thing I can work out is that the sculpture is of Dorothea, and the red paint on her hand must signify blood.

Is she trying to say she had blood on her hands? Yet only one hand is painted red. Is that significant?

And then an item on one of the magpies catches my eye. It's the lighter. A miniature version of the one I'm holding in my hand.

I run back up the steps to tell Rachel.

She's standing between the dogs, looking a little freaked out, and I can see why. A magpie is perched on a branch staring at her, head cocked to one side. When it sees me it flies away.

I hand her the lighter and explain about the tiny version I'd found on the sculpture.

We both examine it properly for the first time.

It looks as though it could be silver, or silver plated at least, but most of it is tarnished.

'Look, there are initials,' she says in a low voice, rubbing at the front of it with her finger.

'RF.'

'We need to find out who RF is,' she says, her eyes widening. 'Because those initials could belong to her killer.'

19

DOROTHEA

Four Years Before

Rosemary walked into the dining room carrying a silver tray with a turkey so huge that her slender arms in her sleeveless dress looked like they were about to buckle under its weight.

'Everyone, please sit,' she announced, and Dorothea was forced to suppress a sigh. Oh, how she hated Christmas Day. So full of expectation that it was always a disappointment. She often wondered if it was only a disappointment for her because she didn't have any family to share the day with. These three women were her family, she supposed. Her chosen family. She'd known them the longest, after all. And, like family, they in turns delighted and irritated her.

There was Annette Baker-Hume in her uniform of tweed and pearls, her hair in a sleek chignon, sitting at the head of the table as always even though this wasn't even her house, with her grandson, Warren, next to her.

Aged seventeen, he had been living with Annette for the past year after falling out with his parents. Annette was long widowed although she still carried her husband's surname along with her trauma.

And then, next to Annette was Maisie. Lovely Maisie Hill, Dorothea's favourite. A sweet-faced woman who, despite being in her late sixties, had smooth, rosy cheeks and a childlike glint in her marble-blue eyes and who was rarely found without her crocheting. Dorothea and Annette had met Maisie back in the late 1970s when she came to one of their art therapy classes. She had bonded with Annette because she too had an ex-husband who was in prison. (Annette's husband had been sentenced to fraud a few years before Dorothea had met her. He later hung himself in jail.) It was only later they discovered Maisie's husband had been sent down for almost killing Maisie. Fifteen years ago she had met a lovely, kind man called Aiden with big shaggy eyebrows and a moustache to match. He sat opposite her and every now and then would reach across the table to pat Maisie's hand. And then there was Rosemary Farrington. Posh Rosemary, as Dorothea used to secretly refer to her. She was now Lady something or other, ninety-eighth in line to the throne. Rosemary had started off as Annette's friend but had become close with all of them when they realized their philosophy on life aligned. For years it was just the four of them, meeting every week in Annette's outbuilding which she'd set up as an art studio. And after Dorothea found some success as an artist, they used her name to expand the group, guided by Annette, and started offering classes in the West Country. Then, in the late 1990s, Rosemary's father died and, as his only child, she inherited his wealth, some of which she ploughed into making the art therapy business a franchise. This meant they could all step away from it, apart from Annette, who was unwilling to relinquish control completely. It was like a child they had all spawned together which had grown and evolved into an adult they no longer recognized. But those first few years, when all they'd had was each other, they'd taken their hurt and despair and trauma and turned it into something good, something worthwhile.

Now Rosemary had turned her hand to helping reform young offenders, offering them board and shelter in her huge house. Her most recent, Peter, who wasn't much older than Warren, came into the room with a bowl of roast potatoes that he'd cooked himself and set them down in the middle of the table. He grinned at Warren as he took a seat beside him. Dorothea noticed Annette's smile disappear for a few seconds, worry flashing in her eyes. Annette didn't really approve of Rosemary's new venture and Dorothea could tell her friend was concerned that Peter was a bad influence.

'Merry Christmas, you lovely lot,' announced Rosemary, placing the turkey onto the table. 'Warren, would you mind doing the honours?'

Warren blushed self-consciously but seemed more than capable of using a knife – Annette once told

Dorothea that her son and his wife owned a farm – and expertly carved the turkey.

Dorothea wished that they could, at least once, hold Christmas lunch at her place, not always at Rosemary's. Annette said it was because Rosemary was lonely living in Greywalls Hall with just herself and whatever new lost soul she was currently helping. Although Peter had stayed around longer than most. Dorothea thought he was a nice lad, a bit awkward and not great at making conversation, but he seemed fond of Rosemary and helped her bring the logs in for the fire and did odd jobs around the house. Rosemary had never married or had children. She'd been engaged once, in the early 1970s, but had been left devastated after discovering he was a con artist with a wife and was using Rosemary for her money.

Greywalls was Tudor in appearance with its vast, draughty rooms and high ceilings. It was on the outskirts of Bristol, near Bitton, and was a schlep to get to. But Dorothea knew all about being lonely so she always ended up agreeing. And it would be like old times in the evening, drinking around the open fire and reminiscing about the past. That was the best part of Christmas Day for Dorothea, the last few hours before bed.

But Dorothea also wondered if there was a darker reason for Rosemary always insisting that they have Christmas here. An excuse to force them all together in the very place where Ruth had spent her last few hours. A painful reminder of how they were unable to save her.

That had been their speciality, after all. Helping vulnerable women through art. Looking for the small, tell-tale signs of abuse. Dorothea had prided herself on seeing those signs in Ruth when she had employed her as her cleaner, but even so, they had failed her.

After they'd eaten, Annette and Dorothea offered to clear the plates. The others were all in the drawing room, Warren setting up the Monopoly board, and, not for the first time, Dorothea felt sorry for the teenager surrounded by a load of oldies and an ex-con. Not that he seemed to mind.

As Annette stood at the sink she started to sneeze.

'Cold?' asked Dorothea as she scraped the unfinished food into the bin.

'Allergies playing up. Rosemary's house is always so dusty.' Annette was hunched over the sink, rinsing one of Rosemary's fancy glass dishes that wasn't to be put in the dishwasher. She reached for a tea towel and dried her hands. 'Let me just get my nasal spray,' she said, moving to the counter where her handbag stood open. Annette always favoured oversized handbags that resembled doctors' cases. Dorothea could never understand what Annette had in there. She watched, bemused, as Annette rummaged around inside the bag and pulled out her spray and some eye drops. 'Excuse me a moment, Dot, I'll do this in the bathroom.' As she hurried out of the kitchen, Dorothea noticed something that must have fallen out of Annette's bag when she pulled out her medication. Dorothea bent down to pick it up. It was a small Christmas card with a robin on the front. She was about to put it back into Annette's cavernous bag when the name inside caught her eye. *Surely that can't be right*, she thought as she opened the card fully. But yes, there it was. No full name. Just a 'Bobby' as a sign-off. And the card wasn't addressed to Annette like she'd assumed, but to Rosemary.

She read it again with a growing sense of unease.

Hope you're keeping well. Bobby

No, she thought, shaking her head. *It could be anyone. Bobby isn't exactly an unusual name.* Was that what happened with age, the past and present converged? It was being here in this house. It always made her imagination shoot into overdrive. And it was this time of year which made her reflect on her life, and her past mistakes.

She stood for a few moments with the card in her hand. Perhaps it hadn't come from Annette's bag after all, but from a shelf above the microwave where Rosemary had placed a few of her cards. Dorothea found a space for it there. Annette must have knocked past it by accident and sent it flying to the floor. See. She was being ridiculous.

20

IMOGEN

DI Erica Shirley is staring at me steadily as I hand her the lighter. I can't tell if she thinks I'm over-reacting or if she's pleased I brought it in to the police station. She drops it into a plastic bag and carefully seals it. She has this way of making me feel nervous. Her gaze is too forthright, too unblinking, and she always takes a beat too long to speak, which inevitably means I begin gabbling to fill the silence.

'Whoever took this lighter has been in the woods. I don't know if they dropped it or left it for me to find, but you'll see the initials on it. RF. It could . . . it could mean something.'

'You've done the right thing bringing it in,' she says. She hesitates, as though she's contemplating saying something else. I wait, willing myself not to rush in and speak. It's a tactic I employ when I'm interviewing someone about a sensitive subject. 'You know, I interviewed Dorothea once, after your mother's death.'

I sit up straighter, waiting to see where she is heading with this.

'The initials on the lighter are RF. Did you ever meet a woman called Rosemary Farrington when you stayed with Dorothea that summer?' she asks. 'She was a friend of Dorothea's.'

We both stare down at the plastic bag. 'Yes, once that I can remember,' I say. 'Do you think that's who this belongs to?'

She remains predictably non-committal and I realize she's not going to answer. 'I know it was Rosemary's house that my mum was walking home from on the night my dad . . .' I trail off.

That Halloween I'd arranged to go trick or treating and then have a sleepover with my school friends. While I was packing a bag I could hear my parents arguing downstairs – something I had to later testify to in court. My father was kicking off because he didn't want to go to the Halloween party at Rosemary's house and he expected Mum to stay at home with him. Mum, dressed in her vampire costume (we'd watched a lot of *Buffy* that autumn) had dropped me off at Ava's and I'd noticed how unsure she'd looked, which made me hesitate as I was getting out of the car.

'Mum? Is everything okay?' I knew it wasn't.

'I don't know,' she'd sighed. 'Maybe I should stay home with Dad. Things have been good between us lately. He's not been drinking . . .'

And I'd cast my eyes over my beautiful mother in her figure-hugging velvet costume – one of the reasons, I'd later realized, why my dad hadn't wanted her to go – and felt a surge of defiance against my father for always trying to ruin her fun. So I convinced her to go. I told her that it sounded like it was going to be a brilliant party and how I wished kids were allowed. I'd only met Rosemary once, but I'd been impressed by her Gothic mansion and knew it would be the perfect venue. It wasn't until the next day when, instead of Mum coming to pick me up, it was a grey-faced Dorothea, that I learned what had happened: Mum had gone to the party in the end, but Dad had followed her there. He'd slipped in, unnoticed in his skeleton costume, and had tried to force her to come home. Witnesses at the party said that he was grabbing her arm and calling her names. In the end Dorothea and Rosemary were forced to kick him out, and Mum walked home later. Dad's car was seen on CCTV not far from where Mum was found the next morning on the towpath with a fatal head injury and my father's skin under her fingernails. Police later found the fabric mask of my father's Halloween costume tossed into the river.

DI Shirley continues to assess me in that quiet, studious way of hers. The way she's looking at me is almost maternal, like she's picturing me as the fourteen-year-old I was during my dad's trial. 'I liked Dorothea,' she says, running the ribbon on her lanyard through her fingers. 'It was obvious to me that she really cared about you and your mum.' And then her face darkens. 'I really want to catch the bastard who killed her.'

'Me too,' I admit. 'You don't think . . . you don't think it could be Rosemary, do you?'

She pulls at her lanyard, her expression grim. 'I don't know. But I would like to speak to her regarding this lighter and to see if it could be hers.'

I would like to do that too, but I don't say as much to DI Shirley.

'I'm glad you've got more security around the house, but please still be vigilant,' she says, her features softening.

'Did forensics find anything at the house when they came yesterday?'

'The report isn't ready yet,' she says in that same non-committal tone as earlier and I can already tell this conversation is over, that she's said as much as she's going to on the subject of Dorothea's murder. She stands up and I follow suit. 'If anything else happens, please don't hesitate to call me. Let me show you out.'

As I walk back to Josh's car it starts to rain lightly and I quicken my pace. I don't know if I've done the right thing not mentioning the sculpture to DI Shirley. I'd asked her about Dennis when I'd first arrived at the station and she said he was still in intensive care. If he was attacked, I'm worried it's all linked to the bunker and that sculpture, and by keeping it from the police I could be making matters worse.

Last night I re-read Maria Hensley's article about Dorothea, hoping that I might have missed something. The piece had been accompanied by some lovely photographs: a recent one of Dorothea sitting in her wing-backed kitchen chair, looking wistfully out onto the garden with Solly at her feet. Another of Dorothea when she was very young, in her twenties with three other women, sitting around a Formica-topped table in a kitchen. By the clothes the women are wearing, it looks like it was taken sometime in the 1970s. Dorothea is leaning forward, elbow on the table and looking serious, her gaze slightly off camera. The piece had the names of the other women under the photograph: Annette Baker-Hume, Maisie Hill and Rosemary Farrington. I'd met Annette and Rosemary that summer, but never Maisie. I peered at the photo of the sweet-faced young woman. She had been crocheting what looked like a bird, or a butterfly. Something with wings anyway. I had to read it furtively, under the sheets when Josh had fallen asleep.

I cross the road towards the car park when I notice a man in padded biker clothes barrelling towards me. The visor on his helmet obscures his face. Unease crawls across my skin. There's something sinister in the way he's striding towards me. Why is he wearing a helmet if he's not on his bike? I move aside to make way for him. He instantly moves as well so that he knocks right into me, roughly shouldering me as he storms past so that I have to stop myself stumbling into the road. My heart is thumping with anger and fear. I glance about me in shock. A woman on the other side of the road is hunched under an umbrella but doesn't seem to have noticed, and nobody else is around.

'What the actual fuck, arsehole,' I mutter under my breath when he's far enough away not to hear me. I watch him as he continues down the street. He doesn't look back.

I don't know if I imagined it, but I'm sure he said my name as he pushed past me.

21

It's a Wednesday, five days after we moved in, and it still feels like we're just visiting. The house still very much feels like Dorothea's, especially as it's filled with all her furniture. Josh has an app so he can assess the camera footage, and he's promised he'll show me how to set it up on my phone as well – not that he's done it yet. He has snuggled right up to where I'm sitting on one of Dorothea's velvet sofas, the dogs laid out on the faded Persian rug, and he's getting closer despite me angling my phone away.

'What you looking at?' he asks, moving even closer.

'Oh, just scrolling.' I try and sound nonchalant, not wanting him to know I'm researching Rosemary because of the initials on the lighter. I've already found her address and now I'm looking into her background. I've discovered her on Companies House – she's had numerous small businesses since investing in the art therapy centre with Dorothea, Annette and Maisie, but there are no red flags. If it was her secret Dorothea wanted to expose, then it doesn't look like anything financial judging by what I've seen. There are no CCJs against her name, no criminal convictions. She's never been married but there is another name on the electoral roll under her address. Someone called Peter Bryce.

I close the page I've been reading and move away from Josh. He flops back against the sofa. 'Anyway, I'd better take the dogs out for their evening walk,' I say. 'Want to come?'

'Nah, I'll make a start on dinner. Remember the security firm is coming back tomorrow to check a few things, so I'll work from home.'

I try not to look disappointed. 'Twice in one week! What will your boss say?' Josh never worked from home when we lived in the flat and neither did I. There was only one bedroom and just not enough space. I hope he's not going to suddenly make this a regular thing now we live here. He'll only get under my feet while I'm trying to investigate what happened to Dorothea.

'He's on holiday this week, so what he doesn't know can't hurt him.' He chuckles. 'I bought a book on Agas as I have no idea how to use one.' He stands up too and loosens his tie. 'I was going to do something on the hob. One-pan chicken and rice okay for you?'

Things I love about Josh: his caring nature. How he cooks so I don't have to.

'Thanks,' I say, kissing him quickly and then heading out the room. I can hear him follow me into the hallway.

'Don't be too long.' He hands me the dogs' leads. 'It's getting dark already because of the bad weather.'

'Okay. See you in a bit.' I throw on my raincoat and head outside, being pulled roughly by both dogs.

'Maybe I should come with you . . .' he says from the doorway.

'No, it's fine. I won't be long,' I call back. I give Josh a little wave and leave through the side gate, the dogs pulling ahead.

The lane is pretty and tree-lined with hedgerows on one side and detached and semi-detached Georgian properties lining the pavements on the other, all in the same creamy Bath stone. At the end of the lane is a small church and then beyond that fields with views of the Royal Crescent and the city of Bath. I take the dogs to the field via a kissing gate and let them off their leads. I stand looking at the view as a fine rain dusts my hair and jacket. The rain stops but the sky gets darker and I'm aware I'm out here alone. I call the dogs and head back down the lane. As I pass Mick and Sue's house, I see someone in the driveway. The gates are open and a man around my age walks towards me.

'Imogen? Is that you?'

'Harry!' My heart twists. He's taller and even better looking than I remember since I last saw him all those years ago, his dark curls stylishly tamed, and the roundness of his teenaged face has disappeared into a well-defined jaw and prominent cheekbones. But he still has that toothy grin that I'd once fallen for. He is wearing a knee-length overcoat over jeans, a maroon scarf tucked into the collar. He has a college student air about him. He's holding a pile of books in his arms and I'm pleased to see his love of reading hasn't changed. I remember how many hours we spent in the woods that summer discussing books and arguing over whether we preferred His Dark Materials to Harry Potter.

His smile is broad yet I instantly feel like that awkward, gawky fourteen-year-old I'd been the last time we saw each other. So much has happened since.

'Mum said you'd inherited Dorothea's house,' he says. 'So tragic what happened to her. I'm so sorry. I didn't realize you'd stayed in touch.'

'We didn't. It's a long story. Do you still live at home, then?'

'Only temporarily. My girlfriend and I split up, and Bath's so bloody expensive and the rent on my flat was costing me a fortune.' He shifts the books to his other arm.

'Sorry to hear about your relationship ending.'

He shrugs. 'Thanks. Just one of those things. So, what have you been up to over the years? Mum said she saw your byline a couple of times. So you ended up in journalism after all? I remember you said you wanted to be a writer.'

'Yes. I've been working for a news station in Bristol but I'm . . . well, I'm on leave at the moment.' I look down as I dig the toe of my boot into the gravel, guilt tugging at the lie.

'Oh, is that a good thing? It doesn't look like it from your expression.'

I'd forgotten how direct Harry could be.

I glance up at him. 'Not really. I suppose I was a bit of

a workaholic and now I hate having all this time on my hands.'

'I can understand that. So, um . . . are you living at Dorothea's villa alone, then?' He's definitely fishing. 'Apart from the dogs, that is?' he adds with a laugh, glancing at Solly and Cady at my feet. 'Wait, isn't that Dennis's dog?'

'Yes. I'm looking after her.' I'm grateful to change the subject. I realize I don't want to talk to him about Josh. 'Did you hear what happened to Dennis? He's in intensive care.'

His face falls. 'Oh, yes, Dad told me. It's awful. Is he going to be okay?'

'I don't know. I hope so . . .' I trail off, realizing I can't say more without revealing the bunker and the sculpture. There's an awkward beat of silence before I ask, 'So, what did you end up doing jobwise?'

'I'm a book editor. Hence why I've got all these.' He adjusts them in his arms. 'I work for an indie publisher in Bristol. Non-fiction. I specialize in history.'

'Oh, Harry, that's amazing.' I feel a burst of pride. 'So you did it. You said you always wanted to.'

'Well, it was always that or an astronaut.'

'I think a book editor is safer.' I laugh.

'I'm also writing my own history book. World War One. Trying to do that around work, but it's taking me a long time. Lots of research.'

'I can imagine.'

He falls silent and his eyes soften as he adds, 'I was so very sorry to hear about your mum. I wish I'd been

'. . . better . . . you know, after. I wanted to reach out so many times, but I was this stupid teenage boy who had no clue how to handle anything deep or my feelings . . .' He glances down at his trainers and blushes. He looks so guilty that I rush to reassure him that I understand.

'Harry. God, it was a messed-up time. I was living in Keynsham, and back then, you and Dorothea and this place all seemed a world away from what I was living through.'

'Dorothea was so worried about you . . .' He looks up at me. 'She tried, you know. She tried to see you but your sister sent her away.'

I stare at him in surprise. 'What?'

'Your sister told Dorothea that she shouldn't contact you. That it would be better for you if she left you alone. I'm sure she did what she thought was best,' he adds quickly, noticing my bewildered expression.

'Alison never told me . . .'

'I'm sure she was just trying to protect you.'

My already complicated feelings towards Alison darken. I swallow and try and brush away my discomfort. 'I better be going,' I say, suddenly noticing it's already dark. And then, as he steps back, the spine of one of the books he's holding catches my eye: *A WOMAN IN TURMOIL? The unauthorized biography of Dorothea Roe.*

'What's that?' I point to the book.

He looks down. 'Ah, yes, this one.' He pulls it carefully from the pile and hands it to me. 'It's a proof copy. For reviews, et cetera. It's not actually published until July. I'm not the editor but I promised to provide notes as a fresh pair of eyes, and also someone who knew her.'

I move both the dogs' leads to one hand so I can take the book with the other. It's a white paperback with red writing and a photograph of a young Dorothea on the front. 'Did Dorothea know about this?'

His cheeks redden. 'Yes, she did. She wasn't happy about it. She asked me so many times if I could give her any info on the author, but obviously I wouldn't be allowed to do that.'

A surge of excitement rushes through me.

'I've made some notes in that version, so I need it back . . .'

My face grows hot. 'Oh, yes, of course. Sorry, I wasn't trying to steal it . . .' I laugh but I don't hand it back.

'I'd give it to you otherwise. But I can get you a copy? From work. You could pop into the office or we could meet for a coffee? Have a proper catch-up?'

I hesitate. I don't want to give Harry the wrong idea. I should have told him about Josh.

His green eyes are hopeful, and, as his gaze meets mine, my stomach does this strange swoop. I glance down at the biography in my hands, feeling disconcerted by the effect he's having on me all these years later.

'Um, could I just borrow this copy? I'd be super careful with it and give it back to you tomorrow?' I know it's cheeky to ask, but I can't bear the thought of giving it back to him. I need to read it straight away.

'Ah, I'm sorry, but I need to finish it tonight so I can give my colleague notes in the morning. But I'll get you a copy ASAP.'

Disappointment gnaws at me but I smile and say thanks anyway. His fingers briefly brush mine as I hand the book back to him. We lock eyes and the years fall away, so that I feel like that teenager again, until I step back from him, clearing my throat, breaking the spell. So much has happened. We aren't the same people, I remind myself. I need to get home. To Josh.

'Anyway, I'd better go . . .' I say.

'Can I have your number?' he says at the same time and we both laugh awkwardly and exchange numbers.

'Don't forget about the book,' I say, backing away with the dogs. 'I'm desperate to read it.'

'I won't. See you soon, I hope.'

I can feel his eyes on me as I almost run back to the villa. The rain slashes down as I let myself into the side gate with the new code. But when I reach the patio doors, expecting to see Josh in the kitchen, the room is dark and the doors are locked. That's weird. I head back around the house to the front porch and ring the old-fashioned doorbell. I can hear it chiming through the house but still no answer. Josh's car is there. Unease tugs at my insides. Has something happened to him?

I pull out my mobile from my coat pocket and see that he's tried to phone me three times. My stomach drops. I call him back but it goes straight through to voicemail.

I ring the bell again, more urgently this time, and then, to my relief, I hear footsteps in the hall. The door is wrenched open to reveal Josh standing there, his expression full of fury.

'Oh, so you've decided to come back then?'

'I haven't been gone that long, have I?' The dogs run past him into the hallway and I chase after them to unclip their leads and usher them down the stairs to the kitchen. I turn on the light, shrug off my wet coat and hang it over the chair. I'm soaked through and freezing. He follows me. An empty bowl and pan sit in the butler sink.

'Your dinner is in the bin,' he announces.

I turn to stare at him, shocked at this sudden, cold change in him.

'Don't look at me like that. What do you expect? I'm not your sodding chef.'

'I'm sorry. I lost track of time. I bumped into . . . next door . . .'

He crosses his arms. 'Yes. I saw. I came out looking for you but you didn't notice me as you were too busy flirting.'

Has he been spying on me? I feel a burst of indignation. 'No, I wasn't. That's Harry. He was my friend when we were kids. When I stayed here with Dorothea that summer . . .'

His eyes harden. 'Was he your boyfriend?'

'No. Not really. I was fourteen and he was a year older, so we just . . . you know, hung out.'

'So you never kissed?'

Why do I get the impression he already knows? 'Well, yes, once or twice, towards the end . . . but it was all very innocent.'

'You never mentioned him before.'

'You never asked.'

He shakes his head. 'Well, it's obvious where your priorities lie and they're not with me. What a fool I am. You can sort yourself out.'

I notice the look of spite and righteousness on his face and anger sears through me. He left me outside in the cold and rain on purpose. 'Josh,' I begin, trying to keep calm. I don't want to say something I'll regret. 'It's . . .'

But he stalks out of the room and I know better than to follow him when he's like this. I slump onto one of the chairs and bury my head in my hands, knowing there will now be a bad atmosphere between us for days. The last time Josh acted this way was when he came to pick me up from work a few months ago, saw me leave the station with a male colleague, and so drove off in a rage, leaving me to get the bus home. He didn't speak to me for nearly a week. I thought things would be different after moving in here. A fresh start. But deep down I know Josh will never change.

I glance at the photograph on the wall of a young Dorothea. Strong, feisty, determined. 'I need to be more like you,' I whisper. I can't imagine she'd let a man treat her like this. I get up and feed the dogs, refusing to let Josh occupy my head any longer. Instead my thoughts turn to Dorothea's biography, wondering how quickly I can get it from Harry. I google the author Sidney S. Crane and can't find anything about him apart from a short paragraph on the publisher's website referencing a history book he'd written before. He's not on Instagram or Facebook, although *A Woman in Turmoil?* is available to pre-order on Amazon.

What secrets are buried in that biography, and how does this Sidney S. Crane know about them?

22

DOROTHEA

Nine Years Before

Dorothea dreaded telling Annette about Gabe, but she needed her friend's advice.

They were in Annette's apartment in Clifton. A recent purchase. At the end of last year she'd surprised everyone by selling her huge detached house in Sneyd Park, claiming it was now too big for her. Dorothea wondered if Annette – like Gabe – was also suffering financially. The whole place was immaculate, the complete opposite to Dorothea's villa. Sometimes she wondered if she should downsize too and release some money. But Villa Oiseau was her sanctuary. She couldn't imagine ever selling it.

'I think Gabe's business is in trouble,' she blurted out as Annette took a seat on the sofa next to her and handed her a glass of wine.

Annette, to her credit, didn't react at first. She sipped her Chablis before speaking. 'What happened?'

Dorothea sighed. 'He said he'd made some bad investments.'

'And he wants you to help bail him out?'

'He wants me to be a silent partner.'

'What? Like put some money in but you won't be involved in the running of the business?'

'Yes. At least, I think so.'

Annette leans back against the cushions. 'Oh, Dot.'

'I know.' Dorothea twirled the glass between her fingers. 'I don't know what to do.'

'That man takes too many risks,' Annette said disapprovingly. Annette and Gabe had taken an instant dislike to one another all those years ago and nothing had changed. Now she turned to the window, a shadow slicing through her profile. Dorothea couldn't help but smile to herself at the sight of Annette's familiar golden chignon – she'd had the same hairstyle and same dress sense since they'd met forty years ago.

Annette turned back to her. 'He's not your responsibility, Dot.'

'I know he's not,' Dorothea replied with an edge of irritation. 'But I owe him a lot. He was the one who took me on. I owe my career to him.'

'You're talented. If it hadn't been him it would have been someone else.'

But Dorothea didn't believe that. She had met Gabe at the right time in her life. A time when she needed more than the art therapy group. A time when she needed something just for her. And, although she was too modest to voice it to Annette, if he hadn't taken her on, she wouldn't have made a name for herself and the art therapy company they'd set up wouldn't have had so much publicity and kudos. Dorothea didn't feel it the right time to point this out. If Annette thought that a man – any man, but particularly Gabe – could have, in any way, been instrumental in her success, she'd refuse to admit it. 'I don't want to buy into his business, anyway. I'm too old for all that.'

'And he's not a great businessman,' added Annette drily. 'So what are you going to do?'

'Lend him some money to get him out of this hole, I suppose.'

'You'll never see the money again, you know that?'

'But what choice do I have? I don't want him to lose everything.'

Dorothea's eye went to the company papers stacked neatly on Annette's coffee table. 'I need to keep my brain active, Dorothea,' she'd often say. 'And I like helping women.' Nobody was as gutsy, as single-minded as Annette Baker-Hume. She was a woman who got things done. No mountain was too high to climb. And all conducted with an air of sophistication with her twinset and pearls and impeccable smile. It was that smile that had helped countless other women feel they had someone to go to, someone to help them, or just some place to find peace.

'You're too kind, Dot. That's your problem.'

'It's not like I have anyone to spend my money on,' replied Dorothea wistfully. 'No family.'

Annette flashed her a look. 'It's funny, isn't it? That out of the four of us, it's only Maisie that found love.'

'Aiden is perfect for her.'

'Yes, she was so damaged when we first met her. But she opened up her heart again. Do you ever get lonely?'

Dorothea looked at Annette in surprise. Annette was usually so closed about matters of the heart and had never trusted men after what had happened with her own husband, Brandon.

'Sometimes,' Dorothea admitted. 'But I've got my animals and my art. And there is a man who moved in a few doors down from me last year. Dennis. He's about my age, loves animals too. We've bumped into each other walking the dogs a few times and he's been over for a cup of tea . . .'

Annette's eyes lit up. 'You dark horse! Do you like him?'

'As a friend. But he seems gentle.'

'Hmmm, they all do at first. That's the problem.'

Annette sipped her tea and then changed the subject, her brief exposure of vulnerability brushed over as though it had never happened.

Dorothea knew that, however lonely Annette got, however much she might miss a romantic relationship, she'd never allow herself to trust again.

And most of the time, Dorothea felt exactly the same.

After all, how could she after everything that had happened?

23

IMOGEN

Josh's mood lasts all of the next day. It's like I'm invisible, and if I try and make conversation he just leaves the room. We shared a bed, but his back was to me all night, and we eat separately, whatever we can find in the fridge: mostly cheese on toast for me.

He's working from home and he spends most of the day dealing with the security team on an issue with one of the cameras, like the house belongs to him and not me. It feels as though he's deliberately keeping me out of the loop and it's grating on me. He hasn't even shown me how to use the app to access the camera footage yet, even though I keep asking. I can see him now in the garden, laughing with one of the men from the security firm. I turn away to find my trainers, tugging them on, so I can go out there and demand to know what's going on, but when I open the patio door they're nowhere to be seen.

Josh's words from last night play over in my mind. Had I been flirting with Harry? It's true that I still found him attractive. That I still liked his sensitive nature. That I was impressed when he told me he'd pursued his dream and was writing a book. Talking to him reminded me of the past, before everything changed. But that's all. Despite Josh's occasional moods, and I suppose you could call it over-possessiveness, he's insecure. His dad walking out when he was a kid really made it hard for him to trust people and he's terrified of losing the ones he loves – not that he would admit that to me, but I just know, because I know him. Better than he thinks I do.

The quote from the alarm company has been left on the kitchen table for me to see. The money Dorothea left me hasn't been transferred yet so I use our joint account to pay it.

I'm in Dorothea's study, arranging some of my books on her shelf, when I hear Josh go back into the room he's using as his home office and slam the door behind him. He obviously wants me to know he's still in a mood and I'm filled with indignation. *How dare he.* I need to get out of the house. I hate not having my own car, but I'm insured on Josh's. Before I can talk myself out of it, I'm flinging open Josh's door and storming into his room.

'I need to go out so I'm going to have to use your car,' I announce to a startled-looking Josh. I don't wait for an answer before closing the door again. I hear him calling me from the top of the stairs as I grab the keys from the dish by the front door and leave before he can stop me.

My hands are shaking as I turn on the ignition, but relief floods through me as I back out of the driveway and away from Villa Oiseau and Josh.

I park up outside Rosemary Farrington's Gothic mansion. I've been here once before. Dorothea had taken me and Mum when we were staying at her villa that summer. It was only a few weeks before Mum decided to go back to my dad, and I'd been blissfully unaware that our new charmed life was about to come to a grinding halt. I'd thought Rosemary a little odd, eccentric with a voice as posh as the royals. She was very tall, even taller than Dorothea, and she had thick copper hair cut in a blunt bob that highlighted her pointy chin. She hadn't been able to keep still. She'd kept jumping up, asking if I wanted some squash, or a biscuit, or if my mum wanted more tea. Her living room was cavernous and smelt of lavender perfume. She had these cotton doilies on every polished wood surface, and despite its size the room felt small and claustrophobic with all the clutter. Even as a teenager the exterior of Rosemary's house had seemed spooky, like something Edgar Allan Poe would write about with its grey walls and stone gargoyles peering down from the rooftops. I didn't believe in ghosts, but if I did I'd have expected them to be lurking in here.

I've parked on the kerb but there are no gates to keep people out, just a vehicle-sized gap between two stone pillars. There is no car in the driveway, but I decide to knock anyway, hoping that if she's in then she'll remember me. I wonder if DI Shirley has already spoken to Rosemary about the lighter and if so, whether Rosemary might be guarded.

When nobody answers I knock again. Eventually I hear footsteps in the hallway, and the door opens slowly, a man peering through the gap. He's around my age, maybe a bit older, with tawny hair scraped back into a ponytail and a bony face. I wonder if this is the Peter Bryce that was on the electoral roll, and who he might be to Rosemary. His dark eyes narrow suspiciously. 'Yes?'

'Hi. I was wondering if Rosemary was in, I'm . . .'

'She's not here.'

'Oh, okay. Do you know when she'll be back?'

'In a few days. Sorry.' He closes the door on me before I can ask any more questions.

I step back and assess the house, wondering if he's telling the truth about Rosemary being away.

As I walk back through the stone pillars, it hits me that this was one of the last things my mum did the night she died. I try to imagine what she was thinking as she left Rosemary's Halloween party all those years ago. Did she know my dad was waiting for her on this very street, ready to follow her home after he was chucked out of the party? Why hadn't she just stayed the night with Dorothea or Rosemary? I think again of Alison and her doubts surrounding our father's conviction. How could she go and see him? After everything he put us through. And then I remember what Harry told me about Alison keeping Dorothea from me and a fresh wave of betrayal washes over me.

When I get back to the car I type Alison an angry text. *Why did you tell Dorothea to keep away from me?*

My finger hovers over the send button, imagining Alison's reaction when she gets the message. I've never sent a confrontational text to her before. We've never really fallen out – we've never been close enough for that. I press send before I can change my mind.

Frustrated that I can't get hold of Rosemary, I try calling Annette. Her number was easy to find as it's still on the art therapy centre's website. But it goes straight through to voicemail. I leave a message stating who I am and that I'd like to talk to her about Dorothea and then I toss the phone onto the passenger seat.

I'm just about to pull away when the phone rings, making me jump. I grab it, expecting it to be Alison or Annette, but it's DI Shirley.

'It's Dennis,' she says without any preamble as soon as I answer. My heart plunges. Has he died? 'He's out of intensive care and he would like to see you. He's very insistent and won't talk to the police until he's spoken to you.'

I exhale in relief. Thank goodness he's okay. She tells me he's at the Royal United Hospital in Bath and I say I'll head straight there.

Dennis is asleep when I arrive on the ward.

'Sit down, lovely, and wait for him to wake up,' says a nurse, pulling out a chair by his bed. 'He didn't get much sleep last night. It's all comings and goings in here.' She gives my shoulder a reassuring squeeze and then wanders off to help a man calling from the other end of the ward.

I take a seat, wishing I'd had time to get something to bring in, but I have no idea what Dennis likes. I sit awkwardly, waiting for him to wake up, thinking how strangely intimate it is, me being here when he's dressed in his pyjamas and in a vulnerable state when I hardly know him.

Eventually he opens his eyes and takes a few seconds to register me before his face breaks out into a smile. 'Imogen. Thank you so much for coming.' He's propped up on a mass of pillows and I ask him if I can get him anything. 'Oh, no. I'm fine. Thank you. I'm lucky to be alive.'

'You are,' I say. 'I'm so sorry this happened to you. I'm looking after Cady and she's doing really well, but she's missing you.'

'That's kind, thank you, dear.'

'What happened? Did you fall?' I ask, already knowing there's more to it otherwise why would he ask to see me?

His expression clouds over. 'It was very odd. I received a knock at the door and it was this delivery guy. At least, I assumed it was a delivery guy. He was holding a small package which he asked me to sign for but he didn't have one of those electronic thingies that the postmen have – it was a piece of paper and he didn't have a pen. So I asked him to hold on for a second while I went to get one and he followed me into the kitchen. And that's the last thing I remember. Because when I woke up I was here.'

'So he attacked you.'

'I'm assuming so, dear, because I woke up with a crack to my skull and a doctor hovering over me telling me how lucky I am to be alive.'

'God, Dennis.' My lungs feel like they are being squeezed. 'Do you think it might be the same person that locked us in the bunker? This has to be all to do with Dorothea, doesn't it?'

He pats my arm which rests on his bed. He has a cannula in his hand and I'm taken aback by how old and frail he looks, his skin paper-thin with purplish bruises staining his wrists. 'Be careful, my dear. I don't understand what's going on, but yes, I think this is the same person who hurt Dorothea. I haven't told the police that yet because I wanted to speak to you first. I noticed you didn't tell that detective lady about the sculpture. Do you still want me to keep quiet about it even if it's probably linked?'

I hesitate, unsure of what to do.

He pats my arm again. 'I won't say anything about it for now. But please, be careful. Don't go in the bunker again.'

I nod. 'Thanks, Dennis. I will tell DI Shirley soon. I just want to see if I can figure out what the sculpture means first.' I don't say it, but I can't help but feel I'd have betrayed Dorothea somehow if I told the police about the sculpture. She left it for me to find. She wanted it kept a secret.

'The man who attacked you. Did you see his face?'

'Well, no, that's the thing.' And his next words give me goosepimples. 'He was wearing full-on biking gear. And a helmet, with the visor down.'

I can't stop thinking about Dennis's words all the way home. Was his attacker the man who'd shoved into me when I was in Bristol – and also the person who'd locked us in the bunker? But why? And why attack Dennis of all people? It doesn't make any sense.

The security team have left by the time I pull up on the driveway. As soon as I step out of Josh's car, he appears at the front door, his face contorted in anger.

'I can't believe you just took my car,' he says as I walk towards him. 'I might have needed it.'

'Why? You're working from home,' I say calmly even though my heart is beating fast. I dump the car keys in his hand as I walk past and he follows me down into the kitchen.

'Where did you go that was so urgent?'

'I went to see Dennis in hospital,' I say without missing a beat. I bend down to stroke the dogs who have rushed up to greet me. 'I should take them out for a walk.'

'You're going out? Again?'

I turn to face Josh. 'If that's all right with you?' His eyes widen at my sarcasm and for a moment he looks confused. Usually when Josh is annoyed I keep out of his way until his bad mood has passed. But not this time. Being here in Dorothea's house – *in my house* – has empowered me. I clip the leads onto the dogs' collars. Josh opens his mouth to say something but then thinks better of it. He storms out of the room, his footsteps heavy on the stairs, and then a slam of a door.

'Come on then,' I say to the dogs. 'Let's get out of here.'

I take them through the newly secured side gate, breathing deeply to steady my nerves. Despite my bravado with Josh, I hate it when we're not speaking. At least I don't have to worry about feeling unsafe now the security system is up and running. The villa now feels like the kind of prison Dorothea surely never envisioned for her home but that might have kept her alive.

I step onto the pavement and it all happens in a flash. The roar of the gears, the squeal of tyres on tarmac, the smell of petrol, the glint of metal as the motorbike veers onto the pavement and drives straight for me.

24

At least one way of getting Josh out of a mood is being almost killed.

The motorbike had mounted the pavement so that I had to slam myself against the wall, letting go of the leads so that Cady and Solly could get away unhurt. The biker's foot grazed my hip as he weaved around me and sped off, and I had sunk to the pavement in a trembling heap. The dogs, thankfully, came running back to me and I hurried them into the house, calling for Josh.

'What's happened?' he asked as soon as he saw the state of me, his anger forgotten.

Josh has gone into full-on alpha mode, trying to comfort and protect me. He seems to like me best when I'm vulnerable: it's an unpleasant thought and I'm determined not to pick over it now. He's already made me report what happened to DI Shirley, who must be getting bored of me. My mind went blank, predictably, when she asked for details like reg plate or any distinguishing features. Hard to notice such things when a motorbike is charging full speed towards you. Josh looked through the new security camera footage, but it's set to only trigger if someone tries to get in through either of our gates.

Now we've ordered a Chinese takeaway and I'm trying to eat it despite my queasiness. Cartons of noodles, egg-fried rice, pork balls and prawn crackers are spread out over the table and Josh has lit two of Dorothea's candles which cast flickering shadows on the walls. It's not quite dark outside, the sky a watercolour mauve.

'Does the detective think it could be the same person who attacked Dennis?' Josh asks through a mouthful of rice.

'She's so non-committal. But it has to be, doesn't it? How many visor-wearing bikers are out there battering old men and trying to mow down women?'

'Do you think it's the same person who broke in here that day too?'

A noodle slides down my throat and I want to gag. I wish he'd change the subject. It's making my brain hurt. I just want to sit and watch something comforting on his huge TV and not think about murder and attackers on motorbikes. 'Maybe. I only saw his face briefly.'

After we've eaten I go with Josh into the big living room and snuggle up to him as we watch one of the *Mission Impossible*s, the dogs lying on the rug next to us. Josh is riveted, his arm draped over my shoulder, but I can't concentrate. My mind is racing with thoughts of Dorothea, the sculpture, the bunker, Dennis and the biker. I need to work out what to do next. Rosemary is apparently away for a few days, so I need to try Annette again, and Maisie too. They are the people who knew Dorothea the best. I have a vague memory of Annette coming here when my mum and I were living with Dorothea that summer, but I'm sure none of them came to Mum's funeral, unless they did but I've forgotten. I only remember seeing Dorothea there.

I'm itching to look again at the photographs of the sculpture that I have on my phone, but I don't want Josh to see. He still knows nothing about Dorothea's hidden piece of art and I want to keep it that way.

When the film is over, Josh stays up glued to some football thing while I retreat to bed. I scroll through the photographs of the sculpture, taking in the magpies and the little trinkets attached to each one: there's the lighter which must be significant, but what do the other things mean? The cat brooch and the miniature Christmas card. The pearls, spade and the crochet butterfly. 'Dorothea!' I whisper into the dimly lit room. 'Why were you so bloody cryptic?'

'What are you doing?'

I jump and hurriedly lock my phone. Josh is standing in the doorway.

'Oh, nothing. Just reading.'

'You really should get a Kindle instead of using your phone. Blue light isn't good for you before bed.' He steps out of his trousers and peels off his shirt so that he's just in his boxers. Then he climbs onto the bed and his eyes twinkle at me, an eyebrow raised suggestively. I know that look. I've obviously been forgiven. For now.

I turn my back to him and pull the duvet further over my shoulder. 'Good night,' I say pointedly as I reach over and turn off the lamp.

25

ALISON

It's not until Alison has left the salon, picked up Lila from school, and returned home that she notices Imogen's text. Her heart lifts at first, until she reads it.

Why did you tell Dorothea to keep away from me?

A familiar desolate feeling presses down on Alison as she's instantly dragged back to the moment of their mother's funeral and that conversation with Dorothea. She'd only met the woman twice and both times were fraught with grief and misery. Alison had been a frightened twenty-one-year-old who had lost her parents in what felt like a nano-second. Imogen was all the family that she had left, and she'd been so afraid that Dorothea, with her big house and her wealth, was going to take her sister away. Had she done the right thing by insisting Dorothea didn't contact Imogen? Probably not, in the grand scheme of things. But that's what fear does to you. It makes you act irrationally. Selfishly.

How did Imogen find out? Did she find a note from Dorothea or some sort of diary in the house?

Alison glances out of the kitchen window where she has a view of her scrubby back garden. Lila is jumping up and down on the trampoline with her friend. A playdate after school on a Thursday isn't something Alison usually encourages, but it was thrust upon her as the girls came out of school, and she felt she couldn't say no in front of the other mum. And, she reasons, it's important for Lila to have lots of friends over, being the only child. She wants her daughter to have the carefree childhood both she and Imogen never had. Her father might not have yet turned into that violent drunk when she was Lila's age, but he never liked them having friends over. He was possessive of his family's time, even then. It should have been a red flag to her mother. It's a trait that Alison recognizes in Josh.

As soon as Gareth walks through the door later that evening she tells him about the text. He always looks as though he's been wrestling with zoo animals after a day's teaching at St Saviour's Primary, which he jokes is what his Year 6 class is like. His shirt is hanging out, his hair is messed up and he has that familiar school corridor smell about him. He dumps his cross-body bag onto the floor, pulls off his tie and throws it onto the kitchen table. Then, noticing her raised eyebrow, good-naturedly picks it up, folds it carefully into his palm and shoves it in his trouser pocket.

'Immy's already pissed off at me for going to see our dad,' Alison sighs, handing him a mug of tea and joining him at the table. Lila is already in bed asleep, exhausted after her playdate. 'And now this whole thing with Dorothea. Honestly, that woman. She's dead and she's still coming between us.'

'She's not coming between you,' says Gareth rationally. 'You just need to explain to Immy what happened and how afraid you were.'

Alison remembers how impressed Imogen had been with Dorothea back then. Every time Alison rang to speak to her sister that's all she'd hear. Dorothea this and Dorothea that. It had made Alison feel as though her mum and sister had a whole other life that she wasn't a part of. She was pleased her mum had left her dad, but she was suspicious of Dorothea's intentions. Her mother had been Dorothea's cleaner, for goodness' sake. Why was Dorothea letting them live rent-free in her house?

'I should have gone home when Mum left him,' she says taking her hand away from Gareth's and chewing her thumbnail. 'I shouldn't have stayed in Cardiff. I shouldn't have told Dorothea to stay away . . .' She swallows a lump in her throat.

'You did what you thought was right at the time,' says Gareth softly. 'You were good to Imogen.' A beat and then, 'I know,' he announces, his eyes lighting up. 'Why don't we pay Immy a visit? Drive over there, see the house? It will be better for you to speak face to face. Iron things out properly. She can't storm out of her own home now, can she? She'll have no choice but to listen.' He looks so pleased with himself for coming up with the idea. Gareth is never happier than when he's problem-solving.

'Hmmm, I suppose. It means I'll have to see Josh.'

He laughs. A big booming sound that instantly cheers Alison up. 'You can't choose her boyfriend for her, Al.'

She sighs. 'I know, but he doesn't help matters. I bet he hasn't been encouraging her to talk to me. She refuses to even entertain the idea that Dad might be innocent, and Josh will be stoking that, I'm sure. If he can alienate her from all of us then he gets her all to himself.'

'I'm sure he's not trying to do that . . .' begins Gareth, ever the optimist. He doesn't particularly click with Josh but he's always trying to see the good in people. '. . . but just in case, let's turn up when they're not expecting it. Then Josh won't have the chance to persuade her not to see you. And you know how much Immy loves Lila. It will all be okay.'

But Alison fears it will never be okay. If she believes their father is telling the truth and Imogen doesn't, then where does that leave them?

26

IMOGEN

When I wake up on Saturday morning Josh isn't beside me. It's 8 a.m. Early for us on a weekend. I assume he's downstairs making breakfast, so I slip on my dressing gown and head to the kitchen, but it's empty. And the dogs are gone too. Anxiety gnaws at me. Josh would never leave without telling me where he was going and certainly not with the dogs. I picture him off in a mood somewhere. Has he discovered that I'm secretly researching Dorothea's death or has he found out about the sculpture?

I search the house with a knot in my stomach, even though it's obvious he's not here. And then I hear barking. I'm in Dorothea's study which overlooks the front of the house and I can see Josh in the lane with the dogs. He's bending down and stroking them tenderly while talking to them and the sight of it tugs at my heart. I knew he'd fall in love with the dogs once he'd given them a chance. And then I see a figure joining him in the lane and my heart sinks. No, no, no. It's Harry. Shit. I hope Josh won't be rude to him. I hover at the window, willing Josh to come back into the house. I can't hear what they are saying but it appears as though Harry is introducing himself and they are shaking hands. Has Harry come over to give me the proof? I texted him yesterday to remind him to get me a copy and he said the few they'd had in the office had been sent off to reviewers so he'll give me his when he's finished with it. It felt like he was making up excuses, which has, naturally, made me even more eager to read it. I hope he doesn't hand a copy to Josh as then I'll have to admit that I am researching Dorothea.

I move away from the window and grab my mobile. I call Josh and pretend I don't know where he is.

'Josh?' I say when he answers. 'Where are you? I was worried.'

'Oh, I'm sorry, babe, I woke up early and thought I'd take the dogs out – yeah, cheers, mate, good to meet you too – sorry, was just talking to Harry, but he's gone now.' He's breathing heavily and I can hear the wind buffeting in the background, the punch of the keypad as he taps in the code for the side gate, the crunch of gravel underfoot. He doesn't sound annoyed, which I'm surprised about after how he reacted the other night. 'We were out of milk and eggs. I thought I'd try and make those Scotch pancakes on the Aga. I found one of Dorothea's recipes in the drawer.' Then his voice changes again, becoming more formal. 'Oh, hello,' he says to someone else. 'Yes, she is. I'm her boyfriend, Josh.'

I rush back to the window. Josh is standing with a smartly dressed woman, her shiny silvery-blonde hair in an old-fashioned up-do. She's wearing a tweed suit and has on a pair of leather gloves. She looks rich and important and I recognize her straight away from the photographs. 'Yes, please come in . . .' I can hear him say. He's putting on his telephone voice to speak to her, which makes me smile. I wonder why she's come over rather than just calling me back?

I quickly dress in yesterday's jeans and jumper and run my fingers through my tangly wavy hair. I quickly assess myself in the mirror. I'm not exactly groomed and I could use some eye make-up to make myself look more awake. No time. I take a deep breath, trying to curb my swooping stomach, and then I head downstairs.

I can hear Josh and Annette in the kitchen. When I walk in she stands up and her face freezes in shock. 'Goodness,' she says, touching the pearls at her throat. 'You look the spitting image of your mother.' She holds out a gloved hand. 'Lovely to see you again. I don't know if you remember me coming to the house when you and Ruth were staying with Dorothea?'

'Yes, I do. Lovely to see you again too.'

I notice something like disapproval behind her eyes and again, I feel like an intruder in Dorothea's beautiful home. I hope she doesn't mention to Josh the phone message I'd left for her.

I turn to Josh with a frown. He's pouring a jug of batter straight onto the Aga's stove top. 'Shouldn't you use a frying pan?'

'Apparently I don't have to. Annette has kindly shown me how.'

She beams at him. 'Dorothea loved her Aga. The times we sat here in this kitchen . . .' Her bright eyes gleam and I realize I had assumed disapproval when it was something else entirely. Regret, perhaps, or a sense of discombobulation at seeing me living in her friend's house. She clears her throat and sits down again. 'I'm sorry for the early morning visit. I was going to call you back . . .'

I dart a look at Josh but his body language doesn't change and I hope he hasn't heard.

'. . . but I was in the area and I thought it would be nice to have a chat face to face and, I suppose, to come here again.' She sighs wistfully, looking around. 'It's so full of Dot. It's almost like she's still here.'

I pull out the chair next to Annette. 'Yes. I'm interested to know more about her. As you know, she's left me the house, which came as a surprise . . .'

'Yes. It's a surprise to me as well, but she was extremely fond of you and your mother. Ruth was so effervescent, even when she was going through such a hard time.' She peels off her gloves. 'I remember when Dorothea first talked to me about her. They'd become so close. Despite everything, Ruth was still in love with your father. That was what was so frustrating, I suppose. Dorothea offered her a sanctuary — you too, of course — but then Ruth threw it in Dorothea's face when she went back to Alec.'

'Oh . . .' My heart twists. 'Is that how Dorothea saw it?'

She waves a hand. 'Oh, I doubt it. They remained friends even after that. I just think Dot . . . well, all of us . . . felt we'd failed her.'

'I wish she hadn't gone back to him,' I say sadly. 'Then she'd probably still be alive.'

Annette reaches over and pats my hand. Out of the corner of my eye I can see Josh flipping over the Scotch pancakes and I wonder how much he can hear.

'I'm so sad that I never got the chance to see Dorothea again,' I say truthfully.

'She tried, but . . . your sister . . .'

'Ah yes. I've only recently found out about that. Do you know why anyone would want to hurt Dorothea?' I ask gently. 'Did she have any enemies?'

Annette sits upright and her composure crumbles a little. 'No. She was a wonderful person.' She pulls a worried face. 'Although . . . there were a few things – just little things – that made her a bit paranoid in the year or so before she died,' she says carefully.

'What kind of things?' My mind casts back to the sculpture.

'Well, she found a postcard in the woods advertising an unauthorized biography by this man called Sidney Crane.' She puts a hand to her pearls again. 'There was a message on the back. I can't remember exactly what it said now . . . something about how they couldn't wait for Dorothea's past secrets to be revealed. And she found this old lighter.'

'The one with the initials RF?'

She emits a small sound of surprise. 'Yes, that's right. How do you know?'

'I found it,' I say. 'Do you know who it belongs to? Could it be Rosemary's?'

Her blue eyes sharpen. 'It's definitely not Rosemary's. She's never smoked.'

Her throat flushes red and I get the impression she's lying.

Josh comes over with the plate of pancakes and places them in the middle of the table with a proud look on his face. They look delicious, fat and fluffy.

I take one gratefully but Annette refuses, patting her flat stomach. 'I've already had my breakfast, but thank you.'

'Can I get you a tea or coffee?' I ask and she says she'd love a black coffee. Before I can move, Josh offers to make it.

'What a lovely young man you've got there,' Annette murmurs.

I feel proud of Josh in that moment, although I do wish he'd leave us alone so I can ask Annette more probing questions about Dorothea. He's going to guess what I'm up to at this rate.

We fall silent. Josh hands Annette her coffee before taking a seat at the head of the table. She sips it, leaving a pink lipstick mark on the rim. Then she turns the cup around in her hands. 'This is Dorothea's?' That look again. The one that makes me feel as though we are intruders. She glances around the kitchen as though noticing it all for the first time. 'All her things,' she says quietly.

'We . . . we didn't know what to do with them,' I begin. 'If there is anything you'd like . . .'

Her eyes water. 'Thank you, that's very kind. It's so very sad that all her artwork perished in the fire.'

'I know, it really is.' I glance at Josh but he's stuffing a pancake into his mouth while scrolling through his phone. I lean closer to Annette and lower my voice. 'Did . . . um . . . Dorothea ever talk to you about her new collection?'

Annette doesn't say anything for a few moments; her attention seems to be taken up by the dresser. I follow her line of sight. She's staring at a photograph of Dorothea when she was much younger – maybe around my age – standing in front of one of her paintings in what looks like an art gallery. She's wearing a red headscarf and is half turned towards the painting, her body obscuring a large part of it so that I can only make out a red background and the outline of a prostrate figure.

'Annette? Is everything okay?'

Josh looks up from his phone and raises an eyebrow at me. I suspect he's been listening this whole time.

Annette turns to me. 'Sorry, yes. That photograph. I was there when it was taken. It was at Dorothea's first ever exhibition. It was where she found her agent. The painting she's standing in front of was one of Dorothea's most personal.' She clears her throat and I make a mental note to look up that painting. 'Anyway, what were we saying? Oh yes, Dorothea's new collection. No, she didn't really talk about her work in progress. I only knew what it was about when I read the *Sunday Times* feature. Seven sculptures. A magpie theme.' She gives a half-smile. 'To be honest, a lot of her art went over my head.'

'But aren't you a trained art therapist?'

'Well, yes, I have a degree in psychology and I'm proficient enough at art and making things to have passed my master's in art therapy. But I wouldn't describe myself as an artist. Not like Dorothea.' She tuts. 'I don't know what the police are doing but I truly hope they do speak to that horrid man, her agent Gabriel Mitchell. He took advantage of Dotty something terrible. Always in debt, that man. Always looking to Dotty to bail him out. A bad egg.' She shakes her head. 'A bad egg indeed.'

I've already done some digging on Gabe, and from Companies House I could see that he's set up and then closed down a number of subsidiary companies over the years and is no longer the sole director of his agency. I've even tried calling him a few times, but he's never picked up. 'And did she help him out?' I ask.

'Well, he asked her to become a silent partner a few years back, but she said no in the end. I don't know how he ended up bailing himself out but his business is still going, so he must have found funding from somewhere else.'

'What about the other women who founded the art therapy centre – Rosemary and . . . Maisie, was it?'

Annette nods.

'Was Dorothea close to them?'

'Extremely close. All four of us were,' she says emphatically. 'Sadly, Maisie has just been diagnosed with Alzheimer's . . .'

'Oh, I'm sorry to hear that.' Out of the corner of my eye I see Josh place his mobile on the table, face down. 'Had you suspected that for a while?'

She stiffens. 'Actually, I had no idea. Aiden hid it from all of us, but he's known for a few years. Maisie was always a little scatty, so Rosemary, Dot and I didn't really notice and now, well . . .' She touches her clavicle. 'Dorothea is dead and Rosemary and I don't see each other as much as we once did. She's busy with her lost sheep . . .'

'Lost sheep?'

'She likes to help troubled young teens. It's admirable, but then sometimes they never leave. Like Peter.'

There is a bitterness to her tone, and I wonder if Annette and Rosemary have fallen out.

'Peter Bryce?'

'Yes. He's her lodger.'

'And was he a troubled teen?'

'Yes, he was convicted of assault when he was in his mid teens, but he seems a nice enough lad,' she admits grudgingly. 'I suppose he's company for her. I think he's like the son she never had.'

I want to ask more about Rosemary but I can see Josh glowering at me from across the table. He's not stupid, he must be able to tell by my line of questioning that I'm too interested in Dorothea.

'Maisie is such a talented lady,' Annette continues. 'She wasn't a founder – she was actually one of our first customers, coming to have therapy herself after an abusive first marriage. But it was in the company's infancy and she loved our ethos so much she came on board. We all had different gifts, but we all complemented each other.'

Interesting. I would love to get Annette's input into what the hidden sculpture could mean, but instinct stops me.

Dorothea kept it under lock and key, not telling anyone about it, which could mean she didn't trust those around her, and that included her oldest friends.

27

DOROTHEA

Sixteen Years Before

It was a sunny day for December. The blue skies and chirruping birds were at odds with how Dorothea was feeling. It should be raining with brooding grey clouds, not a beautiful day like today. Not when they were burying such a gorgeous soul as Ruth. They'd all tried to help her escape her abusive husband, but he'd found her anyway.

The horror of it still hadn't left Dorothea in the five weeks since it had happened. Those poor girls. She could see them now, standing at the graveside, the older sister with her arm around Imogen's shoulders. Little Imogen. So skinny in her long black coat, her lovely hair tied back from her drawn, tear-stained face. It was the second time Dorothea had met Alison. The first had been the morning after Ruth's death, when Dorothea had waited with Imogen until Alison arrived from Cardiff. She was willowy with the same dark hair as their mother, although, unlike Imogen's hair, Alison's was poker-straight and fine.

Dorothea bit back her tears. It didn't feel it was her place to cry.

There was going to be a small gathering at the house in Keynsham and Dorothea followed on in her car. She hadn't had the chance to talk to Imogen properly yet, only a quick hug before the service began. The street wasn't unlike the kind Dorothea had grown up in, and she could see which red-bricked semi-detached it was by all the cars parked outside. The front door was propped open and people trooped in and out. She had no idea who any of them were. She'd never met any of Ruth's friends or family apart from her daughters and she felt strangely conspicuous as she followed on behind, wishing, not for the first time, that Rosemary, Annette and Maisie had agreed to come. She steeled herself for small talk and introductions, two things she wasn't great at. She preferred the peacefulness of her villa and the surrounding woods. She'd hoped these things would have helped save Ruth and it broke her heart that they hadn't, that somehow, despite her best efforts, Ruth had ended up back with her abusive husband. And now it was too late . . .

'Dorothea?' A little voice at her shoulder made her turn to see Imogen, looking small and lost in her own home as though she couldn't understand where all these people had come from, or how they'd found themselves in her front room eating egg and cress sandwiches. Dorothea, who had never thought of herself as maternal, had the sudden urge to scoop up Imogen, bundle her into her car and drive her back to her villa.

'Oh Imogen, my love, come here,' she said, pulling the girl into her arms and hugging her tightly. 'I'm so sorry, I'm so, so sorry about your mum.'

'Thank you,' Imogen replied softly, when they'd pulled away from each other.

Dorothea had so many questions. Where will you live? Who will look after you? Will you be allowed to stay in the house? But she didn't want to bombard the poor girl. Instead she settled on, 'How are you coping? Do you need any help?'

'It's okay. Ali is doing it all. She's been great.' She smiled sheepishly. 'Me, not so much.' She twisted one of her curls around her finger and moved from foot to foot. 'Have you . . . does Harry know?'

Harry Starling. The girl was obviously sweet on him. 'I think so, but do you want me to pass on a message?'

She gave Dorothea another sad smile as she reached into the pocket of her dress. 'Would you mind giving him this?' She handed Dorothea a pink scented envelope and Dorothea felt her heart break a little bit more.

'Of course. I'll make sure he gets it,' Dorothea promised, carefully slipping it into her handbag.

'Thank you.'

Dorothea was about to say more when Alison wandered over. 'Immy, would you mind helping Sharon with the teas and coffees?'

'Sure.' She threw Dorothea an exasperated look and then disappeared into the throng of her well-meaning relatives to ask what they wanted to drink, and it struck

Dorothea how stoic Imogen was being, all things considered. She was just fourteen and was keeping it together so admirably, and Dorothea wondered who would be there for her after everyone had gone. Would Alison, at only twenty-one, have the emotional maturity to cope with not only her grief but her little sister's too?

She turned back to Alison, who was now staring at her with a face like thunder. 'Well, if it isn't the infamous Dorothea Roe.'

Dorothea couldn't understand why she provoked such hostility in Alison, but it was obvious that the girl didn't like her. Maybe she blamed her for not being able to save her mother.

'I wouldn't say I was infamous.'

'Famous then. Whatever.' Alison folded her arms across her chest and scowled some more. 'You shouldn't have let my mum go back to him.'

'I couldn't keep her a prisoner, Alison,' she replied kindly. 'Your dad talked her into coming back. At the end of the day she obviously still loved him, despite everything.'

Alison sniffed. 'My sister thinks a lot of you. Admires you.'

'I think a lot of her too.'

'She thinks you're going to swoop in and save us.'

'I will do everything I can to help.'

'We don't need your help,' she said stubbornly. 'We only need each other.'

'But Alison . . .'

'I mean it,' she said coldly. 'We need to be by ourselves. You have to leave us alone. You'll just confuse Immy. She's done nothing but harp on about her "perfect summer",' she used air-quotes angrily, 'ever since she got back in September.'

'It's because she met a boy . . .'

'No, it's not. It's not just that. It's you, you and your arty-farty ways, wafting around in silk scarves or whatever it is you do all day in between your paintings, in your fancy house with your own wood. Who has their own bloody wood?!'

Dorothea thought it best to stay silent.

Alison shook her head angrily, tears springing up in her eyes.

'Alison, love, I don't want to do anything that will cause you or your sister distress.'

'Then leave us alone,' she snapped. 'Leave us alone! You're just making everything worse. You're giving her ideas . . .'

'What do you mean?'

Alison's angry face flushed an even deeper red. 'She needs to get on with her life. Do well in school. She needs to get away from this . . . from this place, Dorothea. And she won't do that if she thinks she can have a life with you and this boy in your, like, magical wood or whatever and . . .' She sniffed. 'And I promised Mum. Don't you see? I promised her that I'd look after Immy if anything bad happened. That I'd get her through school and on to university. She's clever. She's academic. Not like me . . .

but she's also fanciful and she admires you and your life and thinks that she can have it too. But it's unattainable for people like us . . .'

'No, it's not, Alison. I was brought up in a place much like this. We were . . . I didn't have much money growing up and . . .'

'This is what I mean!' An older couple turned around at the sound of Alison's raised voice. 'Please. Just let me handle it. Leave us alone. Promise me, Dorothea. Don't . . .' She gulped down a sob. 'Don't take her away from me.'

Dorothea stared at Alison, aghast. 'I'd never do that. I only want to help. Please don't get upset. I'll do whatever you think is best.' Dorothea could see the elderly couple making their way over to them, their faces concerned. 'As long as you promise me that if things get difficult, if you ever need money . . . or help, or anything, that you'll let me know.' Dorothea reached into her bag and took out a business card, handing it to Alison. 'This is my number and email address. Promise me.'

'Okay. I promise.' Alison took the card and wiped angrily at her eyes with her cuff.

'Is everything okay, Alison?' asked the woman, clutching her husband's arm and eyeing Dorothea suspiciously.

Alison brushed a hair away from her face. 'Yes, thank you, Grace. Everything is fine. Dorothea was just leaving.'

Dorothea hesitated, wanting to say goodbye to Imogen, wanting to protect her somehow.

'Weren't you, Dorothea?' Alison stared at her pointedly.

'Yes, yes, I was. Please say goodbye to Imogen for me, won't you? I don't want her to think that I don't . . .' She swallowed back her sadness, '. . . that I don't care.'

Alison nodded tersely and Dorothea had no choice but to leave.

It wasn't until she was back in her car that she allowed herself to cry.

28

IMOGEN

'Are you planning on writing a piece on Dorothea?' asks Josh as soon as Annette has left. He's clearing away the plates so I can't see his expression, but his tone is cold.

My pulse quickens. 'Why do you ask?' I take the cup Annette was drinking from and place it in the butler sink.

'I could tell you were trying to speak to her quietly, but you were interviewing her, weren't you? I thought you were going to leave it?'

'I'm just interested, that's all.'

'Because of the arson?' He turns to me and narrows his eyes suspiciously. There is a part of me that wants to tell him the truth about Dorothea, about the possibility she was pushed down the stairs, the hidden sculpture she left for me to find, but it feels too late. I've kept too much back from him already.

'Yes, partly, but also because Dorothea was important to me once.'

He laughs cruelly. 'Like, a million years ago. There's more to this, Ims. Admit it.'

'No, there isn't.'

'Then why did Harry give me this to pass on to you?' He reaches under the table and pulls out a dog-eared paperback that must have been on the chair next to him. He throws it at me. I make a clumsy attempt to catch it but it falls at my feet. I already know what it is before I've had the chance to see the cover.

I bend down to pick it up.

'Well? It's her autobiography, isn't it?'

'Biography,' I mumble, unable to meet his eye.

I open my mouth to say something else but he snaps, 'Save it. I don't want to hear any more of your lies.'

Before I've had the chance to reply, he's left the room. I race up the kitchen stairs after him, wanting to explain, but I'm just in time to see the front door slam and the roar of a car engine. I pull open the door. Josh is backing his car out of the drive, leaving me stranded here alone.

At least I can read Dorothea's biography in peace, I think as I settle into one of the sofas, the dogs at my feet. I try and push away the uneasy feeling about my relationship with Josh. Things seem to have taken a turn for the worse since we've moved in here.

I open the book and despite my worries I experience a thrill. There is a short foreword detailing the author's credentials and some of the biographies he's published before, mostly on historical figures. I flick to the back but there is no author photo and the final page just says 'acknowledgements to come'. I've never read a proof copy of a book before. Inside the cover it states that the biography will be published in hardback, but this is a soft copy, cheap and flimsier than a regular paperback you would buy in the shops. I devour the first chapter. Sidney Crane has an easy, accessible way of writing so that I'm immediately transported to Dorothea's childhood, learning about her growing up as Dorothy Bird in the small textile town of Clayton Rocks. It has more details about her father's physical abuse towards her mother which Dorothea had mentioned briefly in the interview with Maria Hensley. It jogs a memory of that summer, one that I had forgotten until now.

It was a day or so after I first arrived at the villa. I had been terrified – I'd been so shy at fourteen and suddenly there we were in this big old house with a woman I had only met a handful of times before: usually when I'd been off school or had an inset day and Mum had taken me to work with her. I'd hidden in my bedroom most of that first day, even though my mum had tried to coax me out, but then, lured in by the most gorgeous cat I'd ever seen, I found my way into Dorothea's studio. She was standing by the glass doors in a slant of sunshine that picked out the champagne tones in her blonde hair. 'Come in,' she'd said, smiling kindly. She'd noticed my eyes on the cat and she scooped him up into her arms. 'He's very gentle. His name's Casper. Here, sit on this chair and you can have him on your lap. He loves a cuddle.' I did as she said and immediately the warmth and weight of Casper in my lap centred me and I felt my anxieties ebbing away. The studio was just on the right side of messy with canvases propped up against white walls, and even now I find the warm smell of acrylics soothing. Dorothea had sat on the chair opposite and told me to think of the place as my home. And then she reached across and patted my arm and said, 'I was in your shoes once. I always wished I had somewhere to escape to so I want this to be your sanctuary. A place you can always come when things get tough. Okay?'

My eyes smart at the memory and I experience that familiar ache of regret that we didn't stay in touch after my mum died. It's something I want to ask Alison about, if only we were talking. She never replied to my snotty message and I'm still angry at her for going to see our dad in prison. I force my sister from my mind. Her betrayal still hurts. I'm reading on about Dorothea's tough upbringing when my phone rings. Dennis's name flashes up on screen.

'Dennis! How are you? Are you home from the hospital?

'Yes.' He gives a little cough. 'I'm all good. I was wondering if you would mind bringing Cady home. It's so kind of you to have looked after her for me, but I miss the old girl.'

'Of course. I'll bring her over now. Do you want me to walk her first for you? Saves you going out?'

'That would be grand if you don't mind?'

'Not at all. I'll bring her over in about forty-odd minutes.'

'Thank you, my dear. You've been a life saver. Quite literally.' He laughs softly. 'See you in a bit.'

I'll miss Cady, it's been lovely company having the dogs with me. But at least I get to keep Solly. I've found a joy I never thought I needed, just tramping over the rough terrain of the fields with the dogs, a kind of calmness despite the biting wind. It doesn't stop my racing brain but it at least gives me an outlet for my energy.

As I lead the dogs through the kissing gate that exits the fields and leads to the lane, I spot Harry emerging from the driveway of his parents' house. When he sees me his face brightens and he strides towards me. He bends down to make a fuss of the dogs and then his eyes meet mine. 'How have you been?'

'I'm good. How are you? Thank you so much for the book,' I reply, noting how polite, how slightly awkward we are with each other, no longer friends, exactly, but more than acquaintances.

'I was hoping to run into you, actually. I wanted to have a chat about Dorothea, but you've caught me on my way out, unfortunately. Perhaps we could arrange to meet up some other time?' He checks his watch. 'Sorry, I really must be off now. I'm supposed to be viewing a flatshare.'

I experience an unexpected kick of disappointment.

I watch as he gets into his car and then I walk past his house towards Dennis's.

Cady starts pulling at the lead as soon as we head down Dennis's garden path, and Dennis is at the front door before I've even knocked.

'Hello, my girl,' he cries as he carefully bends down and ruffles Cady's neck. 'Yes, I know. I know. So lovely to see you too.' Then he stands up and smiles unapologetically. 'As you can see, we've missed each other. Do you want to come in?'

I hesitate, preferring to get home but sensing Dennis might be lonely. He must miss Dorothea and he also might be able to help me with this sculpture.

I step into his hallway. 'Both dogs are a bit mucky, I'm afraid.'

'Oh, don't worry about that. I have wooden floors everywhere. Come into the kitchen and we can towel them dry.'

I follow him down a hallway with dark-green walls and into the square kitchen where I glimpsed him lying in his own blood that day.

He hands me an old towel and I rub down Solly's muddy legs and paws and then do the same to Cady while Dennis makes the tea.

'It's good to be home,' he says as I perch on a leather sofa that's seen better days. There are rips in the arms and it smells of wet dog. He hands me a mug. 'Sugar?'

'No, I'm good, thanks.' He joins me as the dogs loll at our feet.

'Any more news about Dorothea's hidden sculpture? I couldn't stop thinking about it while I was in the hospital. You know, in all the years I knew her she never mentioned working on anything in secret, and we talked about a lot of things.'

I explain how I went back down to the bunker with Rachel and the lighter we found.

Is that a flicker of recognition when I mention the initials? He doesn't say anything. He sips his tea and then smacks his lips together. 'So good to have a decent cuppa. It was weak as piss in the hospital, excuse my French.' His eyes twinkle and I laugh. I'm tempted to tell him about the biography but decide against it, wanting to read it first. I'm itching to get back to it.

'You know, I was always asking Dorothea questions but she didn't always answer. It depended on her mood. She was very private. But slowly, over the years, she began to open up to me,' he says. 'Yet she never told me about the sculpture.'

I reach into my bag and retrieve my phone. I pull up the photos and then pass it over to Dennis. 'I tried to take some close-up shots of different aspects of the sculpture – look, can you see here the magpies? Some have different trinkets on them. Could they mean something?'

Dennis takes the phone and then slowly scrolls through the photographs with his sausage-like fingers. 'Hmmm. Hard to say. I'm not an expert but I think Dorothea's work always spoke of . . . well, turmoil.'

'I've called Gabe Mitchell a few times,' I say. 'You know, Dorothea's agent.'

'Ah yes. And?'

'He never returns my calls. I've left messages.' I'd need to be careful I don't reveal there is another sculpture that wasn't destroyed in the fire, but Gabe, more than anyone, would know how her mind worked when it came to her art.

'These photos aren't very clear,' Dennis says as he reaches for his reading glasses. 'And I'm finding it quite difficult to recall the sculpture. I do think we're right about what we were saying before, you know, about the sculpture being left for you to find. It's quite big. And I imagine awkward to carry. She wouldn't have worked on it down in that bunker only to then transfer it to her studio. It would have been too difficult without help. And we know the others in this series were in her studio because they were destroyed in the fire. I saw them in there myself.'

I'm surprised by this. 'When?'

He looks up from the phone. 'Not long before she died and only very briefly – she was quite secretive about this new collection. We'd been walking the dogs and she wanted to give me back a history book she'd borrowed, and I was standing on the lawn while she went into the house through her studio. Then she pulled back the glass door and I saw them, well, most of them.'

'And? What were they like?'

'I was too far away to see much, but they were life-like and varied in size.'

'Did you see birds?'

He crosses his ankles, which look scrawny compared to the huge slippers he's wearing. 'Yes. I think so. Although I'm not sure if they were magpies, but I assume so. And, like I say, the sculptures varied in size but were all life-like. They were . . .' He pulls a face.

'Macabre?'

'Yes. And strangely glamorous. A lot of fabric and wigs. I'm sure I spotted some kind of headdress. And one . . . yes, I remember now because it was kind of strange – one of the sculptures was in a skeleton costume.'

My breath stills. I instantly think of my dad and the costume he'd worn to Rosemary's fateful Halloween party the night my mum died. They are popular, I know, but this must be a reference to him. If her theme was abuse, had she used my parents as inspiration? The thought sickens me.

'That was it, really. I didn't get a closer look.' He continues to scroll through the photographs, absent-mindedly touching the side of his head. I notice a patch of white hair by his ear which has been shaved, revealing the puckered edge of stitches.

'Please be careful, Dennis,' I say, feeling a sudden rush of affection towards him. 'I'm worried you've been targeted because of the bunker. Do the police have any leads?'

He glances up, his shaggy eyebrows drawn in a frown. 'No. At least, not that I've heard.' He hands me back my mobile. 'I don't really get what she's trying to say in these photographs, if I'm honest, Imogen, dear. I have never really understood art, although I've tried.'

He picks his mug back up and takes a long slurp of tea. I scan his kitchen. The worktops are clean and relatively tidy. There is a stack of old newspapers on top of the microwave, a notepad resting on top of a cabinet by the back door, the kind I always used when I was making extra notes while interviewing someone. When I came in through the front door earlier my eyes had briefly swept the living room on the left, and on the coffee table I'd noticed a glossy book on twentieth-century artists. Is he lying about not knowing much about art?

'Did the fake delivery man give you a package?'

His hand trembles slightly as he puts down his mug and his eyes cloud over. 'Yes. Actually. The police found it after I explained to them what had happened.' He stands up and goes into the hallway. When he comes back he's carrying a small cardboard box. He hands it to me. 'It was empty. The police swept it for fingerprints, but nothing. It was obviously just a ruse so the biker could get into my house. Although . . .' He looks uneasy. 'When I got home I found a tiny piece of paper which must have partially slipped through the gap in my floorboards and it got caught on the sole of my shoe.' He goes over to the microwave and picks it up before returning to me. 'Look at this.'

I take the slip of paper from him. There's only one word typed on it in capital letters. VINDICTA. 'Is this Italian?'

'It's Latin. I did it at school and it means something like vindication. Or justice.' And then he pauses and the energy in the room changes. Dennis looks grey as he adds, 'And . . . it could also mean revenge.'

29

MAISIE

The room is dark, the shutters closed and there is a loud noise overhead, like a rumble; the sky is on fire. Maisie searches hard for the word, eventually finding it. Thunder. That's it. She sits up in bed. She's always in bed these days. Or it seems that way. Although how would Maisie know because her brain hasn't been working properly lately. Everything is always so hazy, like the worst brain fog. Concerned faces often appear in her room, hovering over her so that when she opens her eyes she is startled, scared. They are strangers, all of them. Even the ones who tell her they are her friends, or her husband. She doesn't recognize any of them. Today another of these strange people with their strange faces and concerned expressions comes into her room. A man.

'Hello, my love, how are you feeling?' he asks. He has bushy eyebrows and a moustache that looks like one of those stick-on ones they used to muck about with on New Year's Eve.

She stares at him. She doesn't feel afraid. So maybe she does know him.

'It's Aiden. Your husband,' he explains softly, putting down a cup of something next to her. 'You need to eat, Maisie, my love. You're getting too thin. If you don't eat they'll put you in a home.'

She swears at him. It's more of a reflex than anything else. She can't stop herself doing it these days. She realizes that she must have been the kind of person who never swore because the looks on these strangers' faces when she lets rip are comical. It always makes her laugh, anyway. But today this man, this Aiden, her husband, isn't laughing. His large hazel eyes look sad.

He says something else but she's not sure what he's talking about. She swears again. She likes the way the word feels on her tongue. She wants to throw the drink he's just given her in his face and she doesn't know why. He seems like a kind man. There are photos of them in frames on every surface of her bedroom and in them they look happy. In them they are laughing. He has his arms thrown around her. He is looking at her adoringly, tenderly. There are wedding photos and anniversary photos. He's not a bad man. She's sure he's not. But there had once been a bad man in her life. A man who had hurt her. Oh, but they got their revenge. She remembers those days. With the girls. How they got their revenge on the bad men. How they made sure they got their just desserts.

'Bad men,' she manages and this man, this Aiden shrinks in front of her eyes.

'No, my love. Not me. That was your first husband.'

Her first husband.

'He went to prison, my love. He died there. You never have to fear him again.' He clutches her hand tightly. 'Please drink your hot chocolate.' He takes his hand from hers and carefully lifts the drink to her lips. It instantly makes her feel calmer, the chocolate sweet and reminiscent of her childhood. He sits there, lifting the mug as she drinks the rest. When she's finished he looks pleased. He takes her hand again and pats it. 'Maybe some sleep now?'

She does feel tired suddenly. Very tired. Her eyelids are heavy. She lies back against the pillow and then she hears him leave the room, hears the click of the door as he pulls it closed. She feels safe. She feels warm. And she sinks into a big black hole of nothingness.

30

IMOGEN

Revenge. Why would someone attack Dennis for revenge? I thought he'd been hurt because of Dorothea. Because of the hidden sculpture. I'd assumed that it was the same guy that drove his motorbike at me, that shoved me in Bristol and, maybe, who I found rummaging through Dorothea's study. But what if it's nothing to do with Dorothea at all? What if Dennis has been up to no good? Although I find that hard to believe. I like to think I'm a good judge of character and Dennis strikes me as harmless. But then I remind myself that, really, I know nothing about him. I only have his word for it that he was friends with Dorothea. He could be lying about all of it.

Dorothea obviously didn't trust those around her. Including Dennis. I need to remember that.

Josh's sullen mood continues for the rest of the weekend. He leaves to visit his mum on Sunday evening and doesn't ask me to go with him like he usually would. I'm happy to stay behind and read more of Dorothea's biography anyway. I'm enjoying reading about her upbringing and her passion for art at such a young age, although it's heartbreaking to read about her father and I notice parallels with my own childhood.

Josh still isn't home when I get ready for bed at 10 p.m. I look at the Find My app and see that he's at the Filton flat. Has he decided to stay the night there instead? I'm suddenly very aware of being alone at night in this huge house with a security system I don't even know how to use. But forty minutes later the sweep of headlights illuminates the bedroom and I jump out of bed and run to the window, relieved to see Josh's car pulling into the driveway. I hop back into bed and pretend to be asleep. I can hear him stepping out of his clothes, the sag of the mattress as he gets in beside me. He snuggles up to my back, his arm draping over my waist. 'I'm sorry for being so grumpy, I love you,' he whispers so softly I wonder if I've misheard. Then he moves to his side of the bed and soon I hear his breathing change and he starts to snore gently.

I'm unable to sleep so I pick up my phone from the nightstand, and I'm about to start scrolling through the photos of the hidden sculpture when I notice a text. At first I think it's from Harry and I wonder what he wanted to talk to me about when I bumped into him yesterday. He had said it was something about Dorothea. But then I see it's from Gabe Mitchell's agency inviting me to visit tomorrow at 11.30 a.m. at their offices in London.

Gabe's offices are in trendy Hoxton Square. It doesn't take me long to navigate my way to Old Street and then I walk through the bustling area, enjoying the sun that has come out. I stop for a coffee at a little place on the corner to kill some time before my appointment.

Eventually I arrive at a large, airy reception area which looks like a gallery with photographs spaced evenly on white walls featuring the artworks of Gabe's most famous clients. I can see several of Dorothea's paintings and her most successful sculpture, *Woman in Turmoil*, a young Dorothea standing beside it. The haughty woman behind the desk barely glances at me as she tells me to take a seat. I must look like another young, wannabe artist hoping for representation.

'Imogen! Darling! So lovely to meet you!'

I turn to see a rotund man with rosy cheeks, wearing a jade velvet jacket and a silver cravat, bearing down on me. He must be mid-to-late sixties with still-dark hair and twinkly eyes and a huge smile. I like him instantly. I stand up and shake his proffered hand and the receptionist glances up with interest, assessing me properly for the first time as Gabe ushers me into his office. It's all white walls and blond floorboards and interesting features: a sofa that looks like Dalí's lips, a glass coffee table with ceramic shoes at the end of slim legs, a spotted sculpture of what could be a giraffe but also may be some kind of dinosaur in the corner. I can't stop looking around, picking out different things: the bookends that are fish, the clocks that resemble moustaches, the Jackson Pollock-esque mural on the far wall.

'So, this is the famous Imogen Cooke. The woman who the lovely Dotty left all her worldly goods to.' He says it without any type of malice or judgement; in fact, he seems delighted for me.

'It was a huge surprise,' I say, perching on the edge of an expensive-looking white sheepskin chair, and I find myself hoping the dye from my indigo jeans doesn't rub off on it. 'I'm still trying to get my head around it. Did she . . . um, did she ever mention me?'

'Of course.' He throws his hands up in delight. 'Absolutely. There were no secrets between me and Dot. She was only around your age when we first met and I was five years younger, just starting out. She was my first client that made it big. She had this raw talent, you know, that I recognized straight away. It was me who came up with changing her name to Dorothea Roe.' Then his smile slips and it's like all the light has been sucked from the room. 'I'm still reeling from her death. I can't believe it. I just wish her last collection hadn't perished in that fire. It would have been a wonderful memory, a legacy.'

I know enough about art to realize that an artist's work becomes even more lucrative and sought-after once they've died.

Despite what Annette hinted about Gabe's debts, I can't believe he was the one who killed her. It would serve no purpose for him to set fire to her art. Unless there was something about it that would expose him.

'Did you see her last collection?' I ask.

'I did . . . it was great. Some of her best work.' He gets up from his seat and heads towards a ruby red coffee machine. 'Coffee?'

'Oh, no, thank you. I've just had one.'

It's like the kind you get in a café and he's silent for a moment as he sets about making himself an espresso.

'You know, there are rumours . . .' He returns to his seat.

I sit forward. 'Oh, yes?'

'. . . that one of her sculptures didn't perish in the fire.'

I try to keep my expression neutral. 'Who told you that?'

He waves his hand. 'Oh, just people.' He peers at me, his eyes lighting up. 'Do you know anything about that? Have you found anything in her house? Well, your house now, I suppose.'

'Um. No. No, I haven't.'

'That's a shame.'

Is it my imagination or is there a glint of suspicion in his eyes? Does he know more about the secret sculpture than he's letting on? If he found it and sold it, he'd make a small fortune. I wonder who told him. Is it the person who's been watching me? Who broke into the villa? Who rifled through Dorothea's office? Who locked me and Dennis in the bunker? If Gabe knows anything about the bunker he's not letting on.

'Was her artwork always personal?' I ask.

He frowns. 'What do you mean?'

'Like, was there always a meaning behind her art?'

He laughs. 'Of course. She once told me she used art as a way to figure out her feelings. So yes, it was very personal to her. Is that what you wanted to see me about?' He peers at me with his sharp eyes and I have to be careful what I say next. I can't arouse his suspicions further. 'You came all the way here just to ask me that?' He narrows his eyes. 'She told me you were a journalist. She was very proud of your accomplishments.'

'Ah, that's lovely to know,' I say, genuinely touched.

But now there is an edge to his voice when he adds, 'Are you looking for a story?'

I try and laugh it off. 'No. Dorothea was a friend of the family. Of course I'd love to find out who killed her. Wouldn't you?'

He leans back in his chair. 'Well, of course.'

'But I'm trying to get to know more about her through her art. I'm not great at interpreting it and so I came to you. After all, you'd know her art the best.'

He rests his hands on his stomach, mollified. 'Well, yes, that's true. Which piece of art in particular do you want to know more about?'

'All of them, I suppose. Did they have a similar overarching theme? Other than birds?'

'Yes. Inequality. Abuse of power. She was a feminist. She believed very strongly in women's rights. Most of her artwork is about that in some form or other.'

I picture the hidden sculpture. A woman. Seven magpies. The miniature items.

'Did she hide clues in her artwork?'

He frowns. 'Clues? I don't understand. What kind of clues?'

I fidget. 'Hidden messages.'

'I'm sure she did.' He clears his throat. 'Imogen, darling, are you trying to find this missing sculpture?' His gaze is challenging. 'Is that what this is about?'

My cheeks go hot. 'I don't know anything about a missing sculpture, do you?'

He sits back in his chair. 'Like I said, I only hear rumours. But if you do find anything, it would be in your best interests to let me know.' His voice is steely and a chill ripples over my skin.

31

DOROTHEA

Sixteen Years and Four Months Before

Dorothea knew even before Ruth opened her mouth what she was going to say. She hovered at the edge of Dorothea's studio, picking at her nails, a guilty expression on her pretty face as Dorothea stood at her easel, paintbrush in hand.

'You're going back to him, aren't you?'

Ruth sagged in defeat and slunk into one of the armchairs. Her eyes went to the glass doors and Dorothea followed her gaze. Imogen was sitting on a blanket on the lawn with Harry, Casper on her lap. It was an unusually warm day for mid-September and all Dorothea could hear was the faint chatter of Imogen and Harry's conversation punctuated with a burst of laughter and the tweeting of birds in the trees. Imogen would be devastated. She had bloomed since coming here. Dorothea felt a sudden, uncharacteristic burst of aggression towards Ruth then. She wanted to shout at her, to tell her she shouldn't go back to him. That she was being selfish. That Alec would never change. He would *never, ever* change. But that wasn't Dorothea's way. How she wished afterwards that she'd been able to persuade Ruth to stay, because then she'd still be alive. But instead she'd just nodded sadly.

'I know you must think I'm mad!' Ruth protested, tears in her eyes. 'And I've loved staying here with you, Dot. You've become such a good friend to me. You've done more for me than anyone has in my entire life and I love you for it. But I can't stay here forever. It's not fair on you. I'm . . . I'm your cleaner, for crying out loud!'

'No. No, you're not! You're my friend, Ruth,' replied Dorothea hotly. *And I love you*, she wanted to say. *I love you like the baby sister I never had and Imogen like the granddaughter I never had.* She bit back tears as she placed her paintbrush down and wiped her hands with a rag.

Since Ruth had moved in she'd still insisted on cleaning the house, telling Dorothea it was the least she could do for letting them stay, even though Dorothea was adamant there was no need. She perched on a stool next to Ruth. How could she tell her she didn't want her to go? 'Why are you going back to him after everything he's done?' she asked instead.

Ruth looked down at her hands resting in her lap. 'He's like two different people, Dot. When he's not drinking he's lovely. Affectionate, warm, loving. It's the drink – and he's promised me he's stopped drinking. He's not touched a drop in weeks.'

Dorothea hadn't realized Ruth was even in contact with Alec. How long had they been meeting for? She felt a sudden slam of betrayal. For weeks after Ruth first arrived, they'd sat together talking about Alec and how diabolical he'd been. And now, after everything, she had decided to go back to him?

'Oh, Dot. I can't bear to see you so disappointed in me. I'm weak, aren't I? Do you think I'm weak?'

Dorothea bit her lip to stop herself revealing her true feelings. 'No, Ruth, of course I don't think you're weak. You love the man. But maybe you should stay here for a bit longer? See how things go? Or, you could leave Imogen here . . .'

Ruth shook her head. 'No, I can't do that. The summer holidays are over now. She's back at school and it's a long way for you to drive every day. That wouldn't be fair on you.'

Dorothea opened her mouth to say it was no bother but Ruth continued. 'I can't hide out here forever. It's been so kind of you to put me up, Dot, it really has. It's been nearly four months.'

Dorothea remembered so clearly that day at the beginning of June. Ruth had discharged herself from hospital, taken a taxi to her home while Alec was at work, and grabbed some belongings before turning up at the villa with Imogen. Ruth had been in such a state, scared to press charges against Alec, but also knowing if she stayed he'd kill her. Dorothea had calmed her down and then the two of them had gone to pick up Imogen from school and they had stayed ever since.

'I have to face my own problems,' said Ruth now. 'I need to try and see if this marriage can be fixed. And don't worry . . . if he drinks, if he lays one hand on me ever again, I'm out of there.'

Dorothea swallowed down her anxiety. It wasn't that easy. She knew that from bitter experience. It was on the tip of her tongue to confess all to Ruth. Her darkest secret. But it wasn't fair to burden Ruth with all that. It was a secret she had vowed to take to the grave.

'You promise?'

'Yes, Dot. I promise.' She stood up and walked over to where Dorothea was sitting and took her hands, holding them tightly. 'You've taught me how to be strong, Dot. I feel like I can achieve anything now, thanks to you. It will be fine. If Alec stays off the drink, then I know he'll never hurt me again.'

32

IMOGEN

I'm in a café around the corner from Gabe's office near Liverpool Street. I wanted to grab some lunch before catching the train back to Bath and to gather my thoughts. I can't get the measure of Gabe. And what he knows about the sculpture.

I order myself a panini and a flat white and find a table by a huge glass window. I'm about to take a bite out of my sandwich when my phone screen flashes up with a message. It's from Josh.

What were you doing at the Mitchell Artists' Agency?

I'd told Josh I was going to London for the day to do some shopping. He'd been a bit dubious about it but didn't challenge me, instead offering to take me to the station on his way to work. I should have realized he'd track me rather than take my word for it. I put my panini down with a sigh and, for the first time in our relationship, I wonder what it would be like to be free. Free of someone always checking up on me. Free of having to justify myself. I wonder if Gareth is the same with Alison. Or Matt with Rachel? I know Josh's text isn't just an innocent question or idle curiosity. No, he's always looking for signs that I could be cheating on him. Since inheriting the villa I can sense his insecurities and jealousies bubbling away, just under the surface. I should have turned off the tracking – or better still, my phone – although that might have made him even more suspicious. I'm just going to have to be honest.

I text back:

Decided on a whim to visit Dorothea's agent.

I wait, watching my phone for signs he's replying. There are no ellipses to suggest he's typing. Then eventually the three dots pop up and I hold my breath.

Why?

And then another text follows immediately.

Are you with Harry? I know you've been texting him.

It's like I've been punched. I inhale sharply. I pick up the phone and call Josh. He doesn't answer. I call again. He sends me a text. *STOP CALLING! I'M AT WORK!*

My thumbs fly across my keyboard in frustration.

Of course I'm not with Harry. You dropped me at the station earlier. You saw I was alone.

I don't trust him and neither should you. You know nothing about him, he replies.

Well, that much is true. I'll talk to you about this later.

I call Rachel instead and give her the low-down on Gabe, trying to push Josh from my thoughts.

'If he does suspect there is a sculpture that didn't perish in the fire, he's going to want to get his grubby little mitts on it,' she says. 'Especially if he's in debt.'

'I know.' I take a sip of my coffee.

'I wonder if he's the one who has been prowling about your place,' she muses. It sounds like she's in the car and I hope there is nobody else with her who can hear this conversation.

'Are you alone, Rach?'

'Yes. Of course.'

'Good. I don't want anyone else to know about the sculpture.'

'Chill. You've already said, and I'm not going to go blabbing my mouth off. I'll see what else I can dig up about Gabe, okay?'

I thank her and end the call. I down the rest of my coffee before heading back to Paddington. I sit in the quiet carriage on the train and look again through my photos of the sculpture. My eye goes to a tiny detail that I'd overlooked before. I take a sharp intake of breath right there in the carriage, loud enough for the woman sitting across from me to look up from her book. I notice for the first time that the cuffs of the wool jacket are lacy and there is a patch of denim with a set of three pink hearts on the breast pocket. I had that exact detail on the pocket of the jeans I wore that summer. In fact – I peer closer at the photo and zoom in – it *is* the actual pocket of my jeans, the denim faded almost white. I lived in those jeans that summer and I'd left them behind when Mum went back to Dad because I'd ripped a hole in the knee and Dorothea promised to mend them. But then Mum died and Dorothea never gave them back to me.

I examine the photographs again, zooming in, trying to work out the significance, if there is any. The pocket could mean nothing. She might have found the jeans and thought it would be an interesting touch. But I don't really believe that. She's trying to tell me something – either that or she is hoping I'll figure out this macabre riddle. I only wish I knew why she couldn't have just spelled it out in a letter like normal people. For the first time I feel a burst of annoyance towards Dorothea. I recall what Dennis told me about the other sculptures he'd glimpsed in her studio. The one wearing that skeleton Halloween costume like my dad's. Is Dorothea the magpie, stealing pieces of our lives to influence her macabre sculptures? I swipe away the photographs in frustration and put my phone face down on the table in front of me. I get out *A Woman in Turmoil?* instead and continue reading Chapter Six about Dorothea's first job at a textiles factory in Clayton Rocks in Wiltshire. It's a long and detailed chapter about the origins of the factory and the man who owned it interspersed with short snippets of interviews with colleagues who had worked with Dorothea. I resist the urge to skim-read in case I miss something important. My mind starts to drift until I get to the last line of the chapter, and I sit up in shock.

'And it was only two months into her job as a seamstress that she caught the eye of the man who would later become her husband,' I read. *'His name was Robert Falkner.'*

33

I close the biography as the train approaches Bath Spa station, my mind reeling.

Dorothea was famously single. How could she have had a husband that nobody knew about? I remember her telling me and my mum that she'd never been married when we stayed with her.

Robert Falkner. RF. Was the lighter his?

When I got on the train earlier I'd texted Josh to let him know I was on my way home, but there's been no answer. It's only 3 p.m. and he won't be leaving work for another few hours, but I still expected him to reply. Although he can obviously see from Find My where I am.

An unwanted scene from my childhood suddenly pops into my memory. Me, in bed, trying and failing to block out the sound of my parents arguing downstairs after a night out with the neighbours. 'It was the way you spoke to him,' my dad ranted. 'All flirty, like. All . . .' He put on a high-pitched voice that was supposed to be an imitation of Mum, '*Karl, you're so funny.* And *Karl, that's such a good point.* It's obvious something's going on between the two of you.'

My mum, pleading, telling him it's not true, that he's just the neighbour who happens to be married to Val. That it's him she loves. Over and over again, his accusations, her denials. And then the inevitable sound of something being thrown and then a fist slamming the table, escalating to him using her as a punchbag. And me, hiding under the covers, not protecting her. Not doing anything to help or to stop it, even though I knew what was going on. A coward. I was a coward. And then I remember another conversation, in Dorothea's studio, where I admitted to her how I felt I'd failed my mum and she had taken my hands in hers and assured me I wasn't a coward, that I was just a scared little girl who had felt powerless. Dorothea was the one who built me up, gave me the confidence and the belief in myself. I spent years after that, fighting for justice, exposing corruption through my job, and now I owed it to Dorothea to do the same for her.

Josh has never hit me. He's never hit me. He's never hit me. He's not my father. I don't need to feel afraid to go home. I repeat this to myself as I step off the train and onto the platform. I almost expect to see Josh, rigid with anger, waiting to make sure I'm not lying about being alone, but he's not around – that I can see anyway. I check my Find My app and see that Josh is at work in Filton. And then I look again. I'm mistaken. He's in Filton, yes, but not at work. He's in our old flat.

I can't get rid of this anxious, twitchy feeling all the way home in the taxi. When I get in, Solly greets me eagerly and I make a fuss of him and then change into Dorothea's old hiking boots and take him for a walk across the fields. I trudge over the uneven ground and then stand looking over the views of Bath in the distance. I inhale deeply, trying to breathe the stress away, to rid myself of this nerve-jangly feeling. The sky has darkened as I head back and thunder rolls overhead. I'm on high alert for any sounds of motorbikes, or footsteps, thinking how lonely this little area on the outskirts of a city centre can be with its winding lanes and narrow passageways, hills and woods.

It starts to rain as I pass Dennis's house and I decide to pop in to check on him. I turn into his gate, pulling the hood of my rain mac up over my hair. His old Skoda is in the driveway but he could be taking Cady for a walk. I head around to the side of his house, where the entrance is, and then freeze. I can just make out the back of someone peeking around the corner from the side return to his garden. He is crouched low, and a big waxed coat like the sort fishermen wear is pulled up, obscuring his head. Is this the same guy who attacked Dennis before? Is he lying in wait, hoping to pounce as soon as Dennis leaves his house?

Solly pulls at the lead and I get out my mobile and find Dennis's number. I quickly punch out a text. *MAN OUTSIDE YOUR HOUSE. DON'T COME OUT. CALL POLICE.*

I continue to back away, inwardly praying that Solly doesn't bark or alert the person crouching in front of us that we are here. Solly, thankfully, backs away with me. I hope Dennis is calling the police but he might not see my text. I back out the driveway, almost bumping into the Skoda. And that's when I notice the motorbike almost hidden by the hedge. Fear seizes me. I need to do something. I call DI Shirley straight away.

'Imogen? Are you okay?'

I explain the situation as quickly and quietly as I can.

'Don't put yourself in danger. I'm sending a car,' she says before hanging up.

I don't know what to do now. I don't want to leave Dennis but at the same time I don't want to put myself in danger.

Coward.

The thought pops into my head with the force of a bully's taunt. If I'd been less of a coward my mum might still be alive. I should have kicked up a stink when she told me we were leaving Dorothea's house and going back home. To him. I should have done more.

We stand there, Solly and me, on the edge of Dennis's driveway. Where are the police? From my viewpoint I can still make out the figure, no longer crouching but now standing to reveal his full height. He is tall, and broad. I watch in dismay as he rounds the corner and disappears from view into Dennis's back garden.

I begin to pace nervously. And then, thankfully, a police car turns up and two uniformed officers step out.

'He's over there,' I cry, pointing wildly in the direction of the back garden.

Without saying anything they rush off around the side of the house and I wait, hoping that the man hasn't broken in or tried to attack Dennis. Is this really all linked to Dorothea? The whole thing doesn't make sense.

And then I see the man in the fisherman's waterproof being led around the side of the house, flanked by the officers. It's not until they get closer that I see the man's face. He looks up at me with surprise and I gasp.

It's Harry.

34

'I told you, didn't I? I said not to trust him,' says Josh later that evening. It was the first thing I told him when he got home from work, and his whole demeanour instantly went from hostile to interested. At least I managed to ward off an argument, although I don't admit how gutted I am. Harry had been so important to me all those years ago, a safe haven. Kind, thoughtful, sensitive. But what is he up to? Again I think about the brief conversation we had when I bumped into him on Saturday and how he'd said he wanted to talk to me about Dorothea.

We're sitting on one of the faded pink velvet sofas. We've lit the fire and Solly is lying at our feet and the room is warm and soporific. For such a huge room with high ceilings, the effect of Dorothea's furniture and the marble fireplace is cosy.

Josh appears in high spirits, happy, no doubt, that Harry is no longer a contender for my affections, what with him being a possible killer.

'It would have been easy for him to attack Dorothea, living next door to her,' he says. I don't want to think that the boy I was once crazy about could drive a motorbike at me and kill an old lady. 'He's been lurking around here too . . . I've seen him with my own eyes,' continues Josh gleefully.

'Wait . . .' I sit up. 'What do you mean, you saw Harry with your own eyes? When?'

'On the cameras, of course. I look through the footage every day. We need to keep ourselves safe, Ims. And Harry is always hovering. Once I saw him in the lane, just waiting outside his house, and then, as soon as you came home, he pounced. And then the other day I saw him trying to get in through the side gate. He obviously didn't realize we have a code now. Everything is secure,' he continues proudly, like he'd installed it all himself. 'Nobody can get in. We're totally safe now. *You're* totally safe.'

'So you think Harry wanted to hurt me but because you've set the place up like Fort Knox he had to go for Dennis instead?'

'I . . .' His eyes flicker to mine and his expression darkens. 'Why do I feel like you're getting at me?' His eyes narrow. 'Oh, I see, you don't want to think that he could be behind all this? I saw you. I saw the two of you in the lane. You all giggly, loving the attention.'

My stomach tightens. 'No, that's not what I meant.'

He stands up, towering over me, and for the first time in our relationship I feel threatened by his physicality.

'You don't need me now, is that it? You don't need my money because you have all this,' he throws his arms out. 'You are a woman of means.'

He makes me sound like a Jane Austen heroine and in no way is it a compliment.

'Josh . . .'

But I can see the more I try and speak, the more riled up he's getting. His face is red, his tie askew, the sleeves of his shirt are rolled up. He's not a broad man but he's tall, and fit, and so much stronger than me. And I feel it between us, this imbalance of physical power. If he wanted to hit me, to hurt me, he totally could. I shrink further into the sofa. He doesn't seem to notice. He continues to rant. He's not shouting, he never shouts, instead it just comes out like a stream of consciousness about how I've used him, how much I take him for granted, that I don't care about him. That I've never cared. That I'm heartless, I'm cold. On and on and on he goes, his words penetrating the insecure part of me that is desperate to please and his words are like tiny little swords jabbing at my self-esteem.

'You just don't see it, do you?' he continues. 'You don't see how you treat me. How you make me feel.'

'I'm sorry if . . .'

'No, you're not. You're not sorry at all. You're fucking not . . .'

And then he does something he's never done before, in the whole twelve years of our relationship. He slams his hand down hard on the table and I wince.

His face instantly floods with shame when he realizes what he's done.

'Oh, Ims. Shit. I'm sorry. I'm so sorry. I didn't mean to scare you.' He slumps down onto the sofa and puts his head in his hands, all his anger dissipating. 'Why do I feel like I'm losing you?'

I shuffle over so that I'm closer to him. 'You're not losing me. I'm sorry. I should have been honest about going to see Gabe. I didn't think you'd approve, but I just wanted to find out a bit more about Dorothea and her life.'

He lifts his head up and looks at me through anguished eyes. 'You're not going to let this go, are you? Dorothea's death?'

I shake my head. 'It was arson, Josh. Dorothea was important to me once. To my mum. I need to know what happened to her.' I need to know what the hidden sculpture means, I add silently.

He gives a resigned sigh.

And then we just sit there on the sofa in silence, the weight of all the unsaid words floating between us until Josh reaches over and turns on the TV. He doesn't ask what I want to watch, instead he puts on a *Match of the Day* he hasn't yet seen. I get up and go down to the kitchen. I make myself a mint tea and then sit at the table, staring at my own gloomy reflection in the opaque patio doors. I try and picture the summer I stayed here: those sun-drenched days that felt like they went on forever, the open doors that made the garden feel part of the house, the dappled golden light that reflected on the ground in the woods where Harry and I used to hang out. And then my thoughts turn to Harry. There must be an explanation for why he was hanging around

Dennis's house. I can't bear to believe he would have tried to hurt Dennis.

I jump when my mobile rings on the table next to me. Alison's number flashes up on screen. I haven't spoken to her since I sent her that text and my hand hovers uncertainly. I consider answering it, telling her about Dorothea, the sculpture. I would love to ask her advice about Josh. It's exhausting keeping his behaviour a secret from everyone. I miss her, I realize.

But then I remember our last conversation. Her keeping Dorothea away from me, going to see our dad in prison.

I reject the call.

35

Josh and I pussyfoot around each other like we're performing a delicate dance. He's obviously still annoyed at me, but I can tell he's feeling guilty too at frightening me. Sometimes, when we are in front of the TV or I'm reading, I sense him watching me as though trying to work me out. When I meet his gaze he forces a smile and turns away.

When he's at work on Tuesday I read more of *A Woman in Turmoil?* While Solly is running up and down the lawn and kicking up mud in his wake, I sit with the patio doors open and flick to the chapter called 'Everybody's Talking about Bobby Falkner'.

> Dorothea was a naïve seventeen-year-old when she first laid eyes on Bobby in the autumn of 1968. A broken bird thanks to her bully of a father. Only three years her senior, Bobby was a strapping, handsome man with a chiselled jaw and gelled-back golden-brown hair and an air of confidence that belied his age. All the ladies at the factory, Cadman's Textiles, were in love with him by all accounts.

'He was the best-looking man at Cadman's by far,' recalled Betty Lyons, now 78, who had worked with him on the factory floor. 'We were all soft about him. He had this commanding way about him. Strong but fair. Yet he wasn't a womanizer. No, he kept himself to himself. He was a chain-smoker, always lighting up in the office, very dapper in his slate-grey suits, and he liked a Scotch or two. We were jealous as hell because we could all see he saw something special in the young Dorothy Bird . . .'

I still can't believe Dorothea was married. I continue reading.

'. . . There was something very fragile about Dorothy. Very innocent. I remember she had these fine-boned hands. Not factory hands, like most of us had back then. She looked like she hadn't seen a hard day's work in her life. But then she'd only been a year or so out of school. She was beautiful too. That classy, understated beauty that the greats like Grace Kelly had. She didn't come from money. None of us did. But Dorothy made her own clothes. She was a great seamstress. She always copied the latest looks. Anyway, it wasn't long before she caught Bobby's eye. We didn't think it would last but they proved us all wrong. And they seemed very sweet together. Like something out of a Hollywood film. They courted for a few years, saved up money to buy their first little house and, well, they just adored each other. There were rumours, of course, later, that cracks soon appeared in their marriage. My friend Carole said she once saw Dorothy with a nasty bruise on her arm. Apparently Bobby had a nasty temper, although I never witnessed it. He always seemed totally charming to me.'

Solly's bark makes me look up from the book, my heart jumping. But he's just rolling around on the grass, a rubber ball in his mouth. I re-read the last sentence.

Was Bobby abusive to Dorothea?

Is that why she was so understanding, so willing to help my mum? The Zippo lighter has to be his. Had he come to visit Dorothea after all these years? Could he have been the one to have killed her? A cold sensation sweeps over me. I need to tell DI Shirley.

I call her but it goes straight to voicemail, so I leave a message telling her about the biography and Robert Falkner's existence.

Solly bounds up to me and nudges my knee with his nose. It's time for his walk so I clip on his lead, lock up the patio doors and head out through the front door. The sun is out and the day feels spring-like. My eyes go to Mick and Sue's house. I am still none the wiser about what has happened to Harry. I was half expecting a text from him at the very least, to explain why he'd been staking out Dennis's house, and I'm disappointed that there has been nothing. I had so hoped against all the odds that Harry would turn out to be innocent, but now doubt has begun to creep in.

I try to imagine Harry dressed in leathers, riding his bike into people and attacking old men, but I can't. I just can't. And yet, how well do I know Harry, really? Sixteen years is a long time. He's not the person I knew when I was fourteen.

I notice a curtain twitching in the downstairs window, and I move on, embarrassed. As I'm walking Solly over the fields my phone buzzes in my pocket.

It's a text from Dennis.

I am sorry for not replying earlier, he says, rather formally. *I wasn't at home yesterday. I have spoken to the police and all is good now. Dennis.*

He couldn't have gone far yesterday as I remember seeing his car in his driveway. I wonder why he hasn't given me any further information about Harry.

My mind turns again to Robert Falkner and the lighter and I decide to call Rachel.

She answers in that booming voice of hers. I can hear the familiar ringing of phones and murmur of voices behind her and I feel a sudden, sharp pang of regret that I'm not there. I'd give anything to be back in the newsroom again. It already feels like a lifetime ago since I was there, despite it only being last month. Being out of work is giving me too much time to obsess about Dorothea, her death and the past. Not to mention my relationships with Josh and Alison, both of which feel like they are crumbling – not that Alison and I have been close for a long time. I suppose, if I'm being honest with myself, the same can be said about me and Josh.

I explain about the biography. 'I'm wondering if this Robert – Bobby – was abusive. What if he was the one who murdered Dorothea?'

'So the lighter could belong to him? Not Rosemary after all?'

'It makes sense. He smoked, according to the biography.'

I can hear her tapping on the keyboard. I notice a man walking through the kissing gate. He doesn't have a dog with him so I call Solly over to me. On hearing my voice his eyes slide towards us and then he turns away and continues trudging across the field, hands in his pockets. He's older, around Dennis's age, and tall with a mop of grey hair. He's dressed in a navy-blue wool coat, a maroon scarf wrapped up to his chin. He tucks his head down as he passes me. Usually when I'm out walking with Solly passers-by will call out a cheery hello, especially if they have dogs with them. Yet this man avoids eye contact and hurries away from us towards the Bath skyline.

I turn my attention back to Rachel. 'Do you think you could find out where this Robert Falkner is living now? I've called DI Shirley to tell her about his existence but she hasn't called me back.' I follow Solly across the field, wrapping Dorothea's scarf further around my neck. The wind is biting up here.

'Yes, I'll have a look and see what I can find out.' She clicks her tongue, a habit she has when she's thinking. 'Falkner . . . hmmm. That's interesting. Dorothea has birds on her sculpture.'

'Yes, and in her art in general,' I say. 'Dorothea was born Dorothy Bird.'

'That must explain it. And Falkner, of course.'

'Falkner?'

'Yes. Doesn't it derive from falconer? Someone who trained falcons?'

I frown. The thought had never occurred to me. I always think of William Faulkner, although I know that's spelled differently. 'But they're magpies, not falcons.'

'Hmmm. Anyway, leave it with me. I'll see if I can find out where this Robert Falkner lives now.'

'I've tried googling him and nothing. Would be good to find out if he has any family still alive.'

'I'm on it. Have you mentioned the sculpture to DI Shirley yet?'

A pang of guilt. 'Not yet. I know I should. If this ex-husband ends up being the one to have murdered Dorothea then I'll tell her about the sculpture. It's just . . . I know Dorothea is trying to tell me something.'

'Are you overthinking it, Immy? Don't take this the wrong way, but if Dorothea really wanted you to know her secrets, wouldn't she have written to you? Left you a letter somewhere? Maybe a diary? Would she really have made a sculpture with hidden clues? It all seems a bit . . . Sherlock Holmes.'

Doubt sets in. 'Maybe. I don't know. I keep coming back to the hidden key and the whatthreewords. Perhaps she was worried a letter would get into the wrong hands, or didn't trust that it wouldn't get destroyed? Who knows.'

We say our goodbyes, and I end the call. I walk slowly back to the villa, thinking about what Rachel said. I picture Dorothea's study and all those empty box files. Is that why someone emptied them? Had she left a letter for me? I guess I'll never know.

When I get home I make myself a cup of tea and then google Clayton Rocks, where Dorothea grew up. A Wikipedia page comes up with the history of the town and the notable persons who lived there. I'm happy to see that Dorothea's name is on the short list, but there is nobody else I recognize.

And then, under nearby places, I notice a name. Magpie Hill. I click on the link and see that it's a set of hills famous for hiking. It's only a twenty-minute walk from Clayton Rocks. A burst of excitement hits as I pull up the photographs of the hidden sculpture. Yes, the woman in the sculpture is wearing hiking boots. Surely that must mean something?

An idea forms. It's a bit of a long shot but it's worth it. I check my watch. It's not yet midday, plenty of time before Josh gets home to do a bit of door knocking. I grab the biography, turning to the pages I've just been reading about Dorothea's marriage and find the street in Clayton Rocks where she lived with Bobby. I still have my press pass and I tuck it into my pocket. I check train times. There is a train every half an hour from Bath Spa to Clayton Rocks which apparently takes twenty-five minutes. I book a return on the app and then call a taxi to the station. I decide to take Solly with me. He might soften people up and then they might be more willing to talk.

36

DOROTHEA

Sixteen Years and Seven Months Before

Ruth and Imogen Cooke stood on her front step like two defeated, traumatized refugees from a war-torn country with their suitcases and bags. There was fear and wariness in the young girl's eyes, but Ruth's face was set determinedly despite the arm in a sling: a broken collarbone thanks to that brute of a husband.

Ruth had been working for Dorothea for over two years as her cleaner. Dorothea wasn't great at being an employer – she always felt that working-class guilt every time Ruth appeared at the door armed with her cleaning products and her cloths. At first Dorothea hid in the studio – a place Ruth was told didn't need to be cleaned – but as the weeks and months passed, they fell into a routine: Ruth would have a cup of tea with Dorothea before they both started work and soon, each time Ruth arrived, it became the favourite part of Dorothea's day.

It wasn't long before Dorothea spotted the tell-tale

signs of domestic abuse: a bruised wrist, a mark on her cheek that she'd tried to hide with foundation, a jumpiness at sudden, loud noises. Dorothea knew she had to tread carefully. She couldn't insist that Ruth leave – she had to gain her trust first. It took nearly two years and then, one day, Ruth cracked. It was while they were having their morning cup of tea that Ruth started to cry silent tears. Dorothea watched as they ran down Ruth's lovely face.

'He hits you, doesn't he.' She handed Ruth a tissue.

'How did you know?' Ruth dabbed at her tears.

She hesitated. Could she tell Ruth the truth? She's kept it to herself for so many years. Instead she found herself saying, 'My . . . father was abusive to my mother, and somebody once offered me a way of escape, a sanctuary, and I want to do the same for you and Imogen.'

'In what way?'

'You can both come and stay here. I have plenty of space. You'll be safe here and you can stay as long as you like.'

It had taken Ruth several more weeks to pluck up the courage. And then, when Alec broke her collarbone and one of her ribs, putting her in hospital, she realized she had to leave him.

And now, here they were. Finally.

'We left while he was at work,' she said breathlessly as they followed Dorothea through the hall and into the kitchen. 'I left him a note.' She laughed manically. 'A note. What a coward!' She looked hot and flustered in her floral maxi dress, a grey suede jacket flung over her arm. Imogen was carrying a floppy pink and white cat that looked very well loved. In some ways she looked a lot younger than fourteen but there was something knowing in her eyes, a maturity that spoke of too much seen.

'And he has no idea you've come here?'

'He might work it out, but he doesn't know we've become friends. As far as he's concerned this is just work.'

Ruth was an attractive woman with eyes so dark they looked like pools of chocolate and with the kind of skin that appeared poreless, but Dorothea could detect the tell-tale greenish tinge of an old bruise at the outer edge of her cheekbone. Dorothea had met Imogen before, but hadn't seen her for a while. Imogen was like a mini version of her mother, although her expression was more haunted and she stooped as she stood behind Ruth, as though wanting to go unnoticed, hugging the soft toy against her chest. And then her eyes went to the cat, Casper, lolling in the chair by the window, and she darted a look at Dorothea who nodded encouragingly before she went over to pet him. When she saw Florrie, the Golden Retriever, flopped by the French doors, sunning herself, she let out a squeal of delight.

'An animal lover,' laughed Ruth, but there was a sadness to her tone, aware that Imogen had lost some of her innocence. She turned to Dorothea, gratitude in her eyes. 'I can't thank you enough for doing this. For opening up your beautiful home to us.' She lowered her voice so that her daughter couldn't hear. 'It's been so hard on Immy. So hard. I can't do it to her any more, I have to protect her. I hate Alec and I love him. It's just so complicated, this feeling.' She clutched at her heart.

Dorothea had taken the younger woman's hand then and squeezed it.

And Dorothea had watched both Ruth and her daughter bloom as the weeks went by. Imogen seemed to grow up and gain confidence before her very eyes. As she struck up a friendship with the lovely Harry next door, she began acting more carefree, like a fourteen-year-old girl should, her reservations and fear falling away like a cape.

In the weeks and months that Ruth stayed with her, they never talked much about Alec, not really. Although Ruth didn't need to tell Dorothea of the fear, the walking on eggshells, the self-disgust, the anger, the hurt, the betrayal, because she'd been there. She'd felt it all. And she had the same question looping around her head as Ruth: How could someone who was supposed to love you hurt you in such a way? It was unthinkable and yet it had happened, over and over and over again.

Until you had no choice but to act.

37

IMOGEN

As I board the train I make sure to sit in a busy carriage, Solly at my feet. I get out the biography and continue reading. I'm so engrossed that when my mobile buzzes it makes me jump.

I reach into my pocket and see DI Shirley's name flashing up on screen. 'Imogen. I'm just returning your call. Thank you for your info on Robert Falkner. We are looking into it. Do you know when they were married?'

I cover my mouth and turn to the window so that the other passengers can't hear me. 'Early 1970s. The biography also alluded to the fact he might have been abusive.'

'Do you have a copy of this book?'

'Yes . . .' I hesitate. I don't want her to take it from me. 'It's written by an author called Sidney Crane, and Harry works for Crane's publisher. That's how I managed to get a copy. Talking of Harry, has there been any news?'

A pause, and then, 'We've released Mr Starling without charge – for the moment anyway. He convinced us it was all a misunderstanding.'

'What was he doing?'

'He said he was checking on Dennis. That he'd seen an individual outside Dennis's house. A smartly dressed elderly gentleman. Have you seen anyone matching that description?'

I'm about to say no when I remember the man I saw earlier when I was out walking Solly. 'Actually, yes. He was in his seventies, grey hair. Navy-blue wool coat. I don't know if it's the same man that Harry saw but . . .' I trail off as I notice the train is pulling into Clayton Rocks station. 'I have to go, I'm afraid.'

She doesn't ask where I am, which is just as well because I don't think she'd approve of my door knocking. Not that I imagine it will lead to anything, it was all so long ago.

'Thank you for telling me about Robert Falkner, Imogen. That's very useful information. I'll be in touch.' She ends the call before I've had the chance to say goodbye.

The town centre is only a five-minute walk from the station. Magpie Hill is in the distance and I can just about see a trail of hikers with poles making their way up a jagged pathway, like figures from a Lowry painting.

The town isn't as pretty as some of the places I passed through on the way here. The area has an industrial feel to it, with former mills turned into apartments overlooking a river. I walk through a small high street with a few boarded-up shops and a homeless man lying on a bench with a dog at his feet. I stop on the grass verge to let Solly have a wee and then we wander around until we find the street where Dorothea lived with Bobby. A terrace of red-brick Victorians with neat front gardens. From the biography, it sounded like she'd worked in a textiles factory which has long since closed down. I stand at the end of the long street looking at the rows of terraces, wondering where to start. I doubt anybody will still be living here fifty years later. I'm not even sure which number Dorothea and Bobby had lived at. I decide to start at the end and work my way down one side of the street and then along the other. It's long and tedious and people either don't answer the door or look at me suspiciously, even if their demeanour softens at the sight of Solly.

Just when I'm thinking this is a complete waste of time, a woman answers the door with a sleepy toddler in her arms.

'Hi,' she says softly. And then she glances at Solly and addresses her toddler in a sing-song voice. 'Oh look, Lola, what a cute doggy.' The woman doesn't eye me cagily, like all the others.

'Sorry to bother you. My name is Imogen and I'm looking for information about a woman called Dorothea Roe. It's a long shot, I know, but she used to live on this street and it was before your time and everything, but . . .'

Her eyes light up. 'You're the second person in the space of a week to come here asking about Dorothea Roe,' she says eagerly, moving her daughter further up her hip.

I try and keep my demeanour calm. 'I see. Who was the other person, out of interest?'

'A man. Older. He said he's written a biography about her and was doing an . . . oh, what did he call it? Like an appendage. Or an epilogue.' She giggles. 'I can't remember what it was called, but apparently she died since he finished the book and he wanted to add something . . .' She trails off, looking uncertain.

'Did he tell you his name?'

She frowns. 'Yeah, he did, but I can't remember. Something beginning with C . . . that's it, Crane, I think. I can't remember his first name.'

'Okay.' I manage to keep the excitement from my voice when I ask her to describe the man.

She considers this for a moment. 'Smartly dressed. Grey hair. Older. Like in his seventies.'

Could it be the same man Harry told DI Shirley about? The man I saw out walking earlier?

'Thank you so much for your help,' I say, about to walk off, my mind racing. Why would Sidney Crane be hanging around the lane? It can't be a coincidence that he just happened to walk across the field this morning at the same time as me.

'Wait.' She steps onto the path in her fluffy slippers; her daughter is quietly sucking her thumb, her eyes not leaving Solly. 'This was my grandmother's house. She's in a home now but she's still as sharp as a tack.' She taps her temple. 'Let me take your number and I'll speak to her and ask if she remembers this woman.'

My spirits lift. 'That would be amazing, thanks so much.'

'Wait there and I'll get my phone.'

She plonks her daughter down, who toddles off behind her in the direction of the kitchen. The woman comes back with her phone and we exchange numbers. 'I'm Scarlett, by the way,' she says, flashing me a smile. 'My grandmother is Esme. She might not remember Dorothea, of course, but it's worth a shot.'

'Absolutely. Thanks so much. She was called Dorothy back then. Dorothy Falkner. Did you, er . . . did you do the same for this biographer who called earlier in the week?'

She shakes her head and pulls at her ponytail. 'No. It was only after he'd left that I thought of it.'

I'm relieved. If her grandmother does remember Dorothea, I don't want this Sidney Crane to be told anything. I have to give it to him, though: he's definitely done his research on Dorothea. Although I wonder why he's left it until now to come here. He knew she used to live here – he was the one who wrote it in his book. So, what else has he found out since her death that warrants a visit now?

As I walk back from Bath Spa station my palms start to sweat and, for the first time, I realize I don't want to be at the villa by myself. What if the biker man is still lurking around? Or if he's somehow managed to circumnavigate the alarm and break in? It's only 3 p.m. so Josh won't be back for a while yet.

I slow down as I pass Harry's parents' house. I can see him in the front driveway, tinkering with his motorbike.

My feelings oscillate: I want to be able to trust him, but I have to remain on my guard.

Harry turns around in surprise when he hears my footsteps. 'Imogen!' He stands up. He's wearing old jeans with a rip in the knee and a hoody which makes him look younger and more vulnerable than when he's in his work clothes. Maybe it's because he reminds me more of that teenage boy I'd once had such a crush on. He's holding a cloth which he uses to clean his hands. 'I've been meaning to call you. I'm so sorry about yesterday. It wasn't what it looked like, I hope you know that. I've explained it all to the police.'

I decide to pretend I haven't spoken to DI Shirley so I can hear his version of events. 'What were you doing?'

'Dennis wasn't even in. He had gone out for the day and asked my parents to keep an eye on the house. That's all I was doing. I'd seen this guy . . . that's one of the things I wanted to talk to you about, you know, the other day when we ran into each other.'

'What guy?'

'Hanging around here. Dressed smartly. Older.'

'I've seen him too,' I admit. 'How often have you seen him hanging around?'

'Quite often. I saw him even before Dorothea died.'

'Really? Do you think it's Sidney Crane?'

He frowns. 'What makes you say that?'

I explain about my visit to Clayton Rocks and what Scarlett told me.

'Well, I mean, it's possible. I never thought of that. I can ask my colleague tomorrow if he has any photos of

Sidney. I really thought I saw him walk onto Dennis's driveway that day but when I went to investigate he wasn't there. I thought I was being stealthy.' He smiles sadly. 'But I've never been very good at that.' He tosses the cloth aside and I take a closer look at his motorbike. I know nothing about bikes, but this looks more like a moped than the kind of powerful bike that drove at me the other day. 'You know,' he says carefully, 'Dennis has lived next door to my parents for the last ten or so years, and yet we don't know much about him. Not really.'

I step back, puzzled. 'What do you mean? That we should be suspicious of Dennis?' I laugh incredulously. 'He's a lovely old gentleman. *I* know quite a lot about him. Maybe you should take the time to ask him some questions instead of lurking around his house.' I realize I sound harsher than I intended and Harry looks taken aback.

'I don't know what I'm saying really. You're right. I've never really had any deep and meaningfuls with Dennis,' he replies stiffly.

'I'm sorry, I didn't mean it to come out like that.' Heat travels up my throat. This was not how I envisaged our reunion going.

'It's fine. It's just . . . the attack, it's . . . well, it's odd, don't you think?'

I recall the note that came with the delivered package. Vindicta. *Revenge*. 'I suppose it is. The same guy who attacked Dennis tried to run me over. So it has to be linked somehow to Dorothea.'

He eyes me warily, opens his mouth and then closes it again. I get the impression he wants to say more.

'What is it? Last week you told me you wanted to talk about Dorothea. What did you want to say?'

He sighs heavily. 'Only how I saw that smartly dressed man hanging around her house before she died.' He lowers his eyes. 'I told the police at the time.'

'Is there something else?'

'No. I've told you everything I know.' His glance rests beyond my shoulder and then he turns away from me to pick up his cloth. It's a gesture I recognize from when we were teenagers – he'd literally turn his back on me when he didn't want to answer difficult questions. I remember him doing just this at the end of the summer when I asked him if we'd see each other again.

He kneels down and continues to clean around the wheel arch of his bike.

'I'll see you later then,' I say, puzzled.

'Yeah. See you.'

38

ALISON

'Blimey,' exclaims Gareth as he pulls the car up in front of the wrought-iron gates. 'This is much fancier than I was imagining.'

'Fancy!' echoes Lila in awe.

A heavy feeling presses down on Alison. The stone wall is inscribed with the name Villa Oiseau. Through the gates she can see that the front of the villa has a portico and she takes in the creamy stone walls and the sash windows with a stab of envy. It looks like a manor house. She can't believe Imogen owns all of this. She feels suddenly uncertain. It had seemed like a good idea when she and Gareth discussed driving over to see Imogen. It worries her that Imogen hasn't returned her phone call. Despite being very different people, they have rarely argued over the years and, since Lila was born, Imogen has been a devoted aunty, travelling over to Cardiff for Lila's birthdays and school plays, sending texts asking after her niece.

'It must have been hard on you both,' Gareth had said once regarding their complex history. 'You went from being Imogen's sister to effectively being her parent overnight. You had to take on that role when you were only twenty-one.' And even now, all these years later, Alison still can't shake that feeling of responsibility towards her sister. That she's somehow failed her. Failed their mum. At twenty-one she hadn't known how to be a mother and the two of them had just rubbed along side by side, until Imogen met Josh and ran off to university over three hours' drive away. At the time Alison had felt relieved that she finally had her freedom back. She'd helped Imogen reach adulthood, get into university. She'd been nearly twenty-five by then, her life had been on hold for the last few years, but she'd done what she said she would. She'd kept her promise to her mum. It was finally her turn to have fun, so she'd returned to Cardiff and the two sisters had settled into a more grown-up relationship.

Gareth leans out of the car window to press the intercom. Alison clocks Josh's car on the driveway and hopes they haven't gone anywhere on foot. But then Josh's disembodied voice floats towards them. Alison can hear the shock in his tone. Alison has never turned up unannounced before. The grand gates slowly creak open to reveal the house in all its Bath stone splendour. Alison experiences another kick of jealousy.

'Wow,' says Lila. 'Is Aunty Immy rich now?'

'Seems that way,' says Alison. 'I bet it's a nightmare to maintain.'

'Absolutely,' agrees Gareth as he pulls in next to Josh's car. 'I don't envy them that.'

She glances at him to see if he's taking the piss, but he doesn't seem to be, and the thought warms her.

'I can't believe this is Aunty Immy's house,' gushes Lila. 'I want to see the fairy wood.'

'It's not a fairy wood, love,' says Alison. 'It's just a wood.' And then, feeling bad, she adds, 'But we can have a walk in it later and see if there are any fairies.'

Lila grins. 'You know I don't really believe in fairies. It's babyish!' She jumps out of the car, making shapes in the gravel with the toe of her shoe. Alison grabs the bottle of wine they'd picked up at Tesco on the way over and clutches it to her chest. Gareth takes her hand and squeezes it reassuringly.

Imogen flings open one of the large double doors at the front of the house and steps out. If she's shocked or annoyed at their unplanned visit on a Saturday, she doesn't let it show. She steps out onto the gravel driveway in just her socks. Lila runs into her arms and Imogen swings her niece around. Josh hovers behind her, looking uncertain. They are dressed for their new country life in jeans and warm jumpers and the kind of woolly socks you buy to go camping in.

'Come in, come in,' cries Imogen, taking Lila's hand. But she avoids eye contact with Alison.

Alison follows her sister, who is still holding Lila's hand, over the threshold into a spacious hallway with intricate mouldings, ornate coving, antique sideboards, gilt-edged mirrors and paintings on the wall. The floor and the stairs are carved from Bath stone and Alison can hardly breathe as she takes it all in.

'Shoes off, Lila,' Alison says and her daughter immediately slumps to the floor and pulls off her favourite glittery pumps she'd insisted on wearing.

The four adults stand stiffly, watching Lila. Imogen looks relieved when her niece jumps up again and grabs her hand. Alison can hear Imogen telling Lila that Josh made a delicious lemon drizzle cake last night. Lila excitedly claps her hands, saying she loves lemon drizzle cake, while Josh continues to smile uncertainly. He's crap with kids, Alison observes. He's hardly spoken two words to Lila in her whole life.

They head downstairs and Gareth presses his hand into her back, leaning in to whisper in her ear, 'Are you okay?'

She turns to him and nods. 'It's just all so . . .'

'I know,' he says, still whispering. 'Be nice. She's your sister and she's happy. You need to make it up.'

Alison grimaces in response but she feels like the worst person in the world. She wants to be happy for Imogen and she's trying, she really is.

The kitchen is beautiful in a vintage boho kind of way with lace at the side window and an Aga and delicate bone-china cups hanging from a dresser. There's a butler sink and a large wooden table with mismatched chairs. In the corner by the French doors is a high-backed armchair in a floral-patterned fabric. The sun streams through the glass and the doors are open onto the huge garden, the edges of the wood visible in the distance. It's idyllic and Alison never wants to leave while simultaneously fighting the urge to run to the car and drive back to Cardiff.

A gorgeous pale Golden Retriever is laid out in a patch of sunlight. So this must be the famous Solly that Imogen is so taken with.

Lila squeals as soon as she claps eyes on him and rushes over to throw her arms around his neck. 'Be careful,' Alison warns. She dumps the bottle of wine on the wooden worktop.

'Oh, he's a teddy bear,' says Imogen, taking cups from the dresser. 'Sit down, both of you.' Her voice is more clipped when speaking to them. 'Do you want some cake?'

Alison sinks onto one of the chairs, Gareth next to her. Josh is faffing around by the Aga with a pair of oven gloves, muttering something about putting in a casserole for dinner. That's one thing Gareth can't do – cook – and, for a moment, Alison allows herself to imagine what it would be like if this was her life: if she had this house and a man who cooked delicious cakes and hearty casseroles, if money was no object. If they had a wood for Lila to run about in and a polar bear of a dog to cuddle up to and take out for walks. She glances at Josh as he picks up a pretty cake stand with the lemon drizzle on top and carries it to the table. He's handsome, she supposes, if you like that kind of floppy-haired, wide-eyed boyish look. She prefers rugby types like Gareth, personally. And Josh lacks Gareth's warmth. She'd always been under the impression that Josh didn't like her. He never made the effort to come to see them in Cardiff, and when Alison, Gareth and Lila visited them in

Bristol – usually meeting at a restaurant – he'd be vacant, almost, like he was going through the motions but didn't actually want to be there. As a result Imogen usually overcompensated for him by chatting too much, all hand gestures and desperate attempts to bring Josh into the conversation.

Josh makes a ceremony of cutting the cake and giving out slices on the delicate side plates. He cuts an extra-large slice for Lila and hands it to her, smiling at her shyly. Then he sits next to Gareth and does what he always does – starts talking about football – which is really the only thing they have in common, even though Alison knows Gareth prefers rugby.

'So what do you think of the villa?' asks Imogen. Their conversation is stilted, and Alison knows her sister is being polite for Lila's sake.

She swallows the cake. 'It's stunning. It really is,' she says truthfully. She wants to get Imogen on her own so they can talk properly.

'I love it!' exclaims Lila, finishing off her cake. 'I wish we lived here.'

'You were lucky to spend that time here with Mum,' says Alison, stabbing her cake with a dessert fork. 'It must have been special.'

Imogen doesn't say anything for a few seconds, but then she nods and says that yes, it was.

'Aunty Immy. Can we go for a walk in the wood?' Lila asks.

'Yes, of course, if it's okay with Mummy?'

There's something calming about being here, in this beautiful kitchen that speaks of a bygone era and which isn't as stuffy and old-fashioned as Alison was expecting. Her sister has always loved that chintzy look whereas Alison preferred a more modern aesthetic, but she can feel this house take hold of her and she relaxes into its embrace. 'Come on then. Let's go and see this famous wood, before the sun goes in. It's supposed to rain this afternoon.' This is the ideal opportunity to get Imogen by herself so they can really talk.

They leave the men still discussing football, and as Alison passes Gareth she squeezes his shoulders gratefully for making an effort. She can see that Josh is trying too, and, for the first time, has noticed a shift in power between him and Imogen. It has always struck Alison that her sister walked on eggshells around him, with her quick, worried glances in his direction, always checking if he was okay.

They take Solly and Lila into the woods and Alison's glad she brought a jacket as it's chilly in the shade of all the towering trees. 'I still can't believe all this is yours,' says Alison, keeping her eyes on Lila who has thrown a ball for Solly to catch. 'It's lovely to think of Mum here. She must have felt safe.'

Imogen nods but doesn't say anything. Alison wonders if this is the right time to bring up their father. She has to clear the air between them.

Instead Imogen says, 'I'm sorry I sent you that text message. But I was so angry when I found out.'

'I've tried to call you a few times to explain.'

Imogen purses her lips together.

'I should never have told Dorothea to stay away. I regret it now. But I wasn't thinking of you. I was worried she'd try and take you away . . .'

Imogen's head shoots up. 'What? But I was a burden to you. It would have been easier for you if I'd stayed with Dorothea.'

'Don't be ridiculous,' scoffs Alison. 'I . . . I needed you too.' Tears spring to her eyes and she blinks them away.

'Oh. I never thought . . .'

'It's okay. It was selfish of me. There was enough room for both of us in your life. I really am sorry, Immy.'

Imogen stops walking, her face pained. 'I understand.' She gives Alison a half-smile. The subject of their father hovers between them but Alison doesn't want to bring him up and spoil this moment. They begin walking again.

Imogen suddenly blurts out, 'Can I ask you something?'

'Sure.'

'Does Gareth ever get jealous?' and then she cries out, 'Lila! Don't go too far ahead.'

'She's fine. In what way?'

'Like with other men. People you work with?'

'I mostly work with women.'

'No male hairdressers?'

'Well, yes, there are. I work with two and one is gay.'

'And the other?'

'He's young enough to be my son!' She laughs. 'Well, not quite. But no, Gareth doesn't get jealous. I mean, I'm sure he would if I was hanging out with Ryan Gosling on a regular basis. Why do you ask? Is Josh the jealous type?'

Imogen nods and looks troubled. 'He's always been a bit possessive, but he . . . I dunno . . . he just seems to be getting worse lately.'

Alison glances at her sister. She's never once said anything negative about Josh in the whole twelve years they've been together. 'Is he controlling?'

'How can you tell the difference between controlling and just caring too much?'

Alison stops walking. 'Really? You need to ask that?'

Imogen toes the ground, her cheeks reddening. 'After what happened with Filcher, Josh insisted he come and pick me up every night, even when I wasn't working late. And once, when he saw me leaving the building with a male colleague, he started questioning who I was working with. Then he started to insist on meeting me for lunch and then wanted to track me on my phone – I mean, he's on the Find My app too, so it's not just one-sided. And since we moved in here he's been acting even more possessive. He doesn't like me talking to Harry . . .'

'Harry?'

They begin walking again, slowly. Up ahead Lila is skipping and twirling, Solly by her side.

'Yes. Remember me telling you about him? He was the one who I had that summer romance with when I was staying here with Mum. His parents still live next door and he's staying with them at the moment after his relationship broke down. Anyway, Josh didn't like it when

I was late home one night because I got talking to Harry. He didn't speak to me for ages.'

A growing sense of unease creeps over Alison. She'd had a bad feeling about Josh, but she'd give anything to be wrong. 'Why didn't you ever say anything before?'

Imogen touches one of her hoop earrings. 'I don't know. We moved here, and we were so excited, but it seems to be getting worse and then the other night he . . . he . . .'

'He what? Did he hit you? If he hit you I'll fucking kill him.' Alison feels a rage so intense she's tempted to stomp off and throttle Josh right this moment. She can't believe this is happening again after what they went through with their parents. She wants to scream at Imogen. *How could you have let things get this far?*

'No, no, he didn't hit me,' she says hurriedly. 'Of course not. But he slammed his hand onto the table in anger, just for a brief moment, which scared me.'

'What the fuck. Immy . . . that's not okay.'

'I know. But he was so full of remorse and things are better between us now.'

Alison knows her sister wouldn't have told her all this if she really believed things were better. Imogen is too proud. She's telling her this now because she's scared.

'Do you love him?'

'I love part of him. He can be so kind and thoughtful. I love how he takes care of his mum. And I do think he loves me in his own way. He's scared of losing me, that's all.'

'I'm sorry, but if he really loved you he wouldn't treat you this way.'

'It's not as simple as that.'

'It is from where I'm standing.'

'We hurt the people we love all the time.'

Alison takes a deep breath, trying not to be reactive when Imogen is clearly asking for advice. What she really wants to say to her sister is that she should dump his sorry arse right now, but she knows that's not going to help and it might just make Imogen retreat further into herself. 'The thing you need to ask yourself, seriously, is if he makes you a better person. If being with him brings out the best in you. Gareth makes me a better person. He is the calm to my storm. He is my moral compass. He makes me nicer, less prickly. He softens my edges.'

Imogen nods thoughtfully and then her face falls. 'I don't think he does. I'm not my honest, authentic self when I'm with him. I find myself lying so he doesn't get angry and then I hate myself for it. And I don't bring out the best in him either, do I? I make him insecure, jealous, controlling. I make him spy on me.'

'You don't make him do these things. That's on him.'

Imogen sighs. 'You know what I mean.'

It's on the tip of Alison's tongue to tell her sister she is in a toxic relationship and that Josh is being emotionally abusive, but she knows she has to tread carefully. The fact Imogen opened up about it is a massive leap in their relationship and the most honest they have been with each other for a long time. She swallows down her anger. 'Do you want to end things with him?'

'I don't know. I can't imagine him not being in my life but I also can't carry on living like this. There are so many things I'd like to do with my life. I'd like to travel, maybe work abroad. But Josh is so stagnant.'

'Steady Eddie.' Although in light of what Imogen has just said, not that steady at all.

'Right. And it's not as if we even talk about marriage or babies – I don't even know if I want those things. Or just don't want those things with Josh. But we don't really talk about the future at all. It's like we are in limbo. This house has been a great distraction but . . .' She stops talking and Alison wonders why and then she realizes it's because a dog is barking. 'Is that Solly?' She slows down and grabs Alison's arm in panic. 'Wait, where's Lila?'

Alison scans the vicinity. She's always prided herself on not being a neurotic parent, but Lila is only six. Still, the woods are enclosed and they aren't very big. Plus she's with Solly. 'She can't get lost in here . . .'

But Imogen has charged ahead, her expression tense with anxiety. 'Come on,' she cries. 'You don't understand what's been happening around here. We need to find her, now!'

39

IMOGEN

I run through the woods, my heart hammering. I can hear Alison calling Lila's name behind me. From somewhere in the wood Solly barks again. Is it a bark of warning, or distress? I follow the winding path to the bunker, almost tripping over a fallen branch, and then, thankfully, there she is, sitting cross-legged on the ground, twirling the stem of a rose between her fingers, Solly next to her pawing at the door to the bunker.

'Are you okay?' I say breathlessly to Lila. And then I notice it's not just one rose; there's a bouquet next to her.

Alison sprints up behind us, holding her ribcage. 'Bloody hell, Immy.' She bends over, trying to get her breath back.

'I saw a man,' says Lila.

'What do you mean? What man?' I hunker down so that I'm on her level. 'Where did you get these flowers, Lila?'

'The man dropped them.'

'What did he look like?'

Lila shrinks back, her bottom lip wobbling. 'Am I in trouble?'

Alison glares at me. 'Of course not, sweetheart,' she says, kneeling down, not caring that the knees of her jeans are getting muddy. 'Aunty Immy was just a bit worried, that's all. Where did you see the man?'

'He was over there . . .' She indicates the hatch.

'What did he say to you?'

'Nothing. When he saw me and Solly he dropped the flowers and ran off. That way . . .' She points towards the fence.

'Do you remember what the man looked like?' I ask, gently this time.

Lila pushes a silky strand of hair out of her eyes and blinks up at me.

'Was he old? Young?'

'Old,' she says.

'Like your daddy's age old or like Grandpa old?'

'Grandpa old. But he didn't look like my grandpa. He had hair.'

If he's as old as she thinks he is – and Gareth's dad has got to be in his mid-to-late sixties at least – then he might not have got far. 'Stay here a minute,' I say, standing up. I call Solly to my side.

'Where are you going?' asks Alison.

'I want to see if he's still here . . .'

Alison frowns and stands up too. She angles her body so Lila can't see her face. 'What if he's dangerous?' she whispers.

It can't be the youngish guy I saw rifling through Dorothea's study – or the biker (if they aren't one and the same person). 'I'll shout for you if there's a problem,' I promise. 'I won't be long.'

Before she can object further, I walk quickly with Solly towards the back of the wood, where I know the high fence is. I wonder how the man got in. I doubt a man in his sixties could scale a six-foot fence, unless he's some sort of athlete. Did we forget to close the electric gate, or not close it properly after letting in Alison's car, and he managed to slip through?

Solly trots in front of me and my heart picks up speed as we approach the fence. It's the only other way in, but I can't see anyone. Unless he's hiding somewhere. I stand still, repressing a shiver of fear, and glance around, jumping at every sound, listening out for the crack of a twig or a shadow behind a trunk. But nothing.

I return my gaze to the fence, surveying it carefully, and then I see it. A gap in the bottom corner that definitely wasn't there before. It's big enough for a person to squeeze through and, as I take a closer look, I can see that it's been made deliberately. I wriggle through it and into a field which I know belongs to a neighbouring farm. There is no public right of way, so whoever did this knew their way around. Lila said the man was near the door to the bunker.

'There you are! I was getting worried.'

I whip around to see Alison walking towards me, holding Lila's hand.

'This is how that man got in and out,' I say, showing Alison the gap.

'What's going on, Immy?'

But I don't answer her because my eye catches something colourful attached to a nail in the fence. I move closer to inspect it. It's a scrap of fabric in a teal-coloured satin.

I'm quiet as we walk back to the house. The fabric could be part of a tie, or a shirt. Maybe a jacket. Who would wear something so fancy? My mind goes back to my visit with Gabe. He was wearing a striking velvet jacket that day and he's the only man I know who I could imagine wearing something in that kind of colour. I believe he knows about the sculpture in the bunker, although I'm still not sure how. Maybe Dorothea accidentally hinted at it before she died. Either way, was it him in the woods with a bouquet of flowers? Or the smartly dressed man Harry and I had both seen in the vicinity?

Lila runs into the house to join her dad, Solly following behind, and I'm just about to go in too when Alison stops me. 'Can I have a word with you before we join the others?'

My heart sinks. I regret opening up about Josh because now she's going to worry. I should have chosen my words more carefully; it sounded a lot worse spoken out loud. Josh isn't a monster but I made him sound like one.

'Look, don't worry about me and Josh. It will be okay. We will figure it out.'

Her expression darkens. 'You can't let him treat you that way,' she hisses.

'It's a totally different situation to Mum and Dad.'

She looks sceptical and I hold my breath, expecting a lecture, but instead she says, 'We need to talk about Dad.'

I've been dreading this. 'Alison . . . I can't.'

'Please, go and see him. I'll come with you. It will probably be your last chance.'

'He's never going to tell us what really happened that night.'

'Please . . .' She grabs my wrist. 'For me.' And then, to my surprise and horror, her eyes fill up with tears. Alison isn't the crying kind. It was always me that teared up when we watched a sad film, with Alison taking the piss.

'Why is it so important to you?'

'Because . . .' She swallows. 'I think you might regret it. He's going to die and then it will be too late. He's the only family we have left and I . . .' She sniffs. 'He sounded so heartfelt, so honest when I saw him. I think you need to hear his version of events from his own mouth.'

I stare at her, chewing my lip. I don't know if I can bear to set eyes on that man ever again. 'I'll think about it,' I say. 'I promise.'

This seems good enough for Alison. She gives me a half-smile and nods, looking relieved. And then her expression switches to concern when she adds, 'Wait. Earlier, you said I didn't know what has been going on around here. What did you mean? What's been going on?'

I glance back towards the house. Lila is sitting on Gareth's lap and Josh is back at the Aga. My gaze flickers back to Alison. 'I need to show you something,' I say.

40

DOROTHY

Forty-Four Years Before

The gallery smelled of sweat and salmon vol-au-vents and Dorothy was beginning to feel claustrophobic in the small space. More people had arrived to see her first exhibition than she was expecting.

Annette had driven them all up to Chelsea yesterday. Dorothy had hoped it would just be the two of them – she was nervous enough about her work being on display for the first time – but Maisie and Rosemary had insisted they come along too for support. It was kind of them but also unnerving considering the subject matter. Would they think she had taken their trauma, their experiences, and used them for her own gain? Then she had to remind herself that their experiences were also her own.

Felicity, the gallery owner, had put on a great event. There were waiters in bow ties weaving through the crowds with trays of champagne and canapés. She noticed Maisie reaching for a vol-au-vent every time a waiter passed by. Dorothy still couldn't get over the fact that her artwork adorned the walls, and it was her papier-mâché sculpture that stood on a plinth in the centre of the room.

If only Bobby could witness all this. He'd see that he hadn't broken her.

'These are truly remarkable, Dotty,' said Annette, standing in front of one of her abstract paintings, and she reached for her friend's hand, squeezing her fingers gently in acknowledgement of what this piece represented. Then she moved so close to her that Dorothy could smell her expensive perfume and the mint on her breath. She spoke out of the side of her mouth in a hushed tone. 'But you don't think people will guess what this signifies?' She pointed to the red paint, the horizontal figure.

Dorothy eyed her in astonishment. 'How ever could they? Only the three of us know about that night.'

'Your *Woman in Turmoil* sculpture is getting some attention!' Rosemary appeared by their side, her face flushed with pride. Her coppery hair was held back by two combs and, for the first time since Dorothy had known her, she was wearing make-up. The turquoise shadow brought out the colour of her eyes.

Dorothy tucked a strand of blonde hair underneath her paisley headscarf, wondering if she should have worn something dressier.

'What is *Woman in Turmoil* about?' asked Maisie, gazing up at the sculpture, sipping a tonic water. 'Why does she have so many heads?'

'It's to convey her many different states of mind,' explained Dorothy. 'Her confusion. Her guilt. Her fear. Her love.'

Maisie's frown deepened and she didn't look any the wiser. Maisie was brilliant at crocheting and making things, but modern art tended to go over her head. She sipped her drink silently, not taking her eyes from the sculpture.

Annette sniffed loudly and rummaged around in her bag, pulling out a small bottle of eyedrops. 'Just going to the bathroom to put these in. My hay fever is playing havoc tonight.'

'So, it's about a woman with a lot on her mind?' Maisie turned and blinked at Dorothy.

'Yes. Basically.' *It's about me*, she silently added. *Me and my feelings.*

'There's a man . . . over there . . .' Maisie nudged Dorothy in the side like an excited schoolgirl. 'He keeps staring at you. Ooh, he's coming over . . .'

Dorothy turned to see a man around her age in a dapper burgundy jacket making his way over to them. He was short and stout with a little moustache and dark hair, parted at the side like Tony Hadley from Spandau Ballet.

'Dorothy,' he gushed, striding over to her and thrusting out a large hand. 'So lovely to meet you. I'm Gabe Mitchell and I'm an art agent. I love your work. It's so eye-catching, so rich and deep. Tell me, do you have representation?'

'Um . . . no . . .' Dorothy felt very provincial suddenly and out of her depth. She self-consciously tugged at the waistband of her corduroy trousers.

'I would love to schedule a meeting with you, here in London. What about tomorrow?'

'Fine. I'm staying here for a few days with the girls.' She cast her eye around for Annette but she must have still been in the loo and Rosemary was nowhere to be seen.

'That's fantastic. I have this feeling, Dorothy Bird, that you could be huge. There is just one thing. The name. It's a little . . .' He pulled a face.

Dorothy didn't know whether to be offended or amused. Although a name change would be a great way of keeping herself hidden, she thought. The perfect way to distance herself from her past.

And from what she had done.

'What do you suggest?'

'Oh, I don't know. You decide. Something more grandiose, memorable.' He thrust his card at her. 'Shall we say eleven a.m. at my office? We can talk about it then.'

'Sure, that sounds good,' Dorothy replied, even though she wasn't sure at all. Even though this whole thing terrified her. She couldn't afford to be huge, could she? It would be better for her to stay in the shadows. Anonymous.

41

IMOGEN

Alison gasps, blinking rapidly in the dull light. The papier-mâché figure stares back at us. I've burdened her with all of this: psychopaths on motorbikes, dead magpies in trees, the attack on Dennis, the man snooping around the woods, the intruder I found going through Dorothea's study, the general, unsettling feeling of being watched. She'd listened in silence, somehow not commenting until I'd finished.

She shudders. 'This is really creepy,' she announces. 'What does it mean?'

'That's what I've been trying to find out.'

'And Dorothea left this to you? Like a message from beyond the grave. Wow.'

'A message I'm trying really hard to decipher.'

She moves forward and reaches out to touch the sculpture tentatively, as though it might suddenly come to life. 'Have you asked Dorothea's friends? There was one who Mum really liked. Jeanette something.'

'Annette Baker-Hume. I don't know. I worry that Dorothea didn't trust anyone else with this.'

The bunker smells damp and metallic and the cold air wraps itself around us. I can almost picture Dorothea down here in her trusty paint-splattered overalls and Birkenstocks with her hidden secrets layered beneath all the paint and fabric, breathing life and meaning into this papier-mâché figure.

'It's just so . . . weird,' Alison says, lightly touching the crochet butterfly on one of the magpies. 'Who is the woman supposed to be?'

'I think it's Dorothea with the hiking boots and blonde hair . . .'

'I can't decide if it's hideous or a work of genius,' she says, touching a strand of blonde wig before recoiling.

'A bit of both,' I laugh.

'Seven magpies. A secret, obviously.'

'Yes! That's exactly it,' I say, enjoying this moment with Alison, both of us trying to work it out together. 'She kept it back from the rest of the collection on purpose. She wanted me to find this.'

I indicate the miniature Zippo lighter and explain about the one I found by the bunker. 'Dorothea was married to a man called Robert Falkner and I think the lighter I found belongs to him.' I then fill her in on what Harry told me about seeing an elderly man hanging around the villa a few days before Dorothea was murdered. 'Maybe that's what Dorothea has been trying to tell me through this sculpture. That Bobby was back. And she suspected he was going to kill her.'

Her eyes widen. 'Was he abusive to her?'

'I'm not sure, but the biography made it sound like a possibility.'

Alison is silent for a few moments while she takes it all in before saying, 'It must have taken her so long. All the little details.' She looks up at me. 'And you think this guy on the motorbike is trying to find this? Do you think he could be this ex-husband?' She looks doubtful. 'Although he'd be at least in his mid-seventies, wouldn't he? Isn't that a bit old to be zooming around on a motorbike?'

'I don't know. And why would he attack Dennis?'

Her eyes dart towards the bunker door, which I've left propped open with a heavy rock, leaving Solly as guard dog.

'Do you recognize this?' I ask, pointing to the denim patch on the wool jacket.

Alison shakes her head. 'I don't think so . . .'

'It was from my favourite jeans. I wore them all the time that summer we stayed here.'

She doesn't say anything. Instead she touches all the small items attached to the magpies: the miniature Christmas card, a cat brooch, the tiny replica Zippo lighter, two small pearls, the crochet butterfly, and a toy spade.

And then I watch in horror as she unpins the brooch from one of the magpies.

'What are you doing?! You can't mess with the sculpture.'

She spins around to face me. 'This was Mum's.'

'What? No . . . it can't be. I've never seen it before.'

'I'm telling you, it is. I remember playing with it when I

was a kid. She never wore it but she kept it in her jewellery box. Apparently her dad gave it to her for her eighteenth.' She hands it to me. It's small and gold-plated with two green gems for eyes and two crystals on the collar.

I touch the gems. 'I wonder how Dorothea got hold of it?'

'I don't know, but it's weird, because Mum wore it on Halloween. I suggested she wear it. She was going to pin it to her costume,' says Alison.

Had she been wearing a brooch? I really can't remember.

'If you say this was Mum's brooch then I believe you. I just don't remember it, that's all. Maybe she gave it to Dorothea?' I pin it carefully back onto the magpie.

'She wouldn't have done that. She knew I loved that brooch,' insists Alison, looking troubled. We stand silently for a moment, each of us assessing the sculpture.

'You need to write this all down,' she says eventually. 'You should do, like, a spider graph or something.' She rolls her eyes when I laugh. 'I know! It's being married to a teacher. Gareth loves a spider graph!'

A noise from outside makes us both jump and we spin around to face the open hatch. 'Let's get out of here,' says Alison hurriedly. 'It's creepy as fuck in here.'

I head up the steps first, expecting Alison to be behind me, but then I hear her calling my name from below. I turn to see her holding something in her hand, a piece of fabric, a strange look on her face.

'What is it?'

She holds it up. 'It's a mask. It was in the sculpture's hand.'

I'm just about to chastise her again for pulling things off the sculpture when she adds in a strangulated voice, 'It looks exactly like the mask Dad wore the night Mum died.'

42

'Why does Dorothea have a mask like the one Dad wore that night?' she asks, shaking it at me.

We both know it can't be the actual mask our father was wearing, because that will still be in a police evidence cupboard somewhere.

I take it from her. 'They're a common Halloween outfit,' I say, trying to push my unease away.

'Why would Dorothea include this in the artwork? First Mum's brooch, then your jeans pocket and now this!'

My mind scrambles to join the dots. 'It's a theme, about abuse. Dad, Bobby . . .'

Alison doesn't look convinced. 'You said you think Dorothea left you this sculpture because she was trying to tell you something, so what is it?' She sweeps the light from her phone over the sculpture, illuminating the waxy face, the blonde wig, the wool jacket. 'Something about Dad?' And then she reaches down and touches the hand with the red paint. 'What does this mean? Is this supposed to symbolize blood?'

'I think so. It's only on one hand.'

She pulls herself up to her full height. 'I think you have an idea what Dorothea is trying to say here, but you don't want to admit it to yourself.'

I stare at her, aghast. 'Don't be ridiculous.'

'This isn't just about abuse. I think Dorothea knows more about what happened to Mum . . .'

I open my mouth to protest but Alison shoots me down.

'You don't want to admit that, because then you'd have to concede that Dad might not be guilty after all.'

'No, it's not that at all.'

'I don't know what all these little details mean – the pearls, the spade and the rest. But a lot of this points to the Halloween party,' she insists. 'If Mum was wearing the brooch that night, how did Dorothea end up with it?'

'Maybe she dropped it at the party. I don't know. Anyway, this sculpture can't just be about Mum. Why would someone kill Dorothea to stop that getting out?'

Before Alison gets in the car later she pulls me in for a hug and whispers in my ear, 'Promise me that you'll think about coming with me to visit Dad. We need answers now more than ever.'

I nod and say I'll think about it, and then she releases me. She knows not to say anything about the sculpture in front of Josh. 'I'll ring you in the week,' she says, closing the passenger door.

'Should we stay in the flat for a few days?' I suggest to Josh as we go back inside after waving Alison, Gareth and Lila off. 'Just until this is all sorted?' I wasn't going to tell him about the man in the woods, but as soon as Lila went back into the house she told Gareth.

'Nah, we don't need to do that. We have cameras in most areas now. Although not the woods. We're fine. And I'll fix the fence to stop anyone getting in.'

'Can you put the app on my phone, then? I'd like access to the cameras.'

'I'll show you later.' He waves his hand dismissively and then starts clearing away the plates and cups. I help him, biting back my annoyance that he still hasn't downloaded the app for me. I'd assumed he couldn't be bothered, but now I'm beginning to think he doesn't want me to have the app for some reason and I wonder if it's a control thing.

'I'm glad Alison came today,' I say as I carry the plates to the sink. 'It gave us the chance to have a heart-to-heart.'

He doesn't say anything, but I can tell by his expression that this isn't what he wants to hear.

'I think I might go with her to visit my dad in prison after all.'

He stops what he's doing and stares at me in horror. 'What? Why would you want to open that old wound up?' He dumps the cutlery in the sink where it clatters loudly.

I don't mention what we found on the sculpture, so I say instead, 'He's still insisting he didn't kill her, even when he's served the majority of his sentence and is dying.'

'He would say that,' he scoffs. 'What, you're saying you believe him now?'

'I don't know what I'm saying.' And it's true. I don't know how to feel. The thought of visiting my dad makes me feel sick, but on the other hand it would be good to hear what he has to say, especially in light of what we've discovered today.

His face floods with concern. 'Ims. Don't go. Seriously. I think it would be a head fuck. I don't know why Alison is so intent on talking you into this. If she wants to see him then that's up to her, but . . .'

'And if I want to see him it's up to me,' I say, trying to stop my voice from quivering.

'Fine,' he says, turning away from me to continue stacking the dishwasher. 'Do what you want.'

On Monday, while Josh is at work, I go up to Dorothea's study and do what Alison suggested: I draw out a spider graph, with the sculpture in the middle and bubbles coming off in different directions with all the clues. There are a lot of question marks but hopefully I can fill some of them in over the next few days.

I decide to call Annette. She was one of Dorothea's best friends. She might have some insight into Dorothea's relationship with Bobby.

She answers straight away, but before I can explain why I'm calling, she says, her voice wobbling, 'I've had some very distressing news about Maisie. She's died.'

'Oh no, I'm so sorry . . .'

'Her husband, Aiden, has been arrested.'

I reel. 'Why?'

'They think he killed her. Maybe assisted dying, I'm not sure, but she had dementia.' I remember Annette telling me this before. 'The way she died is suspicious but they won't . . .' her voice catches, '. . . they won't say how she died. I just can't believe Aiden would ever hurt Maisie. He adored her. He would have cared for her to the very end.'

'Oh Annette, I'm so sorry,' I say again. 'Is there anything I can do? Do you have someone with you?'

'Warren. My grandson. But thank you. That's very kind.' She hesitates and when she speaks again I can hear the fear in her voice. 'First Dot and now Maisie. I can't help worrying that I might be next.'

43

I can't stop thinking about what Annette told me yesterday. That's two of their friends group who have now been murdered. I think of Rosemary. Is there a more suspicious reason why she's gone away?

'You look tired,' says Josh the next morning at breakfast. 'You fidgeted all night. Are you okay?'

I watch as he puts a bowl of food down for Solly and ruffles his fur affectionately. He has taken over Solly's morning feeds and it warms me that Josh has bonded with the dog, despite not really wanting one.

'I'm fine,' I say, sipping my coffee.

'Are you worrying about Dorothea?' He turns to face me, leaning against the worktop, one leg bent flamingo style.

'No,' I lie, but he doesn't look convinced.

His expression softens. 'I know things have been a bit . . . tough between us lately,' he says to my surprise. Josh doesn't usually like to admit when things are wrong. 'It's been an adjustment living here and especially in the shadow of the arson and everything, but . . . I do love you, you know. I know we haven't really talked much about marriage but I was thinking . . .'

The coffee curdles in my stomach. A few years ago I'd have been elated at this, but not now.

The realization hits me like a punch.

I don't want to marry Josh.

He walks over to me and kisses me. I tense. He notices because when he pulls away I see confusion, and maybe fear, in his eyes. 'I better go,' he says. 'I'll be late for work. I'll see you later.'

'Yes, see you later,' I reply woodenly.

When he's gone I breathe a sigh of relief.

As I'm getting changed my phone rings. 'Is this Imogen?'

'Yes.'

'My name is Esme. You spoke to my granddaughter, Scarlett, last week.'

Excitement bursts through me. 'Yes, that's right. I was asking about Dorothea Roe.' I sit on the edge of my bed.

'Dorothy Falkner as she was then,' Esme corrects me. 'She lived next door to me in the mid-1970s. Her and her husband, Bobby.'

Finally, someone who knew Bobby.

I hurriedly explain that Dorothea left me her house and now I'm trying to find out exactly how she died. 'I was just wondering what you remember. About Dorothea – Dorothy – and her husband.'

'I was already married with a second baby on the way when they moved in, so it must have been around 1975. She was probably five or so years younger than me,' she says loudly and without a pause, and I get the impression Esme doesn't have many conversations and is relishing this one, 'and Dorothy was friendly to me, but her husband was standoffish. Very handsome. But kept himself to himself. Yet the things I heard from the other side of that wall . . .'

I hold my breath.

'He was a wrong 'un, that husband of hers. I'd hear him shouting at her late into the night. Accusing her of this and that. As soon as they wed, he made her give up her job and I could see how bored she was, drifting around the house all day. We would chat when we bumped into each other and she told me she had dreams of doing something creative and that she missed working at the factory. She admitted to me once that marriage wasn't what she thought it would be. Their rows got worse and she started standing up to him and, well, it was a bad business, but he hit her. She tried to hide it from me but I saw the signs.'

So it was true. He *was* abusive.

I think again of the Zippo lighter. Not Rosemary's then, but definitely Bobby's. It's not surprising Dorothea had been so intent on portraying domestic abuse in her sculptures. In her art. Why else would she set up an art therapy centre for traumatized women? Why else would she have bonded so strongly with Annette, Maisie and Rosemary? All women who had suffered some form of domestic violence. Why else would she have helped me and my mum?

'Do you remember Bobby leaving?' I ask Esme.

'Pardon, my love? You need to speak up. The line's bad.'

'Did Bobby leave her?' I shout.

'She came to me and admitted that they'd had a huge row one night and he'd walked out.'

'Did he ever come back to the house?'

'No. Not that I saw anyway. There was talk around the village that he'd done a runner. He didn't turn up for work. He just seemed to vanish into thin air.'

A dark feeling presses down on me. 'So, nobody ever saw him again?'

'There was talk he'd gone abroad. Had another family. But who knows. And no. Nobody saw him again. Not after he walked out on Dorothy.'

'And what happened to their house?'

'It belonged to the council, back then. There were all kinds of rumours about Bobby. That he was involved with gangsters, that he owed money, that he was a bad 'un.' She laughs drily. 'I was just glad for Dotty. Her life was so much better without him in it. So much better.'

And yet it seems he had come back. To kill Dorothea.

When I'm in the garden washing the dirt from Solly's paws after our morning walk, my phone buzzes again. I let Solly go so that I can answer it and he runs into the middle of the terrace and shakes himself dry.

It's Annette.

'I'm so sorry I couldn't talk to you properly yesterday,' she says. She sounds much more composed today. 'I had just found out about Maisie and I was in bits. I still am. But the shock. You know.'

'I totally understand, Annette. It's just dreadful news. I can't imagine how you must be feeling.' I take a deep breath. Part of me still isn't convinced I'm doing the right thing, but I'm getting nowhere with this sculpture and Annette might be able to help. Especially if she is also in danger. And then I'm going to have to tell DI Shirley about its existence. What if I'm withholding evidence? I couldn't live with myself if anyone else got hurt. 'Um, Annette. I haven't been completely honest with you.'

She takes a deep breath.

'I didn't know who to trust,' I say. 'I still don't, not really. But I need your help.'

'What's this about?'

'Dorothea left me some co-ordinates after she died. And they led me to a bunker in her woods. In that bunker was a piece of artwork. A papier-mâché sculpture.'

There is a shocked silence at the end of the line.

'Annette?'

'Yes. Sorry. Yes, I'm still here. I'm just very surprised. I thought all her work had been destroyed in the fire.'

'I think she left this piece back on purpose. And I need your help to work out the clues. You knew her better than anyone.'

'Clues?'

I explain about the magpies and the trinkets attached.

'Someone has been looking for this sculpture, Annette. I think whoever killed Dorothea knows of its existence and is trying to stop the truth from coming out.'

'I'm finding this so hard to believe . . .' Her voice sounds small.

'Did she ever say anything to you about a secret sculpture?'

'I . . . I don't know. I can't remember. She might have but . . . I don't know. When can I see it?'

Is she lying? She sounds rattled.

'Are you free now?'

'I'll be there within the hour.'

Annette is silent as she surveys the sculpture. She's slipped a pair of gold-rimmed glasses on and I watch as she examines every detail, gently touching the papier-mâché and fingering the fabrics. She lingers over each trinket, folding back the sleeves of the wool jacket and touching the lace beneath. I almost expect her to try and undo the buttons of the jacket, but she stops short of doing that, thank goodness. The buttons are just for show.

She shakes her head and takes a step back. 'I can only surmise. Dotty had such a cryptic mind. I never really did understand her art.'

I point to the brooch. 'Alison says this belonged to my mum. Do you recognize it?'

She moves closer and presses her glasses further up her nose. 'The light isn't very good in here. How Dot managed to work in here is beyond me.'

'I think she used a head torch. One was left on the bench over there.'

She doesn't say anything but goes to her handbag and gets out her phone. 'This will have to do.' She sweeps the torch over the brooch. 'No, I don't recognize it. But these pearls . . .' She touches the necklace at her throat. 'Is this about me? And the crochet butterfly is Maisie's. Dear Maisie. She went through a phase of making them. And the lighter . . .'

'Belonged to Bobby, didn't it? Her ex-husband.'

She spins around to face me. 'How do you know about him?'

'It was in the biography.'

'You've read it?'

I explain about the proof.

She frowns. 'Right. Well, I told you about the postcard Dot found, didn't I?'

'Yes, who do you think left it? The author?'

She rolls back on her stout heels. 'I don't know. Maybe. Dotty hated the fact that man was prowling around,' she says with feeling. She turns to the miniature Christmas card on the first magpie and slowly prises it open. 'There's writing in here. It's too small for me to read, even with my glasses on.'

I move forward to take a look, surprised that the card opened. I hadn't thought to look before.

'Oh yes. It says . . . "To Rosemary, Hope you're keeping well. Bobby".'

Her face drains of colour. 'That would be impossible.'

'Why? The lighter was found in the woods. Could Bobby have dropped it there? Could he have come back to hurt Dorothea?'

Annette moves forward and gently strokes one of the sculpture's hands. The one covered in red paint.

'It's a confession. Oh, Dot.'

A flame of heat rises up my throat. 'Confessing to what?'

'Something she didn't want the world to know, but for some reason she wanted you to know it. You need to understand, Dorothea was like a sister to me. To Maisie and Rosemary too. We'd been through so much together, the four of us. We would have done anything to protect her.'

I feel like I've been doused in cold water. 'Protect her from Bobby? Because he's come back?'

'No, my dear, he hasn't come back. That's why he couldn't have sent this Christmas card to Rosemary, unless he sent it before July 1976.'

'What do you mean?'

'He's dead. Buried up on Magpie Hill.'

44

DOROTHY

Forty-Eight and a Half Years Before

Ripples of panic flooded through Dorothy, spreading to every nerve ending in her body. She wanted to scream and rage and cry, but all she could do was stare down in disbelief at the body at her feet. And then the shaking began, uncontrollably, so that she had no choice but to sink to her knees on the carpet next to him in the darkening front room.

'Dotty, love, you need to hold it together,' said Annette gently from where she stood beside her. She placed her hand on Dorothy's shoulder as if anchoring her to the room. 'We need to figure out what to do.'

Dorothy's hands flew to her mouth. 'Is he dead? Is he actually dead?'

'Yes, my love. I'm afraid so.'

Just then headlights from outside swept over the body of her husband, illuminating the blood that matted his temple, scarlet against his too-pale skin. She froze in terror at the sound of an engine being shut off, the bang of a car door and then footsteps. Someone must have called the police. Dorothy turned to Annette in fright.

'It's okay. It's only Ro.'

'You called Rosemary?'

'We're going to need some help,' Annette stressed in a hushed voice. 'When you rang me you said you'd hit him and he'd collapsed . . .' They both automatically turned towards the heavy glass ashtray that lay a few feet away. Dorothy could see a dark patch on the corner and a fresh wave of nausea washed over her.

'I should call the police . . .'

'Don't be stupid. You'll be charged with murder. You'll be sent to prison. Is that what you want, Dotty? When it's him that should be the one in jail for what he's done to you.'

Dorothy reached out and gently touched Bobby's cheek. He looked like he was sleeping. How could she have done this? She'd taken another person's life. The man she'd once loved with every part of her. Oh, how she'd loved him once. It had been all-consuming. How had it come to this?

'Stop it, Dot. Pull yourself together,' snapped Annette, batting her hand away from Bobby's face. 'He hurt you. He hit you and terrorized you and made your life a living hell. He deserves this. In fact, this ending is too good for him.'

Dorothy hadn't set out to kill Bobby that evening. Their rows had become more and more frequent. It was as though, once she'd let him get away with it that first time, it had opened some kind of floodgate where all bets were off. He wasn't even apologetic after he hit her any more. That first time, a few months after they were married, he was beside himself with guilt and remorse: crying and begging for her forgiveness and promising her the earth. And she'd had no choice but to forgive him. She had nowhere else to go. She couldn't leave this man with his film-star looks and his charm without causing a scandal. Her father had been glad to see the back of her and her mother was too weak to stand up to him. As it turned out, she'd been more like her mother than she thought. Bobby didn't hit her again for months, and she'd begun to hope that it was a one-off, that he was so mortified, so contrite, that he'd never do it again. But once he realized that being married to her wasn't as exciting or as glamorous as he was expecting, that they wouldn't be populating the planet with their beautiful offspring, that she wasn't content to sit around all day playing house, once he realized that he was bored, bored, bored, then the violence began to escalate.

And then, tonight, it had been worse than ever.

He'd been out drinking with some of his mates down the club, as he'd started to do on a Saturday evening, and he'd come home smelling of another woman's perfume. She'd foolishly thought that, despite the arguments, despite the fact he hit her, that he was faithful, but how naïve, how stupid she'd been. She had accused him of cheating and he'd denied it, of course, but when she refused to believe him, when she wouldn't shut up about it, he'd grabbed her around the throat, pushing her up against the wall, slowly choking her, and she'd felt more afraid than ever. He was actually going to kill her, she was going to die, and as he squeezed the breath out of her she'd searched frantically around for something to hit him with, her hands finally finding the glass ashtray that had been a wedding present and which sat on top of their television. And as her vision started to recede, as everything began to turn black around the edges, she grabbed the ashtray and crashed it hard against his temple. He released his grip instantly and she coughed and spluttered, clutching her throat with both hands, as he staggered backwards, his eyes wide with surprise, and then his legs gave way and he'd crumpled to the floor.

And then, with a dawning sense of horror at what she had done, she called Annette.

'Stay here and be quiet while I let Rosemary in,' Annette instructed now. And then she added, more kindly, 'You can't afford to lose it, Dot.' She squeezed Dorothy's shoulder again, as she walked past.

Dorothy could hear Annette in the hallway, speaking quietly to Rosemary. 'What will Rosemary think?' Dorothy muttered to herself, still on her knees in front of Bobby. She hated him and she loved him, but despite everything she didn't want him to die.

'I'm so sorry,' she whimpered, tears pooling in her eyes. 'I didn't mean it.' She watched his face, his beautiful,

beautiful face, half expecting him to sit up and make a grab for her, but he was so still, so silent. She stood up, dusting down her cheesecloth dress, and glanced down at her bare feet. There was a spot of blood on her big toe. Was it Bobby's or hers? She couldn't tell.

'Dot, oh Dot, what have you done?'

She turned, as though in a trance, to see Rosemary rushing into the room, her eyes round with disbelief.

'She's in shock,' stated Annette to Rosemary, as though Dorothy wasn't there.

'Come on, my love. Sit down and I'll get you a cup of sweet tea,' said Rosemary, as if that was the answer to everything. She guided Dorothy to the settee and then disappeared into the kitchen. Before she knew it Rosemary was back and practically forcing the sweet tea down her throat. 'I've put a little something in it to settle your nerves.'

Dorothy didn't know how much time passed as she sat there staring into space. She was having an out-of-body experience and she felt numb as she dispassionately watched her two friends wrap her husband's body up in sheets like a Swiss roll. She could hear them muttering amongst themselves about Magpie Hill and burial sites and waiting until the early hours of the morning before carrying him out to the car. Dorothy couldn't believe that this was now her life. When she woke up this morning she'd been a married woman. She'd been Bobby Falkner's wife with their own home and a future, but now what would become of her?

'You don't think we should tell the police and say it was self-defence?' Rosemary asked.

'Of course not,' Annette replied impatiently. 'They wouldn't believe it. They'd chuck Dorothy in prison and throw away the key. We've seen it happen before. Come on, Ro. You know the way things are for us.'

There were more low-level murmurings but Dorothy zoned out. She felt incredibly tired all of a sudden. Rosemary must have noticed her slumping sideways because she helped Dorothy lie down on the orange settee. 'Here we are, that's it,' she said, adjusting the cushion so that it supported her head. 'Have a lie-down and don't worry, we will sort it out.' She threw a blanket over her and despite the oppressive heat of the evening, Dorothy shivered. Her eyes felt heavy and her throat, where Bobby had choked her, still felt sore. She must have eventually fallen asleep because when she woke up it was light and she could hear Annette and Rosemary clattering around in the kitchen. The scent of frying bacon drifted over to her and she sat up, kicking the blanket away from her, confused. She glanced around the small front room. It was immaculate. The ashtray had been cleaned and was back on top of the television. In fact, the only sign that she had killed her husband and the whole thing hadn't been a terrible nightmare, was a tiny patch of blood on the mushroom-coloured carpet.

45

IMOGEN

I stare at Annette, pristine in her tweed and pearls, and I try and imagine her and Rosemary dragging Bobby out to their car and digging a grave on a lonely hillside. They would have been much younger and fitter back then, of course, but still, I can't picture it.

She wrings her hands, regret on her face. 'I shouldn't have told you.'

'No. I'm glad you did.'

'Will you . . . will you tell the police? Rosemary and I . . . we would be prosecuted.'

'Of course I won't tell the police,' I reassure her. 'Why do you think Dorothea wanted me to know this?'

She shakes her head, causing one of her silky icy-blonde strands to come free and dangle by her ear. She tucks it away. 'I think she was just unburdening herself. I'm not sure . . . and I don't mean any offence to you . . . but I think this sculpture was more for herself.'

'Then why would she leave me the co-ordinates?'

'Maybe she thought you could sell it, use the money. I don't know.' She coughs discreetly into her hand. 'Do you mind if we get out of here? The damp isn't doing wonders for my chest.'

We're both sombre as we walk out of the bunker and I lock it up behind me. Solly is waiting for me patiently at the top, his head resting on his paws.

'So you don't think Dorothea was killed because of this sculpture?' I say as we make our way back through the woods.

'I don't see why she would have been.'

'Then who do you think killed her? And why?'

She rubs her hands up and down her arms. The day has turned chilly and a fine mist hangs over the roof of the villa. 'It could have been Gabe. To do with money. Or it could have been random. A burglary gone wrong. Although, now with Maisie . . . Rosemary is also worried someone is trying to pick us all off.'

I lower my voice. 'Did Maisie know about Bobby?'

'It happened before we met her. But, yes, eventually we had to tell her.'

'Did Bobby have any family? Someone who knows what you did and is looking for revenge, perhaps?'

'He had a sister, I think. Older than him. But I can't imagine she'd come out of the woodwork now, after all these years.'

I offer to make Annette a drink, but she says she needs to leave. I walk with her to her car – a beautiful oyster-pink Lotus that I know Josh would love. Just as she's about to get in she turns to me. 'Other people's secrets are a burden.' She looks about her as though worried she's being watched and her whole demeanour changes to one of paranoia. Then she grabs my hands in her gloved ones. 'If anything were to happen to me, know this, Imogen. We believed we were doing the right thing. All of us. All we ever wanted to do was help women who couldn't stand up for themselves. I'm not saying we were always right, there are so many things I regret, but our hearts were in the right place.'

Before I can ask her what she means, she gets in her car and backs out of the driveway as though being chased by demons.

After Annette has gone I call DI Shirley. I need to be honest with her about the sculpture. I believed I was doing the right thing in keeping it from her, but now others could be in danger. I feel a strange discombobulation at the thought that the Dorothea I knew was also the same person who killed her own husband. I think of Rachel, or Alison. Would I bury a body for them? And then I think of my mum. What if she had been the one to kill my dad because she'd snapped after years of abuse? Would I have protected her? I like to think so.

'I'll be there around four p.m.,' DI Shirley says after I've explained everything to her, leaving out the part about the murder and cover-up, of course. 'I need to see this sculpture for myself. And, I have to warn you, Imogen, you could be in trouble for withholding this information, considering it could be evidence in a murder investigation.' Her voice is stern and my stomach flips with worry.

'I know, I'm sorry. I didn't realize . . . not at first.'

'You had the prime opportunity to tell me that day I let you and Dennis out of the bunker,' she admonishes, making me squirm. 'I don't know what you were thinking, quite frankly, keeping something like this to yourself, hiding it from me like that. I'll see you later.' She ends the call and I stare at my phone, my heart sinking, wondering what I've got myself into. I recall the fear on Annette's face when she left earlier.

I think of my boss, Chris, and my job that still hangs in the balance. I'd been so sure I was going to write a piece about Dorothea after her killer had been caught. But how can I now when there is so much I'd have to leave out, to protect her and her friends? And her killer might never be caught.

I make myself a late lunch, heating up the last of the casserole Josh made at the weekend, and then I take Solly for his afternoon walk to clear my head.

The wind picks up as I head over the fields with Solly. I let him off his lead and he runs in front of me, his ears back, his tongue hanging out. I'm the only one here and I feel a sudden kick of apprehension and the hairs at the back of my neck stand on end. I pull my duffel coat further around my body. It's nearly June but the weather has turned colder.

'Hello, Imogen.'

I jump and spin around to see Dennis standing behind me with Cady by his side. I didn't even hear him approach.

'Dennis!' I laugh in relief. 'You scared me. I haven't seen you for a while. Have you been visiting your daughter?'

'Sorry. Yes, I got back last night. You looked lost in thought. Are you still trying to figure out Dorothea's sculpture?'

He bends down to let Cady off her lead and she bounds towards Solly and they run off together. We fall in step behind them.

'Have you told anyone about it?' I ask, thinking of Gabe.

'I've kept schtum.' He mimics his lips being sealed.

I tell him about showing it to Annette. 'Did Dorothea ever tell you she was once married?'

'Yes, of course. We were very close. She told me about her father. About Bobby and how much she had once loved him.'

She must have trusted Dennis more than I thought.

'Did she ever tell you Bobby was abusive?'

'Um... no, she didn't.' I sense his shock. So she hadn't told him about the abuse. Dorothea had kept that secret right up until she died. Maybe they weren't as close as Dennis is trying to make out.

'How long ago did you first meet her? Did you say ten years ago?'

'Yes, that's right.' He whistles for Cady and she comes scooting over with Solly. He pats them both, gives them a biscuit and then they charge off again. He sighs again. 'I always thought there was something so fundamentally sad about Dorothea.'

'In what way?'

'It just seemed ingrained in her, you know? Her childhood wasn't good by all accounts. A violent father who ruled the roost and then, obviously, all the stuff with Bobby leaving her. She was a broken bird . . .'

A broken bird. I've heard that before.

'No, she wasn't,' I find myself saying. 'She was a strong, capable woman, Dennis. She was a badass.'

He laughs. 'Okay then.'

'No, really. The stuff she did.'

'I know what she did,' he says mildly with a fond smile.

No, you don't, I think but I keep quiet. She helped Mum and me. She didn't rush into another relationship or another marriage. She was strong. I don't buy the 'broken bird' crap. It smacks of a man trying to put her down.

We walk back down the lane together and as we pass Dennis's house he invites me in for a cup of tea. I've still got an hour or so before DI Shirley comes over so I accept. As he's making tea and I'm perched on his sofa with the dogs at my feet, he says, 'Thank you for your help last week when you thought my attacker was back. Did Harry tell you about the misunderstanding?' He hands me a mug that feels heavy and thick-rimmed after Dorothea's fine bone china.

'Thanks,' I say, taking it. 'Yes, he did. I got the feeling that there was more to it, but Harry kind of clammed up.'

Dennis takes a seat on the other end of the leather sofa and crosses his legs. 'It was a shame I was out. I missed it all.'

We chat a bit more, about his daughter and grandchildren and the dogs. But as we talk something is niggling away at me and I can't work out what it is.

'Actually, Dennis . . .' I lean forward to place my mug on the side table. 'Do you mind if I use your loo?'

He looks up. 'Um . . . sure. It's upstairs, the first door on the right.'

'Thanks so much.' I leave the room. As I pass the bookshelf in the hallway, I notice again the books on contemporary artists. Why so many when he professes to have no interest in art? I then head up the stairs. The house has that air of an older man living alone: musty and old-fashioned with no feminine touches. The walls are painted a pale green and the carpet is brown, which reminds me of the chocolate limes my dad used to eat when I was a kid. Dennis said he's lived here ten years but it looks as though the place hasn't been decorated in a long time. When I reach the top of the stairs I head straight past the loo and tiptoe down the long corridor. Like Dorothea's villa, Dennis's house has high ceilings and Georgian sash windows but it's not as grand. I poke my nose around the second door I come to and see it's a spare bedroom. The next room is Dennis's bedroom, sparsely furnished with the bed neatly made. I pop my head around every door I pass until I come to a small room at the end of the corridor. I don't even know what I'm looking for, I'm just following my instincts really. I push the door open. It's Dennis's study and, by the looks of it, he's currently working on something. He has notepads and Post-it Notes littered all over his desk. I remember him telling me he was a retired history teacher. And then, in a pile on his desk I notice the same proof copy of *A Woman in Turmoil?* as Harry gave me. I pick it up and then exhale in surprise. There are four more of them stacked underneath. Why does Dennis have so many proof copies?

Unless . . .

Author copies.

Broken bird. That's why it was so familiar when Dennis said it. He'd written it in this unauthorized biography enough times.

'Ah,' says a voice from behind me and I freeze. 'I see you've discovered my secret.'

46

I step back in shock as Dennis walks further into the room.

'I'm sorry I didn't tell you before,' he says. He looks so benign, so grandfatherly standing there in his cable-knit cardigan, trousers and checked slippers, yet, for the first time ever, I feel afraid of him.

I shrink back against his desk. 'Did . . . did Dorothea know who you were?'

He shakes his head sadly. 'I thought you might work it out. The anagram. Sidney S. Crane. Dennis Creasy.'

Of course. I've always been rubbish at anagrams.

'I wanted to tell her, but I . . .' He looks unsure. 'I was hoping, when it was finally published, she'd see it for what it is.'

'And what's that?'

'A love letter, of course. I loved her, you see. I loved her from the first moment I saw her, and my love for her only grew stronger day by day.' He looks so sad that, despite everything, I feel a twinge of pity.

'Was it you who left that postcard in her garden?' I suddenly ask, remembering what Annette had said about it. 'It had something scribbled on the back, apparently, alluding to the past.'

He looks genuinely baffled. 'No, I didn't. But I did drop off a batch of postcards to the local bookshops in the area, and they promised to put them out on the counter.'

'Is that why you were attacked, Dennis? Because of this book?' I'm still holding it in my hands and I jiggle it in front of him. He steps forward and calmly takes it from me and places it back on his desk on the neat pile.

Then he turns back to me, rubbing his beard thoughtfully. 'I don't know why I was attacked. But I don't think it's because of the biography.'

I can't get all this straight in my mind. Did Dennis know that Dorothea killed Bobby?

'Did you move here on purpose? To be closer to her?'

He hangs his head and thrusts his hands into the pockets of his trousers. Despite being in his seventies there is something little-boy-lost about the gesture. 'No, I didn't even know that she was this famous artist when I first met her. But then we got talking, and over the years she revealed more and more about her life, and she was so fascinating.'

'But she didn't tell you everything, did she, Dennis? She didn't tell you Bobby was abusive.' *And she didn't tell you that she killed him*, I add silently.

'No,' he admits. 'She never told me that.'

'So how did you get your information? I can't believe Dorothea would have told you her innermost secrets and all about her childhood.'

'She told me bits and pieces over the years and I did my own investigations. When she said she'd been born in Clayton Rocks and worked at a textiles factory there, it wasn't hard to find someone to talk to in the area who once knew her. That's how I found out about Bobby. I'm afraid I wasn't entirely truthful with you earlier – Dotty didn't ever talk about him to me.'

I was a fool to trust this man because he looked like a kindly grandad.

Then something occurs to me. 'It was you! You were the man who visited Scarlett in Clayton Rocks, weren't you? Is that where you were when Harry was hanging around your house?'

'I wanted to check I hadn't missed anything. For the epilogue.'

'You must also have had a source. Journalists always do. So who was yours, Dennis?'

'Oh, now, I'm not a journalist . . .'

'Was it one of Dorothea's friends? Was it Gabe? I know he's not doing well financially. Did you pay him to leak information to you?'

It's a shot in the dark but I can tell by his expression that I'm right.

'Did you tell him about the secret sculpture?'

A flush forms on his cheeks and he picks at his beard. 'It slipped out. I didn't mean it to.'

'For goodness' sake, Dennis. Does he know where it is?'

He nods.

'Her death is suddenly quite lucrative for you, isn't it? Now that it's been released to the press that she was murdered.'

His head shoots up. 'What I do isn't so different to what you do, my dear.'

'What do you mean?'

'You were a journalist. You wrote exposés on people all the time.'

'Yes. Bad people,' I splutter, shocked that he's comparing us. And I know Dorothea killed Bobby. I know she's not innocent but she wasn't a bad person. 'Dorothea didn't do anything to deserve you probing into her life like a . . . like a snake. Pretending to be her friend!'

'It wasn't like that.'

'Well, if it was all above board then why weren't you honest about it?' I snap. 'Now, if you'll excuse me, I need to leave.' Despite my bravado I feel a flash of fear when he steps in front of the door.

'I thought – hoped – we could try and figure this thing out together. We need to find out who killed Dotty.'

'I need to leave, Dennis.' My heart races when he doesn't move. 'Dennis?'

He steps aside and lets me pass and I run downstairs and grab Solly, taking him out the back door before Dennis can follow.

When I reach the villa I double-lock the front door and call Josh. He doesn't pick up. I check the Find My app. He's not at the office but at the Filton flat again. I need to ask him why he keeps going there. I've mentioned a few times that we should go over and sort it out, ready to rent it out, but he said we need a few repairs done before that can happen.

The house suddenly feels too spacious, too silent, and when someone buzzes the intercom on the main gate I jump in fright. Dennis must have followed me here. It buzzes again, and I run up the stairs and down the hallway to speak into it. I relax when I see it's DI Shirley.

I open the front door as she drives through the gates. She gets out of the car and follows me down to the kitchen. I can tell by her body language she's still annoyed with me. Once she's sat at the table I tell her everything that has happened, right up to finding out Dennis is Sidney S. Crane.

'Wow, you really have been a busy bee,' she says as she scribbles this all down in her notebook, and she doesn't make it sound like a compliment.

'You need to show me the sculpture.' She eyes me sternly; her fluffy hair is a puffball around her face and she looks like she slept in her clothes. She's a police officer, a detective, I remind myself. She helped put my dad away. She was kind to me and Alison during the trial.

She looks up at me expectantly when I don't say anything. 'Well? Can I see it?'

'What . . . what will happen to it?'

'We'll have to take it away, of course. For evidence.'

Reluctantly I get up and grab my keys and together we walk through the woods. As we do so, I tell her about Lila seeing a man with flowers on Saturday and

I explain about the patch of teal satin I found. 'Dennis told Dorothea's agent, Gabe, about the sculpture and I think it might have been him, looking for it.'

'I'll talk to Gabe Mitchell, don't worry.'

DI Shirley looks perturbed when I show her the sculpture. She takes a series of photographs with her phone from all possible angles. Of course she's going to be interested in the sculpture, I tell myself. It could give clues as to who killed Dorothea.

I wait by the bench while she examines it and then she turns to me, her expression serious. 'Please don't allow anyone else down here. I don't want this contaminated any more than it might already be. I'll be sending a team in to carefully remove it.'

Then she climbs the stairs out of the bunker and I follow her. Solly, as usual, sits guarding the door.

'Can I ask you a question?' I say as I show her out.

'Of course. But don't expect me to answer if it's about this case.'

'It's about my mum.'

She stops by her car. 'Go on.'

'Alison has started to doubt that my dad killed her.'

DI Shirley's eyes narrow. 'I see.'

'She wants us to go and visit him in prison. But you were one of the officers on that . . . case . . .' I swallow. It sounds so sterile calling it a 'case' when it's about my own parents. 'Could there have been any doubt?'

'A jury found him guilty, Imogen. They found him guilty beyond reasonable doubt. Can we ever be one hundred per cent sure? Of course not. But all the evidence supported his conviction.'

'And . . . the evidence was . . .?'

'You were at the trial,' she says gently.

'Not all of it. I was too young. I didn't sit through all of it.' And I've never wanted to know the full details, deeming it too painful.

'Oh,' she frowns. 'Right, yes. You were there for the verdict, I remember that.'

I nod. My stomach clenches when I think about that traumatic time.

She touches my shoulder and her expression softens. 'There was enough evidence to suggest it was him. Testimonies from people at the party who heard him threatening her. CCTV along part of the road that captured his car. The mask he wore to the party found nearby.'

She hasn't told me anything I didn't already know.

'The mask though', I say. 'Why would he be so careless, leaving it at the scene of the crime?'

'It wasn't premeditated. I think they got into an argument, and he pushed her. But his violent past, his threats to kill . . . it all went against him, Imogen.' Her voice is kind as she adds, 'I can see why you'd want to believe he didn't do it. But he did. I'm sorry.'

I nod.

'I'll be in touch about the removal of the sculpture.' She has her detective voice on again now. 'Remember what I said. Please don't allow anyone else down there.'

I watch as she reverses out of the driveway. I close the gate behind her.

When I'm inside I check Find My again. Josh is now back in the office. He won't be home for a few hours, and I don't want to stay in the house by myself.

'Fancy a trip, Solly?'

He looks at me with his head cocked to one side.

I call a taxi and fifteen minutes later we are driving away from the villa towards Bristol.

It's only been two weeks since we moved out of the flat, but it feels like a lifetime ago, and as I let myself in, it's as though I'm breaking into someone else's home. The flat is smaller than I remember and Solly looks too big for the space. I poke my nose around the kitchen door. There is a take-away Costa cup left on the breakfast bar. Solly follows me eagerly into the living room. Most of our things have been taken to the villa so I'm shocked when I see our old coffee table covered with some kind of equipment. I move further into the room. Yes, there's Josh's laptop next to a monitor and a small computer. I place my hand on top of the Apple Mac. Expensive. When did Josh buy all this? And with what money? I open the laptop and straight away it asks for a password. We've been using each other's names as our passwords for years and I tap it in, confident he hasn't changed it. And why would he? He wouldn't expect me to come here. The fact he has all this here and not at the villa means he doesn't want me to see it, so naturally my curiosity is piqued.

But nothing prepares me for what I find.

At first I assume it's just photos of the rooms in the villa. But then I click and see that he has Camera 1. LIVING ROOM, Camera 2. BEDROOM, Camera 3. DOROTHEA'S STUDY and Camera 4. KITCHEN, and when I click on each one I can see it's a live stream. There are also cameras in the garden, side gate and driveway. Obviously I knew about those, but I didn't realize he'd set ones up inside the house too. He'd done all that without telling me.

The truth hits me like a punch to the gut.

Josh has been using the cameras to spy on me.

47

I think I might be sick. Josh has been spying on me. *He's been spying on me.* I can't breathe for a few seconds and then my eyes go to the monitor. I press enter on the keyboard and the monitor wakes up. He hasn't even bothered to close it down properly and on it I can see that he's somehow linked my phone to his. With dawning horror, I can see that all my text messages, emails and search history are mirrored onto this monitor. A fresh wave of nausea washes over me. How long has he been spying on me? He'd accused me of texting Harry. I didn't twig at the time, but he knew because he could read the messages for himself.

I hear the turn of a key in the lock.

Fuck. He must have been alerted to the fact I'm here. I get up, wondering if I can pretend I haven't seen all this but knowing it's impossible. I can't run away from this any longer. I can't bury my head in the sand or ignore any more red flags. For once in my life I'm going to have to face up to what's going on.

I'm going to have to be more like Dorothea.

And right at this moment I'm so angry and repulsed I could actually kill Josh.

Josh rushes into the room and his face pales as he sees me standing there. 'I can explain,' is the first thing he says.

I swallow down the bile in my throat.

'I just wanted to make sure you were safe, that's all. I promise.'

'What? By snooping through my text messages and emails? What the hell, Josh!'

'I had to. With Harry prowling around. It's obvious he still fancies you, it's obvious he . . .'

'For fuck's sake!' I cry. 'Stop it. This is ridiculous.'

He stops, his eyes widening. And then his expression changes from panicked to sanctimonious. He takes a deep breath. 'You don't need to shout, Imogen. At least give me the courtesy of hearing me out. You're being over emotional, as usual. Jumping to conclusions. Why am I always the bad guy? You're the one who's being dishonest. You're the one who pretends you're going to London to do some shopping when you're really going to see that stupid agent of Dorothea's. You're obsessed with her. Wearing her clothes and those hiking boots. And I know you've been researching her and lying to me about it and trying to find out who killed her. It's really quite sad. You're not a journalist any more, don't you get it? You were given the boot. So why are you running around playing at being Miss Marple like some silly little girl?'

I blink at him. Was he always this passive-aggressive and cruel? Did I think, just because he didn't shout and wasn't violent like my dad, that he was *somehow better*? That his words were somehow justified? Had I really sleep-walked through this whole relationship? Anger bubbles and I clench my fists.

'Come on,' I say to Solly who is standing by my side. 'Let's go.'

Josh folds his arms across his chest. 'You're just going to walk away?'

'There's nothing to say.'

'Oh, there's plenty.' His face darkens. 'You really need to take a good, hard look at yourself. Stop playing the victim. I know you've told Alison all about me. I could see it in the way she looked at me when you came back in from the woods. Thanks for your loyalty. You only told her one side of the story, typically.'

'Well, you ought to know,' I say. 'You've got it all on camera!'

He glares at me, his face reddening. 'I did all this for you and for your protection. You need protecting from yourself, don't you see? You can't look after yourself, Ims. You need me.'

'I don't need anyone,' I reply. 'And I don't need you. It's over, Josh.'

He stares at me in surprise. 'What? Don't be ridiculous. Of course it's not over. You're going to end a twelve-year relationship over this?'

I sigh. 'It's not just this. It's you . . . and me. We're not right together. We bring out the worst in each other. Don't you see that?'

'No. I've been nothing but great to you. You've used me. Now you have this inheritance you don't need me any more. Is that it?'

'Josh . . .'

He continues to glare at me, his eyes flashing. 'That's what all this is about. Now you can live your life in that old hag's house with all her money. God, you're a bitch.'

'I'll give you money if that's what you want, Josh . . .'

'Oh, that's right. Now you get to be magnanimous. Saint Imogen. Always the victim. Poor little Immy. No mummy and a daddy in jail. And now a big, bad boyfriend who spies on her. That's what you'll tell people, no doubt. You won't say I was doing it for your own good. This is all just an excuse so you can run off with that Harry, you slut.'

I need to get out of here. Despite my bravado I don't want to argue with him, and he's getting nastier and nastier. I clip on Solly's lead. 'I think it's best I leave.' I concentrate on sounding calm but underneath my heart is hammering so hard I worry he'll hear it.

He's standing in front of the living room door. 'I don't think so. Not until we get all this sorted.'

'Josh, please let me pass.'

'*Josh, please let me pass,*' he says in an imitation of my voice. 'No, I'm not going to let you fucking pass. Not until we've sorted this out.'

'Fine. It's sorted. I'll see you back at the villa.'

He laughs angrily. 'Do you think I'm stupid?'

'I don't know what you want me to say.' I can feel tears

pressing behind my eyes, but I refuse to cry in front of him. I need to stand up to him for once.

'God, you're cold,' he says.

We stare at each other and then I hear a low growl from Solly. I reach down and touch him gently on the head. 'It's okay, boy. Josh is going to let us pass, aren't you, Josh?'

Despite the situation I want to laugh when I see the fear on Josh's face. He steps aside to let me pass. 'Ims...' His chin wobbles. 'Don't do this. You make me this way.'

I feel braver with my hand on the doorknob. 'No, Josh. You made yourself this way. I would never cheat on you. And I only ever lied to you because of your reactions to things. The mood swings, the punishing me for days if I didn't do exactly what you wanted...' I swallow back my tears. 'And I've had enough. I've had enough of feeling afraid all the time.'

He looks genuinely surprised. 'I wasn't trying to make you afraid. I was trying to protect you.'

'No. You don't trust me and you're trying to control me. We're in this weird, toxic cycle and we need to break it. You were spying on me, Josh! Don't you get how fucked up this all is?' I indicate his laptop and monitor. We'd latched on to each other in our late teens because we'd each desperately needed someone, but it was a relationship that was never meant to last. He must know it too, deep down.

His face crumples. 'I'm so sorry, please don't end things, Ims. I need you.'

'Oh, Josh. You don't need me . . .'

He wipes his eyes with the back of his hand. 'I'm sorry . . .' He slumps onto the sofa, his head in his hands. 'I don't know what I was thinking.'

'I'm sorry too,' I say quietly. We need to break free from each other. Two damaged people in a damaged relationship.

He lifts his head up, his eyes red-rimmed. 'I'll stay here tonight. Will you be okay in the villa by yourself?'

I hesitate, imagining the villa without Josh. Can I really do this? Can I really end things? And then I think of Dorothea, and how strong she was. She lived there alone for years. I can't stay with Josh just because I'm scared of being on my own. 'I'll be fine,' I say. And then I leave with Solly, closing the door behind me.

48

AIDEN

The bedroom where his precious Maisie died still looks and smells the same and Aiden can't bring himself to clean it. Even the bed is still unmade, the silk eiderdown bunched up at the bottom where she'd kicked it off that last night, the lace curtains still closed. He eyes a framed photograph of their wedding that sits on her bedside table: her in a long, pale-blue dress and him in a dapper suit. It had been a registry office affair; neither of them wanted a traditional wedding, both having been married before. He sits on the edge of the bed and picks up the photograph, running his thumb gently over Maisie's smiling face.

She's at peace at last. Whoever killed her did her a favour. But it wasn't him.

Yet how can he tell the police? If he does then he's breaking a promise that he made to Maisie. He'd kept it close to his chest all these years and the truth would tarnish her memory and undo all the good.

But if he doesn't tell the truth then he'll go to prison for a crime he didn't commit.

He's been sleeping in the spare room since he was released from custody. He hasn't been charged with anything yet. There isn't enough evidence to suggest it was him who had poisoned his wife's hot chocolate and he'd done just as his lawyer had advised and met every question with a No Comment answer. But that will only work for a while. He's an easy target. An open and shut case.

But maybe there is a way around it. Maybe there is a way he can keep his promise to Maisie but help himself as well. Because he doesn't want to spend years behind bars for a crime he didn't commit. And he doesn't want the world to think he killed his beautiful wife.

49

IMOGEN

Another night without much sleep. My body feels like it's going through cold turkey without Josh. I know it's for the best, that it's over, but I've been with him most of my adult life. He made me feel like I'm not safe without him and now, every creak of the house, every slam of a car door, every sound in the garden, makes me break out in a cold sweat. In the end I let Solly sleep upstairs with me and I'm relieved when I hear the morning birdsong and see the sliver of light between the curtains.

The kitchen feels sterile without Josh here cooking pancakes, without the comforting smell of his coffee machine, and I experience that tug of loss again. And then I remember. Is he still spying on me now? I glance around the kitchen, trying to work out where he's hidden the camera, but I can't see anything. Then my eye focuses on the smoke detector. Isn't that where spyware is usually hidden? It is in films. I pull back one of the chairs and stand on it, twisting the plastic case away from the detector, and peer inside, almost disappointed when I don't see anything other than the battery. I replace the case and step off the chair. I cast my eyes around for another hiding place. Could it be in one of the photo frames? I recall the things he'd called me yesterday too – a slut, a liar – and feel a thump of anger. Was he always this way? Surely not. Although I've always been good at sticking my head in the sand. The truth is, I didn't want to see Josh for the person he is because to do so would mean examining our relationship and I wanted to believe everything was perfect. Josh and his mum have been my family since I was eighteen. I leaned heavily on them, and I was terrified that if I left Josh I'd have nobody. But now I realize that isn't true. I have Alison, and Gareth and Lila. And I have Rachel. And I have a future that's free of a man controlling my every move, telling me who I can and cannot be friends with, distrusting me, spying on me, slowly chipping away at my confidence.

Yet, despite all this, I still feel too sick to eat and I just sip at my morning coffee.

My phone pings with a text and my heart lurches in case it's Josh. But it's Alison.

I'm visiting Dad tomorrow – I've got us a visiting pass just in case you have a change of heart. I'll be outside the prison at 11 a.m.

My resolve wavers. Can I really do this? But it could be my last chance and I still have question marks around the replica mask and the brooch found on Dorothea's sculpture. I tap a quick text back telling her I'll be there even though the thought makes me feel like vomiting.

The doorbell rings and my nausea intensifies. *Josh?* I can't face him right now. I go to the front door, my heart pounding, relieved when I see it's not Josh standing at the front door, but Harry. How did he get through the gates?

'Sorry to call so early,' he says when I open the door. 'I hope I didn't wake you up.'

'Not at all. Truth is, I've been awake for hours.'

'Your side gate was open. Hope all's okay?'

I frown. Did Josh open it? Or maybe the keypad isn't working properly. I'll need to take a look at that but the thought of trying to figure it out without Josh's help makes me feel overwhelmed. 'Just a rough night.'

He looks down at his feet awkwardly and then back up at me. 'I wanted to talk to you about Dennis.'

'Do you mean Sidney S. Crane?' I raise an eyebrow.

'Ah. You know!' He thrusts his hands in his pockets.

'Yep. Come in.' I show him into the kitchen and make him a coffee.

'When did you realize that Dennis was the one behind *A Woman in Turmoil*?' I ask when I've joined him at the table. Solly, after his run around the garden, is flaked out by the back door in a patch of morning sunlight.

'Something about Dennis niggled away at me. He asked too many questions about Dorothea and when I told him I was reading a proof of her biography he kind of looked weird about it, started mumbling about not being aware I worked at the same publishers as Sidney Crane. That day you saw me hanging around his house – well, I knew he was planning to go out and I thought maybe he'd left the door unlocked, or a key under his plant pot, and I'd have a little poke around,' he admits sheepishly.

'Harry!' Although I know I'm not one to talk after what I did to Dominic Filcher.

'I know. I'm not proud of it.'

'Couldn't you have asked around at work?'

He brings his mug to his lips and takes a big sip before lowering it again. 'I did. They described him to me and it matched Dennis's description, but I couldn't be sure until I'd seen some proof. I've since found out that the address we had on file for him was his daughter's. And then, last night, his author photos came in. And that's when I knew for definite.'

'Wow.' I digest this information.

'I was going to text you but I wanted to talk to you about it face to face. I didn't think I'd be welcome last night. Josh . . . you know.' He flicks me a knowing glance.

'Well, you don't have to worry about that any more, Josh and I have split up.'

His eyes widen in surprise. 'I'm sorry to hear that,' he says, not looking sorry at all.

I brush over it. 'There's something I haven't told you. But now the police know, it's going to get out.' I pause. 'Not all Dorothea's work was destroyed in the fire.'

'What?'

I tell him about the hidden sculpture and then I hand him my phone. 'I took photos. Scroll left.'

'Wow,' he says, thumbing through the photos. 'This is . . . weird as hell.'

'I know.'

'She has a lot of birds in her art.'

My phone pings with a text message and Harry looks awkward as he hands it back to me.

The message flashes up on screen. It's from Josh and my heart sinks.

AND YOU WONDER WHY I DON'T TRUST YOU!

Are the cameras still connected? I place the phone face down on the table, anger coursing through me. 'Do you fancy a walk?' I say to Harry, who looks surprised to be asked but agrees. I call Solly in and lock the French doors. He curls up in his bed and I decide to leave him here.

When we reach the side gate I notice the keypad has been smashed in, rendering the lock useless. Did Josh do this in a moment of anger? For revenge? I stare at it in dismay.

'Oh, shit,' exclaims Harry, following my line of vision. 'Who would do this?'

'I don't know. But I'm going to have to call the security company back.' I pull the gate to, a knot of anxiety in my stomach.

As we step onto the pavement, Harry turns to me and says, 'So will you show me this sculpt—'

But he doesn't get the chance to finish what he's saying as the roar of a motorbike makes us both jump.

'Look out!' Harry yells, pulling me away from the road as the motorbike swerves out of nowhere. He grabs my hand and we sprint towards the fields, the motorbike chasing after us. For a quick, paranoid moment, I wonder if it could have been Josh all along but then I dismiss this immediately. Josh doesn't know how to ride a motorbike.

Harry almost pushes me through the kissing gate that leads to the fields just as the motorbike skids towards us and crashes, throwing the biker into the air. I stare in horror as I watch him land hard onto the tarmac, the bike coming to a halt by a tree trunk, wheels still spinning.

'Shit!' Harry runs towards the biker.

'Be careful,' I cry, still in between the kissing gate, wondering whether to join him or not.

Harry kneels beside the biker. 'He's badly hurt. Call an ambulance.'

I pull back the gate and join Harry. The biker is lying on his side, helmet still on. I call 999 and explain what's happened.

'Is he breathing?' the woman on the other end of the line asks.

'I'm not sure. He's still got his helmet on.'

Harry turns to me with a look of alarm. 'I can't find a pulse.'

I repeat this to the operator. 'You're going to have to gently take his helmet off to administer CPR,' she says calmly. I repeat this to Harry. 'And someone needs to support the head.' I bend down and do as she says while Harry gently lifts the helmet away. The man's head feels sweaty and he has a buzz cut, the bristles rough against my hands. Harry shrugs out of his jacket and places it between my feet and then I lower the man's head gently onto it so that Harry can administer CPR.

I stand up, finally getting a good look at the man's face.

And I gasp.

Because I know who this man is and why he's been trying to frighten me.

50

DI Shirley meets us at the Royal United Hospital in Bath. Harry and I sit in the corridor nursing plastic cups of lukewarm coffee.

'Is he alive?' I ask as soon as she walks towards us, her long coat fanning out behind her. She has a harassed look on her face and her hair is even more dishevelled than usual.

'Yes. He's very lucky – or unlucky, depending on how you view it.'

Ironic that Harry saved his life when he was trying to take ours.

'And is it him?' I know it is, but I want to hear her say it.

'Yes. It's Dominic Filcher. He's told me what happened and how you helped put his father away for corruption and then went after him too.'

Jeremy Filcher's son. All this time I'd assumed this was something to do with Dorothea's death and it was all about Filcher.

I've already told Harry all about it on the drive over.

'And Dennis? Did Dominic admit to attacking him too?'

'Well, no. That's the strange thing. He's adamant he had nothing to do with Dennis's attack. He said he only ever wanted to frighten you, not hurt you.'

'And you believe him?'

'I'm not sure, yet. He'll need to be questioned further.'

'I know it wasn't him who broke into Dorothea's study. That man was a lot younger. But what about locking me and Dennis in the bunker? Did he admit to that?'

'He said he's never been on your property.'

'And it wasn't him who damaged the keypad on the gate?'

'Apparently not.'

'So we're still no closer to finding out who killed Dorothea?' I can hear the disappointment in my voice. I feel like I've failed her.

'There is no "we", Imogen,' says DI Shirley sternly. She takes a seat next to me on one of the plastic chairs and leans forwards to put her empty coffee cup on the lino. 'Now can I take a statement from you while you're here? I need to know everything that happened with Dominic Filcher. Start at the beginning.'

Harry pulls up outside the villa. A shimmer of sunlight beams in through the windscreen, highlighting the tawny patches in his green eyes.

'Will you be okay?' His face fills with concern. 'All a bit of a shock.'

I'm tempted to say no, I won't, mainly because I don't want to be on my own in the villa, especially now anyone can gain access through the side gate. But I decide against it. It's about time I stood on my own two feet.

'Thanks, Harry. But I'll be fine.'

I notice the flash of disappointment in his eyes.

'Thanks for the lift.' It feels too final to end it there, so I say tentatively, 'Maybe we could go for dinner one evening?'

His face brightens. 'Sure. I'd love that. Let me know when you're free. And, if you need anything, please don't hesitate to call me.'

I touch his arm in thanks and then head back to the villa, alone.

As I'm letting myself into the house, I receive a call from Rachel. I'm so excited to hear from her that I tell her everything: about Josh and the cameras, about Dennis being Sidney S. Crane, about Dominic Filcher. She's suitably shocked.

'Do you want me to come over? I can stay?'

'That's kind, honestly, and I'd love you to stay soon, but I feel I need to face up to being here on my own if I want to make my life here, you know?'

'I get it. I do have some positive news,' she says. 'It might be nothing, but I think I've managed to track down Robert Falkner. In Australia.'

My heart falls. How can I tell her that she's been wasting her time? That Bobby is dead and that Dorothea killed him, when I promised Annette I'd keep it to myself?

'Oh, that's great,' I say with false enthusiasm, guilt tugging at me that I can't tell her the truth.

'I mean, it's a long shot,' she says. 'But he's around the same age and is a British national, and he has a sister who doesn't live very far from you.'

My interest stirs. 'Oh my God, really? What's her name? Where does she live?'

My eyes go to the old photograph of Dorothea sitting around the table at the art therapy centre with Maisie, Rosemary and Annette. Could this sister know that they covered for Dorothea and be seeking revenge?

'Her name is Irene Fuller,' she says. 'I'll text you her address.'

51

DOROTHY

Forty-Nine Years Before

Dorothy stood in front of Rene's house. Her knees were shaking beneath her long skirt and not just from the cold. She pulled the scarf further around her neck, to hide the bruise on her skin. Bobby's violent outbursts were getting worse, and she didn't know what to do. He hadn't started hitting her until six months into their marriage, when, she supposed, the honeymoon period of them living together had worn off. For the two years they had been courting, he'd been the model boyfriend, and she'd loved him with every fibre of her being. She had been so excited when, on their wedding day, she finally moved out of her parents' house. She thought she'd burst with happiness. She'd thought she'd found her happy ending.

Her wedding day had been the best day of her life.

Bobby adored his big sister, Irene, and vice versa. She was four years older than Bobby and was the only person he ever seemed to respect. It was now obvious he had no respect for his wife. In the years since Dorothy had met Bobby, she'd become close to his sister as well. Rene was a chain-smoking, outspoken woman who took no nonsense. Married to the cowed Edwin Fuller, who was several inches shorter than her, she definitely ruled the roost. She was childless by choice and, unlike Dorothy, hadn't given up her post office job after she married.

Annette had advised her she must tell someone close to her what was happening. Annette had become Dorothy's closest friend since they met a few months ago, the only person who knew what was really going on in Dorothy's marriage. Annette had been through something similar and was struggling alone with a three-year-old son after her husband was arrested for embezzlement. Luckily Annette's family money was untouched, but Dorothy knew if she left Bobby she would have nowhere to go. She didn't have money like Annette. She didn't have the same choices.

So, here she was. Hoping that Rene could talk some sense into her brother. She was the only person he ever listened to, after all.

The streetlamps had come on and their amber glow illuminated the ice crystals that crunched beneath Dorothy's boots. She knew Rene's shift would have ended now, and she blew on her hands, her breath clouding in front of her. It was now or never. She couldn't lose her nerve.

She took a deep breath. The cold air hurt the back of her throat and she coughed. She swallowed down her nausea. This was her only option. She had no choice.

Slowly, her legs heavy and feeling like she was trudging uphill, she made her way down the front path and knocked on Rene's door.

'Give us a minute!' she heard Rene call. The hall light flashed on. Dorothy blew on her hands again, her resolve seeping out of her like the heat from her body. She couldn't do this. She couldn't do it. What if Rene turned against her?

Bobby's power lies in the secrecy, Annette had said. She repeated it over and over in her mind, her heart thumping, her hands damp despite the chill.

And then Rene threw open the door, a terrifying figure in rollers and a dressing gown. Standing there she seemed to tower over the petrified Dorothy.

'Dot, my love, what're you doing here?'

'Can I come in?'

'Sure. I hope everything is all right with that bleedin' brother of mine.'

Dorothy stepped over the threshold and Rene ushered her into the small front room. Edwin, thankfully, was still at the factory. He worked with Bobby but in a different department.

'I'm just getting ready to go out,' she said, tying the belt of her dressing gown tighter. 'Meeting the girls. Sit.'

Dorothy did as she asked and watched as Rene perched on the arm of the settee and lit up another cigarette. She smoked even more than Bobby did.

'What's up, Dot? You've got a face on you like a slapped arse.'

Dorothy's stomach somersaulted. 'It's Bobby.'

'Bobby? What's that brother of mine done?'

Dorothy slowly peeled the scarf away from her neck to reveal the angry purple bruise.

Rene's eyes widened in horror. 'He did that to you?' The disbelief in her voice was clear to hear.

Dorothy nodded.

'When? Why? What happened?'

'He'd come home from work last night. I could see he was tired and stressed and we got into an argument – I can't even remember what started it. It doesn't . . . it doesn't take much any more.'

Rene's eyes bulged. She stubbed out her cigarette into a standing ashtray. 'Are you saying this has happened before?'

'Yes. Infrequently at first, but lately it's more often.'

Dorothy held her breath, wondering what Rene would say. Would she believe her? She had to, surely. The evidence was right there in the bruising on her neck.

Rene closed her eyes and exhaled slowly. When she opened them she said, 'Leave it with me, Dot. I'll talk some sense into that thick-headed brother of mine. Don't you worry. Now, if you don't mind, I've got to finish getting ready.'

She stood up and almost manhandled Dorothy out of her house. She didn't say anything more about it. She waved Dorothy away as though what she'd admitted had been nothing more anodyne than what she'd had for supper.

And she knew, somewhere deep inside her, that Rene wouldn't help. Her loyalty would always be to her brother. She'd hoped for some female solidarity. She'd hoped that the feisty, straight-talking Rene would be on her side.

But now she realized she was on her own.

52

IMOGEN

A few minutes after Rachel has ended the call, my phone pings with a text: Irene's address in Corsham. I make myself a cheese sandwich – *Are you watching, Josh? Are you laughing at my crap attempt to cook for myself?* – and after I've eaten it I leave Solly snoozing in his bed and call a taxi. I really need to get myself a car. I have the intrusive, petrifying thought that Josh might sneak in while I'm out and do something. Add more cameras, hurt Solly in some way. Then I tell myself that no, Josh might be controlling and crosses boundaries, but he'd never hurt an animal. I saw the way he was with Solly when he thought I wasn't watching; he was caring towards him, giving him an extra treat or bending down to ruffle his neck. Josh is many things, most of which stem from insecurity. But he's not a psychopath.

The taxi drops me off in Corsham half an hour later. Irene Fuller lives in a modern house on the edge of a rabbit warren of an estate. As I step from the taxi a wave of uncertainty washes over me. How am I going to handle this? I can't very well ask her whether she knows that Dorothea killed her brother and if she's hell-bent on revenge. I could say I'm writing a piece about Dorothea's life. I decide I won't tell her I've inherited Dorothea's house. The less she knows the better. Although, if she was the one to send someone to break into Dorothea's studio, she might already know the truth. I shake the thought out of my head. No. I'll stick to the journalist story.

I knock twice before I hear a shuffling from behind the door and then it's wrenched open by a tall woman with white hair clipped back from her face. She's less old and frail than I'd been imagining. Her eyes are a bright, startling blue and she's dressed in varying shades of creams and neutrals. From over her shoulder, I see a navy wool coat hung up over the end of the banister.

'Yes,' she barks. She has a lot of lines on her face, particularly around her mouth.

'Hi, are you Irene Fuller?'

'Yes,' she says again in the same loud tone.

I explain that I'm a journalist writing a piece about Dorothea Roe. As I talk she narrows her eyes at me, and I experience a ripple of anxiety that she can see right through my lies.

'Dorothea Roe?'

'She was married to your brother, Bobby. Dorothy Bird as was.'

Her expression closes up. 'I have nothing to say about that woman.' She has a faint London accent.

'You didn't like her?'

She purses her lips together which I take as a no.

'My brother took off because of her. Moved to the other side of the world. Lost contact with everyone.'

I think of what Rachel said about a Robert Falkner in Australia. It can't be her brother if he's dead. But has someone – Annette perhaps – made her think the Robert Falkner in Australia is her brother to stop her being suspicious?

'Had you seen Dorothea in recent years?'

'Absolutely not. Why would I want to see her?' She takes a step back into the hallway. Worried she's about to close the door on me, I blurt out, 'Did you know any of Dorothea's friends? Annette Baker-Hume or . . .'

'I met Annette once or twice. She was the one who encouraged Dorothy. She stirred in their marriage, if you ask me. Things were fine until she became friends with Annette.'

'In what way?'

'That woman gave Dorothy ideas.' Her expression softens a touch. 'Don't get me wrong, I understood Dorothy's predicament, I really did. But Bobby was my brother. My family. And if it wasn't for her, I wouldn't have missed out on all those years with him. All those wasted years.'

'But . . .'

Her expression hardens again. 'I don't want to talk about it any more. Now if you'll excuse me . . .' And she shuts the door in my face.

53

The next day I meet Alison outside the prison as promised. It's an hour's train ride away and by the time I arrive I feel sick and stressed and I'm regretting agreeing to this. I hardly slept last night worrying that the person who had smashed in the keypad was prowling around the garden, planning to break in. The security firm have said they will try and come out this afternoon to replace the lock.

Alison squeezes my hand before we enter. Everything about this place makes me want to run away. We're ushered through security and then we find ourselves in the waiting room that smells of too many bodies and stale food. It's too hot and the murmur of voices adds to my anxiety. I try and block out the other inmates in my peripheral vision, clutching my tote to my chest like armour.

'I never thought I'd come here again,' says Alison. 'But we need answers.'

'Yes,' I whisper. 'I just don't think he's going to be able to give them to us.'

Our father is already sitting at the table. He looks unrecognizable and I'm so shocked that I can only stand, rooted to the spot, until Alison pulls my arm and guides me to one of the chairs facing him.

He doesn't look like the same man. He's shrunken and his skin has a yellow tinge to it. He's lost so much weight in his face that his nose looks hook-like and his cheeks sunken. He's wearing a navy sweatshirt with jeans, his eyes hooded and bloodshot, his once-dark hair now white and thin, revealing the shape of his skull. It's a shock to realize he's no longer that big, hulking man from my memory. The man who hit Mum, who screamed at us. Despite everything, nestled within my hatred and loathing is a very tiny knot of sympathy. He wasn't always a drunk, I remind myself.

He looks like a benign old man. How many other men out there, now aged and frail, were once like him? How many of the old men I might have noticed and felt sorry for as they wobbled their way across the road with a cane were once abusers? It's an unpleasant thought.

'Ali. Immy.' His eyes swim. 'I wasn't expecting to see you today. Or ever again.' His voice is thirty-cigarettes-a-day croaky.

'I hear you're dying,' I say dispassionately.

He nods. I notice his wrists are stick-thin, the skin papery and marred by blotches of dark red and black. I look away, appalled.

'I'm glad you've come to see me. There is so much I want to say. Especially to you, Imogen. I've already apologized to Alison.' To my surprise his eyes film with tears. 'I have so many regrets, so many. I have had therapy in here and I understand now why I was so angry, why I had all this rage and resentment that I took out on all of you, why I drank, and I wish – God, how I wish – I could go back and change it all. But I can't. I can never make it up to you, I can never make amends for what I did. But all I can do now is be honest with you.'

'In that case, you need to tell us the truth about Mum. Did you kill her? I want to hear you say it. I want you to admit it, for once.' My voice is getting shriller and Alison reaches over and lays a hand over my forearm.

'I have no reason to lie to you now,' he says. He flicks a glance at Alison. He must have said the same thing to her when she last visited him, and despite everything, I still feel that same kick to the guts that she did that without telling me.

'I was a bad husband. I'm not going to deny that. I hit her. I won't deny that either. But I didn't kill her that night. I have no reason to lie to you about it. I. Did. Not. Kill. Her.'

I wish I could believe him. But how can I?

'I wouldn't have put you girls through a trial if I'd killed her. I like to think I'd have protected you from that at least. I was a drunk and I was violent and I hate myself for it. But I'm telling the truth about that night. This is why I wanted you to come and visit, what I needed to tell you.'

'Will you tell us your version of what happened that night?' Alison says gently. Why is she being so kind to him? I jolt my arm away from her hand and clench my fists. I want to punch him, and all the men like him. A white-hot surge of rage floods through me. But then I remember my doubts. The mask. The brooch. I can't allow my hatred of this man to overshadow the truth.

He closes his eyes. My ears are ringing, and my face feels flushed. I put a hand to my hot cheek. When he opens them again he fastens them on me and his gaze is so intense I have to look down at the table.

'That night, the night of the Halloween party, we had rowed. It was the first row we'd had since we got back together. I hadn't been drinking that night. So, yes, I was angry, but I'd been off the drink for months. It's not an excuse, I know, but I was only violent when I was drunk. This was just a normal argument.'

'Why did you row?' I find myself asking, looking up at him.

'Because I didn't really like those women she had started hanging around with. Dorothea and the others. I felt they were trying to keep us apart. They didn't like the fact that we'd got back together.'

'Can you blame them?'

He hangs his head. 'No, of course not. But it was how I felt. I'm trying to be honest.'

'Go on,' urges Alison.

'Anyway, she went by herself. I didn't like what she was wearing. It was a vampire costume and it was very figure-hugging. I was jealous. I thought her friends would try and set her up with another man. So I waited until she'd dropped the car back home after taking you to your friend's house. She wanted to walk. It wasn't far. I sat at home, brooding, imagining all sorts. I was supposed to go with her to the party but during the argument I said I'd stay at home. But then I changed my mind and realized that's what I needed to do, to keep an eye on her. So I put on the skeleton costume she'd bought for me and jumped in the car.'

I think of Josh and his cameras.

'When I arrived at the party I tried to persuade her to come home with me, but she was having none of it. She was spurred on, I think, by those women.'

I bite my tongue.

'One of the women, Rosemary, I think, told me to leave. And Ruth just let me go. She let her friends throw me out. I got in my car but I didn't want to go home, so I decided to park up, near Rosemary's house, and wait until Ruth left.'

'The road where you were caught on CCTV?'

'Yes. The main road. When I saw your mum walk by – it wasn't very late, not even ten-thirty – I jumped out the car and tried to persuade her to get in. But she was furious with me, started shouting. I pulled her arm and she scratched me on my wrist. I could feel the row escalating but I stepped away . . .'

I can't help it. I make a pah sound.

'When did you ever step away?'

'I was stone-cold sober. I had control. So I stepped away and got back in the car. I was spotted on CCTV getting back in the car.'

'Yes, but then you knew there was no CCTV by the towpath. So what did you do, take the car home so it looked like you were there and then lie in wait?'

'No. I didn't. I went home to cool off and I stayed there, waiting for her to get back. I promised myself that when she got home we would talk about it.'

I find this hard to believe.

'What about the mask? It was found near Mum.'

'I never left with the mask. I left it at Rosemary's house. I told the police at the time, and it was used in my defence, but I couldn't prove it and the jury didn't believe me. There was too much other evidence. My past mistakes, the scratch to my arm, us arguing on CCTV.'

I sit back in my chair and watch his expression carefully. He sounds so sincere but he might be lying... *Why would he lie now though?*

Did he leave the mask at Rosemary's?

He looks up at us, his eyes beseeching. 'I have no reason to lie. I've lost everything. Do you think I killed her? Honestly?'

'Yes,' I say.

'No,' says Alison at the same time.

I turn to her with a raised eyebrow.

'Please, listen to me, girls. Please.'

His face looks so earnest that it's hard not to believe him.

'I want you to know this because I'm going to die. I'm going to die and the person who murdered your mother is still out there.'

54

'You're not going to like what I'm about to say,' warns Alison as we walk back to the car park. 'But I think, deep down, you've been wondering it too. And that's why you came with me to see Dad.'

'I still hate him, even if he didn't kill Mum,' I spit. 'He still made her life hell.'

'Immy...'

I stop and spin around to face her. I don't want to hear it but I know what she's going to say. 'You think Dorothea knew what happened to Mum, don't you? You think that's what she's been trying to tell me in her sculpture. You think that's why she left me the house? Out of guilt?'

'It makes sense,' she says gently. 'It makes sense as to why she left you the sculpture. And the house.'

'That's if she did leave the sculpture to me. It could all just be a mistake. Something that was supposed to be part of her collection, but she never finished it in time...'

'Immy...'

I toe the ground, refusing to look at her, like a petulant child.

'You need to tell DI Shirley.'

'Dad was found guilty,' I mutter. 'There is no evidence Dorothea knew who killed Mum. Or was the one to kill her. Why would she? She loved her.'

'Maybe that's why? I don't know.'

'I can't . . . I can't do this right now. I need to go home.'

'How're things with Josh?'

I hesitate. 'We're finished. He's moving out. It's a long story.' My head is pounding. I just want to go back to the villa and cuddle Solly and bury my head beneath my duvet and not have to think about my father being innocent or Dorothea being guilty.

Her eyebrows shoot up in surprise. 'Oh, Immy. I'm sorry, although I think it's the right thing after what you told me. Do you want me to come home with you?'

'No. I'll be fine.' I want to be on my own.

'Okay, I'll ring you later. Go home and get some rest.'

She pulls me in for a quick, awkward hug and then we go our separate ways.

I don't want to believe that Dorothea had anything to do with my mum's death, but the only way I'll find out for sure is from Annette. She covered for Dorothea once before with Bobby. Would she do it again?

I call her but there is no answer and so I look her up on the TV station's electoral roll and find an address for her in Clifton. I decide to do a detour to Bristol Temple Meads on the way back from the prison. It's a long journey so I get out the biography, still shocked that Dennis was the one to write it. I flick through the pages but there is nothing earth-shattering in it. Dennis didn't know about Bobby's death. I remember Annette telling me about the postcard and how someone had scribbled on the back about finally getting the truth about the past. But what truth? Apart from Dorothea having an abusive husband in the past, there is nothing much here. I turn to a chapter called 'The Fab Four'.

> Who knows what would have become of the young, heartbroken Dorothy after her marriage failed if it hadn't been for Annette Baker-Hume. Only a few years older than Dorothea, Annette took the broken bird under her wing. Sensing that Dorothea needed a purpose in life, and knowing she would have empathy for the women seeking shelter after what she had witnessed with her parents, Annette asked if Dorothea would like to be part of something.
>
> Annette, whose own husband had gone to prison for fraud, before taking his own life in his cell, had retrained as an art therapist and was looking for a like-minded individual to set up an art therapy institute for women. Dorothea, having not yet made her name in the art world but being talented and experimental, agreed and the art therapy centre was born.
>
> 'Annette Baker-Hume was a woman to be reckoned with,' explains her one-time neighbour, Lydia Smith. 'She used her money wisely to help others. Annette and Dorothy bonded over their commitment to the institute.'

One of their first clients, Maisie Hill, whose ex-husband at the time was serving a long prison sentence for attempted murder, joined Annette and Dorothea to become a founding member of the institute. While Maisie wasn't a gifted sketcher or painter, she was very talented at knitting and crocheting. The other member was Rosemary Farrington. She started out as a classics teacher specializing in Latin at the expensive all-girls school in . . .

I look up from the book. Latin. I think of the word printed on the piece of paper Dennis found. Could his attack have had something to do with Rosemary? Revenge? But for what? Another thing to ask Annette.

I drop the book into my bag as the train pulls into Temple Meads and then take the bus to Clifton. As I walk down Annette's street, exhaustion sweeps over me. Was it only yesterday that Harry and I were chased by Dominic Filcher on the motorbike? It feels like weeks ago. But I can't sit around the villa by myself. If I keep busy then I can stop thinking about Josh and the end of our relationship.

My throat is dry by the time I've reached the door of Annette's mews house, and before I've pressed the buzzer I go over and over my rehearsed speech. I'm so psyched up for having it out with Annette that when the door opens revealing a young guy wearing a baggy T-shirt, jeans and clumpy trainers, I just say, 'Oh.'

'Can I help you?'

There is something familiar about him. 'Who are you?' I blurt out rudely. 'I was looking for Annette.'

He looks taken aback but then laughs. 'I'm Warren. Annette's my grandmother and she's not here at the moment.'

'Oh, okay.' I'd been so eager to speak to her, so intent on coming all the way to Bristol, that it never occurred to me she might not be in. 'Would you mind giving her a message?'

'Sure.' He opens the door wider to reveal a long, elegant hallway: an extravagant orchid sits on a black console table and a large chandelier glistens above Warren's head. He's very tall. And rangy. Something tugs at my memory. 'Who shall I say is calling?' He smiles at me again in a slightly flirty way.

'Um. Imogen. Imogen Cooke.'

His smile slips. 'Okay. I'll pass it on. Thanks.' He steps back and closes the door abruptly in my face.

It's not until I'm back in the car that I realize who that man is.

He'd been wearing a hoody, but that rangy figure, the way he holds himself with his left shoulder lowered, his awkward gait . . .

Warren was the guy who broke into Dorothea's office, I realize with a sickening thud. What the hell is going on?

As I walk back along the lane I'm still reeling about recognizing Warren. Questions loop around and around my head. Has it been Warren who was looking for the sculpture all this time? And if so, was he doing it for Annette?

I trusted her. I even showed her the sculpture and asked for her help.

It doesn't mean that she killed Dorothea, I tell myself.

And then I stop walking abruptly.

A man stands at my gate, not caring that he's getting soaked by the rain. He's around Dennis's age and he waves when he sees me.

My stomach tightens. 'Can I help you?' I call.

'Imogen?' The man steps forward. I don't recognize him. He has a thick moustache that contrasts with his greying hair, but he has kind eyes.

'Yes?'

He takes a step towards me. 'I'm Aiden. Maisie's husband. I was wondering if I could have a word with you?'

Aiden. The man the police suspect of killing his wife.

'Um. Now isn't a good time,' I say, moving around him to open the gate, conscious he's hovering at my shoulder and hoping he doesn't notice the keypad is broken.

His face is desperate. 'I didn't kill Maisie. She was poisoned, Imogen. We had a visitor that day.'

'Have you told the police?'

'Yes. I'm not sure they believe me though.'

The wind picks up and I feel a surge of fear. I just want to get inside the villa. I don't know who to trust any more.

'Who was the visitor?' I ask, dreading the answer. Because somewhere, deep down, I think I know who he's going to say.

'Annette.'

Of course. Has Annette played me this whole time? I think of her grandson going through Dorothea's office. I think of her standing next to me in the bunker, calmly telling me how she buried Bobby for her best friend. 'But why would she want to kill Maisie?'

'Annette couldn't trust her any more. Not with the dementia. Maisie was a loose cannon. Who knows what she was going to say about what happened all those years ago?'

I can barely hear him above the rain. I waver, wondering if I should invite him in. But he could be lying. I don't want to be on my own with him.

'What did Maisie know?' I ask, thinking of Bobby. Would Annette really kill Maisie to keep that a secret? And if Maisie did tell someone, then surely they would assume it was the dementia talking?

He hangs his head. 'This is going to be hard to hear. And I'm sorry to have to be the one to tell you this, Imogen. But Maisie knew the truth about what happened to your mum.'

55

There is a strange buzzing sound in my ears as his words sink in. 'What do you mean?'

'Maisie helped cover it up. All of them: Dorothea, Annette and Rosemary. They . . .' He coughs and looks ashamed. 'They set up your father, for revenge for how he treated your mother, but it wasn't him who killed her. Her death was an accident . . .'

The sky tilts and I have to hold on to the gate for support.

'What happened?' I cry, my voice almost lost in the wind.

'I'm sorry. That's all I can say. I have to go. I just wanted you to know the truth. I've already said too much – but I'm worried for my own life. If anything happens to me, please tell the police what I've told you.'

'Aiden! Wait!'

But he hurries off down the lane, his head tucked into his chest, his hands in his pockets. How could he throw a grenade at me like that and then just run away?

A shard of white-hot panic slices through me as I let myself into the villa. My hands are shaking as I peel off my wet jacket and hang it up. I think of Annette's response to the sculpture, her telling me it was about domestic abuse when that wasn't the full story at all. Did she know Dorothea was going to reveal the truth in her sculptures? Is that why she was stopped? And what *is* the truth? I still don't know. Aiden said my mum's death was an accident. Was it caused by one of them – Dorothea? – or all of them?

I kick off my trainers and slump onto the bottom step, my head in my hands, trying to process all this information. Annette killed Maisie. Does that mean she killed Dorothea too? And is Rosemary next? But the Latin? Dennis's attack? I'm missing something. I just can't work out what it is.

I get up from the stair, my body heavy. I picture the sculpture again: the red paint on one of the hands, all those miniature items, and I try and assimilate them in my mind. The Zippo lighter must be about Bobby, then there is the toy spade – a reference to the fact they buried Bobby? The pearls – Annette always wears pearls.

I head down to the kitchen. I'm surprised Solly hasn't rushed to greet me. He usually does.

And then I step into the kitchen and realize why.

Sitting alone at the table, calmly drinking a cup of tea from one of Dorothea's bone-china cups, is Annette.

56

I freeze. 'Annette? What are you doing here? How did you get in?'

Solly is spread-eagled under the table. Some guard dog.

'Why don't you sit down, Imogen. I think we need to talk.'

A burst of anger mixed with fear.

'How did you get in?' I ask again.

'I have my ways, Imogen.'

She must have damaged the keypad on the side gate, or got her grandson to do it. Did she smash a window to get inside the house? Why didn't she trigger the cameras and the alarm system? She probably did, but I wouldn't know, because Josh never gave me access to the app. Maybe I had to press something to switch on the alarm. I realize I relied too much on Josh to sort it all out for me. I should have insisted he showed me how to do it.

'Please sit,' she says, more sternly now, ignoring me. 'Warren said you wanted to see me. He rang, and luckily I was already in the area, so I came straight over.'

'And thought to let yourself in.'

'Well, it was raining and I didn't want to sit in my car and wait. I'm not getting any younger. Here, I've made you a cup of tea.'

I think of Aiden's claims that Annette visited Maisie the day she was poisoned. 'No, thanks. I know you poisoned Maisie.'

I'm still standing at the exit to the kitchen. I mentally plan my escape if needed. Solly, who can sense something is amiss, is now sat up, his ears forward as though on alert for my command. Has Annette asked Warren to come here? Is she just keeping me talking until he turns up to do her dirty work?

'Maisie was becoming a problem,' she says calmly as though she's talking about the weather, not murdering her long-term friend. 'I had to keep her quiet. She was saying all sorts.'

'But why? Everyone would have dismissed anything she said, wouldn't they? She had dementia.'

'I couldn't take that risk. Maisie knows where the bodies are buried, so to speak. I knew poisoning her hot chocolate would do the trick. Easy to do. Just a squirt of my hay fever meds in her drink. Aiden's told the police, of course, but I've denied it and there is no proof I was ever at their house that day. And isn't it always the husband? Are you going to sit down?' She looks so prim, sitting there with ankles crossed in her tweed suit and the pearls at her neck.

'Did you kill my mum? And Dorothea?'

She sighs and pats her hair. She's still wearing her leather driving gloves. Her handbag is open by her feet, and I notice a bottle of eyedrops nestled next to her purse. I remember reading a case about a man who poisoned his wife with her own hay fever medication as some brands of eyedrops contain tetrahydrozoline, which can cause death if too much is ingested.

'Your mother's death was an accident. Nobody wanted to hurt her. We were all very fond of Ruth.'

A jolt of dread shoots through me. 'Please, Annette. Please tell me what happened.'

'Please sit down, Imogen, you're making me nervous.'

I slump into the nearest chair.

'I was cross with your mother for going back to that man. I thought she'd been very disrespectful to Dorothea, to all of us who had escaped abusive relationships. But she was willing to give your imbecile of a father another chance. And then, at the Halloween party he came charging in, effing and blinding as usual, trying to get her to leave with him. We threw him out. But not long after, she left too. I followed her. I was furious with her, but I also wanted to make sure she was okay. I found her on the towpath, she told me what had happened, how they'd rowed, and how he'd tried to get her in the car. I said then that she should come back with me and stay at Rosemary's or move into Dorothea's. Or mine. She was welcome to stay at mine. You have to believe me when I say I was desperate to save her from your father. But she refused. Said that he was different – she was deluded, of course, he wasn't different. His behaviour that night proved that. But she wouldn't listen, and I tried. I tried to make her listen.'

My stomach flips. 'What did you do?'

'I got angry with her. I didn't mean to. Things became heated and I tried to pull her back along the towpath, in the direction of Rosemary's house. She wrenched free, stumbled backwards and fell, hitting her head. It was an accident.'

'Then why didn't you explain that to the police?'

'Because I was scared, Imogen. I didn't want to go to prison.'

'So you thought you'd set up my dad instead?'

'I had his mask in my pocket. He dropped it as he left the party. It was a spur-of-the-moment decision and he was a bad man. An abuser. We all felt it was the right thing to do to put the blame on him. He needed punishing, one way or the other.'

I stare at her open-mouthed.

'Oh, don't look so shocked. Don't worry, your precious Dorothea tried to convince me to go to the police and tell the truth. But she owed me, you see. She owed me for Bobby. Her hands were tied.'

Annette had robbed me and Alison of both of our parents. The realization is guttural and painful, and I experience a stabbing sensation in my chest.

'And the others? Rosemary and Maisie?'

'They found out later. It was Dot I told first. Dot who helped me.' It's obvious to me that Annette Baker-Hume doesn't do anything unless there is something in it for her.

'Why did you help Dorothea cover up Bobby's death? What was in it for you?'

She blanches. 'I don't know what you mean. I was being a good friend. We kept each other's secrets.'

Annette sips her tea and then carefully places the cup back in its matching saucer.

'I think you killed Dorothea, Annette. You killed Maisie to stop her talking. You – or rather your grandson . . .'

She stiffens at the mention of her grandson.

'. . . pushed her down the stairs and set fire to her work.'

'I didn't mean to push her downstairs.'

'What, like you didn't mean to kill my mother?'

She gives me a withering look. 'You're making it all sound premeditated, and it wasn't like that at all. Dorothea had become . . . strange in the months before she died. Paranoid. Untrustworthy. She pulled away from me, and I didn't know why. When I read in the newspaper that she had come up with this magpie collection and hinted at secrets, then I had to see for myself. I couldn't risk her exposing all our secrets, could I?'

'You mean *your* secrets?'

She doesn't say anything.

'And then, what? You pushed her?'

'I didn't realize she was in the house. She told Rosemary, who told me, that she was going away for a few days. It was an instinctive thing, an involuntary reaction at finding her there. She . . . she didn't even know it was me . . .' To my surprise, her eyes tear up. 'I was only supposed to destroy her sculptures and the letter . . .'

'What letter?'

'She'd been writing a letter to you, Imogen. It had sat unfinished in her studio. But it read very much like a confession. I think she was planning to give it to her solicitor to give to you in the event of her death. The sculpture was added insurance, apparently.'

So that's how she knew there was a sculpture.

'I caught your grandson going through her box files. I'm assuming you put him up to it? Why would you drag your grandson into all this?'

She looks visibly annoyed at this. 'I've not dragged Warren into anything. He's very protective. It was his idea . . .' She stops herself. 'This isn't about Warren. It's about Dorothea and her not being able to keep to her word. She didn't say in the letter to you where the sculpture was. Since her death Warren has kindly been helping me find something, anything, that might say where she'd hidden it. She never once told me about the bunker.' She smiles enigmatically. 'It seems Dorothea liked to keep secrets of her own.'

'But Warren found out about the bunker, didn't he? He was the one who locked me and Dennis in that day.'

'He didn't realize the sculpture was in there at first. He's not the brightest spark, unfortunately. It was only when he told me about it that I guessed. But that bunker is impossible to access without a key.'

'How did Dorothea end up with Bobby's lighter?'

She fidgets. 'She said she found it in the woods but I think she was lying about that. I think she must have kept it after his death.'

'Why did Warren take it out of the box?'

'He liked the look of it.' She rolls her eyes. 'When I realized what he'd done I told him to put it back. But he must have dropped it when he was looking for the bunker. He should never have taken it in the first place. Warren had been watching the house for me after you and your boyfriend moved in.'

'You got Warren to do your dirty work for you? Your own grandson?'

'Oh, he didn't do anything illegal. It wasn't like he was the one to push Dorothea.'

'No, that was all you.'

She crosses her arms. 'I loved Dorothea. And hurting her was a last resort.'

'Who attacked Dennis? Was that Warren too?'

She doesn't say anything.

I remember Dennis's grey face, the slip of paper bearing the word VINDICTA. 'Or was it Rosemary? Afterwards, Dennis found a note with the Latin word for revenge written on it, and Rosemary once taught Latin.' I picture the man with the tawny ponytail who answered the door when I visited Rosemary's house. 'Or was it that man who lives with her, Peter Bryce? I know he's got a previous conviction for assault when he was a teenager.'

When she remains quiet, I add, 'Let's say I'm right about Rosemary's lodger . . . did she hurt Dennis because you'd asked her to?'

'I think we should keep Rosemary out of all this. Dennis deserved what he got. He was a user. He used Dorothea and then wrote a book about her.'

'So you knew he was the one writing the biography?'

'I worked it out. Yes.'

'I bet that terrified you, didn't it? Were you worried Dorothea would let slip something to him about what you did to my mum?'

'You're being ridiculous.'

'I don't think I am. Rosemary isn't really away, is she, Annette? I think you've silenced her too.'

She scoffs. 'What an imagination you have. As if I'd hurt Rosemary.'

'Why? You thought nothing of hurting Dorothea and Maisie. They were your friends and you killed them to keep your nasty little secrets.' I shift from foot to foot. 'I don't think it was an accident at all, what you did to my mum. You wanted to control her, and you didn't like it that she didn't listen to you. You didn't give a shit about my mum. You didn't even bother coming to her funeral.' My heart pounds in anger. I scrape my chair back and get up. 'I'm calling the police.'

Her laugh reverberates around the kitchen. 'Oh, Imogen. It will be your word against mine and who do you think the police will believe? A grubby journalist and the daughter of a convicted killer, or a fine, upstanding member of the community renowned for her charity work?' She stands up and dusts down her skirt. 'I felt like I owed you the truth about your mother. And about Dorothea. But leave it now. You can't prove any of it, and Rosemary will back me up and give me an alibi if I need it.'

'The police know about the sculpture, Annette. It's no longer secret.'

She rocks on her heels slightly and I realize this has unnerved her.

'I think that sculpture doesn't just hold clues. I think there's evidence hidden there somewhere that could implicate you in my mother's death.' It's a guess but by her stunned expression I can tell I'm on to something.

She recovers herself. 'Well, the police haven't figured it out yet, have they? And I'll make sure Warren destroys the sculpture. If you would just kindly give me the key?'

'I don't think so.'

She takes a step towards me, her eyes hardening as I hear the sound of footsteps in the hall outside the kitchen. And I realize that her intention was never to let me go.

57

Warren steps into the room. He's in the same hoody he was wearing when he broke into Dorothea's study and I want to laugh at him and say, 'What, seriously? I've already seen your face!' And then I see he's holding a knife.

He brandishes it at me. It's one of those flick-knife things. Is Annette intent on making her grandson a murderer?

With one swift movement Annette pushes me back onto the chair. From beneath the table Solly starts to growl.

'Where's the key?' asks Annette.

'It's on my key ring. In my coat.'

'Which coat?'

'It's upstairs in the hallway. On the coat rack. Yellow raincoat.'

Without saying anything further, Warren leaves the room.

Annette looks down at me. 'Don't look so worried, Imogen. We're not planning on hurting you. I never wanted it to come to this.' She smiles at me sadly. 'I never wanted any of this, you have to believe me. I loved Dorothea. She was my best friend and I never wanted to hurt her. Or Maisie. This wasn't planned. I never thought any of it would end like this.'

'What are you going to do?'

'Burn the sculpture. Destroy it.'

'It's a waste of time. Like I already said, a detective has already been here and taken photos.'

'I don't care about photos . . .'

I realize I was right when I hit on the idea of evidence buried in the sculpture. What is it? And where? Is it one of the trinkets? My mum's brooch? But I dismiss this idea. How could the brooch implicate Annette? I think, whatever it is, it must be hidden in either the wool jacket or the hiking boots.

I'm relieved that DI Shirley's team have already collected the sculpture. Although I won't be telling Annette that.

Warren reappears with a petrol can. 'Got the key. Come on, Grandma. We need to go.'

'I'm sorry, Imogen,' says Annette, not looking particularly sorry at all.

And then I realize. They're not only going to set fire to the sculpture, but they're also going to start a fire inside the villa.

'Annette . . . don't do this. Don't make Warren your accomplice and ruin his life too . . .'

Warren starts pouring petrol around me and I make a dart for the door, but Annette blocks my way. She pushes me backwards so that I stumble against the chair. She's stronger than she looks. Solly stands up and starts to bark at her.

I try to get up. The smell of petrol fills the air, making me cough.

And I collapse onto the floor, the fumes filling my lungs.

58

My head is spinning from the fumes. I can hear Solly barking, Warren shouting, feet on stairs and then, to my surprise, four uniformed officers burst into the kitchen. They swarm around Warren, simultaneously removing the petrol can from his hand as another snaps handcuffs on his wrists and leads him from the room. Annette just stands there, watching it all unfold with a neutral expression. She presumably thinks she can talk her way out of this, but then I see DI Shirley appear at the bottom of the stairs. She flicks her eyes to me, still lying on the floor, and then promptly reads Annette her rights.

'You've made a mistake,' Annette calls over her shoulder as she's led away by another officer. 'This is all a terrible misunderstanding,' but the officer ignores her and ushers her out of the kitchen.

I don't understand. How did they know? How did they get here so quickly?

'Are you okay?' DI Shirley says as she helps me up from the floor. All the other officers have left and it's just the two of us. 'Come on, let's get you out of here.' She takes my arm and gently steers me upstairs to the living room. Solly follows us.

'Who rang you?'

'Josh,' she says. 'He seemed very well informed. He said your life was in danger.'

'What? But how? How would he know that?'

And then I remember.

The hidden cameras he'd set up in the house. The ones I hadn't been able to find. They must still be working.

Josh would have caught, not only my conversation with Annette, but her confession, on film.

For once I'm thankful that Josh was watching me.

Forty-five minutes later Josh has turned up looking ashen and breathless. He instantly relaxes when he sees I'm alive and well and sitting drinking coffee in the living room with DI Shirley. I don't know whether to swear at him or to thank him.

'Thank goodness you're okay,' he says somewhat sheepishly.

DI Shirley gives him a disapproving look. I'd filled her in on everything before Josh arrived, asking her if what Josh had done was illegal and she said it was a grey area. Apparently you are allowed to install cameras in your home if you own it. But Josh doesn't own this house. I do.

Josh notices DI Shirley's hard stare because he reddens.

'I understand you have cameras set up inside Imogen's house,' she says to him as he stands there holding some kind of gadget in his hand. 'While you've helped us out on this occasion, it is most irregular . . .'

He hangs his head.

'. . . and I'd like you to remove every single one of them while I'm here, otherwise I'll arrest you, is that clear?'

I can see Josh squirming. He hates being told off, especially by someone in power. I flash DI Shirley a grateful smile.

'I'm sorry. I'm really sorry, Ims.' He unfurls his fingers to show a small black device in his palm. 'I've got it all on a USB stick. Annette's confession. Everything.' He pushes the USB stick across the coffee table to DI Shirley with an eager expression. Does he expect a pat on the back? Although, of course, I am grateful. It would have been her word against mine otherwise.

DI Shirley picks up the USB stick. 'Right, I'll take this down to the station.' She addresses me as she leans forward to put down her coffee cup. 'And thanks for the statement, Imogen. I'll speak to Aiden Hill as well, although, thanks to this,' she brandishes the USB stick, 'we've got her confession about what she did to Maisie as well.'

And then she instructs Josh to show her where he's hidden all the cameras and I follow them around, watching in shock as he removes them from places I never thought to look: a glass vase in the living room, a picture frame in the dining room, a small hole in the wardrobe in the bedroom and in the Aga's hood in the kitchen.

'I trust that's all of them?' DI Shirley fixes her piercing gaze on Josh.

'Yes, I promise.'

'I think you should also hand over your key to Imogen.'

Josh looks at me questioningly and I nod. I can see how reluctant he is to part with it, but with a detective watching he has no choice.

He burns with humiliation, and I can sense the lack of control is killing him.

'Thank you,' I say as I take the key.

'I'll come and collect my stuff at the weekend,' he mumbles. 'If that's okay?'

I tell him that it is but I make a mental note to ask Alison or Rachel to come over when he does.

DI Shirley tactfully suggests that I can show Josh out while she mops up the petrol in the kitchen.

Josh is quiet as we walk down the hallway, and I can see him gazing around wistfully. 'Will you be okay on your own, here?' he asks as I open the front door.

'I'll be fine, Josh,' I say, hoping it's true.

'I heard what Annette said. I heard all of it. I'm so sorry, Imogen. I'm so sorry for what happened with your mum . . . and your dad. And Dorothea. What will become of your dad now?'

'I don't know.' I haven't had the chance to wrap my head around the repercussions of all this.

'I can't even imagine what you must be feeling.' He touches my arm gently.

A tear slides down my face. 'My mum trusted Annette and so did Dorothea. How could she have been so cold? How could she have just left Dorothea to die like that? After everything they'd been through together?'

'I don't know,' says Josh.

'I feel like I've let her down, somehow.'

'Of course you haven't.' He shuffles awkwardly. 'I know I've done so many wrong things in this relationship, Ims. And I'm not asking for another chance. But . . . you've been in my life for twelve years. I can't bear the thought of us not staying friends.'

I almost want to laugh. There is no way Josh could just be friends.

'Anyway.' He flushes. 'What I'm trying to say is . . . I'm here if you ever need me.'

I smile a thank you and then I watch as he gets in the car and reverses out of the driveway. And I feel a mixture of sadness and relief that he's gone.

As DI Shirley is leaving I ask about the sculpture. 'Did you find anything else? All this time I thought the little miniature items on the magpies meant something, and they did, in part. But I also think Dorothea hid some evidence somewhere on the sculpture. Maybe the boots or . . .'

DI Shirley holds up her hand. 'We're already on it, Imogen. We've found a blouse underneath that wool jacket.'

The lace sleeves. I'd assumed the jacket was just fabric pasted onto the papier-mâché and that the buttons were false.

'The blouse is part of a banshee costume,' she continues, 'and pinned to it was a Polaroid of Annette wearing the same blouse at the Halloween party back in 2008. The blouse has a large bloodstain on the front, which . . .' her expression softens in sympathy, '. . . I think will belong to your mother. I'm hoping Annette's DNA will also be on the blouse. That, along with her confession, should be enough to charge her.'

Dorothea must have kept it all this time. Insurance. She didn't trust Annette.

After DI Shirley has gone, promising to be in touch about my dad, I ring Alison. She's at the salon but I tell her as much as I can.

'I'm coming straight over after work. I finish today at five p.m. Lila has a playdate after school so Gareth can pick her up.'

'You can stay the night if you like?'

She must sense the hope in my voice because she tells me she'll bring an overnight bag and that Gareth's mum can help out with Lila.

When she's ended the call I stroll across the fields with Solly, grateful for the fresh air. The scent of petrol lingers in my nostrils. There are so many questions going around in my mind. I'm still puzzled by who left the postcard for Dorothea in the woods, and why. It doesn't sound like it was Warren. Why would he? And who was the man Lila saw in the woods? Gabe apparently (according to DI Shirley) had an alibi for that day. It doesn't sound like he fits Dennis's description either. Another thing that niggles is why would Dorothea decide she needed to make the magpie collection now? It's been sixteen years since Annette killed my mum. Had something happened in the months before Dorothea's death that gave her a reason to rat out Annette?

I still feel I'm missing something.

I decide to call Rachel. In the distance I spot Dennis with Cady but I deliberately turn and walk in the opposite direction. I'm not ready to talk to him yet.

Rachel picks up but I can tell she's distracted.

'Sorry, Immy, I'm on a deadline.' The newsroom is a blur of noise behind her.

'Just a quick one. Did you ring that number you had for a Robert Falkner in Australia?'

'I did, yes. I'm so sorry, I meant to call you about it. I think it must be the right man. I spoke to a woman who said Robert Falkner was her husband and that he was in the UK on business. The ages definitely line up, and this woman said Bobby has a sister called Irene who lives in Corsham. Sorry, Immy, I've got to go. Can we talk about this later? OKAY, I'M COMING . . .' she screams at someone. 'Sorry,' she says to me. 'Chris is being a prick . . .'

Before I can reply or ask for the number, she's ended the call.

My whole body fizzes with adrenaline as the pieces of the puzzle finally click into place. When I went to visit Irene she said how she'd missed Bobby so much and something about all those wasted years. *And if it wasn't for her, I wouldn't have missed out on all those years with him. All those wasted years.* They would only have been wasted years if she knew she could have spent them with him.

At the time I'd dismissed it as her not realizing he was dead. But what if Irene had seen Bobby recently? Harry and I had both spotted a smartly dressed older gentleman near the villa. And Lila saw the man in the woods that day. Was that Bobby? What if Annette had lied to Dorothea about his death so that she had a hold over her?

What if Dorothea hadn't killed Bobby at all?

59

RENE

February 2024

When he sauntered down her path that crisp, cold morning she thought she must be hallucinating. But no. It was him. All the flesh and blood and bones of him. After nearly fifty long years, there he was. Her brother.

He looked surprisingly well – all that sunshine, she imagined. Living it up on a beach somewhere. He still had his thick head of hair, grey now instead of golden brown. But he'd kept his looks, albeit with more lines and jowls. He was dressed in a beautiful cashmere coat with a satin teal lining and polished brogues that looked handmade.

He'd always resembled a movie star, had her Bobby.

When he disappeared that summer of 1976, she hadn't asked too many questions, even though she suspected it had something to do with Dorothy and her allegations.

'You need to promise me, Reney,' he had said as he called her from a phone box in the countryside somewhere, 'not to tell anyone you've heard from me. Not even Edwin. You gotta promise. I'm being paid handsomely to disappear. It's what I want. What I need.'

She knew Dorothy didn't have the money or the means to pay him off. And she never really got to the bottom of what had gone on between them. But she'd kept her promise; not that anyone came looking for Bobby. That was what had surprised her the most. Nobody reported him missing. Everyone just assumed he'd left his job and his marriage and buggered off somewhere.

But Rene blamed Dorothy for all of it. She was the one who had sent her brother away. She was the reason why they'd only had sporadic contact over the last five decades. Rene had no choice but to watch in disgust as Dorothy Falkner, née Bird, became Dorothea Roe, a famous artist. The resentment had burned and burned inside her.

And now here he was at last.

When she opened the door she fell into his arms, pressing her face into his soft coat, taking in the expensive scent of tobacco and Marc Jacobs.

'Oh my Gawd,' she cried. 'I can't believe it's really you.'

'Surprise,' he laughed. 'Can I come in?'

She ushered him inside out of the cold. She'd been lonely since Edwin had passed on five years ago and her world had become very small. She was hoping Bobby was back for good, to give her a new lease of life.

'What are you doing here?' she exclaimed, taking his coat and fussing over him, making him tea and then cranking the heating up. 'After all this time.'

'I had some unfinished business to attend to,' he said with a wide smile showing off a perfect set of white teeth. 'And I could use your help, Reney.'

She clasped his hand between hers. 'Anything,' she said. 'As long as you promise to stay.'

'Tell me everything you know about my ex-wife,' he said, his eyes lighting up. 'I'm thinking of paying her a visit.'

60

IMOGEN

Irene opens the door and doesn't look surprised to see me. Her gaze travels over my wayward hair, my jeans that smell faintly of petrol, and the duffel coat I hurriedly threw on to walk Solly. She looks pristine in a beige-and-cream-toned outfit, similar to what she'd worn the other day, and a face full of make-up.

Her eyes narrow. I can see that her fingers are nicotine stained. 'I knew you'd be back,' she says. 'You better come in.'

The same expensive wool coat is hanging over the end of the banister. As I pass it I take the opportunity to peel the corner back so that I can see the lining. It's torn, a patch of teal satin is missing.

'Is Bobby alive?'

She arches an eyebrow. 'Of course he's bleedin' alive. He's in the living room.'

My stomach flips. I'd been half-expecting this, but excitement surges through me at the prospect of seeing him.

'Hello, Imogen,' he says as I walk into the room. He's

sitting on a floral sofa nursing a hot drink. With his expensive clothes and his coiffed hair, he looks out of place in this old-fashioned living room. 'Please sit. I've been expecting you.'

'I'll leave you to it,' says Irene, quietly closing the door behind me.

'So. You're the lucky one who has inherited all of Dot's wealth,' he says with a grin. 'I was hoping to meet you at some point.'

'It was you I saw walking the fields that day, wasn't it? Have you been following me?' I perch on a matching chair opposite him and next to the fireplace. Sun streams through the leaded windows, glinting off a photo frame on the hearth. It's a black and white picture of Irene and Bobby when they were kids.

'We grew up in Tooting Bec,' he says, indicating the photograph. 'Our parents died young. Reney basically brought me up. And, in answer to your question, no, I haven't been following you. I was just keeping an eye on the place.' He flashes me a charming smile. Even though he must be getting on for eighty, he's still handsome. He has an elegant gold Rolex on his wrist. I can see why Dorothy would have been so enraptured with him all those years ago. He has this way of making you feel at ease. His body is angled towards me, and his voice is husky with a faint trace of cockney.

And then I remember. This is the man who abused Dorothea. This is the man who almost choked her to death.

'Dorothea thought she'd killed you,' I say in amazement. 'Why did you let her think that?'

'Annette paid me off. She was once a very wealthy woman. Unfortunately, not any more, much to my disappointment.'

'But . . . I don't understand. Why would she let Dorothea think she'd killed you?'

He shakes his head as though disappointed in me. 'Annette is a conniving woman. She'll do whatever it takes to make things as she wants them. She wanted me to disappear so that she could have Dot all to herself, to mould her and manipulate her, and, ultimately, to have a hold over her, and that's what she did.'

All this time Dorothea had been trying to escape an abusive man, only to end up with a controlling woman.

I stare at him blankly. 'Do you know that Annette has been arrested for, amongst other things, the murder of Dorothea?'

'Ah, well, I'm not surprised about that.' He waves a hand in the air. 'Poor Dot. She didn't deserve that, but then . . . that's what you get when you trust people like Annette.'

I want to wipe the smug smile from his face. 'Can you start from the beginning?'

He leans over to put his mug down. 'What's in it for me?'

I glare at him.

'I'm only joking. I've got enough money, thanks to Annette.' He chuckles. 'Okay. Well. Short version. Dot hit me over the head with an ashtray after we argued.

Left me for dead. Annette and her sidekick Rosemary whatshername apparently carried me to the car, although I was unconscious at that point so I only have their word for it. I woke up in the middle of Magpie Hill with the two of them looking down at me. Their faces when they saw that I was alive. It was hilarious. Anyway, Annette offered me a lot of money to disappear. She said it would be better for Dorothea to think I was dead. I didn't care why. I just wanted the money. I was never going to make much at the factory.' He crosses his ankles. 'So I went along with it. She paid me to go to Australia and set up home. And then she made sure I had a monthly income. Every now and again the payments would lapse so I'd send a little reminder to her, or Rosemary . . .'

'Like a Christmas card?'

'Yes. Exactly.'

'But why Rosemary?'

'She was a rich old bird too and she didn't want a scandal. Can you imagine if the world knew that Lady Rosemary Farrington was willing to clean up after her friend? She didn't want the truth coming out any more than Annette did. I must have bled Annette dry, because about eighteen months ago she told me she had no more money left. I threatened to tell Dot the truth if she didn't come up with more cash.'

Revulsion towards this man rips through me.

'But they didn't seem bothered. It was like something had shifted. Maybe they thought, hoped, that all these years later I wouldn't be believed.' He shrugs.

They were probably more concerned about the truth coming out surrounding my mum, but I don't say this to Bobby.

'I had no choice but to pay Dot a visit.' He leans back against the sofa, smiling at the memory.

'It was you who left the postcard?'

'Yes. And my lighter too. I'd like that back, actually, if you have it. And then, after I left the items for her to find, I decided to drop in on Dot. Oh, you should have seen her face when she first saw me looming out of the mist. She really thought she was seeing a ghost. After the shock had worn off I told her everything. About Annette and Rosemary, and what they'd done. How, for all those years, they'd let her believe she'd killed me. She'd already begun to suspect the truth, though, thanks to the lighter and the postcard. Some friends, huh? We actually had a nice chat, in the end. Parted as . . . not exactly friends, but not enemies either.'

'Did Dorothea talk about going to the police and telling them the truth about Annette?'

'She never mentioned the police. But I doubt that crossed her mind. She'd get into trouble either way because she'd helped cover it up.'

'You were in Dorothea's woods on Saturday, weren't you? Why?'

His cornflower-blue eyes glint. 'I wanted to pay my respects.'

'Were you also looking for the sculpture?'

He throws his hands up in the air and laughs. 'Okay,

you got me. I was hoping I'd find it. Or something of value in that bunker. When I tried to escape through the fence I ripped my favourite coat – well, the lining anyway.

'Haven't you got enough money?' I splutter.

'You can never have too much money, Imogen.'

I stand up, feeling grubby. I need to get away from this horrible man. 'The police have taken the sculpture away and there is nothing else of value in the bunker, so you're wasting your time.'

He raises an eyebrow at me.

'Goodbye. Thank you for your time,' I say stiffly. 'I'll show myself out.'

'What do you think you're going to do now?' Alison asks later that evening. We're on the sofa in the front room and I've got the fire going. We've spent hours discussing Annette, Dorothea, Mum. I'm exhausted and my throat is sore from all the talking. Was it really only this morning when we went to visit Dad?

I'd only been back home a short while when DI Shirley rang.

'I'm afraid I have some distressing news,' she said, her voice grave. She then proceeded to tell me that Rosemary's body had been found at a bed and breakfast near Hastings. 'It looks like she'd taken her own life, but we're not ruling out foul play either in light of what has happened to Dorothea and Maisie. Police searched her house and found a bloodied metal ornament that we think her lodger, Peter Bryce, used to attack Dennis. He has a previous conviction as a teenager for assault although he's been living with Rosemary for years.'

'Did Annette and Rosemary come up with the idea to hurt Dennis together? Because of the biography?'

'We're not sure, but it looks that way.'

'And you think Annette killed her?'

'It's a possibility.'

The only way to ensure her secrets were safe. I've wondered since whether Warren knows the full extent of Annette's crimes.

'I'm going to call Chris tomorrow and ask if I can go back to the TV station soon,' I say to Alison now, with resolve. 'Especially now we know that Annette killed Dorothea.'

'You'll have to be careful what you write though, won't you? Because Annette will be put on trial. She's bound to plead not guilty.'

'I can start working on the story, ready to publish after the trial.' I feel confident Chris will go for it.

'And what about Dennis and his book? Will you take up his offer?'

Dennis must have got wind of Annette being arrested as he'd called me while I was on my way home from seeing Bobby to tell me the publisher has put his book on hold for the moment. He'd wondered if I wanted to write it with him in light of all the new developments. I said I'd think about it, but it's a way of making certain Dorothea's voice is heard.

'I'm still not sure,' I admit.

'How are you feeling about it all?' Alison asks. 'Dad will be released . . .'

'It still feels so much to take in. Annette killing Mum . . .'

We both stare at each other, our expressions mirror images of one another. And then Alison says, 'I just can't believe all this. I feel strangely numb.'

'Me too. I don't think it's hit us yet.'

We sit drinking the bottle of wine I'd opened. We're already on our second glass.

'What will happen with Dad?'

'I think he'll have to go into a hospice or something.'

I nod and take another gulp of the sauvignon blanc.

'I've been thinking,' I say, eyeing her carefully, not sure that she'll agree. 'It doesn't feel right that Dorothea just left this house to me. It was your mum who died too. I want us to split it.'

Alison almost spills her wine. 'What? No! You can't do that.'

'I want to. It's too much for me. I've already told Josh I'll sign over my half of the flat to him. We can't sell the villa for a year . . .'

Alison frowns. 'Oh yes, that's a weird stipulation. I wonder why Dorothea did that?'

'I reckon it's because she wanted there to be enough time for me to find the sculpture. But anyway, you're welcome to come and live here. You, Gareth and Lila. The place is big enough that we all get our own space. I know it means you'd have to get new jobs and find a new school for Lila. But the schools in Bath are great. Think about it, yeah? Talk it over with Gareth.'

Alison glances out of the window to the large garden only just visible in the gloaming. I can tell she's imagining Lila playing on the lawn.

My feelings towards Dorothea will always be conflicted. I'm so grateful to her in so many ways, but I'm also angry that she never told me the truth before, about what happened to Mum. I realize that Annette had a hold over her, but it still burns.

Yet that summer had been so perfect. The memory of it is what keeps me going and I feel sad for Alison that she never experienced it. But then I remind myself she has her own memories of our childhood, before I was born, before the drinking and the abuse.

'This house deserves to be filled with love. Like it was that summer . . .' I sip my wine to hide a sudden burst of sadness.

Alison reaches out and lightly touches my arm.

'I agree,' she says. 'That's what Dorothea would have wanted.'

61

DOROTHY

Fifty Years Before

Dorothy wasn't supposed to go to the meeting. She hadn't even known it was happening, but when she saw the flier attached to a tree she found herself heading for the town hall.

She was so deeply unhappy with Bobby. Her prince had quickly turned into a monster not long into their marriage and she was at her wits' end. She just wanted to hear the talk on women's rights, that was all. To feel empowered, even for just a moment. To take back some control. She wasn't planning on saying anything about her own situation. Bobby would never need to know.

The hall was already crowded when she arrived, full of women in their warm coats and woolly hats, stamping their feet together against the cold and blowing on their gloved hands. The talk was already underway and Dorothy slipped in next to a woman around her own age wearing a smart tweed jacket. The woman turned to look at Dorothy with kind eyes, her gaze roaming over Dorothy's face and the fading bruise on her cheekbone. Their eyes met in mutual recognition, and for once in Dorothy's life she felt that she was being seen. Really seen.

'Hi,' said the woman, smiling kindly and offering a gloved hand to Dorothy. 'I'm Annette.'

'Dorothy,' she replied, taking the woman's hand in her own. And she felt a spark, like they were kindred spirits. She felt instantly that this woman understood her and that she would help her. She could tell that Annette had been through something similar.

And so, after the talk, when Annette asked Dorothy if she'd like to grab a drink, Dorothy had said yes.

Since marrying Bobby, she had lost most of her friends, but with Annette, it was like having a sister. A soulmate. During the day when Bobby was at work she would arrange to meet Annette and they would talk, really talk, about everything. Sometimes in cafés with Annette's toddler on her lap, other times in Annette's beautiful kitchen overlooking the river. Slowly, as the weeks wore on, they became more comfortable with one another.

'You know, Dot,' she'd often say. 'You're the first person I've met that I feel I can truly say anything to. I know you won't judge me.'

And Dorothy felt the same.

Then, one evening while Bobby was away for the night with work, Dorothy had gone to stay with Annette. Over copious amounts of wine in Annette's kitchen, with her son asleep upstairs, they opened up to one another. Annette leaned into Dorothy, so close that she could smell the booze on her friend's breath, and admitted the truth about her husband. She had set him up for fraud. He was serving a prison sentence because of her. 'It's something to think about with Bobby,' she said with a wink. 'Sometimes it's the only way to get revenge. By the end I hated him, Dot. I hated him and I wanted him out of my life, and this was the only way. You know what the police are like. They wouldn't have done anything. He was clever. He hid his abuse behind respectability. But our wealth came from my side of the family. Not his.'

'I don't know if I could do that to Bobby. What if he gets out of prison and comes looking for you? He must know that you set him up?' Dorothy was genuinely worried for her friend.

'He won't come looking for me. I made sure of that too.'

'What do you mean?'

'I know people who know people.' She tapped the side of her nose. 'He won't be getting out of prison. That's all I'll say.'

Two weeks later, Dorothy heard that Annette's husband had hanged himself in his cell.

'Was it . . .?' she'd dared to ask.

'What do you think, Dot?'

Dorothy hadn't known whether to be terrified or impressed. One thing she did know was that she respected Annette. She was taking back her power. She was an inspiration. And Dorothy felt, for the first time ever, that she could change the course of her life. That there might, somehow, eventually, be a way out.

Yes, she was supposed to meet Annette on that cold winter's night. It was fate, and for the first time in a long time she felt hopeful for the future.

Annette was going to save her.

THE END

ACKNOWLEDGEMENTS

This is the tenth year I've been published with Penguin Michael Joseph – *Local Girl Missing* came out in the summer of 2016 – and what an amazing journey it has been. The wonderful MJ team, led by my brilliant editor Maxine Hitchcock, have really taken my career from strength to strength and I can't thank them all enough. Thank you, Maxine, for always believing in me, for your insightful edits, and our wonderful chats over cake before lunch. Thank you also to Clare Bowron and Stella Newing for their brilliant notes and advice. Also to the rest of the amazing team: Ellie Morley, Frankie Banks, Vicky Photiou, Beatrix McIntyre, Deirdre O'Connell, Hannah Padgham, and Katie Corcoran. To Lee Motley for the striking book jackets – this one is my new favourite! To the audio team who do such a fantastic job on the audiobooks, the fabulous narrators who have bought my characters to life over the years, and to Sarah Bance for the copy-edits.

A huge thank you also to Juliet Mushens, dream agent. Thank you so much for steering my career all these years – thirteen years now, where has the time gone! – for taking a chance on me and for changing my life. Thanks to you and the talented Mushens Entertainment team – Catriona Fida, Alba Arnau Prado and Emma Dawson – my books are now published in over twenty-two countries, and have film and TV options with the help of Jenny Bent and Mary Pender in the US.

Also a huge thanks to my US editor Sarah Stein and the brilliant team at Harper, and all at HarperCollins Canada for continuing to publish and push my books across the pond and to Eva Schubert and all at Penguin Verlag for the wonderful job they do in getting my books into the hands of German readers and ensuring they hit the bestseller lists over there.

To all my lovely friends who have been so supportive over the years, and to all the authors who have given their time so generously to read and quote for my books.

To the West Country author crew, Gilly Macmillan, Tim Weaver, C L Taylor, and Chris Ewan. Thank you for the lunches, messages of support, the word races, and laughs.

To the booksellers and librarians for getting my books into readers' hands, and to book bloggers for the reviews and cover reveals.

To my readers who have been on this journey with me. I am so grateful to you all for continuing to read my books, pick up my backlist, and for all your lovely messages, reviews, and posts.

To my family, Ty, Claudia, and Isaac, who make me so proud every day. And to Sam and Jeff, Dad, John, Laura, Sharon and Mark, and the Williams'. I'm so thankful for you all.

Finally, a huge thank you to my amazing mum. You are one of the strongest, most caring, and loveliest women I know and I'm so lucky that you're my mum. This book is for you.